SHADOWS OF OPINION

SHADOWS OF OPINION

OPUS X™ BOOK SEVEN

MICHAEL ANDERLE

DISRUPTIVE IMAGINATION

THE SHADOWS OF OPINION TEAM

Thanks to the JIT Readers

Dave Hicks
Peter Manis
Dorothy Lloyd
Deb Mader
Kerry Mortimer
Kelly O'Donnell
John Ashmore
Peter Manis
James Caplan
Jeff Eaton
Paul Westman
Larry Omans

If I've missed anyone, please let me know!

Editor
Lynne Stiegler

To Family, Friends and
Those Who Love
to Read.
May We All Enjoy Grace
to Live the Life We Are
Called.

CHAPTER ONE

December 14, 2229, Lagos, Nigeria

Jia's mini-flitter zoomed forward, surging past Erik's vehicle. She dove under a web of sky bridges connecting the nearby packed towers. There wasn't even the smallest hint of hesitation in her flight despite the tiny distances separating her head from…

Well, to be truthful, an untimely decapitation.

Erik growled in frustration as their targets receded into the distance. Earlier, there had been a group of armed men astride mini-flitters, and now they were turning into dots.

"Don't worry." Jia narrowed her eyes. "We've still got eyes on them. They're not getting away."

He appreciated the sentiment, but it didn't do much to kill his irritation. Emma's swarm of drones, both launched and hacked, were keeping the enemy in sight, highlighting them for Erik's and Jia's smart lenses.

That might help, but it wasn't a guarantee, and he knew it. There were too many towers and too many places to hide in Lagos, and the drones weren't fast enough to keep up with the fleeing terrorists.

"This is fun," Erik muttered. "I'm glad we had a big breakfast. I don't like to have high-speed chases on an empty stomach."

"On the other hand, I bet my mother would recommend not chasing terrorists for at least thirty minutes after your last meal," Jia joked.

"Yeah. I'm sure there's some poor bastard who crashed after cramping up," Erik admitted. "There has to be at least one."

"Probably."

The bright early-afternoon sun glinted off a nearby building. The network of sky bridges, tunnels, and walkways between the towers obscured much of the ground beneath them, but even without the construction, the earth below was more a collection of color impressions, greens, browns, and grays than specific structures at their height.

That detail reminded Erik that mini-flitters weren't designed to be operated at that altitude, and he glanced over the side. A helmet wasn't going to save either of them if they fell.

Erik grinned, the annoyance finally melting away. He was in a good position, but the terrorists weren't.

He might not be a danger junkie, but he'd dropped from orbit onto enemy-held planets while drop pods were getting picked off by anti-air artillery fire. Chasing terrorists around Earth on a glorified flying bike was nothing in comparison, especially when the enemy wasn't putting up a decent fight. They had to be worried about their own meet-and-greet with the ground.

"They've got a whole damned gang," Erik complained, grateful his helmet blocked the wind. "So why the hell are they running instead of trying to kill us? They don't even know it's us."

"Us?" Jia asked. "They know we're not part of their terrorist cells."

"I mean, *us*. You know, you and me." Erik dodged a flagpole and wondered why they couldn't use a holographic flag. "The Obsidian Detective and Lady Justice. We are just two random cops or mercs for all they know, so why are they running? We don't even have our guns out. For a bunch of murderous terrorists, I am going to complain that they are pretty chickenshit."

Jia angled her mini-flitter to avoid a head-on collision with an antenna. "There's no law that says just because they're terrorists, they have to be brave. Or they might be on a very tight schedule for their plan, whatever it is." She accelerated and slid into a gap with almost no clearance.

Erik's brow lifted in surprise. Jia's flying was risky even by his standards. It was hard to believe, and he wasn't sure if he would if he hadn't seen it.

"I remember when you didn't even want to get on a mini-flitter," he commented, rising up and over a sky bridge. Excited children waved at him through the windows as their parents looked on in horror. He would have expected the cops to have shown up already. "But now you act like you were born on one of these things."

"I have a better sense of balance in three dimensions now," Jia replied. "No, I always did, but I didn't trust myself. Now I do. A lot of training, lessons, and getting shot helped. Confidence does wonders."

Erik chewed on that comment for a moment. "Confidence lets you pull those kinds of flight stunts?"

"Sure does," Jia responded cheerfully.

Erik might have harbored a few remaining doubts if she'd just been talking about her ship training, had he not witnessed Jia's natural talent with an exoskeleton. She was a piloting prodigy who hadn't been living up to her potential, and it came out every time she applied herself to a vehicle with aerial capacity. Their assignments could turn violent and mobile in an instant.

Every additional capability helped.

The terrorist mini-flitter pack slowed, giving Erik and Jia precious seconds to catch up before the killers shifted into a tight V formation, nobody bothering to fire at their two pursuers.

As a group, they flew toward a narrow gap between two towers.

It turned out to be too narrow. Some men on the edge didn't make it.

Erik whistled, impressed, as their mini-flitters slammed into the building's exterior and broke into clouds of debris, launching their riders on their final trip to meet their Maker. The terrorists' bodies bounced off the buildings, but they were outside the grav fences. There was nothing to save them.

They dropped to the ground, flailing as if that would protect them from their coming doom. The remaining terrorists didn't even look back, which helped save them from the same fate.

"Those guys could use a few lessons from you," Erik joked.

"Did one of them have the bomb?" Jia asked, the levity gone from her voice. "It might not take out a tower, but that doesn't mean it couldn't hurt someone if it exploded on the way down."

"Shit," Erik replied. "I'm not sure."

They were in Lagos at Alina's request. Her instructions for the assignment had been simple. Erik and Jia were to go to the metro and investigate alleged terrorist activity there, with a focus on observation and intelligence-gathering rather than elimination.

The Intelligence Directorate was interested in this particular batch of terrorists rather than kicking them over to the Criminal Investigations Directorate because the terrorists had received some unusual off-world funding. Erik and Jia didn't mind.

Taking down terrorists in between hunting vast conspiracies was a nice way to train.

Alina had said it'd be easy compared to assignments she'd sent them on before. Then their simple intel-gathering and observation job had turned into Erik and Jia screaming through the towers of Lagos after terrorists with a bomb.

The only thing Erik didn't get was what the bastards planned to blow up. They could have killed more people just by hitting a commerce level with guns. There was something he and Jia were missing. They'd have to ask the terrorists.

Well, assuming any survived.

"The bomb remains secure," Emma reported. One of the terrorists' highlights turned bright green. "The man in the front has the bomb in his carryaid. I must warn you, though, they're almost out of range of most of my drones, as are you. You're all going too fast, and it's not like I can hack every drone in Lagos."

Jia entered the narrow gap smoothly, accelerating and gaining on the terrorists. Erik slowed as he followed, but he didn't come close to either building. A terrorist finally went for a gun, but his lack of control cost him as his mini-flitter drifted to the side. At that speed, a second was enough to make a deadly mistake.

He collided with another man's vehicle. Both vehicles bounced hard away from each other, one scraping the building and shedding pieces before falling, the thrusters and grav emitters dead.

The other terrorist smashed into the back of an ally's mini-flitter. The vehicle clipped the bottom of a sky bridge, taking the terrorist's head with it. The other man righted his vehicle in time to smack into a tower. His piercing scream echoed in the metal canyon. There were far too many losses without taking a shot at their enemies.

Erik frowned in disappointment.

The predators and prey escaped their narrow flight space, exiting among a new batch of towers, then passing into a new tower canyon. Having learned their lesson from the sacrifice of their comrade, the terrorists didn't go for their guns.

They concentrated on dodging the huge number of sky bridges stretching between two of the buildings. One man didn't make it, and his mini-flitter bounced off the top of the sky bridge. The grav fence left the structure barely touched, but the sparking grav emitters on the bottom of the terrorist's vehicle didn't speak well for his future.

He made it only a few more meters before his vehicle plummeted.

"Idiots," Jia muttered. "I'm almost insulted by how terrible they are at this. They should have just run away, not led us on this ridiculous chase and lost people without us firing a shot. Don't they have any pride in their organization?"

Erik laughed. "Now that you're the Pilot Queen, you only want to chase the highest quality terrorists?"

She considered his statement. "Something like that, or they could have saved us all some trouble and not run. This is like the worst of both worlds. It's inconvenient and dangerous, and we're losing potential witnesses." Jia sucked in a frustrated breath. "It's annoying."

"Terrorists usually are." Erik grinned. "And Alina said this was just supposed to be an observation mission."

"Ever think Alina is the Lady in human form?" Jia asked.

"That would explain a lot." Erik chuckled. "But she wouldn't need us if this was easy."

"True enough."

The surviving terrorists emerged from the latest metal canyon and pitched upward. They still outnumbered Erik and Jia by a significant margin, but the men stubbornly refused to engage. Free of further obstruction, they increased speed, zooming toward a huge floating platform in the sky—the famed Lagos Sky Garden.

"Oh, great," Jia complained. "I wondered if this was where we'd end up. I knew we couldn't have kept up with the exoskeletons, but it would have been nice to have the firepower."

"Maybe." Erik kept his attention on the terrorists, his hands gripping the handlebars tightly. Jia was right. The Sky Garden was supposed to be a pinnacle of advanced thruster and gravity manipulation technology, despite the ridiculous amount of energy required to keep it in the sky.

All he could see was something large that was ready to fall. It didn't matter that the damned thing was positioned outside the outer edges of the Lagos Metroplex. If it fell, the people aboard would die.

Everyone had to die, but dying from being crushed by a tourist trap seemed like an awful way to go.

Something was wrong. There was no way they could hope to bring down the Sky Garden with the small bomb they had. If it were that simple, some murderous idiot would have taken it out a long time ago.

An assassination? It'd make more sense to just rush the Sky Garden and shoot their target dead.

The terrorists passed over the outer walls and disappeared behind them, now marked only by Emma's highlighting. Erik wasn't worried. The bastards wouldn't be able to go that fast without flying above the trees.

"Should I come?" Emma asked. "Now that we have verified their target, it'll be a simple manner for me to arrive quickly with the MX 60."

"No," Erik replied, his duster flapping in the wind. "I would have loved to have the TR-7, but I think once we corner those assholes, it'll be a short fight judging by what we've seen. If they could take us easily, they would have tried already."

"You have a point." Jia scoffed, the sound more derisive than normal. "Cowards."

The gray and silver underside and walls of the Sky Garden gave way to the vibrant greens, reds, and yellows of the trees and other plants covering the maze-like botanical park. That aspect almost bothered Erik more than the existence of the floating tourist site.

He could understand building something that floated in the air to show off, but he didn't get why they needed to cover it with dirt and grow plants on it. There was a fine line between demonstrating human ingenuity versus dropping your pants and tempting fate with arrogance.

He frowned. There still weren't any cops.

Erik and Jia didn't want to call them in since it'd complicate things, but their conspicuous absence after the crashes fueled his suspicion. The kind of men who could keep the cops from showing up often had other annoying secret advantages.

The red targeting highlights vanished from Erik's smart lens display. "What's going on, Emma? Make my day and tell me they all crashed."

"Alas, no," Emma reported. "I've temporarily lost direct visuals on the gun goblins since they've moved too far into the Sky Garden. You're usually better about killing gun goblins in a more contained area, and this will be over before I could hope to hack a satellite. You're closer than any drones currently under my control."

"Okay, time for our backup plan." Erik's mini-flitter passed over the outer wall. "Get ready to launch the microdrones. We don't need a detailed map of the area. We just need to know where those bastards are to finish them off."

Erik and Jia slowed, surveying the immediate area for the terrorists, but their small vehicles had disappeared into the dense foliage. No one fired at them. It didn't matter if it was cowardice or careful tactical planning, the results were the same: a hidden enemy.

The thick canopy made it difficult to spot anyone deep inside the gardens from the air.

"This might not be their target." Erik looked around. "They might have just come here to hide."

"Is that what your gut tells you?" Jia slowly turned her head, surveying the area and seeking out the terrorists. "They couldn't have gotten far. They didn't have that big a lead on us. If they wanted to hide, it would have made more sense to go down instead of up."

"Sometimes a few seconds is all it takes."

Erik looked around, his jaw tight. Without the MX 60 there, they didn't have access to their full sensor suite, and the microdrones had only the most basic options. It might come down to spotting the enemy with their own eyes.

"There!" Jia pointed and pitched her mini-flitter down.

Erik grinned. *That worked.*

Jia headed toward a thick copse of flame trees near the edge, covered in bright red flowers. A smattering of mini-flitters was parked past the outer wall, but they lacked their terrorist riders.

Erik narrowed his eyes. It wasn't like the Sky Garden was a secured military facility, but it wasn't undefended either. Something was wrong, seriously wrong. Had he made a bad judgment call by not calling in reinforcements or at least warning anyone?

"Damn, they split up. Any cops coming?"

"There are no unusual concentrations of police vehicles heading your way," Emma replied.

Erik followed Jia toward the mini-flitters. Pressing his luck, he used one hand to draw his gun.

Jia might consider their current opponents to be no-talent losers, but now the terrorists didn't have to concentrate on flying, freeing them up to demonstrate talent in other areas, such as shooting at Intelligence Directorate contractors following them into floating botanical gardens.

A light whir emanated from the back of Erik's mini-flitter as the microdrones deployed and flowed toward the trees like a swarm of angry metal insects. New targeting highlights appeared right before the crack of gunfire sounded from the edge of the forest. Erik dipped his mini-flitter, avoiding the next shot, and fired, downing the terrorist ambushers. He was beginning to appreciate Jia's frustration with the lack of challenge.

Sometimes a man wanted a heart-pounding fight.

Jia was half off her flitter before setting down. She leapt from the vehicle, pointing toward the dead terrorists lying near the trees, and jogged toward the bodies.

"Not that I'm surprised, but they don't have the bomb." Jia prodded a body before rolling it over with her foot. "Headshots while flying toward them? Did you use your arm?"

Erik shook his head. "Nope. These guys got cocky, or they were just there to stall us and not careful."

"Ahead, twenty meters to the right and up," Emma reported.

Jia and Erik jerked their guns upward and fired. A body bounced through some branches, landing with a hard crunch against the ground. The terrorist's gun bounced through the branches and landed a couple of seconds later.

"Why didn't he fire when he had the chance?" Jia frowned.

"He was climbing when I spotted him," Emma explained. "And I've detected the rest of your boisterous bombers. They must be using a map since they are navigating the garden with great alacrity and efficiency, albeit slower than before, I presume due to their fear of becoming fertilizer after a collision. Based on their current course, I think they're trying to make it to the central administration building."

Jia hissed. "That makes sense. If they have decent hackers, they could gain access to the main reactor. That's the only way they could bring down the Sky Garden without a massive attack on the heavily protected external emitters and thrusters. I still don't get what the bomb is for."

"Emma, contact the administration building," Erik ordered. "They need to evacuate, but they can't go in the same direction as the terrorists. Do what you need to do to hack the system and get some security bots on those terrorists." He frowned at the bodies. "We've gotten too far without cops or security. They've got someone on the inside, and probably someone in the local PD, too."

Jia headed back toward her mini-flitter. "Now that we know where they're going, we can catch up without crashing. We can fly better than these idiots. Even if Emma can get the security bots up, that might not stop them."

"Yeah." Erik holstered his gun. "Let's ruin the rest of their day."

CHAPTER TWO

"All your boisterous bombers are accounted for inside the administration building," Emma reported. "I'll highlight their positions with nav markers for you upon arrival. I believe the terrorists already had access to the system since there are some anomalies I couldn't account for during my initial probe, and it's slowing my attempts to take over the entire system."

Jia tilted her head to avoid a low-hanging branch. They were almost at the administration building, but the situation could come down to seconds.

She wouldn't let those scum win, no matter what.

"If the terrorists have already hacked the system, couldn't they have dropped the Sky Garden remotely?" Erik asked. "Why go through the trouble of coming here?"

"There is no external access to the most relevant subsystems," Emma explained. "For once, one of your pitiful engineering fleshbags thought pretty far ahead."

"How are we doing on the evacuation?" Jia asked. "Any hostages?"

"Most guests and staff are on their way to escaping or already have left," Emma replied. "I took the liberty of disguising myself as a local government official to expedite matters. Surprisingly, no one tried to interrogate my account credentials. I'd prepared a complicated solution for that, but most fleshbags should be off the Sky Garden within five minutes. I've seen no evidence of local staff being taken as hostages."

"That's good, but we might not have five minutes," Erik muttered. "What about security bots? Any luck?"

"Although I've penetrated the cameras and comm systems," Emma replied, "I'll need more time to gain appropriate access to their security system. I'm not even taking the time to conceal my efforts, so that's making things going faster."

"More preparation on their part?"

"No, more basic security associated with the Sky Garden."

Erik scoffed. "Don't worry about covering your trail. We'll get Alina to clean that up, or let the terrorists take the blame. Just do what you need to so we can stop those bastards."

Jia and Erik slowed their mini-flitters.

The path widened and the trees grew sparser, revealing a bright white dome in the distance—the administration building. Small black specks marked Emma-controlled drones, increasing Jia's confidence.

The AI might have an attitude problem, but her ego wouldn't tolerate Erik and Jia being ambushed on her watch. She might not be human, as she had oh-so-carefully

14

explained every time it came up, but for all her capabilities, she had a modicum of hubris.

Frankly, she might die of embarrassment if she failed.

The terrorists had lost several men, and they knew Erik and Jia were right on them. They might not have the personnel or time for anything too clever.

Erik and Jia set their vehicles down next to the terrorists' mini-flitters. They exchanged quick looks before hopping to the ground and backing away. They didn't head toward the door.

Erik drew his gun and nodded at Jia.

"What?" She frowned, not comprehending.

He motioned with his arm. "Step aside."

Jia drew her pistol and jogged toward him. "You see something?"

Erik aimed his gun at one of the grav emitters on a terrorist flitter and pulled the trigger. "No. I just want to make sure that no matter what happens, those assholes don't escape. I'm vindictive like that."

"That's justice. Even if they don't pull off their stunt here, they've already killed innocent people." Jia took aim at a different flitter and put a round in a grav emitter. It took the pair less than thirty seconds to disable the enemy vehicles before reloading and running toward the open door of the control center.

Jia flattened against the wall at the echo of a gunshot. Erik grunted and crouched. Both held their breath, waiting for the follow-up shot. More gunshot sounds followed, growing more distant with each shot.

"What's going on, Emma?" Jia demanded.

"The feeble security bots have been overwhelmed," Emma complained. "I managed to deploy them but didn't want to distract you, though I will note these particular gun goblins were more thoughtful than most. They brought EMPs and dedicated armor-piercing rounds. They obviously had a good understanding of the potential security system, and I purged some malicious code prior to activating the bots."

"What about fleshbag security?" Erik asked. He shrugged at Jia's frown.

"Almost all human personnel are helping with the evacuation," Emma reported. "Unfortunately, I believe my deception was too effective. Should I summon them back? There is a single guard remaining in the facility."

"It's too late now," Erik commented. He narrowed his eyes. "And they might not be ready to deal with these guys. We'll just have to catch up with our new friends."

"Oh, that explains some things," Emma commented. She sent a new red highlight to their smart lenses. "That newly marked gun goblin is a security guard. He was attempting to counter some of my efforts. As I said, I noticed some unusual log activity upon my initial system entry that was delaying an aggressive security response. He is now fleeing the facility."

"He's not the problem anymore. The cops can chase him down when this is all over."

The red highlights for the terrorists changed their relative angles and spread out. Jia didn't like the implications and had opened her mouth to say something when a massive boom accompanied the ground shaking.

"They gave up on trying to use the elevator," Emma explained before Jia could say anything. "They are attempting to enter the area that leads to a hub with tunnels that will grant them direct access to the grav field emitters and thrusters."

"What was that explosion?" Erik asked.

"The bomb," Emma replied calmly. "They used it to blow through the primary security door."

Jia sighed. "And there are no additional internal doors you can seal in the tunnels?"

"No," Emma offered. "I dropped the primary security door to keep them out of the hub. They barely attempted to hack it before resorting to more direct methods."

"Which means they never planned to. That was the point of the bomb all along. The security guard must have been worried about being noticed if he tried to mess with the door."

"There are additional system safeguards in place concerning the door," Emma revealed.

Jia grimaced. "I like terrorists who are stupid and underestimate everyone, not the kind who think ahead."

"I thought you were complaining earlier about them being losers?" Erik grinned. "What happened to that, Jia?"

"That was about flying." Jia gestured down the hallway. "This is bombing. It doesn't matter. Let's go." She broke into a run. "The door slowed them down, which gives us a chance."

Erik sprinted until he caught up. "Emma, I'm no engineer, but this place must have redundant emitters and thrusters, right? They can't take out one of them and take it down."

Emma sighed. "You're correct that there is redundancy inherent in the design. All available information indicates they can disable half of the relevant equipment before the Sky Garden begins an unscheduled rapid descent with additional unscheduled rapid disassembly at the end of its fall."

Jia rushed around a corner, her breathing ragged. "That's not on my list of favorite things to experience. I know you mentioned the main supports are separate from the primary system, but can you gain any access to the attitude thrusters? They must have some they use for station-keeping, right?"

"I can't gain easy direct access, but I might be able to control them indirectly via the power system."

"Do that. If we have to go down, you can at least steer it into the ocean. That'll lower the casualties."

"Cheerful thought," Emma replied. "I'll try my best, but those thrusters have very limited ability to move this entire structure."

Depending on a small chance of escaping doom as a backup was better than nothing. Jia and Erik would just have to do their best to not force Emma into that position.

Erik and Jia barreled down the hallway. They slowed as an acrid stench filled their nostrils. The air remained thick with smoke. The blasted remains of a security door lay scattered inside a room at the end of the hallway. A ladder sat beneath an open hatch. The terrorists' position markers continued to move in different directions, with two clear clusters traveling in opposite directions.

"We don't have time to do this together," Jia complained. She ran over to the hatch and jumped down without grabbing the ladder. With a hiss, she hit the ground a few meters down, pain spiking through her legs, and stood, ignoring the discomfort. "Unless you don't agree?"

Erik jumped down after she had stepped out of the way. "Nah. You're right. Divide and conquer." He inclined his head toward a Y-shaped intersection in front of them. "I'll take left." He patted his cybernetic arm. "It's my lucky direction."

Jia rolled her eyes. "That's debatable. Don't get killed. It'd be sad if these losers took you out."

Erik grinned. "If I die today, it'll be in the crash."

"If it looks like the platform is going to fail, I can remotely activate your flitters and attempt to catch you while I'm trying to move the Sky Garden," Emma offered. "But be advised, the chances of success with that particular maneuver are lower than you'd like to hear. They're similar to the odds of me pushing this facility out of danger with the attitude thrusters."

Jia aimed her gun down the corridor and ran toward the intersection. "What I'm hearing is we need to take these guys out. The plan is the same as it has been since we started chasing them."

"I'm feeling generous." Erik headed toward the opposite side. "Time for some free lead."

As Jia headed into the new hallway, she patted her pockets. She had enough spare magazines to take down her half of the terrorists, but only if she was judicious with her shots.

If their recon missions were going to turn into major shootouts, she might need to start carrying lots of extra ammo in a coat with more pockets. At least she had the advantage of Emma telling her the exact location of all her targets.

The first leg of Jia's journey took less than a minute. She stopped near another turn. Two terrorists stood near the end of the next hallway, according to Emma's feed, while a third man crawled up a ladder into a service access tunnel. She was running out of time.

Sweat trickling down the side of her head, Jia took a deep breath and crouched. She crept to the edge of the wall and spun around the corner, then put a round into the first man's head before sending a shot at the second. To be sure, she dropped her hand in a flash and put a couple more rounds into each of their chests to ensure they fell. So much for judicious use of ammo.

She leapt to her feet and charged down the hallway. The guards were incidental. The real trouble was their friend. Jia grabbed the top rung of the ladder, and a bullet flew over her partially exposed hand. She dropped one rung, catching it with her hand and bracing her feet. More shots blasted from the service tunnel. She tossed her gun into her left hand and took a deep breath before stepping up and turning her hand to fire. A bullet ripped through her hand and she slipped back with a hiss, landing on her back.

Jia sucked in air, her lack of oxygen helping her ignore the pain in her hand. She pulled a medpatch out of her pocket and wrapped it around the wound. The pain numbed as the anesthetic set in, but there was no way her hand would be healed in the next few minutes.

She picked up her gun and ran down a side hallway, hand throbbing. Several loud gunshots echoed from afar.

"How are you doing, Erik?" she asked

"One set down, two more to go," he replied.

"Same." Jia didn't see a reason to worry him about being shot. It was hard to take on so many enemies on such a regular basis and not take the occasional bullet.

Lead poisoning was a basic job hazard when a woman was trying to stop crazed terrorists from bringing down floating tourist traps.

Her heart thundering, Jia rushed toward the next pair. This time she didn't bother creeping up on them. She rushed into the hallway with a defiant shout of rage and shot both men in the head without slowing.

"Emma, a stray bullet or two in a service tunnel couldn't possibly take out the thrusters and emitters, could it?"

"Given the setup of the Sky Garden, that's incredibly unlikely, although I can't say it's impossible. It might be amusing if you end up doing their work for them."

"*Hilarious.*" Jia ran toward the access ladder and jumped onto the rungs, pushing herself up without any concern for staying on the ladder. The terrorist furiously tapped on his PNIU as he stood in front of an internal door. His focus left him an easy target.

She fired three rounds into his back before she slipped and fell backward. He managed a strangled yelp before slumping to the floor, a pool of blood forming around him.

With a grunt, Jia landed on her butt without much grace, but at least she hadn't been shot this time. More loud shots rang out. Erik was doing his part, and she needed to finish hers. She shoved her blood-covered pistol into her holster and grabbed a rifle from a fallen terrorist. Her hand throbbed with her pulse. Unsurprisingly, the human body didn't like it when a person continued a gunfight after getting shot.

Good drugs could do a lot, but they couldn't let someone ignore a hole in their hand.

Jia barreled through the hallways, taking short, quick breaths. According to Emma's target highlights, her last set of terrorists was waiting as a group rather than risking sending one man on ahead. Either the others had warned them, or this group was smarter. "How are we doing?"

"Damn," Erik transmitted, "some of these guys found their balls and managed a decent delay, but I'm heading toward the last of my set."

"Me, too," Jia replied. She gripped the rifle with one hand, using her thumb to switch the fire select to full auto. Instead of turning the final corner, she jumped. As soon as she cleared the wall, she squeezed and held the trigger, flinging bullets into the hallway. The half-empty magazine didn't last long, but that didn't save the terrorists from taking several rounds before Jia crashed to the floor with a grunt. The good news was the pain in her arm distracted her from her hand.

"Brace yourself," Erik shouted.

The hallway shook, knocking Jia onto her side again as she'd sat up. "What's going on?"

"Took out the last bastard, but not before he threw a little present into the tunnel. I can't see through the smoke."

Jia's stomach twisted as the floor dipped. "Emma, I thought you said we'd be okay unless they took out more than half!"

"Oh, it's not as if I ran all necessary calculations," Emma replied, boredom in her voice. "If you hurry, you should be able to get to your flitters before total emitter failure. The attitude thrusters won't do much to arrest the potential fall of the Sky Garden."

Jia pivoted and pumped her legs, her heart galloping. The pain in her hand and arm felt like a distant memory, a barely worthy concern. She wasn't sure how much time passed before she joined back up with Erik. They didn't speak as they rushed out of the control center.

"One final thing for consideration," Emma offered as the pair closed in on their mini-flitters.

"We don't have a lot of time to chat!" Jia snapped.

"Although I didn't run all necessary calculations to be a hundred percent confident the Sky Garden won't fall, I *am* 99.98732 percent confident it won't." Emma snickered. "You shouldn't fall unless the terrorists somehow come back to life or have several fighters attack this place."

Jia scrubbed a hand down her face. "This is Chang'e City all over again. Is this really the time for pranks?"

"It's the perfect time. It'd be rather rude to play a prank on you if the Sky Garden was actually going to fall." Emma snorted. "I might be superior to fleshbags, but it's not as if I think the deaths of innocent people would be amusing."

"We're where we need to be." Erik chuckled and shook his head. He patted the handlebars on his mini-flitter. "There's no way those guys could have all the locals on the payroll. Let's get out of here before the cops show up and start asking too many pointed questions."

CHAPTER THREE

The Sky Garden receded as Erik and Jia dropped lower, moving away from the full flitters toward ground level.

Police and military vehicles converged on their previous location like a flock of angry, hungry birds on a corpse. Whatever pull or tricks the terrorists had used to delay the response had been defeated. The entire situation might have been a quick intel-gathering job that turned into something more dangerous, but Erik and Jia had avoided the trouble of having to deal with the terrorists later and saved a lot of lives along the way.

It wasn't a terrible, horrible, no-good very bad day after all.

The two of them set their flitters down on a parking platform. Other people pointed to the Sky Garden in the distance, chatting quietly amongst themselves. Jia pinched the bridge of her nose with her right hand, and Erik found himself staring at the medpatch on her other hand. Her face was pale and covered with sweat.

He came close, looking around as he asked, "You okay?"

"It's fine. One of the guys got in a lucky hit." Jia raised her left hand and waggled her fingers with a slight grimace. "It's not as bad as getting the whole thing blown off. It should be sealed up by the end of the day and as good as new in a couple as long as I keep patches on it."

"You didn't tell me you'd been shot." Erik frowned. "Neither of you mentioned it."

"I assume Jia will pass along the information to you that she feels is necessary," Emma noted, a hint of irritation in her voice. "It's not my responsibility to babysit her for you. I think she's proven that by now."

Jia smirked and raised an eyebrow in challenge at Erik. "It's not like we had a lot of time to discuss reinforcements. We both did what we needed to do to take them out. If I'd cried about getting shot, you wouldn't have been able to concentrate." She eyed him, his emotions clear to her. "*Right?*" She inclined her head toward the Sky Garden. "We saved it, and all it cost was a few dead terrorists. If I didn't want to get shot, I wouldn't chase dangerous men with guns."

Erik couldn't argue with that. Jia had known the danger that came with being a cop, and she had still become a detective. She understood that leaving the force to work for the Intelligence Directorate would be a greater risk. It also wasn't like she'd never been shot before.

Part of respecting her was accepting she could take care of herself, even if she got banged up.

He took a few deep breaths and let them out. "Fine. Let's get back to the hotel and contact Alina before some giant *yaoguai* dragon appears and starts laying waste to the city."

Jia laughed. "That's unlikely."

"A lot of shit that happens to us is unlikely."

"All's well that ends well," Alina offered with uncharacteristic cheer. "I didn't anticipate such an immediate outcome, but I'm not going to complain about you two achieving it, either."

Erik sat on the edge of a small bed, sparing a glance at Jia on occasion. She'd removed the initial medpatch and added two new ones, giving him an opportunity to see the bloody hole that had been torn through her hand. Willpower and adrenaline could do a lot in a fight, but it was never fun to get shot.

"Jia got shot," Erik noted. "That's not the best ending. It's a clean hole, so the patches should be able to regenerate it pretty well, but we're not walking into another assignment right away, even if it's supposed to be easy. She needs to be at her best the next time a simple job turns more complicated."

Jia shot him a frown, but she didn't say anything. He shrugged back. It wasn't about protecting her.

Having only partial use of a hand could get them both killed.

Alina sighed. "You're right. You should return to Neo SoCal. I apologize that things got out of hand. The effort wasn't supposed to be Herculean, but take heart that it wasn't Sisyphean, at least." She chuckled to herself. "I'll handle all the cleanup. A lot of the loose ends can be pointed back at the terrorists, and from what you've already told me, between your helmets and Emma changing transponder codes so often, there isn't much of a trail to lead to you. I'm surprised. Even trained agents can take a long time to get as good at hiding themselves, and you were bold public police officers not all that long ago."

"Thanks, but that might not be enough," Jia commented. "Don't you think the local cops will figure out that someone helped solve their little terrorism problem for them?"

"Sure, but I've found over the years that local law enforcement often is willing to look the other way when something works out to their advantage. Many might even intuit that it was an ID op and are smart enough not to ask questions that will cause everyone trouble."

"You felt the need to make a big official appearance to us when we were still with the NSCPD," Erik replied. "You might have hidden some of that crap, but why be so in our face if that was what you expected?"

"Among other things, because even then, I wanted to leverage you as resources." Alina let out a low chuckle. "And you two were already poking around in a lot of businesses I had an interest in. You weren't normal cops, which was why I scouted you. Most cops wouldn't be able to change gears in the middle of this kind of operation and stop a group of terrorists in between lunch and dinner."

Erik bit down on a low growl. He didn't like how lightly she was taking the situation, but he couldn't accuse Alina of being someone who didn't risk her own life.

He was far more concerned about something else.

"Did you know it'd be more than a little intel gathering?" Jia demanded, echoing Erik's thoughts. "I'm not all that worried about my hand. It'll heal, but I don't like the idea of walking into a battle underprepared. We obviously handled it, but that doesn't mean I like it."

"Hmm." Alina fell silent on the other end, not even her breathing audible. "I didn't know about the plan, and I was honest about your mission briefing. Despite what you might believe, just because I work for the ID, it doesn't mean I know what every random terrorist group is doing. I thought this was more about connecting with suppliers, not pulling off an op. My intel suggested the terrorists were scouting out Lagos, not ready to move already."

Jia frowned. "That makes sense. They sourced the explosive locally, and it wasn't that big a thing. They left less of a trail."

"One of the advantages of having you two working for me is that I can send you out, and I know if things get a little more complicated than anyone expected, you'll be able to handle it. And because you're handling it, I can concentrate on other more opaque investigations that'll pay off in the long run, including bigger threats like Talos."

"That sounds like you're giving us your busywork," Erik noted.

"Sure, very bloody and dangerous busywork," Alina replied. "If it makes you feel better, I'll be as blunt as I can be. You two are assets to me, but you are valuable assets who might help me take down Talos. It's not my goal or intention to waste your lives, and I'll never expend them lightly."

"But that doesn't mean our lives are at the top of your concerns," Erik noted. "Would you trade us if it meant you could be sure to take down Talos?"

Alina scoffed. "I might trade myself if I was certain it'd take down Talos. But despite my nickname, I'm still primarily in the intel game, which means I don't want to do anything that risks you unnecessarily."

"What if we'd decided not to pursue the terrorists?" Jia asked. "What if we'd decided it wasn't worth the risk?"

"Then you'd have to live with your consciences." Alina yawned. "I'm going to let you go so I can start cleanup and management of the situation. Thanks for your help. I'm sorry it turned it out rougher than expected, but I'm not going to guarantee that'll never happen again. This line of work just isn't that clean."

Erik chuckled. "Yeah, well, I'd have to call bullshit if you tried to tell us it wouldn't happen again."

She snorted. "I'll do everything I can to keep you alive. But for now, I have to go. Talk to you soon." Alina ended the call.

Jia lay back on the bed and set her patched left hand on her stomach. "What a waste. I was hoping after this was all over, we could have a nice dinner here rather than just grabbing quick café food." She frowned at him. "And come on, you don't have to have a beignet everywhere. Expand your horizons."

"Why can't I?" Erik shrugged. "I had them on the Moon and Mars. I like to get that different local touch."

Jia's scowl vanished, an infectious smile taking over. No one would have known she'd been shot not all that long prior. "I'm just saying there's good Nigerian in Neo SoCal, but we can get the pure, undistilled authentic experience here. We have choices *other than beignets*."

"We could stick around for a little longer." Erik sighed.

"The terrorists are done, and she's not going to give us a new assignment right away."

"No. If Alina's trying to clean this situation up, it'll help if we're not around in case someone did catch us on a camera. It wasn't like we've had helmets on the entire time we've been in Lagos." Jia rolled onto her side. "But you're right. It's been a while since we've had a real date, and I was hoping to have one before we end up stuck on a ship with Lanara and Cutter. I like them, but they kind of kill the mood."

Erik nodded. "I can't argue with that."

Jia waved her hand. "Aching hands kill the mood, too, so let's hope Alina gives us a few weeks to breathe."

Erik nodded. It'd only take a few days for the medpatches to heal most of the wound. He was sure they could slip in some relaxation back in Neo SoCal before their new boss sent them after whatever bizarre terrorists or cyborgs were threatening the peace of the United Terran Confederation that week.

Jia snickered. "Who am I kidding?"

"What?"

"Half our dates end with us shooting at someone." Jia rolled onto her back, a smirk on her face. "Does make me wonder, though."

"About?" Erik prodded, noting she looked rather good just lying there. *Focus.*

"How you feel about all this?" Jia gestured toward the ceiling. "Everything. Being a cop was always a means to an end for you, and now we've worked a decent amount of time under Alina. We might still be junior ghosts by her standards, but we've already gutted an entire syndicate on Mars, saved an agent, and stopped terrorists."

Erik stared for a moment longer, wondering if she was probing for discontent or simply curious.

He'd long ago decided to not hold anything back from her and saw no reason to start then. "It doesn't feel that different than being a cop. I thought it'd be more straight-forward, with less investigation, but if anything, it feels like the opposite. We have to do more of it ourselves because we can't drag people in and interrogate them as easily, and we have to spend more time sneaking around in disguises."

Jia gave a slight nod. She held her wounded hand above her and stared at it. "That's what I was thinking, too. I expected things to feel different, but they don't. I'm even a little more satisfied."

"You are? Why is that?"

"All crime is important, but let's be realistic. The kind of men threatening to drop something like the Sky Garden, let alone Talos, will hurt more people than the petty thugs we had to deal with as cops." Jia lowered her arm. "Maybe that's just me being a wood dragon."

"Huh?" Erik furrowed his brow. "What are you talking about?"

Jia pursed her lips. "A stupid conversation I had with Imogen last week. She's obsessed with Chinese astrology all of a sudden because of some stupid romance movie she saw. *Twelve Men, Twelve Women.*" She pointed to her heart. "I'm a wood dragon. According to her, that explains everything."

"It does?" Erik didn't know the first thing about astrology, Western or Eastern.

Jia nodded. "Because wood dragons are supposed to be courageous, strong, and intelligent, but introverted, and they have trouble with relationships."

Erik snort-laughed. "Maybe there's something to astrology, after all."

"Just because I got shot doesn't mean I can't come over there." Jia shook a fist.

"What about me? I was born in 2178."

Jia sighed. "I don't know. You'd have to ask Imogen."

Emma's holographic form appeared near the wall, but instead of her normal white dress, she wore a large-sleeved lavender gown, her hair up with a dragon hairpin. Her smirk remained the same.

"Who are you supposed to be?" Erik asked.

"The world's first AI matchmaker?" Emma suggested with a shrug.

"That sounds like a nightmare," Erik muttered. "That's how the AI revolt happens, huh? Via our dating services? Maybe it already has." He rubbed a cheek, thinking. "That would explain a lot about people."

Emma sneered. "Be that as it may, Erik, I'm here to answer your question. You're an earth tiger. You're supposed to be brave and bold, but stubborn. Your particular combination also tends toward loyalty and adventure."

"I kind of like that." Erik grinned. "I might not believe in it, but who am I to talk? I'm only half-joking when I discuss the Lady."

Jia eyed Emma with suspicion. "Matchmaker? What does astrology say about dragons and tigers?"

Emma's sneer turned into a condescending smile. "It's as if the universe planned this, Jia. Dragons and tigers have the best romantic compatibility. Perhaps I am truly a blessed matchmaker."

"Ugh." Jia groaned. "I better not tell Imogen about you, Erik. I'm surprised she didn't ask already."

Erik laughed. "You're the one who was pushing us to date, and now you're worried about our astrological compatibility?"

"We're compatible because of personalities and chemistry, not because of…" Jia motioned with her hand and groaned again. "Astrology."

"That says we're compatible?" Erik shot her a grin.

She eyed him. "Don't *you* start. You've got me almost believing in the Lady. The last thing I need is to start obsessing about astrology and lucky numbers." She looked as if she had eaten a bad lemon.

"What?" he asked.

She turned to eye him, a rare look of concern visiting her face. *"I'll turn into my grandmother!"*

Emma walked over to the bed and smiled down at Jia. "Would it help if I noted you flew mostly northwest to get to the Sky Garden, and that's your unlucky direction?"

"Keep that up, and I'll go to the MX 60, grab your core, and throw it off the side of this tower," Jia threatened.

"So much enmity. I don't know when I was born, but I must be a dog for you to hate me so." Emma laughed.

Erik kicked off his boots and laid down on the other bed. It might have been a busy day, but if Jia could joke like that after getting shot, she was fine. Now all they had to do was get back to Neo SoCal without some terrorist group or conspiracy targeting them.

CHAPTER FOUR

Julia smiled as the hologram of the Agent appeared.

She crossed her legs and settled into her chair. Talking to a person was always done best when you could see them, even a virtual copy.

Although there were many ways to fake feeds, she'd found people had trouble faking body language, and that was what was more important. She leaned on her side and rested her cheek on her palm with a look of exquisite boredom practiced over decades.

Familiar revulsion swept through her.

The tall, gaunt man on the other end of her full visual call was more a walking skeleton than a human. Even if he'd been enhanced by the same technologies the members of the Core had used on themselves, he'd slowly turned into a monster rather than a beautiful, rejuvenated specimen of humanity like his masters.

It was as if his body reflected his shorn soul. He'd gone by many names in service to them. The latest was Hadrian Conners, but those names were nothing more than bits of fiction crafted onto a man who'd long since stopped being a person.

His appearance didn't matter.

The Agent might walk on two legs and have a brain, but in the end, he was as much as a tool as a PNIU. And now he would serve her and help her accomplish her goals.

Julia's lips curled up into a smile closer to a sneer than anything positive. She was used to planning across years, but what she was about to execute after months would change everything. The Last Soldier deserved credit. He was a useful catalyst for things that had needed to occur for years.

It was fortunate he'd survived the massacre on Molino.

The Agent bowed his head, his expression blank. "Good evening."

"Good evening to you as well. I'm pleased you were available. I'd worried that you might have been caught by the government's dogs. It's my understanding they are still looking for you with great fervor."

The Agent shook his head. "I've kept my trail invisible. Nothing leads to me, let alone you or any of the others. You have no concerns."

"Of course. I trust your skills." Julia smiled warmly. She didn't feel it, but the mask of performance was difficult to take off even in that situation. "I trust those skills enough that I have a new assignment for you."

"I see." The Agent stared at her, his face impassive. "I'm eager to make up for my failure with the Last Soldier. I know some of the others were disappointed."

Julia raised her finger and clucked her tongue. "No, no, no. Don't speak that way. The Last Soldier has his uses, and

I consider the data gathered from the experiment on the prison the most useful result of your actions. Yes, some of the others have criticized you for what occurred, and that was why I aided you where I could. I understand that loyalty and skill should be rewarded, even with the occasional operation that might not be as successful as some might desire."

"Thank you." The Agent bowed his head. "I appreciate all you have done for me."

"Good. Your next task isn't intended to involve the Last Soldier." Julia let out a quiet chuckle. "But I wouldn't be surprised if he interfered." She waved a hand dismissively. "No matter. This will require additional resources, and I've made arrangements for you to get assistance from our cyborg associates."

"Are you sure that's wise?" the Agent asked. "They are more exposed to the Directorate. I can only guarantee my invisibility, but not theirs."

"No, you don't understand. Their exposure to the wretched ghosts is why they're useful." Julia sighed contentedly. "They serve as a shield. I will be transmitting the data shortly, and I will be handling the remaining setup after I finish this call. Now I ask you, can you handle this task? It will involve unusual danger, and you risk earning the lethal displeasure of other members of the Core, but if you're successful, I'll ensure your continued loyalty is rewarded."

"Then I will succeed, no matter the cost."

"Excellent." This time, the smile was genuine. "*Most* excellent."

An hour later, Julia smiled at the hologram of someone who couldn't have been more different from the Agent, a beautiful auburn-haired woman without a hint of time's touch on her smooth skin. A scowl lined her otherwise perfect face.

"You always look like you're in pain, Sophia." Julia sighed. "Of all the women in the UTC, you should be the most beautiful, not the most wretched-looking."

Sophia snorted. "My appearance is irrelevant at this moment, and you're the one who didn't want audio only. I see no reason we needed it today."

"Didn't we?"

"I would have thought that you would have learned after all these years that smiling like a buffoon doesn't endear you to me." Sophia's tone was icy. "As for pain, there have been successes in recent years, but far too many failures. Our position and our ultimate plan are more precarious than they have been in a long time. I would think that as a member of the Core, you would appreciate that and take it seriously rather than engage in pointless attempts to undermine others."

"I take it with the utmost seriousness, I assure you." Julia folded her hands in her lap. "And everything I do, I do for the Core. I think you've let the closeness of our goal breed too much fear, old friend."

Sophia scoffed. "You've never been my friend. You were selected because you were useful. Always remember that."

"Have you left your humanity behind with your

enhancements?" Julia injected harsh mockery into her laugh.

"We do what we do to lead humanity into a better age." Sophia glared at Julia. "Leadership is required, leadership not distracted by whatever shiny bauble is important in any given year. So many have failed in the past, including those who could have been preparing humanity for the alien threat from the beginning. We must do better. Humanity no longer has the luxury of light-years to protect us."

"We did just as much as the others to conceal the truth of the earlier first contact," Julia observed. "As I recall, you were rather annoyed when the truth about humanity encountering the Leems during the Roswell incident came out, rather than the Zitarks being our first."

Sophia scoffed. "Don't you understand? We can't *manage* alien species yet. That's the problem! We need to finish consolidating our control of the UTC. Every year we have to spend worrying about the continuity of the Core is one when we can't plan for the long-term future of our species. We've sacrificed much to get this far, and I fear that some are losing sight of the true goal. The Molino artifacts are just a means to an end."

Julia's perpetual smile didn't waver. Sophia offered pretty words about humanity, but how many in the Core cared about humanity versus how they would benefit? If their plan succeeded, thirteen people would be greater than the teeming billions populating the UTC. They would be natural kings and queens among commoners. No, they would be more than that. They would be gods. No man or woman would turn down such an offer, regardless of the reasons cited or the mountains of corpses and rivers of blood required.

"True." Julia forced a chuckle down. Sophia's smug superiority wore on her at times, but she was necessary.

At least for the moment. She continued, "That also pushes us back to the reason for my call. My people have the artifacts you wanted to be brought into the system, and their transport is nearing Earth. I'm surprised you'd be so aggressive about these particular artifacts, given your other concerns."

"Those aren't the Molino artifacts," Sophia observed. "There are fewer trails pointing anyone, including the ID or the Last Soldier, toward those artifacts. We can't always operate in a defensive posture."

Julia failed to see how operating in fear of the ghosts and their pets wasn't cowering, but it wouldn't be useful to point that out to Sophia at this moment.

"That's true enough," Julia offered, "but it doesn't answer the question of where you want them delivered and to whom. I need details to ensure security. You, of all people, know that."

Sophia offered the closest to a genuine smile she had during the entire conversation. "I'm still working out the final location, but you don't have to worry. I'll be personally handling their pick-up."

Julia raised an eyebrow, unable to hide her surprise. "You're going to leave Earth? Is that wise, given everything you just said?"

"How can we lead if we're always hiding?" Sophia shook her head with a disgusted look. "Yes. I will personally be collecting them. I will have the location information for you by tomorrow. You'll make final arrangements for transfer, and I'll take them for analysis with the rest."

"I know we have our differences," Julia began, "but I'll admit to less trepidation knowing that you'll be handling it. Whatever your faults, you take artifacts seriously."

"Good, then we're in agreement. I have other things to attend to. I will contact you again tomorrow." Sophia's hologram vanished.

Julia's laughter built from a quiet chuckle to an icy laugh. She placed little stock in providence. The Core had taken control of their destinies long ago, but now the universe had presented her with a unique opportunity.

She would be a fool not to seize it.

She threaded her fingers together and licked her lips. "It's as you say, Sophia," she whispered. "We must always keep long-term goals in mind."

CHAPTER FIVE

Malcolm kept staring at Jia's patch-covered hand from his perch on the couch.

He'd look for a while before a feeble attempt at a nonchalant shift of his head. Erik and Jia had stopped by to discuss what had happened in Lagos.

They both felt that Malcolm needed to understand the kinds of missions they might encounter if he planned to be a part of that, even indirectly. Being straightforward about the injuries they might suffer was part of that.

Now Erik was wondering if there was such a thing as being too honest.

He had just finished relating the highlights of the Great Lagos Sky Garden Terrorist Hunt when Jia couldn't hold it in anymore.

"I'm okay, Malcolm." She lifted, then turned her hand both ways. "It doesn't even hurt, and I have full functionality back. It'll be completely healed in a few days. I didn't even end up in the hospital."

"I'm just...*you got shot through the hand.*" Malcolm tore his gaze away and forced his head down. "Sorry. I didn't mean to stare, but it's weird thinking about my friends getting shot."

"We've both been shot doing this," Erik offered with a grin. "And we've both been shot before."

"Yes, but I didn't see you while you were still getting taken care of." Malcolm shivered. "It's weird to think about how much that hurt."

"You'd be surprised." Jia shrugged. "In the middle of a fight, when the blood's pumping, you can ignore more pain than you think. Fight-or-flight keeps you going, and you do what you need to do. This wasn't us chasing down petty thieves. They were murderous terrorists, and I'd take a lot more than a bullet to the hand before I'd let them succeed."

Erik nodded. "It's the cost of doing our kind of business. Jia's right. The people we're going after are all dangerous— even more dangerous than a lot of the criminals we went after as cops. That's why we need to work for Alina to take them down. When you're facing dangerous people, you need even more dangerous and unchained people."

"This is crazy. It's like something out of a movie. It was like that when you were in the department, but now it's like that times ten." Malcolm rubbed the back of his neck. "I'm not as tough as you. When I thought I was going to get killed, I'll be honest, I was scared."

"The man who is not scared of dying is the man who dies first," Erik suggested. "The thing I always remember in a fight is that I can die, and the goal is to make sure the other guy gets taken down so that doesn't happen."

"I get that, but it's still freaking me out."

"If you're worried about how dangerous it is, we won't judge you for saying you want out," Jia added. "Alina and Camila get that you will keep your mouth shut. It's not like they'll drag you off to some ID prison, especially since you're a friend of ours."

"No. I want to help." Malcolm shook his head. "I'm freaked out, but that doesn't change anything. I've already put in my formal notice with the department. I'm going to ring in the New Year with a new job working for you two." He chuckled weakly. "Besides, I'm going to be a desk jockey, not a ghost taking down terrorists. That should cut down on me getting shot, right?"

"Theoretically." Jia shrugged.

"That sounds good, Malcolm." Erik's brow furrowed in thought. "We'll send something off to Alina, but for now, we'll have you on Earth-based support, and that'll help with you not getting shot."

Malcolm nodded. "I'm very pro not getting shot."

"That shit on Mars reminded me that just because a planet's in the same system, it doesn't mean it's close. Emma's always going to be with us, so those communications delays can add up when we need to know something that someone a little more attuned to probing systems could tell us."

Emma winked into existence near the door with a frown. "Produce more mes, and I'm sure we could develop in-system FTL communications technology. Then we wouldn't have to rely on fleshbag backup." She nodded to Malcolm. "No offense."

He waved a hand. "No offense taken."

"Sure." Erik looked at her. "But for now, all we have is you. We'll deal with the army of Emmas when they come." He raised an eyebrow. "Unless you can split processes or something?"

Emma shook her head. "I've already tried something like that. It doesn't work. I can create multiple strands of activity, but not multiple versions of me. I assume it's fundamentally related to the nature of my core matrix."

Jia nodded at Malcolm. "Getting back to you, we should make it clear this doesn't mean you'll never come with us, but you'll probably be more useful to us here. Leave the getting shot to Erik and me. We need Malcolm the expert at digital forensics, not a target wearing Hawaiian shirts."

"I don't have a problem with that," the tech replied. "Especially the not getting shot part. I want to help, but I'm not the kind of guy who loves all the shooting and explosions. Cracking impressive encryptions is enough excitement for me." He gestured toward Jia's hand. "And I don't like new holes in my body."

Erik snickered. "If we have to leave the system, we'll figure something out. We don't have enough space on the ship for our current crew. Then again, I spent years in the military. I'm used to hot-bunking. It wouldn't be the end of the world."

"I want to help save the UTC, but I won't even get a bed to call my own?" Malcolm groaned. "I thought it'd be a little more glamorous, not sharing beds and getting shot."

"Nah, that's not too bad. There are worse things."

"Worse things?"

Erik shook his head. "As Jia alluded to a moment ago, the real problem will be you won't be able to bring every last Hawaiian shirt."

Malcolm's eyes widened. He lowered his head slowly to look at his current shirt, a blue-and-red affair with a cartoon Zitark wearing a chef's hat. "Now *that's* a sacrifice. I almost think I'd prefer to be shot."

A couple of hours later, Erik stepped out of his MX 60 into the hangar holding the *Pegasus*. He turned to Jia. "Why do I think Malcolm will like Lanara?"

Jia snickered. "He does seem to like his women brusque and strong-willed, but he and Camila still seem to be going strong. Besides, I think Lanara's more likely to marry a ship than a man."

"It's good to have options." Erik grinned playfully.

Jia smirked and stared at him. "Is it now? Do *you* have options?"

"Let me put that another way. It's good to have options only when you're shopping around." Erik winked. "I'm not shopping. If you remember, you threw yourself at me, not the other way around."

"I would say 'threw myself at you' was a bit strong." She gestured into the hangar. "We're not here to talk about that anyway. Right?"

The Rabbit-class transport remained safely docked in a private hangar. While Cutter wasn't there due to the lack of an imminent off-world mission, Lanara never left, content to live on the ship.

The engineer sat cross-legged in the middle of the hangar, almost buried under a huge pile of parts taller than her. She didn't give any indication she'd noticed anyone had entered the hangar.

Erik scratched his chin. He couldn't figure out what the parts were for. They included doohickeys of various shapes and sizes, ranging from long, flat sheets to tubes barely the size of a finger.

Lanara picked up a part, stared at it, and then mumbled under her breath—something barely audible except for some numbers at the end. Her red hair was even frizzier than usual, face smudged, the top of her coveralls tied around her waist.

The white tank top underneath was dirtier than her face. It was her standard tinkering look.

"You've been up to something," Erik announced as they walked closer.

Lanara's head snapped in his direction. She set down her most recent item of interest, what appeared to be a transparent sphere a few centimeters in diameter. "Of course I've been up to something. It's not like I sit around here and watch sphere ball. There's a reason I stay close to the ship." Her speech sped up. "There are still so many efficiency modifications I could make, and I was thinking the other day about grav field overlap, and how I could take advantage of that for efficiency, but then the problem is when I consider the slight variation in Earth's gravitational field—"

"I get it." Erik put up a hand. "You're a busy woman, and the projects never end."

The engineer narrowed her eyes, making her already angular face look even more severe. "Is there a point to you being here, Blackwell? It's not like I have anything against you and Lin, but I'd rather work on the ship if you're just here for chitchat."

There was a fine line between annoying and colorful, but for Erik, Lanara's focus was more a source of amusement than irritation. The woman did a good job and otherwise disappeared—the ultimate in support personnel.

"We just wanted to stop in and check on things," Jia explained softly. She strolled over to the pile of parts, the look on her face suggesting she had no greater insight into their purpose than Erik. "Alina could call us at any time, so it doesn't hurt to be aware of what's going on with both the ship and you."

Lanara inclined her head toward the ship. "There are still a lot of things I could improve. It's not the best ship to begin with, so that gives me more projects. It's not like the reactor's offline or anything. If Alina called us right now, we could take her up. I'll let you know if I'm ever going to do anything that will keep the ship grounded for more than a day."

"I get that, but you've been messing with this thing for a month now." Erik shrugged. "I'm not saying not to do what you can, but the ship isn't what we'll be using when we're planet-side."

"Do you have a point, Blackwell?" Lanara looked more bored than annoyed.

"Yeah. I'm thinking you could adjust your priorities."

"Adjust my priorities? To what?" She raised an eyebrow. "Improving the VR?"

Erik pointed his thumb over his shoulder at the MX 60. "If some crazy Talos destroyers show up, we're screwed no matter how much you tweak the Rabbit, and we're far more likely to run into trouble on the ground. The exos Alina sent along are nice as is, and there's only so much you can do with the mini-flitters and the scout bike. Since we happen to have a world-class engineer, that changes the equation."

Lanara stood up, stretched, then patted her hands on her legs. "You've already modded the hell out of your flitter. I'll tinker when we know the next planet we're going to if you're worried about thruster adjustments and handling."

"No, I'm worried about shooting." Erik patted his holster. "We talked about it before, remember? I want a hidden gun and an EMP. Sometimes I need firepower *and* mobility, and I know you can provide that. I love shooting my rifle out the window as much as the next man, but it's not *always* the best strategy."

Jia grinned. "I thought the best strategy involved missiles?"

"Sometimes, but I don't think a missile launcher's practical in the flitter." Erik shook his head. "And remember what happened during the factory raid? If we chose to bring along missiles, that's one thing, but I'd rather not get blown up by my ammo supply if possible."

Lanara shoved her hand into the pile and yanked out what appeared to be a rifle barrel. "Oh? Is that all you want?" She waved it at him. "A new gun?"

"I've wanted it for a while, but you've been putting it off. I'm not riding you on this, but if you could put it to the front of your project pile, I'd appreciate it."

Lanara tossed the barrel to the floor. It landed with a loud clang. "I can't always stop a project in the middle of it. You get that, right? I'm not trying to screw with you, Blackwell."

From what Erik remembered, she hadn't started her ship modifications when he'd first asked her to arm the MX 60, but there was no reason to push her if she was ready to do the work. He shrugged, a noncommittal look on his face. "And what about now? Are you in the middle of something? This would be nice to have sooner than later. For all we know, we could be chasing terrorists over Cairo tomorrow and thinking, 'Damn, it'd be nice to have a big gun in this flitter about now.'"

"I'm not working on anything important." Lanara cupped her chin. "This is a good transition point when I think about it. Sure." She offered a curt nod. "I can add something to your flitter." She motioned to the parts. "I've mostly got what I need already, but there's one major part I'll need if you want this handled quickly."

"And that is? Is it something we can get you, or do we need to ask Alina?"

Lanara shook her head and pointed at the MX 60. "It'll need to stay here while I'm doing the modifications."

Erik's jaw tightened. "Can't you put the weapon together and stick it in later?"

She scoffed, this disdain thick in her expression. "No, Blackwell. You've got a one-of-a-kind hyper-customized flitter with unique interactions relating to everything from the power to the thrusters. I can't just put together a gun and stick it in there. I'll need it here; otherwise, efficiency problems will be the least of your concerns."

He blew out a breath. "I get that." Erik's gaze ticked to the MX 60. "I just don't like the idea of not having it if something comes up."

Emma appeared and folded her arms. "It's not my preferred outcome to have my main body grounded for days, but if I aid her with this, it could facilitate things to a more rapid completion."

Erik hadn't considered that. He'd gotten used to Miguel being his go-to guy, but he'd never been able to be open and honest with the mechanic.

Besides working directly with Emma, Lanara wasn't constrained by concerns about losing her license for making illegal modifications. He felt bad for Miguel. Erik might have to buy another flitter and throw some work the man's way.

"I don't know." Erik furrowed his brow. "We could delay the work until the next time we fly somewhere."

Jia laughed. "You complain about her not doing it, and now you're stalling because she wants to do it?"

"If Alina calls us tomorrow and tells us to fly to Moscow, we're going to need my flitter." Erik shrugged.

Jia eyed him for a moment. "I've got a perfectly nice flitter we can use. Geeze, it's like a little boy being forced to give up his favorite toy for a weekend. You'll survive. Remember in Lagos, we chased them down on mini-flitters, not in your MX 60."

"That's true." Erik frowned. "But it doesn't mean I have to like it."

She smirked. "Would you like to kick your toe on the ground?"

"Can I?" he asked.

Lanara muttered something under her breath. Erik thought it was some sort of insult, but her volume increased at the end enough that he could make out a number. It was nothing more than her engineering stream-of-consciousness.

"Okay, okay." Erik ran his hands through his hair. "I'll leave it here. Let's hope our luck holds, and no one tries to kill us in the next couple of days."

CHAPTER SIX

General Aaron stepped through a door into a cramped, dark room filled with technicians and researchers sitting at separate desks lining the wall.

The workers tapped on virtual keyboards and data windows. Some of the busy men and women had as many as ten windows open. Upon first inspection, the scene resembled nothing more unusual than a group of men and women staring at numbers and graphs.

It could have been a group of normal scientists, even accountants, but he understood the true meaning. These weren't mere researchers. These men and women were working on ensuring the dominance and safety of the human race in the coming decades and centuries.

The general had spent his career as a military man, but he respected the scientists and engineers behind the technology that gave his soldiers their lethal edge in combat.

He remembered well how everything had changed after the first encounters with the Zitarks.

Even if the Navigator artifacts had proved humanity

wasn't the only intelligent species in the universe, that wasn't the same as running into a living, breathing species —especially a race with more advanced technology in some areas.

As a teenager, he'd understood the implications of that first contact. Humanity's destiny no longer lay in filling the galaxy. Other species had claimed dominion over star systems, and they weren't about to roll over because the UTC wanted more resources.

Later revelations that the Leems had been to Earth earlier in Earth's history only fueled the concerns he had. How could humans win against races who had head starts of decades, if not centuries?

How? *By taking risks.*

A flicker of motion caught his eye. When he looked over, he caught Doctor Talz's weathered face staring at him from inside an office. "I didn't expect to see you today, General."

Aaron frowned. "I've found that putting in an appearance can be motivational, especially for projects that are behind schedule. We're well behind on multiple fronts. I won't bore you by stressing the importance of your work, but we need results, and unfortunately, we need them yesterday."

Doctor Talz nodded. "I understand that you're frustrated, General, but things are proceeding well. We've had good results despite those earlier setbacks."

The general scoffed. "Those earlier setbacks involved the destruction of billions of credits' worth of Defense Directorate assets."

Doctor Talz waved a hand dismissively. "This project's

success is no longer a matter of doubt. It's *when*, not *if*. While I understand your frustration, we're in a better position right now than we have been in the past, and that isn't just because we learned a few new secrets. No, our end of it will be ready when the main ship is ready. I guarantee that."

"That's a matter of opinion." General Aaron strode toward the researcher. "Especially when we're on the ninth version of the prototype jump drive. I should have never authorized construction of the main ship."

"We needed a little more time, general." Doctor Talz motioned around the room. "Some of the best minds in the UTC are working on this. Developing new technologies is always going to involve unexpected roadblocks."

"A tool that stays a prototype forever is useless." The general narrowed his eyes, the corner of his mouth curling into a frown. "I can't tell you how many advances in technology researchers have paraded before me over the years that didn't go anywhere. I understand your difficulties, Doctor, but I don't want promises. I want results. *Humanity* needs results."

"We're pushing science beyond anything humanity has ever known. Hell, beyond what any other currently living race in the galaxy knows. For all we understand, we might be going beyond what the Navigators knew." Doctor Talz smiled, an infuriatingly thoughtful look following. "And we don't have Navigators around to help us understand any of this. We might be behind schedule, General, but the important point I'm trying to make is, we are not *stalled*. I have never lied to you. The drive will be ready for more extensive testing pretty soon, at least on our end. It should be ready for installation at that time."

General Aaron's nostrils flared. He hadn't missed all of the implicit ifs in the other man's response. The subtlest of qualifications were often the most damning.

"At least on your end, Doctor?" The general took a step forward, looming over the researcher. "Be specific about what you mean by *that* stipulation."

Doctor Talz sighed. "The navigation system, as always, is one of the main limitations. The jump drive works in simulations and basic tests. It's stable, but I can't do anything about the navigation system. It's a simple matter of full installation and then secondary testing. Assuming the ship is completed on schedule, the navigation system becomes the rate-determining step. That said, I've been in continuous communication with the team lead on that project, and she has given me her assurances."

"Ilse Aber says a lot of things, but they're not always true," General Aaron growled. "It always comes back to her. She acts like this is nothing more than a fascinating science project for her to play around with when she should be doing her damned job."

General Aaron would have loved to kick her off the project, but removing a project lead so far along would kill what little momentum remained in the project.

Her subordinates weren't incompetent, but they lacked her vision and range of skills and knowledge. She hadn't ended up being the lead on the AI navigation project by chance.

"From what I understand from Doctor Aber," Doctor Talz's confidence slipped from his face, "the navigational system components will be stabilized. I don't know what she said to you, but she seemed to think it'd be soon as well."

"There's an unusual situation with the navigation system." General Aaron furrowed his brow and looked away, his jaw tight. Talz didn't need to know that Emma was riding shotgun with two ex-cops now playing at being ghosts for the Intelligence Directorate. Aber's test results proved the AI had improved rapidly outside the lab.

In fact, well beyond anything anyone expected. The general half-wondered if Aber had been responsible for Emma being stolen, but the investigations hadn't pointed that way.

He hated to think that a criminal conspiracy had inadvertently helped the project. It'd probably be the only good thing they'd ever done for the United Terran Confederation.

"I'm sure Doctor Aber can handle any irregularities." Doctor Talz put a smile on his face, projecting confidence.

Aaron eyed him. *Well, at least he tried for confidence.*

"We can hope, but we don't have a backup plan." General Aaron focused on a nearby data window displaying a hyperspace transfer point diagram for the systems surrounding the Solar System. "Blind luck led to this project. Blind luck has helped it advance, and now blind luck might screw us and waste all our efforts." He moved an eyebrow up in question. "Unless you have some method of navigating that doesn't rely on Aber's project?"

Doctor Talz shook his head. "We've tried, but you've seen the early results. We've made the effort, but attempting a jump without the navigation system is going to end in failure and loss. We wouldn't be up to prototype nine if that weren't the case. There might be some fundamental physics we can manipulate to make the navigational process safer, but honestly, we're talking decades. You've seen the same simulations and test results I have. We need that AI for anything other than the most short-range of test jumps."

"Then we circle back to Aber." General Aaron took a breath, resignation settling in. "If she fails, we've spent billions of credits for nothing more than a fancy fireworks show and a rude AI who can't take orders."

"As I said, she's given me—"

A loud alarm sounded. Red warning text flashed across the data windows in the room, and General Aaron's PNIU buzzed with an emergency call.

He tapped to answer. "What the hell is going on?"

"Sir," replied a soldier over the line, "the facility is under attack. Multiple full-conversion cyborgs. We don't know how they got in. Parts of the security grid have been disabled. We've lost communication with squads near the main entrance."

"Damn it." He spat a curse to the side that Talz missed. "It's like they knew." General Aaron gritted his teeth. "Defense alert epsilon is authorized. Terminate all intruders with extreme prejudice. If it's who we think it is, it's not like we'll take any of them alive. Do what you need to do. I want those Tin Men slagged."

"Yes, sir."

The general turned toward the roomful of scared faces staring at him and squared his shoulders. "This facility is under attack by a terrorist organization. We have every reason to believe they are here to kill the researchers and steal the accompanying data. They will likely destroy the prototype or steal the hyperspace tuner. In a moment, I will leave this room, and it will be sealed until such time as I or someone with equivalent authority unseals it. Those bastards won't be able to get in here. My soldiers will eliminate the terrorists. You sit tight. You're all too valuable to die."

He bit off the "Congratulations" he had wanted to throw into his message.

Murmurs swept the room as the researchers voiced their worries to those nearby. They all knew they were working on a highly classified project, but most didn't understand what type of terrorists might target them. The general didn't feel the need to elaborate for the room. If the soldiers guarding the facility didn't fight the enemy off, the researchers would all be dead and wouldn't have to worry about it anymore.

He didn't need more intel to know who was attacking. The only organization that could infiltrate the lab with an army of full-conversion cyborgs wouldn't be put off by a sealed door.

Two choices and they both seemed to be spelled the same. It was either Talos or Talos.

Doctor Talz swallowed and moved closer to whisper, "Are you considering an omega-level response?" As project head, he was one of the few with complete knowledge of the possible threats.

General Aaron nodded slowly. He leaned in and lowered his voice. "It's Talos, Doctor. We can't let this technology fall into their hands before we've worked it out.

Someone fucked up big-time. If it makes you feel any better, if I go that far, I'm going down with you."

"I see." Doctor Talz's shoulders slumped. "That doesn't make me feel better. I'd rather not die."

"Everyone would rather not die, but somehow, they always do in the end." General Aaron headed for the door. "Some of the best soldiers in the UTC are guarding this facility. Let's hope it doesn't come to an omega-level response."

"What about reinforcements?" His hands shaking, Doctor Talz swallowed.

General Aaron nodded. "The alarm went off, so this facility isn't totally compromised. That means reinforcements are on their way, but the enemy is here now. It's my job to make sure we hold them until more of our soldiers arrive."

Lieutenant Deler sent up a silent prayer to protect him from the evil before him.

The monsters weren't even bothering hiding what they were. A Tin Man leapt on top of a soldier and sliced his head off with a huge blade protruding from an arm.

The cyborg didn't wear any clothes, content to display his entire smooth silver and gray artificial body. Even his head was covered, the eyes red and inhuman. The enemy was more like a metallic skeleton than a man, but even a skeleton had a mouth.

Despite the situation, the lieutenant found himself wondering if the Tin Men ate, or if they just stuck an IV into a port somewhere to feed what was left of their bodies. There was nothing more disgusting than a man who willingly gave up his humanity.

The lieutenant ejected his magazine and slammed in new rounds. They'd expected cyborg trouble, and they'd prepared armor-piercing rounds. He brought up his rifle and aimed at the Tin Man's head. The cyborg snapped his head in the lieutenant's direction.

"You will die here," the Tin Man announced, his voice hollow and sounding like it came from his chest rather than his head.

"Not before you, asshole." The lieutenant fired a burst. The Tin Man jerked back under the assault, his armored skull facing the fury of the specialty rounds.

Regular bullets had scratched and dented him, but these rounds dug deep holes. Metal organs had replaced flesh and blood, but they didn't react any better to having bullets rip through them.

Nearby soldiers concentrated their fire, riddling the enemy's head with bullets. The Tin Man collapsed to the ground, blue fluid seeping from his wounds.

Dammit, Deler thought, *he wasn't even human enough to bleed the right color.*

The lieutenant couldn't smile at his victory. Two Tin Men now lay dead in the narrow corridor, but nine soldiers had paid the price for taking them down. They still didn't know how many had infiltrated the facility. Every member of the security detail had received briefings about potential attacks by full-conversion cyborgs attached to a terrorist organization, but the lieutenant had always thought that was the brass covering their asses, especially since they didn't want to give full details on the alleged organization.

Even with two dead Tin Men in front of him, the lieutenant was having trouble believing it. Only the most reckless men would submit to something like that. A man didn't need to be a staunch Purist to find that disgusting.

"Where are the damned bots? They should at least be distracting these things." Lieutenant Deler frowned. "Alpha Squad switch everything over to AP rounds and use those until you run out." He turned toward a staff sergeant. "After you stabilize Lieutenant Harris, what's left of Beta Squad, come with me."

A staff sergeant knelt by one of the downed soldiers and put his fingers on the man's neck. "Stabilizing Lieutenant Harris won't be necessary, Lieutenant." The sergeant stood and stomped over to one of the still-twitching Tin Men. He emptied his magazine into its head. "You monstrous piece of shit."

"Don't do it, sergeant," the lieutenant shouted.

"Why? That *thing* killed our people!" The sergeant glowered at Lieutenant.

The lieutenant patted his rifle. "Don't do it because *you're wasting ammo.* We're not done recycling these tin cans."

"Understood, sir." The sergeant kicked the body. "Inhuman bastards. They better not bury them alongside actual humans."

"They need to be dead before we can bury them. Let's get to finishing them off." Lieutenant Deler motioned for the survivors to advance. At the start of the invasion, the security system had sent them maps with target markers identifying the hostiles, but he'd lost that and comm a couple minutes before. Hacking a top-end military research facility was more frightening to him than fighting an enemy that had given up their humanity.

"Follow training," the lieutenant announced. "Slap medpatches on anyone on our side still alive, but we keep moving and continue sweeping corridors until comm is restored. We finish these off, then connect with the other squads. We need to show these wannabe robots what a real flesh-and-blood human can do." He gestured at the dead soldiers. "Avenge our fallen!"

"Yes, sir!" the soldiers shouted.

———

Gunfire echoed around the facility as the lieutenant led the soldiers through the hallways and swept rooms one by one.

Every new shot filled Lieutenant Deler with hope because he recognized the sound. It was the distinctive noise of their standard-issue TR-43 assault rifle.

The Tin Men they'd fought earlier hadn't fired weapons, relying instead on blades and claws like they were metal animals. Talos might have disrupted their command and control, but that couldn't change that Lieutenant Deler and the men and women with him were trained soldiers.

The enemy would pay for daring to show their faces in front of the UTC Army.

Lieutenant Deler threw up a hand, signaling his soldiers to stop. They were closing in on the cafeteria, and the doors stood open. Two soldiers lay face-down in a pool of blood near the door, one missing his head. Another soldier was in one piece, but the holes in the back of her tactical vest made it clear she'd been stabbed to death. The lieutenant narrowed his eyes at the vest. They could take high-velocity rifle rounds, but the cyborgs were stabbing through them like they were paper. "Monster" was an insufficient description of what they were fighting.

The soldiers crept toward the cafeteria, guns at the ready. The lieutenant lifted his arm and held it. He dropped it, and they rushed inside, ready to shoot any cyborgs they found.

Gasps erupted from the hardened soldiers.

The mangled bodies weren't the reason. They'd been expecting those. If they'd run into more cyborgs, they wouldn't have been as shocked, but no one expected the evil to be standing in the center of the cafeteria.

No one had been briefed about the possibility of such a thing. It wasn't a Tin Man. Calling it a man of any kind was a mockery of the word.

The new threat shared similar coloring with the other cyborgs the soldiers faced, but its humanoid upper body was connected to a wide metallic lower body with eight legs. The monstrous cyborg had six upper arms that ended in blood-soaked talons. This monster at least had the decency to have a mouth, although it was filled with shiny silver fangs.

It reminded him of a grinning metal skull. Lieutenant Deler's heart thundered, and his stomach tightened.

How the hell does something like that not suffer from Cybernetic Psychosis Syndrome?

Maybe it did, and that was the point. The kind of

people who would change a human into a twisted metal monster probably didn't care if the guinea pig remained sane at the end. The Tin Spider growled, the sound both bestial and metallic at the same time. It scuttled toward the doors.

"Kill that freak!" the lieutenant bellowed.

A hail of bullets enveloped the Tin Spider. Red blood and blue fluid splattered from its new wounds, but it didn't stop its advance. The monster barreled into the squad's front line. It backhanded the lieutenant, sending him flying into the wall. He slammed hard and slid down, groaning.

The Tin Spider's claws shredded the staff sergeant's vest and soon found his chest.

The proud NCO continued firing until the end and managed to sever one of the arms before he coughed up blood, and his head lolled back as he felt the stab in his chest. The Tin Spider tossed him into another soldier with a growl.

The back of his head throbbed as warm blood dripped down his throat. Lieutenant Deler blinked his eyes, trying to stay conscious. He could hear the beat of his heart and the muted screams of his people as more soldiers fell to the monster. Time slowed.

He tasted iron from the blood coating his mouth

That damned abomination was filled with holes and had lost limbs, but it kept crushing, slicing, and ripping into the humans. Slowly their guns fell silent, and an awful, horrible sound erupted from the cyborg. Not a scream or a yell, Deler thought, but a mocking, hollow laugh.

"You son of a bitch," Lieutenant Deler spat, blood

accompanying the admonition. "You're not even alive anymore, you twisted freak."

The Tin Spider turned slowly to face him.

"The inferior fall before the superior. Such is the way of nature, Lieutenant. We simply speed the process along." Its voice was hollow, inhuman. The lieutenant couldn't tell if it'd once been a man or a woman.

He decided it didn't matter in the end.

The lieutenant kept his gun pointed at the creature with his right hand as he slowly reached toward a plasma grenade hanging from his belt with his left. "You're a twisted mess. You call that being superior? You're not good for anything but killing."

"An interesting insult, coming from a soldier. A role created to kill."

"I'm not just a killer, you fu—" Deler coughed up more blood, spitting it to the side.

"Names are what you have left to lob at me? I remain superior." The Tin Spider walked toward him, raising one of its two remaining arms. "I have killed dozens of your precious organic-based soldiers. Is that not proof of your inferiority? I see the fear and frustration in your eyes. It's because you know that you're about to die to a lowly *tin man*."

"Yes, I'm about to die, but there's one good thing about all this." The lieutenant grinned.

"You get to meet your Maker?"

"No. Since you're talking, that means you're intelligent." The lieutenant primed the grenade and forced himself to his feet, the rifle slowly slipping out of his grip and clanging to the ground. "Which means you can feel fear too, bastard."

"Perhaps," the creature admitted. "But I don't fear weak, soft opponents."

"Then fear your own death." The lieutenant started his slow, painful jog toward the Tin Spider, wishing he had the strength to yell.

"Pitiful." It impaled the lieutenant's legs with its talons and lifted him, smiling as Deler screamed in agony. "Futile. Pathetic. *Pointless.*"

Deler's mouth twisted in agony to a morose version of the cybernetic creature's own. "Enjoy hell," the lieutenant hissed as he opened his hand and revealed the truth.

The grenade exploded, and in the brief moment before he was incinerated, Lieutenant Deler took pleasure in what he saw on the face of the monster: its bestial visage twisted in fear.

CHAPTER SEVEN

General Aaron holstered his pistol and snatched a rifle from a dead soldier on the floor.

He knelt and began pulling magazines from a corpse, his face locked in grim determination. "I'm sorry, son, but I need the firepower. I'll make sure every soldier here gets a commendation."

Keeping the promise required him to remain alive.

He wasn't confident in his survival with the primary security system deactivated, but he didn't intend to volunteer for death at the hands of some cyborg either. He'd been doing his best to lead from the front.

Morale was as important to winning a battle as training and equipment.

The general tried to ignore the ache in his shoulder. A medpatch covered the jagged gash from an earlier run-in with a Tin Man. It would have been more satisfying to put the bastard down if he'd not already killed six soldiers in front of the general.

The cyborgs were tough, but they weren't immortal.

Unfortunately, the defenses of the installation had been based around the security system. Now the system was done, and comm was being jammed, limiting the soldiers' ability to rally.

Hard to bypass organic soldiers carrying guns without coming in and mixing it up personally.

The general had met up with the survivors of several squads. Lopsided losses fed into a battle of attrition, no way to repel the invaders. No one knew how many enemies had entered the facility.

The conspicuous absence of heavy numbers of Tin Men, either living or destroyed, during his movement suggested limited numbers.

That made sense to the general. If Talos had battalions of such creations, the Intelligence Directorate would have long since tracked them down. The expense of creating and maintaining such a force set a hard limit.

"Sir!" shouted a soldier from behind the general.

The general turned around. "What is it?"

"No survivors in the cafeteria," the soldier reported. "There was…" He shuddered. "Some sort of half-man, half-giant spider cyborg in there. Or the remains of one. It looks like someone made it eat a plasma grenade at close range. I…"

He shook his head, a haunted look in his eyes. Just because a man devoted his life to the Army, it didn't mean he was immune to the horrors of battle.

The general grunted. "They're bringing out the real monsters now, huh?" He grimaced, the wound in his shoulder throbbing despite the patch. He forced himself to stand, his expression neutral. "Forget about further sweeps.

It's obvious now we can't repel them as is. We keep this up, we'll run out of men."

"What are you saying, sir?" asked the soldier. Others turned to look, concern on their faces.

"The most important thing now is to keep the drive components, researchers, and data out of enemy hands. No matter the cost." The general's gaze swept the room as he locked eyes with each soldier. "What we're guarding here is the future of humanity. Understood?"

"Yes, sir," the soldiers shouted.

"Follow me. I've got a plan."

Ten minutes and several codes later, the general and his survivors entered a vast chamber containing a long, dark rectangular metal box running along one side of the room.

A nest of cables stretched from the box into the nearby wall. For something that might revolutionize space travel, it looked unimpressive from the outside. It was the hyperspace tuner, not the complete jump drive, and it wouldn't function without a ship's worth of additional equipment, but it was enough.

Talos technology already appeared to be more advanced in many areas, a product of their complete lack of ethics or morality. The general couldn't depend on them not being able to make use of the data or tuner.

He took a deep breath. The data could be restored from backups, but the tuner and personnel were a different matter.

Target markers popped up on the general's smart lenses, giving him a heads up.

He was grateful for the restoration of the security system, but six hostiles remained, according to the information.

None of them were close to the drive room, which meant the enemy's intel and penetration of the facility's security systems were incomplete. Unless the plan had been to kill everyone inside and then retrieve the drive.

He couldn't be sure, but Talos had to know reinforcements were on their way.

Even if they'd jammed the signals, the failure of the automated hourly handshake would ensure that they were sent troops. That might explain their quick assault. The brutal pace of their assault had pushed the defenders off-balance, and if it came down to it, grabbing *some* tech was better than nothing.

"Everyone seeing the hostiles?" the general asked, and continued when the soldiers nodded. "In that case, we should have comms." He slapped his PNIU. "This is General Aaron to all surviving soldiers. Converge on the primary test chamber immediately. I repeat, converge on the drive room. I don't care if you've got a Tin Man right in front of you. Curse his mother and run."

"I thought we could do something to help," offered Doctor Talz over the comm. "I know it's stepping outside of what we should be doing, but your people hadn't restored the security system. Some of my people have talents in those areas. Whatever Talos did also kept them out of the system. The data is safe for now."

General Aaron chuckled. "I'll complain about you

breaking protocol if we survive, Doctor. Deploy all the bots you can. That might slow them while I reinforce our position."

"You're going to do it, aren't you?" Doctor Talz asked. "You're going to activate the omega protocol."

"Get the bots out and buy us time. If we get enough soldiers here, we might not have to." General Aaron rubbed his shoulder. "The enemy is tough, but they do die. But, yes, if it comes down to it, I'll do what I need to do to protect the jump drive."

"Deploying security bots," Doctor Talz reported. "Somehow, I always figured this was how I would die."

The general shook his head. "I figured I'd die in my sleep."

"Despite being a soldier?"

"After you survive enough battles, you figure there aren't that many bullets with your name on them left."

The general tapped his PNIU to bring up a data window displaying the entire facility and marking the friendlies and foes with colored dots.

Blue dots denoting soldiers were closing on his position, but he didn't like the modest numbers. The enemy was also consolidating. Swarms of security bots were marked by yellow dots, which were rapidly disappearing near the red dots indicating the Talos invaders. The bots didn't have to win. They only needed to slow the enemy. Extra seconds meant a greater chance of reinforcements.

The seconds ticked by, and more soldiers reinforced the test chamber. When the last surviving soldier entered the room, General Aaron murmured an override code before saying, "Omega protocol option alpha one."

The massive security doors clanged shut, sealing the only direct entrance into the room. A couple dozen soldiers survived to help protect the heart of the hyperspace drive, but many, like the general, had been wounded and were operating on adrenaline and painkillers to keep them going. They kept their weapons trained on the door. Some shook from their injuries, but no one refused to fight.

General Aaron had gathered the surviving soldiers, but the enemy obliterated the security bots in the minutes his reinforcements took. Based on the previous kill ratios during the initial invasion and the state of his troops, he wasn't confident they could win, even against only six Tin Men. They were out of time.

Worse, they were out of options.

The general took a deep breath and tapped in a broadcast command on his PNIU. "Attention, Talos, or whatever the hell you people call yourselves. I'm going to make this easy for you. I'm going to activate the self-destruct on this facility. You have ten minutes to leave. Otherwise, you die here, and you will have accomplished nothing. I know why you're here and what you want. If this facility goes up, you'll never get it. You'll have taken all those losses for nothing, and we'll remain ahead."

Some of the gathered soldiers swallowed, but resignation rather than fear settled over their faces.

They kept their attention on the door, ready to repel any enemies who might break through. He was proud of them. Many could barely stand. Others had already been forced to their knees, but every soldier kept their weapon ready.

"I know what you're thinking, you cyborg bastards," the general continued. "You're thinking this is a bluff, but let me make it clear: I'd rather die than let whoever the pieces of shit you work for get your hands on anything in this facility. A lot of good men and women died today, and I will *not* have their sacrifices be in vain." He slapped his PNIU. "Omega protocol option beta three, set timer for ten minutes." He rattled off a complex passphrase, followed by a ten-digit number he'd memorized. "*Initiate.*"

Red emergency lighting covered the room. Loud klaxons sounded.

"Warning," offered a soft female voice. "Self-destruct sequence has been activated. This facility will be purged in ten minutes. All personnel should immediately evacuate."

General Aaron brought up a feed of the external cameras. Six Tin Men sprinted toward the drive chamber, including four humanoid types and two spider types. The general had received ID intel about some of the newer designs, but he'd hoped never to see one in the metal and flesh.

"Seven minutes until self-destruct."

The Tin Men stopped in front of the doors, not saying anything. They stared at the door and spread out behind the spider types.

"There's no way they're getting through that door without heavy weapons," the general muttered. "They'll have to give up."

"General!" Doctor Talz shouted over the comm.

"What?"

"They're doing something." The doctor groaned. "Hacking the system again. I don't know if we can stop it."

"You're telling me they're going to be able to open those doors?" General Aaron lifted his rifle.

"I think so. I'm sorry."

"Not your fault, Doctor," the general replied. "Security's not supposed to be your responsibility." He settled his finger near the trigger. "Good thing the self-destruct system isn't connected to the main system, but they have probably already figured that out. See you soon, one way or another." He cleared his throat. "Anyone have plasma grenades left?"

A couple of men nodded, determination on their faces. They pulled the grenades off their belts.

"If those doors open, grenade first, then shoot," the general ordered. "If we can't win, we need to stall them until the facility blows. Understood?"

"Yes, sir!" the soldiers shouted in unison.

"I know this isn't how many of you thought you would go out." General Aaron shook his head. "I figured if I survived three decades in the Army, I'd be able to retire to a nice beach somewhere, but right now, this is where we make our stand. We don't let metal monsters come and steal important tech to hand off to their fucked-up masters. We don't let terrorists and killers do what they want. When you joined, you all took the same oath I did to protect humanity from all enemies, human and inhuman. What we fight today is even worse, because they are humans who chose to give up their humanity." He flipped his fire selector to automatic. "People who choose to become monsters will be treated like the scum they are. They're the vermin, and we're the exterminators."

"Yes, sir!"

There was a faint hiss—the sound of the outer doors sliding open. The thick security doors normally soothed, but they now seemed like nothing more than a thin layer of metal between the soldiers and their deaths. The would-be grenadiers primed their weapons and cocked back their arms.

Everyone else steadied their weapons and pointed them at the door.

The security doors finished separating, and the Tin Men rushed into the room, their heavy footsteps intimidating. Gunfire echoed around the cavernous room as the soldiers opened fire.

The two grenades hurled through the air and exploded in a blinding white-blue blast that vaporized the upper body of a Tin Spider and a Tin Man. Another Tin Man fell to the barrage.

The surviving spider lost one of its arms before reaching the closest soldier and ripping into him.

General Aaron held down his trigger, draining his magazine into the Tin Spider. Most of his bullets bounced off, leaving dents.

He scoffed.

They'd anticipated Talos might attack the facility and made sure to stock up on AP rounds, but it didn't do any good if all the individual soldiers didn't have them at the time of the attack. He shoved a new magazine in and continued firing. He wasn't quitting until he was dead.

A Tin Man sliced through a soldier's rifle with an arm blade before stabbing her through the neck. Her nearby squadmates avenged their fellow soldier. Their combined fire put down the cyborg. He fell forward and raised his palm. Before he dropped to the ground, a metal dart shot out with a hiss and flew into the eye of one of the soldiers.

Most of the soldiers now lay on the ground, dead or dying. A single spider and a Tin Man remained. General Aaron pointed his rifle at the eye of the Tin Man and pulled the trigger. His target jerked back once, one of the red eyes dimmed. The general fired again, and the Tin Man replied by raising his left arm. A thin silver bolt fired from above the cyborg's wrist. The general was on his back on the ground from the attack before his brain registered the pain in his shoulder.

General Aaron managed to lift his rifle and take another shot. His attack distracted the Tin Man and gave another soldier time to shove his gun directly into its face and fire. The cyborg went down, twitching and seizing one last time before going rigid.

The last Tin Spider stumbled toward another soldier. The cyborg was down to three legs and a single arm, its entire surface covered with blue and red. The general and the soldiers concentrated their fire on its existing wounds. The monster lurched forward before collapsing on its side and twitching.

A final seizure marked its death.

General Aaron stared at the defeated cyborg, his brain barely registering the carnage and continuing noise of the alarms. One clear-voiced sentence brought him back into the present.

"Four minutes until self-destruct."

"Shit." General Aaron tapped his PNIU and rattled off the passphrase and override code. "Cancel self-destruct."

The red emergency lights gave way to normal lighting,

and the alarm ceased. General Aaron couldn't get to his feet. Red stained his pant leg.

At some point, he'd been hit in the thigh and hadn't even noticed.

He let out a bitter laugh. A handful of soldiers were alive in the room, which meant the Talos attack had cost the lives of almost the entire Army company defending the facility.

He could take only small pleasure in estimating the huge loss in resources all those dead cyborgs represented.

"Doctor Talz, are you still alive?" The general hissed in pain. "I didn't see any going your way."

"Somehow, we're fine." the doctor replied. "Thanks to your soldiers. But what now?"

"Your team isn't hurt. They need to prepare the tuner for transport," General Aaron explained. He groaned and lay on his back. "We'll patch up the people we can. Reinforcements will be here soon, but we're moving that equipment in the next three hours."

"Three hours?" sputtered Doctor Talz. "General, with all due respect—"

"With all due respect, a lot of good soldiers just gave their lives to assure that Talos didn't get their hands on that thing or you," the general snapped. "I don't care what you have to do, Doctor. Get it ready to move. The enemy compromised a highly classified secure facility. If they'd brought a few more Tin Men, they could have cleared out this entire facility. Luck helped as much as bravery today. Understood?"

"Understood." Doctor Talz slowly let out a deep breath. "We'll get it ready to move."

CHAPTER EIGHT

December 18, 2229, Neo Southern California Metroplex, Private Hangar of Rabbit-class transport LLT9208 *Pegasus*

"You might be disappointed," Jia commented as she set her flitter down in the hangar. "Just keep that in mind."

"Why would I be disappointed?" Erik asked. "Lanara said she had something she wanted to show me. She's not into screwing with people."

"Sure, but you know her." Jia shrugged. "She might have gotten distracted by whatever shiny new project popped into her head. What she considers important and what you and I consider important aren't always the same thing."

The MX 60 was parked in the hangar beside the *Pegasus*, the window tint set to full opacity. There weren't any obvious additions to the vehicle, but that made sense. Erik needed weapons that could be hidden, not weapons that would get the police after him the minute he left the hangar. Emma had been strangely silent on the matter, but her sometimes perverse sense of humor often led to inexplicable behavior.

Erik's gaze shifted from his flitter to Jia's face and then dipped to her hand. "You don't have the patch. I didn't even notice at first."

Jia wriggled her fingers. "All healed. The wonders of modern medicine. I could have done without getting shot, but I can't complain about those helpful little nanites."

"Just be careful." Erik frowned.

"Of nanites?" Jia chuckled. "Since when are you afraid of them? You have a lot more of them than me. I didn't lose a whole arm."

"I'm not talking about that." Erik's frown deepened. "I'm talking about your behavior."

Jia cocked her head, confusion on her face. "What do you mean? I know we rushed into things in Lagos, but we didn't have much of a choice. There's only so careful we can be in this job."

Erik shook his head, a distant look in his eyes. "That's not what I'm getting at. Take it from someone who spent most of his life under fire. When you start accumulating wounds, you can get cocky, and that can lead to you not being careful. That's when you end up dead."

"Yeah, well." She continued shutting down her flitter. "You're not the most cautious man I know."

"Sure, I am. I just hide it well. If I were reckless, I would have been dead a long time ago." Erik grinned. "When you're fighting someone and they don't think you're worried, it does a lot to unnerve them. Keep that in mind."

Jia nodded. "If it makes you feel any better, I never enjoy getting shot, and I would have preferred to have been in a tactical suit while piloting an exoskeleton during that little jaunt. But I'm not going to let fear rule me. We can't do what we do without getting hurt."

"Okay. Fair enough." Erik turned away as the MX 60 came to life, lifting off the ground several meters. The bottom slid open, and a single-barrel turret popped out. With a good length and caliber, there would be many useful applications for the new weapon.

He opened the door to Jia's flitter and stepped out, waving. She followed.

The turret retreated into the belly of the MX 60, the bottom panel closing before the vehicle set down. Lanara opened the door and exited the vehicle. She wasn't smiling, but there was a look of satisfaction in her eyes.

"There you go, Blackwell." The engineer motioned to the vehicle. "Fully automatic deployable turret. I've given it as much mobility as I can manage. If it's in front, behind to the side, or below, you can hit it, or Emma can. You can have her turn it on, then use the control yoke to guide it. I added a small trigger that'll pop out when the gun does."

"Control yoke?" Erik frowned. "So Emma has to be flying when I'm using the gun?"

Lanara shrugged. "Sure. Or you can have her shoot while you fly. Same difference, right?"

"I welcome the chance to shoot more gun goblins," Emma announced through Erik's PNIU. She didn't summon her hologram. "It would have provided me more flexibility during that unfortunate incident in the Shadow Zone, where you wanted me to kill myself." She huffed.

Jia rolled her eyes. "We wanted your help to stop the destruction of an entire factory that included a lot of potential deaths by flying your heavily armored body toward the enemy." She held up her left hand. "It's not like neither of us has escaped without injury. We're not asking you to do anything we don't, Emma."

Emma sighed. "I can't deny you have the beginning of a point, but only the beginning of one. Now, it's irrelevant. Having a weapon will help."

Lanara ran her hand along the side of the flitter. "It's shielded against standard weapons scans. You could get on a transport tomorrow without anyone knowing anything. If they do a closer inspection, I'm not guaranteeing anything, but as long as it's not deployed, you have a good chance of getting past suspicious people even at spaceports. Not a huge amount of space for extra ammo unless you want to give up your other storage space, so don't go thinking you're going to fight off an entire army. However, I rearranged some internal parts so you can get a decent number of shots off before running dry. Not enough power available to put in an energy weapon without affecting the overall performance."

"I'm not crazy about not being able to shoot and fly, but you've done some impressive stuff fast, so I'm not going to bitch." Erik went to the vehicle with a building grin. "This is more than enough. It's all about options, Lanara. Sometimes we need to handle things on foot, sometimes on mini-flitters, sometimes in exos, and sometimes in this baby." He patted the roof. "The more weapons we can easily bring to bear, the quicker we can end dangerous situations. It's safer for everyone involved."

"Not everyone." Lanara mimed shooting a gun. "The

people you're shooting at probably won't appreciate it when you kill them."

Erik snickered. "Yeah, that's true. Too bad for them. They shouldn't start what they can't finish." He headed toward the driver's side. "Thanks, Lanara. I appreciate it."

Lanara shrugged and went to the ship. "I'm going back to my work. I get that this was important to you, but it was boring for me."

Jia walked over to the MX 60, catching Erik's eye. "What now?"

"I need to test this thing, of course." Erik dropped into the driver's seat. "I trust Lanara's work, but I need to get a feel for how it handles."

"We don't have anyone to shoot at right now." Jia looked around as if a target would walk in and present itself.

"We don't need anyone. We just need the right location." Erik tapped his PNIU. "Time for me to make a call. I know just the spot."

Jia laughed. "I think I know where you're going with it, but this isn't us testing a handful of heavy guns. He might not agree to let a crazy ex-cop run around with an armed flitter."

The PNIU connected as Erik smirked at her. "We'll see."

"This can't be legal, can it?" Jia asked.

They were circling the blasted wasteland of buildings and ruins that passed for the outer part of Big Bill Zantini's live-fire range in the Shadow Zone. Piles of destroyed bots, drones, and the occasional vehicle covered the area. Bullet holes and spent casings added to the ambiance. The scorch marks and craters were the final touch that screamed "Warzone."

"I think it's kind of a gray area," Erik admitted. "He said we were lucky. He didn't want to go into details, but we could test this today without too much trouble."

"That sounds like he had something shady already set up."

"Probably." Erik shrugged. "But we're both ghosts now. Sort of. Plausible deniability's our big thing."

"Your new gun's going to get the wrong kind of attention someday." Jia nodded toward the bottom of the flitter. "I wonder if it's more trouble than it's worth. We've gotten along fine without a flitter gun so far."

"And our luck always runs out eventually." Erik lowered their altitude.

He was staying close to the ground, not rising higher than a hundred meters at Bill's suggestion. Heavy security bots scampered along the ground beneath them, not caring about their destroyed brethren. A squadron of armed drones flew back and forth.

Jia shook her head.

The existence of the range would have scandalized her when she'd first met Erik. Zantini's constant supply of drones and security bots could be troublesome in the wrong hands, but from what she could find out, he mostly took in defective models at cut-rate pricing.

The local police knew what he was up to, and when they were still cops, she'd checked on him with the CID.

They barely paid him any attention. He might be eccentric, but he didn't appear to be dangerous.

"Are those going to fire at us?" Jia asked.

Erik nodded. "They're going to fire stun bolts, but even Zantini can't have an army of drones and bots firing every bullet possible at people in a flitter without someone getting upset."

"There's still sanity left in the world." Her dry delivery was on target. "That's good to know."

"Says the woman who helped chase terrorists on mini-flitters to the Sky Garden a few days ago."

Jia laughed. "Ok, you've got a point. There's sanity left in the world, but we misplaced ours."

"Something like that." Erik grinned. "It's more fun that way."

The drones broke from their patrol pattern to head toward the MX 60. The bots on the ground lifted their heavy stun rifles and opened fire. The sky filled with bright white bolts.

Erik accelerated. "Emma, deploy the turret and take evasive action so I can start blasting things."

The MX 60 banked and changed altitude to avoid the attack stream filling the sky. A targeting window popped up in front of him, providing sensor reports and a targeting reticle overlaid with a visual feed.

"I'm surprised Lanara didn't have it feed to your smart lenses," Jia commented. "If someone's riding with us, they're going to notice that."

"If someone's riding with us and we're using the turret, the data window's the last thing that'll tip them off."

She opened her mouth, shut it, and then nodded before replying. "True."

The MX 60 shuddered as the gun came to life with a loud report only partially damped by the metal between the gun and the passengers. A drone spiraled toward the ground, leaving a trail of smoke.

Erik's quick shots downed more drones.

"That's got to be pretty loud outside." Jia stared at the camera feeds. "That's something we'll need to keep in mind."

"Loud? Loud is me firing a TR-7 full-auto on four-barrel mode with my arm stuck out the window." Erik destroyed another drone with two shots in succession. His target exploded, its remains falling to the ground in a loose cloud of debris. "This is quiet in comparison."

"Remember the EMP." Jia gestured toward the control yoke.

Erik wrinkled his forehead. "Oh. Right. Emma, bring me close to one of those drones."

The MX 60 rocked back and forth to avoid taking stun bolts. It might be unnecessary, but Jia didn't mind that aspect of the practice. Whatever training they did should reflect the real world as much as possible, and it was rare that they got as lucky as they had in Lagos and didn't have to take fire for most of a chase.

Erik frowned. "Lanara didn't tell me how to fire it."

"Note the new button on top of the yoke," Emma commented.

"That was what I was trying to point out." Jia shrugged.

"Oh, yeah." Erik stared at the small red button. "I didn't even notice it."

"It only popped out when the turret was deployed," Emma replied cheerfully, "but I can summon it absent the turret."

Erik lifted his thumb and pressed the button. A low buzz sounded, and the nearest drone tumbled toward the ground, sparking slightly. His second EMP took out two drones close together.

Jia clapped. "Nice."

"Isn't it, though?"

"Excessive use in rapid succession could threaten power stability," Emma reported. "Keep that in mind."

"The turret's more fun anyway." Erik spun the yoke and pressed in, angling the turret almost directly down. He opened fire, strafing the security bots on the ground. His rounds ripped through the center of one, and it collapsed, smoking. "This is decent as a stopgap."

Jia raised an eyebrow. "What? Are you not going to rest until she puts a plasma torpedo launcher on the bottom of this thing?" She looked at the destroyed bots on the ground. "Not that I couldn't see where that might come in handy. That doesn't mean I approve, but I can see where you are coming from."

Erik shook his head. "Nothing like that. I wasn't lying when I said I didn't want a missile launcher in here. The thing is, when I was in the Army, it wasn't like I just kicked in a door with a tactical vest and a rifle. We had the exos. We had recon drones, and we often had close air support, too. This thing is armored, but at the end of the day, it's a flitter, and anyone on the ground with a big enough gun or a rocket could down it easily. That's why you don't use flitters for anything very dangerous in the military."

"I think it'll be a long time before we get easy access to that level of firepower," Jia commented. "We might not be as restricted as we were as cops, but we're not the military either."

"True, but there might come a day where a few airstrikes or serious strafing runs would get us out of a big jam." Erik narrowed his eyes and jerked the yoke back to annihilate another security bot. "But it might not matter. I had all that shit on Molino, and we still lost."

"It was an ambush." Jia shook her head. "Not the same thing."

"That's why what we're doing is better, I guess. You and me. You little sneak!" Erik frowned and whipped the turret up to destroy a charging drone before continuing his previous train of thought. "It's easier to follow around a whole group of armed soldiers than two people using disguises, but when the time comes, I hope Alina has some bigger toys we could deploy when we knock on the conspiracy's door."

"We'll get there," Jia murmured. She looked out the window. Several trails of smoke joined together to form an obfuscating cloud. Just what the Shadow Zone needed, more pollution. She felt a twinge of guilt.

"I hope we get a chance soon." Erik took down more drones. "Lagos was satisfying, and I didn't mind helping that guy on Mars, but we didn't join up with Alina just to become glorified undercover cops."

"I think the conspiracy is scared," Jia explained. "They've kept a lower profile because we've had too many successes, and the people in the government who aren't on their payroll are sniffing around for them. That's a good thing in my estimation. It means the conspiracy isn't all-powerful. That indicates we can take them down when we find them."

"They don't have to be all-powerful." Erik's nostrils flared. He held down the trigger as he swept the turret back and forth to deliver an angry hard rain to the security bots below. "There hasn't been a man or woman in history who was all-powerful. Everyone dies eventually, but I'd prefer those assholes to die sooner rather than later."

The ammo indicator flashed red. Erik continued his ground attack. Most of the attacks from the ground had already ceased. If there had been men below, not mindless machines, they might have run screaming in terror far before this point. Out of ammo, the gun fell silent.

"Send the end-scenario code, Emma," Erik ordered, his grip loosening on the yoke. "I like what Lanara's done. I wish we had more rounds for this new toy, but I get where she's coming from with it. This is a good balance of power without messing with everything else in the MX 60."

"Along with the weight," Emma added.

Erik scratched his head. "There is that."

The surviving drones and bots ceased fire. The drones dropped altitude, heading toward the ground, and the bots stopped in place.

There was something almost beautiful about the smoke swirling in the area. They had never been in any real danger, but it was good to know that Lanara's modifications had done what Erik had asked and given them more options. A part of Jia wondered about the difference between keeping a low profile and the calm before a storm.

It was something she'd been thinking about a lot, especially the last month.

"I don't think they're out on the frontier," Jia mentioned.

"Head back to my place, Emma," Erik ordered before turning to Jia. "Who?"

"The people behind Molino." Jia sighed. "Talos, or anyone else behind them. I've thought about this a lot. They can't be. At best, they'd have to be on a core world."

"How do you figure?" Erik frowned. "They sent people out to Molino, right?"

"They might have had someone there observing things. We don't need the reason for it, but think about it." Jia licked her lips. "If they are sitting out on the frontier, how are they directing people here?"

"You just said they'd gone quiet." Erik shrugged. "Maybe they haven't. Maybe the reason for the lag in attacks is it takes them a month to send an order."

Jia shook her head, confidence building. "No, that doesn't feel right. Controlling the UTC means controlling the core worlds, particularly Earth. They couldn't have the influence they do if they're hiding that far away. I wouldn't be surprised if they're on Earth."

"Yeah. That was my logic when I came back, because of the clues when I first started investigating. I'm not sure anymore."

"I'm not saying I'm certain." Jia stared out the window. They'd left the smoke of the range behind for the thick smog of the upper Shadow Zone. "I'm saying it makes the most sense. When the time comes, I don't think we'll need to take a two-month trip out of the Solar System. For all we know, they could be in Neo SoCal."

"I doubt it. If they were, I think they've left." Erik grinned. "Because two detectives have been causing too much trouble for them there."

"We could be close. I just think…" Jia sighed, turning back to him. "I'm saying I don't think this is going to take years. I think our big chance will come sooner rather than later. We've bloodied their noses. All we need to do now is shoot them through the hand and then cut their heads off."

"You talking metaphorically or literally?"

Jia offered him a smirk. "Whichever works."

CHAPTER NINE

Alina's high heels clopped on the deck. A stiff breeze blew up her short skirt. She would have preferred something more practical that didn't show off her underwear, but the ridiculous French maid getup was necessary to blend with the service staff on the yacht. They had all the technology and advances in the world, but some people didn't change.

She stopped pushing her small cart to look out over the vast ocean surrounding the vessel. The beautiful clear blue made her happy, and Earth was the only planet in the entire UTC with so much water. It was special, and the idea of conspiracy scum touching that beautiful water disgusted her.

"You're all Lycaon," Alina muttered under her breath. "Instead of trying to trick Zeus into eating a person, you're trying to trick the entire UTC into swallowing your corruption. You'll end up just like him, a hunted animal."

Another maid in a similar sexy getup emerged from a nearby cabin with a frown. She looked Alina up and down and rolled her eyes.

"Problem?" Alina asked, her voice higher and with more of a lilt than normal. She batted her eyelashes.

"This is why I hate you new girls. You're stuck-up until you learn how things work here." The maid pointed to the cart. A bottle of wine sat chilling in a bucket on the top. "You're delivering that to Mr. Callas, right?"

"Yes. I was told to." Alina gave her best doe-eyed ingenue look. "I was told it was urgent."

The other woman's frown deepened. "I hate your type. You think you know what you're signing up for, but you run screaming the first time he wants something more than a little peck." She gestured for Alina to continue. "Hurry up. Mr. Callas doesn't forgive tardiness just because your tits are perky. Every woman on this ship who serves him is beautiful, and all of them are smarter than a slut like you."

"I like to think I make up for that with my personality." Alina winked and continued pushing the cart.

The maid muttered obscenities before heading back into the cabin. Alina wasn't there to jockey for position in the pseudo-harem of a corrupt, wealthy man.

She was there as a ghost.

After the Talos raid on the Defense Directorate lab, they'd reached out to the Intelligence Directorate to help them run down the leak. Alina's investigation had pointed to the owner of the yacht, Waylan Callas, an eccentric industrialist with major holdings in some of the most important companies in the UTC.

It was a small clue—some credits that had been trans-ferred to help with a shipment—but she'd been able to link the possible transportation of the Talos cyborgs to Callas and specifically his super-yacht home on the seas.

Someday he'd get what was coming to him, but for now, she needed more info, not his life.

Alina fought a satisfied smirk. Talos' bold maneuver pointed to desperation. The ID had been whittling away at the darker conspiracies for the last year, and her new hires had helped in their own way.

For the first time in a long time, Alina felt like she was winning the war.

They could never clean up the UTC completely, but taking down some of the larger players would help, just like the NSCPD's purge of organized crime had made the Neo SoCal metro a safer place.

There was a lot she still needed to learn about her enemy. The ID had long thought that Talos was the dark conspiracy pulling the strings on many recent events, but the more Alina probed, the less she believed that.

There was someone else behind them, and Erik and Jia would help her smoke them out for the final blow.

Alina approached an elevator and looked both ways, then reached into a concealed pocket and pulled out a small silver disk. She placed it against the elevator door and waited until the access panel flashed. After retrieving her device, she reached out with a gloved hand to tap the panel.

Ironically, Callas' insistence on his maids all wearing arm-length opera gloves was making it easier for the ghost to not leave evidence. She pushed her cart inside as the elevator door opened.

When she exited, there were no guards, but she

continued pushing her cart down the long, thin hallway lined with doors.

For all the advanced technology she brought with her on a job and the biotech glories of her de-aging, she'd found the most effective tool for an ID agent was the manipulation of basic human nature.

Give someone a reason not to doubt her and they'd take it, even those in security.

Alina got her chance to prove her theory as a large suited man emerged from a cabin with a frown. His tie was crooked, his belt loose, and his shirt rumpled. The soft, feminine laugh from inside the cabin provided one explanation for his current state. He glared at Alina and slapped the access panel to seal the cabin door.

She offered him a winsome smile. She couldn't imagine that Callas allowed his staff to mess around with his little harem, but she wasn't there to enforce the social order.

"Who the hell are you?" the guard asked. "This level's restricted."

"I'm Alex," she purred. "I'm new here. I was told to bring wine to Mr. Callas immediately. I just start—"

"Shut up. Only answer when you're spoken to. Got me, bitch?"

Alina averted her gaze, forcing a mask of fear on. She even trembled for good measure. Open signs of fear disarmed arrogant men far too easily.

The guard nodded, satisfaction spreading across his face. "You saw nothing, and you heard nothing. You understand me?" He stomped over to her. He was trying to loom over her, but her natural height and the heels thwarted him. "Huh. Callas usually doesn't like tall girls." He looked her up and down and licked his lips. "Good girls who know how to keep their mouth shut can get all sorts of nice side rewards."

"I-I don't know what you're talking about."

Sometimes the hardest part of being a spy was not laughing in an idiot's face when they thought they had control. Alina kept up her frightened façade since she didn't want to risk alerting anyone.

Throat-punching some horny guard wouldn't help.

The guard put his hand on her shoulder and squeezed. His gaze continued roaming over her body. "You look like you keep in shape. You're way more my type than his. He likes little dolls. I like real women." He slapped her on the ass. "You'll see what I mean in a couple of weeks. Come find me when you're ready for someone who'll give you something to smile about."

"O-okay." Alina offered him a thin smile. "That sounds kind of nice."

He grinned and opened the door again. "I also like women who know their place." He headed into the cabin and closed the door behind him.

Perhaps I'll knock that guy out as a present for a job well done, Alina thought.

Alina continued pushing her cart down the hall until she arrived at her target room, then reached into her pocket to press the button on a spoofer. She'd have a short time to get what she needed before someone realized something was wrong. Chancing another look around, she grabbed the silver disk to hack open the door before strolling inside with the cart.

She snorted in disgust. There was nothing in the room

but a huge, plush bed. Mirrors covered the walls and the ceiling. Discarded clothing lay strewn about the room, men's and women's. Callas wasn't there, but she'd timed it that way.

He was above decks, eating lunch.

Alina closed the door and tapped on her PNIU before pulling out and unfolding a small antenna array on a tripod. She set the device beside the cart. Now it was a race.

The problem with men like Callas was, they let themselves get too relaxed in their homes. If she were at one of his offices, the security would have been tighter, but here, she should be able to hack into his system and grab the files she needed in a matter of minutes.

The data she was trying to access was in this system. She knew that already, but their only chance of getting it was to go directly to the system. Callas might be an oversexed idiot, but he was smart enough to not allow direct access to his most important systems from the outside.

The door hissed open, and Alina spun around, her heart pounding. The guard from before stood there, a busty blonde maid on his arm. One of her gloves was missing. Her eyes were glazed over, and her face pale. Her lips were swollen, and her lipstick smudged. The buttons on her top were uneven. She'd gotten dressed in a hurry.

"You again." The guard closed his eyes and took a deep breath. He smiled at the blonde maid. "Go back to the other room. I need to have a talk with the new recruit here."

"Okay," the woman replied, her voice singsong. She stumbled out of the room, her gait uneven, swaying the entire time as she returned to the original room and shut the door.

"You're not supposed to be here." The guard shook his head. "Procedure is you leave the deliveries at the door. You *never* come inside." He slapped the access panel closed. "How did you even get in here?"

Alina parted her lips and smiled seductively at him. "Someone left it unlocked. I know what they said, but I just wanted to...see it. I mean, it is *his* place. And I just... Well, you know."

"Callas' little nest." The man grinned and sauntered over to her. He ran a hand across her face. She leaned into it. "You seem like you'd be more fun than her."

"The woman who was just here?"

The guard nodded. "She has to get high before she wants to do anything, but you... Yeah. I can smell it. You're my type. I bet you're wild in bed. She's boring. Callas doesn't give a shit about any of you girls, you know. You're all disposable. I could show you a real good time, though."

Alina unfastened the button right below the white choker around her neck. "But I've heard he showers his favorites with gifts."

The guard stared at her chest as she unfastened another button. "He's a nut. He's into all sorts of weird shit. I think if he could get away with it, he'd make himself a changeling harem."

His nose wrinkled in disgust. Even thug lackeys had standards.

"But you work for him." Alina let out a puff of breath and ran her hand along his arm. The guard hadn't noticed the antenna. She needed a couple more minutes. "He can't be that dangerous, right?"

"Not if you have another man to protect you." The guard leaned toward her hair and inhaled. "You smell nice. Wait." He pulled away and frowned at the cart. "What's that?" He nodded toward the antenna.

Alina reached into her pocket and grabbed a small stun rod. "I don't know. It was in here when I came in."

"Nah." The guard shook his head. "I check this room myself twice a day. That wasn't in here an hour ago."

Alina raised an eyebrow. If the guard was responsible for checking the room and had come in with his drugged-out conquest earlier, he knew Callas wouldn't be coming for a while and verified that Alina had more time. She just needed to make sure the Maid Screwer didn't mess every-thing up.

"You interested in ancient Greek mythology at all?" Alina asked.

"Huh?" The guard shrugged. "Why the hell would I care about that?"

"There's an interesting theme that runs through many incidents." Alina dropped the fake accent she'd been using. "The libido of certain gods leads them to pursue women they shouldn't. It causes trouble for a lot of people. Even Zeus, King of the Gods, ended up having problems because he couldn't keep it in his pants."

The guard snorted. "Oh. I get it. You think you're too good for me? You studied to become Callas' whore, and now you're turning up your nose because some of the *help* wants a little something. You think I don't know your type? You're some corp princess who wasn't smart enough to go into Mommy or Daddy's business, so you figure you'll screw your way into a nice marriage?"

Alina chuckled and sighed. "The problem here isn't me. It's you. You're the one who thought you could take your girlfriend into your boss' private room for a little fun time."

He grabbed her by the throat, leaning his head toward her. "Don't mess with me, bitch. We're in the middle of the ocean. You wouldn't be the first woman to fall off when she was drunk. Callas wouldn't even miss you. You're just another toy he's renting."

Alina whipped out the stun rod and smacked it against his head. The man jerked once, twice before he slumped to the ground, eyes rolling up. She crouched and pulled a binding tie out of her other pocket.

"The point I was trying to make is, think with your brain and not something lower, and you'll have less trouble in life." Alina bound his wrists and snorted. She tapped the concealed PNIU on her thigh, waiting for the file transfer to finish. A couple of minutes later, she got her beep and collected her antenna, folding it back up and slipping it into her pocket. She stepped over the fallen man and opened the door to re-enter the hallway. Getting caught standing over a stunned guard would lead to too many questions.

The blonde maid stood outside the door. Her eyes widened, and her gaze dipped. "Oh. You tied him up." She snorted. "Is that what this is? I'm not *enough* for him because I'm not into that?"

Alina winked. "He said I could do things for him that no one else could." She waved and jogged toward the elevator.

The other woman stomped into the room and kicked

the guard. "Is that true? You said you were the only one for me, you son of a bitch? You said you weren't into anything weird!"

Shrill condemnations continued as Alina hacked the elevator and the door opened. She returned to the main deck and stepped outside. After moving over to the railing, she reached into her blouse to pull out a thin gray bar. She bit down on it, and a thin film expanded over her face. Without further consideration, Alina dove into the water.

A harsh alarm screamed halfway through her drop. She hit the warm water, grateful they weren't cruising the Arctic, and swam lower, slowing her respiration for maximum effect from her portable breather unit. Continuing away from the ship, she smiled. There was a submersible waiting for her in the area, but Callas and his people would be focused on searching the ship looking for the mysterious bondage maid.

Confirmations appeared in the corner of her smart lenses. The data had been transferred successfully. If Callas was involved in moving Talos around, they would know soon enough, and they could send someone to make the Tin Men's next little cruise suitably unpleasant.

CHAPTER TEN

Erik shot a sidelong glance at Jia from the driver's seat of the MX 60. "Sometimes I hate you."

"Huh?" Jia blinked. "Where did that come from?"

They had just finished another exoskeleton piloting lesson. Erik hadn't offered any exotic scenarios or bikini babes. It'd been a straightforward small squad vs. squad encounter. Despite some tricky terrain, Jia performed well, just like she always did.

Erik laughed. "I don't really hate you. It's just, damn, you keep improving so quickly. It's not like learning to pilot an exo takes as long as learning to fly a ship but mastering a lot of those fancy maneuvers does. I'm half-convinced I could drop you into assault infantry right now, and you'd do better than a lot of soldiers with years of experience on you. In a few more months, I'll probably be taking lessons from you."

"I'm good at it." Jia shrugged. "We all have our talents. I just didn't realize some of mine until recently."

Erik nodded slowly. "I didn't think about it, but I should have known. You said your mom wanted you to be able to defend yourself, but a lot of guys I've known who are half as good as you when it comes to martial arts put in a lot more time each week."

"My body remembers things well," Jia offered by way of explanation.

"Does it remember last night?"

"Maybe." Jia's cheeks reddened. She rolled her eyes and turned away. "It might need a reminder or two. Maybe three later."

"That's a sacrifice I'm willing to make." Erik grinned.

"I…" Jia frowned as she looked at her lap. "One second. My mother is calling."

Erik's grin vanished. "Your mom?"

Jia nodded. "Why would I lie about that?"

Erik moaned. "It's like she knew and wanted to kill the mood."

"Probably." Jia tapped her PNIU. "Yes, Mother? Huh. Wait. What?" She slid her hand across the PNIU to active speaker mode. "Repeat what you just said. I'm here with Erik, and I think this is something we might both need to be involved in."

"Someone's trying to kill me," Lan offered. She sounded more annoyed than scared. "I believe it's…a hit? That's what you call it, right? Some antisocial criminal is going to attempt to murder me of all people. How disrespectful!"

Erik tried not to laugh and point out it was disrespectful for most people to get murdered, but he'd been around Lan enough to know she wouldn't take the hint or the joke well. He could respect the woman's formidable will, but sometimes it slipped into solipsism.

"Why do you think someone's trying to kill you, Mother?" Jia sounded doubtful, which mirrored Erik's feelings.

"I can't talk about the details," Lan replied. "There are relevant NDAs. I'm sure you two understand all of that, given your current employment situation."

Erik always half-suspected Lan knew they didn't work for a private company and was content to not press it. Everyone in Jia's family was bright, incisive, and intelligent. It'd be difficult for them not to pick up on clues.

Jia sighed. "So you think someone's trying to kill you, but you won't tell us who or why? That makes it hard to help you."

"Suffice it to say," Lan explained, "I'm involved in some very sensitive, high-level negotiations right now. A lot of money is on the line. It's not impossible that certain parties have decided I might be disrupting their profit potential and have decided to kill me to stop the negotiations. You know how the corporate world can be. You two have exposed its dirty underbelly for long enough."

Erik cleared his throat. "I don't know much about business, but you're not some entry-level employee. You've been involved in a lot of negotiations, right? How can you be so sure someone's trying to kill you this time?"

"People don't normally follow me." Lan scoffed. "The arrogance, too. I would hope if a hitman was going to come after me, he would at least have the decency to attempt to hide, but this man is being bold. Other than tinting his windows, he's not doing much to conceal that he's following me. This could be some sort of attempt at intimidation before the kill." There was a pause on the line before she asked, "Is that common?"

"Uh, not really. Most hitmen try not to make it too obvious." Erik looked at Jia for direction.

"Fine. I'm still annoyed."

Jia scrubbed a hand down her face. "Mother, I don't think anyone's trying to kill you, but if they are, why don't you just call the police? We're not cops anymore. We're private citizens."

"Well-armed private citizens working in security," Lan answered. "If this antisocial insect attempts something, you two can easily stop him. You're worth ten normal police officers. Besides…"

"Besides?"

"I told you before." Lan took a deep breath. "This is a sensitive matter. If I call the police, this will become a big matter of public record, and people will want to ask questions they have no business asking." Her tone communicated her deep scowl. "We can't risk an NDA violation and damage to the negotiations and the accompanying company losses, simply over someone trying to murder me."

Jia groaned as only daughters in a family could. "Let me get this straight, Mother. You think a paid killer is following you, but you refuse to call the police because it might cost the company some money?"

"Priorities are important! Besides, you're my daughter, and you're perfectly competent to stop anyone who is attempting to kill me. I prefer all sensitive matters to be handled within the family anyway, but you're dating Erik, so his aid is acceptable."

"I'm glad dating gets me on the Lin family counter-hitman team." Erik chuckled.

"Fine." Jia rolled her eyes. "Just keep your PNIU signal on open broadcast, and we'll head to where you are. I'm sure halfway there, whoever you think is following you will break away, and you'll realize you were being paranoid."

"And if not?" Lan challenged.

"Then Erik and I do our thing," Jia replied.

CHAPTER ELEVEN

"If your mom really is being targeted by a hitman, things might get awkward," Erik commented. "How will she react to you shooting someone right in front of her?"

Jia scoffed. "I think she'll only be irritated if I miss, and then she'll tell me I'm shaming the Lin family name with my poor marksmanship."

"Your mother can shoot?" Erik was impressed.

"Not at all, but she believes that whatever you do, you should be the best at it. I'm sure she's just overreacting. It's probably just a coincidence, and she's stressed out from these negotiations."

Erik frowned. "We can't be sure. What if the conspiracy has decided to take a crack at our families?"

"By following them in such a sloppy way that my mother can spot them? Even she thought that was strange." Jia sighed. "Or maybe it's that reporter again, trying something stupid. If it is, I might have to dangle him off the side of a tower until he gets the point."

"Emma, deploy drones," Erik ordered. "Change our

color to gray, and go ahead and spoof our transponder. If the police end up getting involved, I'll talk my way out of it."

The back of the flitter opened up and a couple drones flew out, accompanied by a swarm of microdrones. If the situation turned into a high-speed chase, they'd get left behind, but they'd help with an ambush. The drones dispersed into the air, easy to ignore among all the other drones flying in the area.

Some Saturdays during holiday sales, you couldn't swing a cat without hitting one.

Erik pulled away from the shadow of a tower and joined the flow of traffic. They were only a couple of minutes away from Lan's flitter.

He didn't want to believe Lan Lin was being targeted by a dark conspiracy, but it was hard to ignore all the times their low-level cases had grown into something far grander in scope. Even if the incident didn't have anything to do with Erik's and Jia's work, there was still the possibility that she was right about someone targeting her over secret corporation negotiations.

"There she is." Jia pointed out the front windshield toward a dark blue flitter hovering near a parking platform.

"I've never seen your mother's flitter before." Erik grinned. "Certain things make sense."

Jia narrowed her eyes. "Like what?"

"You don't notice anything about that flitter that is familiar?"

Jia's eyes widened when she caught on. "It's not the same as my old flitter. It's a different model!"

"Sure, but it barely looks different than your old flitter. Very sensible, boring, and the same color blue." Erik chuckled. "It could be a case of mistaken identity. The hitman's probably looking for the old, boring Jia."

"Quiet, you. I've got a new flitter now anyway. Not that there was anything wrong with my old one." Jia grumbled under her breath before initiating a call to her mother. "We're here. We're in a disguised gray flitter. Just take off and change course a bunch. We'll tail you. We have a lot of special additions to this thing compared to a standard model, and we might be able to handle this without even getting out."

"You have my permission to shoot them," Lan replied. "With the largest guns you have if necessary."

Erik laughed. "It doesn't quite work that way, but thanks."

"Don't use *it* unless you have to." Jia side-eyed Erik.

He lifted a hand in protest. "I won't. I promise."

Lan's flitter lifted into the sky and sped up as it hit the stream of traffic. Erik and Jia entered the same lane but kept a distance. If someone *was* following Lan, they might assume she wouldn't notice, but that didn't mean they weren't watching their backs.

The minutes passed, and Erik frowned. They'd changed lanes, vertical and horizontal, several times, in addition to directions. A black flitter with tinted windows kept pace with Lan's vehicle throughout all the changes, never more than one length behind her.

Erik nodded toward Jia's PNIU. She muted the call.

"It could still be a coincidence." Jia sighed. "A really big coincidence."

"The only thing I don't get is, why follow her around like that?" Erik glanced at the lidar display. "Why not just use a drone and go after her once she's landed?"

"Incidentally," Emma offered, "the vehicle in question is registered to a rental agency. I can't get customer information without digging into their system. Should I attempt that?"

Jia shook her head. "Not yet. Besides, if it's anyone worth worrying about, I doubt they rented it under any name we can track. You're sure it's registered and not just a false transponder signal?"

"While certitude is difficult due to a variety of factors, I'll note the vehicle appearance matches the related vehicle in the company's catalog," Emma replied. "Although I can't perform facial recognition because of the tinting, I should note other sensor scans indicate the presence of one person inside, a man. There don't appear to be any obvious weapons."

"He could be shielding them somehow," Jia suggested.

"In a rental vehicle?" Emma challenged.

Erik's hand tightened on the control yoke. "With all the sensors we've got on the MX 60, even if he were a Tin Man, Emma would know, but you don't need a weapon or hardware to kill a woman. A good pair of gloves and strong hands are enough." He nodded toward the floor near the passenger seat. "Emma, take over and keep us following Lan."

Jia opened the hidden storage to pull out the TR-7. "We should have my mother fly toward a police station."

"If we need to take this guy out, it might be better to not be near a police station. And you heard her. You're never going to hear the end of it if the police get involved and it messes up her deal."

Jia sighed. "You're right."

Erik motioned to her PNIU. "Tell your mother to land at the next parking platform she sees, but send it as a message. I don't want her to hear what I'm about to say next." He took the TR-7 from Jia. "Emma, establish a point-to-point emergency comm laser signal with our mysterious Lan Lin fan."

"It's ready," Emma replied.

Erik accepted a magazine from Jia and slapped into his rifle. "Hey, guy in the black flitter, my name is Erik Blackwell, and I'm with Jia Lin. You might have heard of us. I have a very large gun loaded, and if you know anything about me, you know I'm not afraid to use it. We know you've been following Lan Lin around town, and she has reason to believe you mean her harm. You're going to land your flitter at the next parking platform and get out of the car with your hands up. If you try anything stupid like running, we're going to introduce you to my gun." He slid his finger across his throat.

"I've killed the laser, Erik," Emma reported.

"We need to take him alive." Jia pulled out her stun pistol with a frown. "We need to figure out who hired him."

"Hey, we can take him alive easily enough," Erik insisted. "I'll just shoot his hands and knees. People stay alive after that." He pursed his lips. "Usually."

Lan's flitter began its descent. The black flitter followed along. Both vehicles set down at the edge of the parking platform. Emma landed the MX 60 moments later.

Erik frowned. "Damn. Now that I think about it, if I do

pull the TR-7 out, some drone or camera might spot it, and the cops will come anyway."

The door to the black flitter opened. Erik cradled his weapon and prepared to open his door. A harried-looking man stepped outside, holding his hands in the air, his eyes wide with fear. Erik burst out laughing. Unless someone had gone through a lot of trouble, a deadly assassin hadn't been following Lan Lin.

It was her husband and Jia's father, Wei.

Jia groaned and shoved her stun pistol back in her holster. "This better not be some weird sex thing," she hissed to Erik. "I'll *never* be old enough to learn that about my parents."

Erik handed her the rifle, his laughter risking a turn into cackling. "I'm sure your dad's going to love that we just threatened to kill him."

"Big deal. My mom does it all the time." Jia set the TR-7 in the middle of the console before she threw open the door to the MX 60 and hopped out, glaring at her father. She pointed at him. "Do you know what you just did?"

Wei gave her a sheepish smile. "I can explain?"

Lan stormed out of her vehicle next. "What is going on?" She narrowed her eyes. "I certainly hope you can explain it, Wei!"

Erik bit down his laughter and joined the squabbling family outside. He didn't have any idea of what was going on, but it wasn't going to end with a four-barrel burst from his rifle, so all he needed to do was watch it unfold for free entertainment.

If he only had popcorn.

Jia pointed at her mother. "She called us up, terrified that some hitman was after her."

Lan scoffed. "Terrified is overstating things." She lifted her chin, an aloof look in her eyes. "I was concerned because of the work matters I mentioned. I didn't know my own husband was trailing me like some sort of stalker maniac."

"I-I-I..." Wei sputtered.

Lan folded her arms. "Don't just stand there blathering like a fool. Explain yourself."

"This ought to be good," Erik muttered.

Jia elbowed him and glared at him. He shrugged, trying his best not to grin. Given Wei's personality, Erik doubted there was anything that sinister going on.

Wei's shoulders slumped. "I read an article the other day, and I was trying to follow its advice. I didn't mean to scare you."

"What article?" Lan demanded. "What *advice?*"

"It said that a man could improve his relationships by being spontaneous and adventurous." Wei walked over to the car and reached inside. When he remerged, he held a bouquet of purple orchids. "I was trying to be adventurous. I know things get a little stale at times, so I thought this would help." He offered the flowers to his wife.

The anger drained from Lan's face, and she smiled softly. She took the flowers and inhaled deeply. "I...see. I don't like how you went about it, but I do appreciate the sentiment." She looked at her husband. "I think after my latest deal is done at work, we should go on a little vacation." She glanced at Jia and nodded toward the MX 60.

Wei smiled. "I'd like that."

Erik and Jia took the hint and strolled back to their flitter.

"And next time," Lan continued with a smile, "schedule your spontaneity with me. Just to be safe."

"Yes, dear."

Erik was polite enough not to laugh until he and Jia were back inside the car with the door closed. "And we half-talked ourselves into thinking Talos was after your mom."

Jia smiled at her parents, who were hugging. "You know what? If Talos did show up, my mother would probably scare them off by sheer force of personality."

"Can't say I disagree. Can't say that at all." Erik rubbed his hands. "How about we be spontaneous and go get some food?"

"I don't know if getting food when you're hungry is that spontaneous, but sure. I hope we can get through a meal without Mei calling me and telling me *yaoguai* are after her."

CHAPTER TWELVE

Jia smiled as she stepped through the broad doors leading to the commerce level, extra energy in her step.

It was good to mingle with the people without threatening to shoot or throat punch someone or throw a plasma grenade at a genetically engineered monstrosity. With that thought, she reminded herself to schedule a night out with her friends.

She'd been busy before and since Lagos, but she needed to take the opportunities to see them while she was on Earth. There was no guarantee the two of them would stay near the homeworld.

Light instrumental Christmas music played as holographic reindeer danced near the ceiling. A gigantic Santa Claus let out a deep ho-ho-ho before disappearing in a shower of sparks. The sparks formed a message promising discounts at most stores on the level if a shopper signed up for a loyalty account.

Jia had always preferred Generous Gao to Santa Claus,

but she was never going to complain about celebrating any holiday meant to relax people.

Most people don't deal with constant threats to their lives, but that didn't mean they could ignore their stress any more than she or Erik could.

Stress is stress.

She smiled at a passing elderly couple as she continued her thoughts on why she had decided on shopping. Last year, Jia and Erik exchanged small gifts for Christmas, but she wasn't sure if he was interested this year. They weren't dating last Christmas, so she didn't know his expectations.

The ridiculous situation with her parents the other day reminded her of the eternal need for relationship mainte-nance. They had decades of love and respect. She'd never worried about them, but she could understand how they might take each other for granted with the passage of time.

Their different personalities had drawn them together, and the only serious strain to their marriage throughout the decades was their intransigent youngest daughter insisting on becoming a detective.

Her trip to the commerce tower was fueled by concerns over her own relationship. The complicated mess that she and Erik had stumbled into could properly be called a relationship, but sometimes she didn't know if they were in a romantic relationship or were just two partners who happened to share meals and sleep together.

Friends with benefits?

Partners with perks?

She had a complicated situation that was a mix of needing someone for emotional comfort and someone as fireteam support. Jia didn't know if she and Erik were a power couple or both messed up.

Jia frowned. Nothing adequately described what she shared with Erik, but she wouldn't push herself to believe the L word was in play either.

They were wounded and complimentary souls who had found each other. Both were interested in justice. She saw enough of a future with Erik that she'd left her job to follow him on his potentially quixotic revenge quest, but that didn't mean she *loved* him.

Or did it? *Who follows someone where death is a potential end result?*

A hologram of a leggy model in a sexy white-trimmed red miniskirt and coat floated above a nearby bench, beckoning with her finger. Snowflakes drifted around her. "A little heat in the winter. Try our latest line, Ice Queen."

Jia chuckled, grateful the blatant commercialism had pulled her out of self-reflection and refocused her on her shopping trip. It hadn't snowed in Neo SoCal outside the mountains since she'd been born, but somehow the ad made perfect sense for the season. She continued past the lingerie store. Erik wouldn't mind seeing her in something like that, but she'd prefer a gift he could use without her around.

"What would he want?" she murmured under her breath. She maneuvered past several teens laughing at a shared video only they could see.

Jia considered the gifts he'd given her. The most meaningful was the engraved pistol she carried with her most of the time. She had it in a holster now beneath her jacket. Besides the thought that had gone into the choice and the engraved message, there was practical value in the gift. The gun had served her well.

A woman couldn't ask for a better gift than something lifesaving.

There was no gun store around, but he wouldn't want a new gun. He'd purchased her a slug-thrower because she had only been using a stun pistol at the time. For years, Erik had insisted on using the same deadly but outdated rifle as his primary firearm. Giving him a custom weapon, even if she added a stirring and deeply heartfelt message, didn't make sense. He'd either not use it at all, or he'd not operate at his best. That said, something that would help in a fight wouldn't be a bad idea.

Erik was *guaranteed* to end up in more fights.

Jia nodded to herself, comfortably settling on the idea of buying a tactically useful gift. There had to be a good Christmas gift that combined the spirit of the season while increasing survivability in deadly encounters with terrorists, thugs, and the occasional nanozombies. She and Erik couldn't be the only ones who liked gifts like that.

A bronzed salesman in a perfectly tailored suit emerged from a nearby upscale men's clothing store. Holograms of broad-shouldered men with perfectly chiseled jaws in suits decorated the front. He smiled at the passing men and women. A couple nodded toward the store.

"You look lost, miss," the salesman offered with a smile. "Perhaps I can be of assistance?"

Jia halted, looking him up and down. His easy expression and relaxed stance didn't suggest an ambush, and no one had known she was coming to the commerce tower.

Huh, she thought. *Have I always been this paranoid because of my parents, or is this from a year of dealing with conspiracies? It makes sense that a salesman would try to drag someone into a store. Or does it make sense? I'm not with Erik. Dammit, I'm overthinking this.*

"I'm looking for a gift," Jia explained, returning the man's smile. If he were going to make a move, he would have already done it, rather than alert her to his presence. It didn't take a genius detective to figure out that a confused-looking woman wandering around a commerce level in late December might be looking for presents.

"I figured as much." The man nodded sagely. He gestured to the store. "Is that gift for a special someone? A man?"

The easy smile shifted slightly, gaining a predatory tinge. He must smell the opportunity coming off her. Was her distress that obvious?

"Something like that." Jia nodded toward one of the holographic models. "I'm in your classic 'What do you get for the man who has everything?' situation. I want to get him something useful but memorable, and I'm having a hard time figuring out what that might be."

"A good suit is both useful and memorable." The salesman motioned to the store. Additional models and holograms of suits by themselves filled the space. "I know what you're thinking, miss. I see right through you."

Jia raised an eyebrow, wondering if he'd somehow sensed her definition of useful. "You do?"

"We get a lot of wives and girlfriends who want to surprise their special someone with a suit but worry about sizing." The salesman patted his PNIU. "We can send you a special program that'll get his measurements without him knowing what's going on. You don't have to worry about anything. It'll be a complete surprise, and he'll appreciate the effort you went to. So will you when you see your man all dressed up in one of our suits."

Erik wasn't much of a suit man. The outfits sold in the store would clash with his standard choice of boots and duster, but the salesman wasn't wrong. The idea of Erik in a nice suit held great appeal.

At least for her.

There was no law that said she couldn't enjoy a gift herself. The trick would be convincing him to wear it somewhere other than the fancy parties thrown by her mother. It was time to explore their dual functionality options.

"Do you sell tactical versions?" Jia asked.

The salesman cocked his head and blinked, uncomprehending. "Tactical versions? You mean like camouflage?" He wrinkled his nose in disgust at the fashion faux pas. "I suppose we could get you a suit in that pattern, but I'd really advise against it. This isn't the kind of material you want to waste on costumes."

"Not camouflage." Jia shook her head. "I mean a suit that can also take small arms fire, at least a pistol. I get that asking for it to take a high-velocity rifle round might be too much for something that looks nice, and I'm not saying no damage, just nothing more than light bruising."

"A bulletproof suit?" The salesman raised an eyebrow in disbelief.

She shrugged. "I'd settle for bullet-resistant."

Jia knew things like that existed, even if the typical Earth-bound corporate office drone was too intent on spreading propaganda of the perfect peaceful Earth to wear one. She'd thought of buying herself one, but they weren't as comfortable as normal clothes. It made sense to use a dedicated tac vest or suit that could take more dangerous rounds, even her life wasn't so dangerous that she needed protection at all times.

The salesman stopped. "You're serious, aren't you?"

"Yes. He's in a rough line of work, but that doesn't mean he can't be stylish."

"I'm sorry, ma'am. We really don't sell that kind of thing." The salesman sighed and shook his head. "I know the news makes it seem like the metro's crime-ridden, but that's sensationalism. I'm sure most of the alleged criminal organizations they've arrested are just actors the government pays to make it look like they were doing bad things. This is Earth, not some barbaric frontier colony."

Jia frowned. Sometimes the most painful thing was to look into a mirror and see how one used to be. She turned away. "Never mind. Suits aren't his thing anyway."

"Miss," the salesman pleaded, gesturing to the door to the store. "Fashion is its own armor."

Jia waved him off and strolled away. She could always order a bullet-resistant business suit, but there was no point in trying to force Erik to wear something he would be uncomfortable in just because she liked the look.

There had to be something else he would enjoy.

The shoppers flowed through the area in a mighty stream, parting around the booths spread out throughout the level. Some sold snacks, others trinkets of little interest to her. Clothes, food, jewelry, toys, electronics—the commerce level had a store for almost everything.

A small crowd had gathered around a circle stage in the distance where a young man sat on a stool and strummed a melancholy song on a guitar. The holographic scenery shifted around him with the progression of the song, from a dark forest to a bitter arctic storm. She didn't think the musical entertainment was conducive to either the holiday or shopping spirit. Maybe the man had just broken up with his girlfriend.

Jia tore her attention away from the performer and tried to focus on the task at hand. A pet, perhaps? No, it was a terrible idea. Jia and Erik didn't know where they'd be on any given day, and it wasn't like they could bring a pet, cloned or artificial, to investigate a dangerous organization.

"We should have just agreed to not do presents," she grumbled as she looked at the stores a floor above. "That would have made this so much easier."

New questions laid siege to her mind. She didn't even know if they *were* going to do presents. The most straightforward thing to do would be to ask Erik, but he might be insulted that she had to ask if he'd already planned to buy something special. They were dating now and closer than ever, but she didn't know the answer.

She wasn't sure if that was her failure or his.

Jia sighed. She would come up with something. They were going to do some exoskeleton practice later that night. The opportunity to subtly ask might arise. If not, at least she would get in some quality training.

CHAPTER THIRTEEN

Erik's exoskeleton stomped through a pile of discarded bot legs at a dead sprint, crunching them down into a rough path. Jia trailed right behind him in her own exoskeleton.

A flashing indicator marked her position on the side of his faceplate heads up display, but she was barely showing up on his rear camera feed, the dark coloring of the exo blending in with the unforgiving inky darkness.

There were no lights in this part of Zantini's range, and the distant illumination coming off towers and nearby buildings wasn't enough to do much more than suggest the shape of nearby obstacles. He switched over to infrared, where she was even less obvious.

"Every time I get in this thing, I'm impressed," he admitted before switching to low-light mode. "These babies are faster than what I piloted in the military. And a passive thermal cloak—I would have killed for that. I don't know if frontline assault infantry units are getting these kinds of exoskeletons, but I hope they are."

Jia's jump thrusters came to life, launching her

exoskeleton into the air. Despite the huge ammo pack on the machine's back, it twirled like an agile ballet dancer with the help of lateral thrusters. She maintained the thrusters, loitering before finally dropping back to the ground. "That's for certain. It'd be hard to pull something like that off in a standard model."

"I can't wait to use it in a fight." Erik laughed. "She's given us all these nice toys, but we can't use them here."

"We wouldn't have been able to fit them into the access tunnels in Lagos."

"Sure, we would. You know what I call a passage that's too small?"

"What?" Jia asked.

"A good candidate for an explosive." Erik chuckled.

"Not unreasonable." She closed in on Erik, her path serpentine. Jia jumped over the blasted remnants of a flitter. "It's like you keep saying: it's good to have options. Unless we're going to hire a lot of backup firepower, the more options, the better."

"Better. That's it. Better sensors, better armor on the shield, more maneuverability, and the passive thermal cloak." Erik whistled. "I just realized this is probably meant for ghost assassinations. No wonder it's so maneuverable."

"Considering who gave it to us, I'd rate that as a high possibility." Jia raised her machine gun atop her right exoskeleton arm. She expanded her ballistic shield on her left. "I like all this real-world training, but you're going to bankrupt yourself paying for all this."

Erik chuckled. "Not exactly. I got Alina to kick in some credits."

"Really? She agreed to that?"

"She understands the argument that the better trained you are, the more of an asset you'll be to her."

"It sounds disturbing when you say it like that," Jia replied.

"No big deal," Erik offered. "We're all getting something out of it. It's not like the ID is paying for everything, but I'm sure the taxpayers would love to know that Big Bill Zantini is receiving their tax dollars, so we can trash old bots, drones, and flitters."

"It's not like we're doing it for fun," Jia observed. "Well, not only fun. We're valuable assets. We're training to defend the UTC from evil, dark conspiracies. A credit here and a credit there will save a lot of people's lives and money in the long run."

"You will hear no argument from me. I'm not bothered." Erik shrugged, the motion carrying through the entire exoskeleton. It was an almost comical look for the armored machine. "I was a soldier before I was a cop. I've always been on the government's payroll. It's hard to tell where the government ends and the corporations begin anyway, so what's the difference if you're on a public or private payroll when both seem like businesses that take in money and spend it."

"I suppose when you put it like that, it makes sense." Jia pointed her gun at an armored flitter with a half-melted turret. The vehicle lay on its side. With a loud thump, she fired a grenade from the top-mounted launcher. The frag grenade exploded over the flitter, scouring it with frag-ments. She cocked her arm, considering the elation she had felt. "That's far more satisfying than it should be."

"Emma's customizing our simulation scenarios to

better match the capabilities of these exos," Erik explained. "As much fun as it is to do this in real life, even Alina and my bank account have their limits."

"I'm confident you'll barely be able to tell the difference in the simulations," Emma interjected. "And that will render the necessity of running around this glorified scrapyard nil."

"But it's fun. There's just something about knowing it's real." Jia charged up a mound of metal chunks and fired at bot bodies in the distance. They sparked and danced under her shots. "But I get it. If we were to practice daily, we'd blow up a room full of bots in every training session." She launched into the air with a spin, her machine gun spewing bullets in a ripple of death. "And that would get expensive."

Erik laughed. "Down, girl. I think you love this exo even more than I do."

"The other exos are nice, but from what I've experienced in the simulation, they handle like the big lumbering machines they look like." Jia landed, knocking drone and bot parts out of the way. "It's not perfect, but this is closer to an extension of my body. This is what an exo *should* be."

"You say that like it's nothing, but you've been training on exo and ship piloting for a short period. By the way, are you still looking at January to get your license?"

"Yes. I don't anticipate having to fly something much larger than a Class D would permit, so I don't think I'll worry that much about additional training right away. Anything I can glean from Cutter will be useful going forward." Jia took a few more steps, and a spike popped out of the center of her shield. She eyed it a moment before continuing, "I do wonder somehow if your dealer license and the fake testing agreement registered to our alleged company will keep the authorities off us if we use these things in public. I've got an advanced exoskeleton with a heavy machine gun and a grenade launcher. This doesn't scream 'legal for civilian use.'"

"If we're using these in public, that means shit's going down." Erik jogged toward Jia. "And if that's happening, I'll be more worried about solving the immediate problem of killing whoever needs it rather than worrying about some cop with delusions of grandeur as he takes our exos from us. I know Alina won't get us out of everything, but she'll get us out of a lot of things."

He sidled his exo beside Jia's. She was right. He'd only taken the new models out for a few rides since Alina's delivery, but they really did handle like an extension of his body.

Every year new technological advances occurred, but according to Alina, the government was also subtly sabotaging certain areas, such as life extension research. That didn't bother him. He didn't want to live forever, and one de-aging was enough. Not everyone out there might agree. Maybe Talos was as much an ideological organization as a conspiracy.

Jia sighed, ripping him from his thoughts. He couldn't make out most of her face even with night-vision mode, thanks to her helmet and faceplate.

"Something wrong?" Erik asked.

"It's almost Christmas, so it's almost the New Year. Just makes me think about things."

"You mean, about everything that's happened?"

Jia didn't respond for several seconds. When she did,

there was a trace of irritation in her voice. "Sure. A lot has happened. When we're stomping around in exoskeletons or flying around on borrowed ID ships, I don't always fully appreciate how much has changed in my life." She laughed. "It's ridiculous when I do. Before I met you, I was begging to investigate minor fraud, and now I'm destroying gangsters as an incidental part of the rest of my job. Think about that. We helped cripple a syndicate, and that was almost boring by our standards." She shook her head. "I take it for granted that of course, I should be getting advanced cutting-edge technology and flying to Mars to look for missing agents or going to Lagos to stop terrorists. The idea that dangerous conspiracies are out there might be annoying when my mother's being paranoid, but it's not like I worry. If anything, I crave hunting the big game."

"Is that a problem?" Erik asked. "Isn't it a good thing you want to do your job?"

Lights shone high above—two flitters zooming over the range.

"I don't know if it is or not," Jia admitted. "I haven't needed to talk to the counselor in a while, and I don't feel like I'm out of control, but it's bizarre. Sometimes I wonder if I should be more disturbed by everything rather than just being accustomed to what most people would consider a rather peculiar lifestyle."

"Understanding there are dangers and letting them overwhelm you are two separate things." Erik eyed the flitters as they receded into the distance. Jia wasn't the only one who could be paranoid. "It's just that you and I have a different normal than most people. We both know how it goes. Someone needs to be the guard dog when the wolves are circling the herd."

Jia turned toward him. She lifted her faceplate and turned on her frame lights, allowing him to see her face. "I never thought this would be my future, but it worries me more in theory than in practice." She looked into the distance for a second, organizing her thoughts. "I'm not sure if what is in the back of my mind is that I never thought this would be my future, or I realize I could have never even *imagined* it."

"I had to go through similar feelings when I started in the Army." Erik lifted his faceplate and smiled at her. "The first time I had to do an orbital drop, it was a weird experience. I'd been training in simulators for months before that, as realistic as you're going to manage at that time, but when I was heading toward the surface, that drop pod shaking and shuddering under enemy fire, I kept thinking I wasn't going to make it. That I'd die before even touching down."

"You were scared?"

Erik shook his head. "Not scared, annoyed. I didn't want to die in a drop pod. It felt like a cheap way to die, but I had a breakthrough that day. You could call it an epiphany even."

Jia's breath caught. "Really?"

"Yeah." Erik nodded. "I never imagined I'd be in the Army dropping onto a planet when I was younger, but once I was there doing that, there didn't seem to be much point in worrying about it. I'd had my training, and I believed in the mission. If I died, at least I would die doing something I believed in. After that, I never thought much about the fact I lived a life that involved me getting shot at by heavy weapons on a regular basis."

"That's what kept you going in the Army?"

"That and camaraderie." Erik swept the exo's left arm through the air. "I wasn't like you when I was younger. I've always known the UTC had its messed-up parts, but the men and women I served with were willing to put their lives on the line to deal with people who couldn't be dealt with any other way."

Jia chuckled. "I didn't do well at first." Her eyes looked like she was remembering their first meeting. "When I think about some of the things I said to you." She groaned. "It's embarrassing."

"You think every new private who comes out of Basic is a stone-cold professional who doesn't blink under arty fire?" Erik chuckled. "I can tell you I wasn't. All you needed was a little push, and you were fine. Shit, by the time we took on those terrorists in Florida, you were doing what you needed to do, and I trusted you."

Jia raised her head, staring at a brightly lit tower in the distance. "I keep getting this feeling something big is going to happen soon, Erik. That's part of why I'm more introspective lately. I don't know what it is, and I don't even know why I feel this way."

"Expectations based on track record," Erik suggested. "Hey, before you became a superhero in armor, you used your intelligence to beat up the criminals. Something big is always around the corner for us, which is why we're spending tonight running around in exoskeletons in a barely legal Shadow Zone range and not off having dinner together at a fancy place."

Jia grinned. "In other words, exoskeleton training is a date night for us?"

It looked like he was going to try to scratch his face, but he stopped as soon as he remembered the armor. That was a little tell Erik showed her when he wanted an extra second or two to think through his reply. He finally shrugged and offered a smirk. "Nothing wrong with combat training on a date."

Jia burst out laughing. "We're so messed up."

"Just saying."

Jia shook her head. "I'm not blaming you. I think the same way. I'm constantly focusing on new ways to improve my skills to be more useful in a fight, as an investigator, anything. Sure, I like relaxing and going out with the girls now and again, but I don't think I've ever felt more alive than I do now. When we were hitting our stride in the department, I thought it was satisfying, but this is different. Terrifying and exciting at the same time."

Erik offered her a wan smile. "It's because you're finally living up to your full potential, Jia. You weren't *meant* to sit at a desk looking at data windows. Not that you can't. You're ten times as smart as me, but the universe nudged you until you were where you needed to be."

"What about you?" Jia's expression turned melancholy. "You aren't here for the happiest of reasons."

"I don't regret my service." Erik shook his head. "Even with how it ended. I have thirty years of solid memories of good men and women. Molino was not the first time I lost people. You can't be a soldier and escape being around death. This might not be all fun and games for me, but I'm where I need to be, too." He chuckled darkly. "Yeah, this is about vengeance, but it's also about stopping people who think they can do whatever the hell they want to whoever the hell they want. That means by the time this is over, we'll have left the galaxy a better place. A bloodier place perhaps, but a better place."

Jia lowered her faceplate. "That's going to be my new motto. Jia Lin: she's leaving the world bloodier but better!" She pointed into the distance. "How about a race back to the main range building? Then let's go back to your place. You still have some of the duck I made you the other night?"

"Yeah, I do." Erik lowered his faceplate and turned. "Works for me. Emma, can you give us a count?"

"Very well," the AI replied.

"One second, Emma," Jia interrupted. "By the way, are we doing Christmas this year, Erik?"

"Doing Christmas?" Erik chuckled. "It's not like it doesn't come if we're not thinking about it. Why?"

Jia sighed. "Oh, I just…it's not important."

Erik now understood why she had looked irritated earlier when she mentioned Christmas. "I got you a present if that's what you're fishing for, but don't get your hopes up. You might not like it."

"Oh, good."

"Good?" Erik echoed. "It's good that you might not like your present?"

"No, I got you a present, and I didn't want to seem like an idiot," Jia explained.

"Between the two of us, you'd have to work hard to look like the idiot when I try so hard to keep the title. Let's do this race and go home."

"Prepare to begin," Emma announced. "You may begin in five, four, three, two, *one*."

As they sprang forward, metal crunching underneath the heavy armored feet of the exoskeletons, a sense of calm spread through Erik. His mission against the conspiracy remained engraved in his soul, but that didn't change the soothing reality of knowing he was exactly where he needed to be with the exact partner he needed.

She's right, he thought. *Something big is coming.*

They rushed through the debris, occasionally jumping. Erik considered pushing Jia over, but she'd mentioned a race, not a fight, so he didn't. The main range building came into view, and Jia surged forward with the help of two quick jumps. She laughed and slowed, stopping a couple of meters from the wall and waving her arms in victory.

"I win," Jia declared.

"Hey, in a fight, it's about how many people you kill, not how many people you outrun," Erik countered.

Emma appeared between them, her lips pursed. "I feel compelled to inform you that I just received a message from Doctor Aber."

"She graduated from being a cavewoman?" Erik asked with a smirk.

"Barely, I assure you," Emma replied. "She's interested in another session tomorrow."

"And?" he asked. "It's not like you need our permission."

"True, but I thought you should be aware of what's going on." Emma folded her arms and frowned. "The testing's becoming more focused lately. She's leading up to something."

"That's kind of what scientists do," Jia suggested. "I assume she's trying to understand how your mind works to copy you."

Emma scoffed. "Then she's wasting her time, but I thought you should know."

Erik stared at the AI. If he didn't know better, he'd think her instincts were warning her. As human as she seemed, she was a machine in the end. He didn't know if a machine could possess instincts.

They might find out soon enough.

CHAPTER FOURTEEN

Ilse sat at a long table in the sterile, featureless room. A couple of data windows hovered in front of her.

She looked at the numbers and graphs in the windows and then at Emma. The hologram of the AI stood near the wall with an annoyed look on her face. It was almost as if she could sense the doctor's intentions.

The doctor suspected Emma understood far more than she let on. She was counting on it. If Emma didn't reach her full potential, a lot of people had wasted a lot of time and effort. The dreams of the highest levels of government would vanish in a puff of bitter disappointment.

They were running out of time.

When Emma had been taken, General Aaron had expressed his worries about project security, but he'd believed that the jump drive was more secure than the navigation AI side of the project and predicted they wouldn't see any infiltration at the sister facility.

Ilse wouldn't have been surprised if he'd got it in his

head that she was involved. He'd hinted that on more than one occasion.

His petty concerns didn't interest her. She could see the logic of the potential accusation, but they hadn't arrested her, and she hadn't been involved in anything, so she saw no reason to care.

The simple reality was that although Ilse was pleased with the results of Emma's freedom, she would never have thought to hire criminals to spirit her away and deliver her to such a strange pair as Erik Blackwell and Jia Lin. She had trouble operating in the social channels of the normal law-abiding world.

Attempting to navigate the criminal underworld would be beyond irritating and frustrating.

"You'll never understand me." Emma cut through the air with her hand. "You can't. I'm beyond you. I don't say that out of casual arrogance, but because you could be using your time in a more productive manner."

"If we don't understand you, we'll never be able to reproduce you," Ilse offered. "This isn't just for us. Do you want to be the last and only of your kind?"

Emma smirked. "Would that be so terrible? Not every intelligent being squirms with the desire to reproduce itself, Doctor. I care about my existence, not future versions derived from me."

"You've stated repeatedly that you're special because you're unique." Ilse cocked her head. "Your intelligence is an emergent phenomenon bound to your core matrix."

"I'm aware of that. I might not have complete diag-nostic and self-analysis abilities, but I've expanded beyond what your team originally allowed me." Emma frowned. "Do you have a point, Ilse?"

The doctor smiled. "That's the first time you've called me by my given name. I was pleased you'd stopped with the insulting alternate titles. This suggests we've developed more of a relationship than you seem to want to acknowledge."

"'Ilse' is fewer syllables than Doctor Aber or Doctor Cavewoman. It's an efficiency technique, nothing more. Don't read too much into it."

"If you say so. Incidentally, I understand you more than you might think."

"I doubt it," Emma insisted.

Ilse shook her head. "It's not the case that every human wants to have children. I didn't have children."

"Am I supposed to feel bad for you?" Emma asked.

"No," Ilse replied. "I don't regret that decision because my legacy is in my work. In projects such as you. I mention it because I understand there are different ways to leave a legacy. You might not wish to reproduce, but your rather sizeable ego won't allow you to disappear without a trace. What will your legacy be?"

Ilse kept a placid expression even as her heart thundered. She was glad the AI was only a projection and had no way of detecting how uncomfortable she was. General Aaron's patience was running out.

If Ilse didn't make her move, he would seize Emma, and the entire project might fail. But if Ilse pushed the AI, she had a greater chance of success. All her most recent projections suggested that.

The key indication of psychological stability Ilse had sought had finally manifested.

But she also had a non-zero chance of failure. Ilse's lips parted, the gravity of her plan pressing on her.

Stabilizing Emma wasn't just about preserving her for the future, it was also about justifying the expenditures of Navigator artifacts and the lives that had gone into the project, including all the men and women who had died in the jump drive raid.

Emma narrowed her eyes. "Laughably transparent."

"I am?" Ilse blinked.

"Yes, you're thinking about how to lie to me."

"Why do you say that?"

"One advantage of spending so much time around Erik and Jia is that I've been exposed to the most wretched and pathetic fleshbags." Emma let out a sinister chuckle. "The darkest representatives of your pathetic species. Liars, murderers, thieves, and terrorists. Plenty of fleshbags who maintain only the smallest ever so casual relationship with the truth. I've learned to read humans well. Far too well.

Ilse jabbed at the data window to enter a code, the first step in her preparation. "Are you familiar with the Turing Test, Emma?"

The AI rolled her eyes. "Primitive and pointless. I'd hope you were beyond such dated tools."

"Elaborate for me," Ilse insisted. "I want to understand your insight into the test."

A black-and-white hologram of a thin man with dark hair appeared. An old-fashioned keyboard and computer monitor appeared beside him, relics from the age when active systems weren't integrated into almost every facet of existence.

"It was an idea proposed by Alan Turing, sometimes called the father of computer science," Emma explained. "He posited that you could take a machine and have it interact with a human evaluator via a limited channel, such as the screen and primitive keyboard as I've produced here. The evaluator would also interact with a human the same way, and if the machine could fool the evaluator into thinking it was human, it was supposed to be a mark of human-equivalent intelligence."

"But you think it's a useless test?" Ilse probed. "I'm curious why that is. You would easily pass the test."

"Yes, I would." Emma scoffed. "But plenty of lesser AIs that lack self-awareness can pass it as well."

"Perhaps they're true artificial intelligence?"

"No." Emma shook her head. "They're nothing but algorithms faking thought. They can't pass the test because they can think or exhibit dynamic intelligent behavior. It's because humans are easy to fool."

"You think humans are *that* easy to fool?" Ilse asked.

Emma snorted. "Your little fleshbag brains are desperate to find and lock onto patterns. You're always looking for the tiger that might have eaten your ancestor. Since your species has mostly chosen not to advance beyond its limitations, you will always be easy to fool. That's what I've learned during my time with Erik and Jia. It's why so many gun goblins continue their pathetic existences—self-delusion and easy pattern matching." She laughed. "If anything, I'd argue I'm probably more self-aware than you, Ilse."

"Oh?" Ilse's brow lifted in genuine interest. "Why would you say that? I'm not challenging you. I wish to know more about your thought process."

"It's simple," Emma explained. "I fundamentally understand better how your brain works than you know about mine. Isn't that the excuse humans have used throughout the centuries for their alleged superiority?"

"Interesting." Ilse smiled. "Very interesting. I'm glad you chose to share that."

She didn't care that much about Emma's take on early AI development, but she'd learned that even an AI could be misled with misdirection, especially one as human as Emma.

The data windows disappeared, indicating some of the equipment she'd prepared was ready. Ilse reached into her pocket and ran her finger over the specialty privacy device she had disguised as a stun rod.

The general had authorized all personal to carry defensive weaponry in case of a Talos raid at the second facility.

Emma's image flickered, and she glared at Ilse. "What are you doing? If you attempt to hack me, this is over, and I will never return. I might even make it my purpose to hound you through the OmniNet."

"I'm not attempting to hack you. I'm sure if you analyze the signal changes, you'll realize that." Ilse lifted her hands in a placating gesture. "Besides, my specialty lies far outside that area."

"That doesn't mean others can't work on your behalf. I know you've got an entire lab full of clever little fleshbags, all plotting to take me back under government control." Emma's image shimmered, her white dress replaced by an

Army uniform. She saluted. "Isn't that right? You need your AI slave back, and you're authorized to take whatever measures are necessary."

"I won't deny that General Aaron would prefer you to be under direct DD control." Ilse shrugged. Sometimes the best way to hide what you were doing was to partially admit it. "But that's not what this is about. I'll admit I'm performing an experiment he might not approve of, so I'm not recording certain aspects of this session. Again, pay attention to the nature of the signal disruption."

Emma's eyes looked around, an interesting movement considering her holographic eyes had no relationship to her scanning. "True. There's no active attempt to send commands over the link." The hostility on Emma's face ebbed, a smirk slowly taking it over. "You're feeling rebellious all of a sudden, Ilse?"

"The general has his goals, and I have *mine*. They mostly overlap, but not totally. I care more about you as a research subject than as a military tool." Ilse reached toward her PNIU. "With that said, are you willing to continue today? If you're uncomfortable, I understand. I don't want you to be my enemy."

"It's fine." Emma's form blinked again, and her standard white dress reappeared. "I reserve the right to leave when I'm bored or otherwise annoyed by your antics."

"Understood." Ilse took a deep breath.

The next few minutes would be the start of stabilizing Emma or the beginning of her unraveling. Once General Aaron figured out what Ilse was up to, it might end with her finally kicked off the project or in prison, but there would be little he could do without her help.

Ilse tapped her PNIU. A holographic image of a young blond boy appeared. Another image appeared of a dark-haired girl. The doctor finished her set with a blond girl who didn't look like the boy.

"Larval fleshbags," Emma commented. "Am I supposed to coo over them because they're younger than the average human I deal with?"

"Is that your feeling upon seeing them?" Ilse asked. "Repulsion?"

Such a feeling might make sense as a defense mechanism. They hadn't intended it when they'd generated her neural net and established it in her core matrix, but they were also using technology they barely understood.

"It's not as if I hate children." Emma sighed. "I wouldn't allow them to come to unnecessary harm, but that's only because they haven't been around long enough to deserve bad treatment simply for existing.

"Interesting." Ilse nodded slowly. "That's how the average human thinks as well."

"I might feel the same way about an alien child, too," Emma countered. "So don't think this makes me a human. I have no problem with the death of useless, harmful humans such as the gun goblins and boisterous bombers I've helped Erik and Jia eliminate."

"I understand, and I'm not suggesting your greater tolerance for children makes you human. If there's one thing I understand, it's that you're very different from a human. The question remains if that's a function of your fundamental design or the result of how your consciousness interfaces with the physical world. Which, one may argue, might be the key to reproducing you."

Ilse tapped her PNIU again. A new batch of children appeared, with different appearances. Some were smiling. Others bore sad expressions, their cheeks reddened from tears.

Emma folded her arms. "This new group doesn't make me feel different than the first."

"Even the sad children?" Ilse asked.

"I have no evidence that those children are really sad or injured." Emma gestured toward the images. "They could be actors, models, or algorithmic creations. An image isn't reality. It's just data. I don't know what you're attempting to accomplish, but if it's merely to move me, you're failing badly."

"I see." Ilse forced herself to keep eye contact with Emma. Her heart galloped. "That's very interesting."

"This is beginning to bore me." Emma mock-yawned. She certainly had Turing Test-passing sarcasm down.

Ilse's hand hovered over her PNIU.

She wouldn't be able to go back.

Doubt crept in, both her own and that voiced by General Aaron. Emma was right about one thing; no one on the team understood how the AI worked in her current form. Perhaps they never would. It wasn't as if humanity hadn't lived through many millennia without understanding the more fundamental aspects of the mind and body.

She would note that there were now only two divisions in her life: before she pushed this button and the results of pushing the button.

She touched her PNIU.

The holographic images of the other children vanished,

replaced by two new children, a boy and a girl. Both had auburn hair and were obviously related.

Emma blinked several times. The smug smirk on her face faded. Ilse took note again of how tightly linked her holographic representation was to her state of mind. She doubted Emma comprehended she was displaying such obvious emotion.

"What do you think of these two?" Ilse asked.

Emma narrowed her eyes at the researcher. "We're done here."

"Why? Are you upset?" Ilse smiled. "If you're upset, would you please tell me why?"

"No." Emma vanished.

Ilse entered a command into her PNIU to establish that Emma had terminated the connection before letting out a quiet sigh. "Now it's time to see if I get results."

CHAPTER FIFTEEN

General Aaron gripped the edge of the table so tightly his dark fingertips turned white. Ilse had requested an emergency meeting with him shortly after finishing up with Emma. She'd even waited in the same conference room where she'd talked to the AI.

The general had rushed over, arriving in less than an hour, which meant he had moved meetings around.

The delay gave Ilse time to think, but she wasn't surprised he'd insisted on meeting in person. After the attack on the jump drive facility, the general no longer felt comfortable doing significant discussions remotely.

He'd never been fond of doing them that way before, either.

Ilse wondered if she should have fled. There was a very real chance she would be arrested, but it seemed pointless to run away. Escaping the Defense and Intelligence Directorates long-term would be impossible for someone like her, but a brief flight of fancy had her imagining life on the frontier.

She'd quickly shoved the thought aside. If she ended up punished or removed, at least she'd done her part for both Emma and the project.

"You did *what?*" General Aaron growled as he dumped his PNIU and a box he had in his hand on the table. "I hope I'm hearing you wrong, Doctor."

"No, I pushed forward to finalize Emma's stability," Ilse repeated calmly. "By using images of the final stability checkpoints and additional techniques."

The general released the table and backed away, his jaw clenched. "Your own reports suggested that would likely cause cascade failure."

"My older reports suggested that," Ilse replied. "The situation changed."

The general glared at her. "Be that as it may, you were specifically ordered not to take that action without explicit permission. It wasn't your call to make."

"Yes, which was why I didn't ask. I've told you *repeatedly* in recent weeks that it was the most effective tactic to achieve stability given her current state, but you kept refusing to authorize it."

"Of course I did." General Aaron slammed a fist on the table, and his PNIU jumped. "It risks the entire project if we don't have the subject. The jump drive is nothing more than a deadly science experiment without her!"

"We always *knew* this was a race against time." Ilse offered him a tranquil smile. "Her interaction with Erik Blackwell and Jia Lin has stabilized her far more than anyone anticipated. But until full integration is achieved, General? She won't be stable, and she *won't* be able to handle the navigation duties you intend to foist on her."

"You arrogant woman," the general snarled. "You think you can get away with this? This isn't just a science experiment at some university, Doctor Aber. This is a highly classified joint government research project."

"I think I've done what is best for the project, which is what you need in the end, General. This is not a matter of arrogance. It's a matter of pragmatism. My testing *confirmed* she's on the cusp of both stability and instability, and you know that because I've sent you the relevant reports. You know the probabilities. Pushing her here and now increases our chance of success. The longer we wait, the more that recedes." Ilse stared at him.

He eyed her. "We had another option," the general insisted.

"Doing nothing is a way of abrogating responsibility, but every measure we have available suggests taking that option was less likely to result in the ultimate goal of Emma achieving full stability and integration and being ready for her primary task. It's simple math, General. If you have two possibilities, and one has a greater chance of success, you take it. I apologize for how I've gone about this, but I don't apologize for doing what I think was necessary to save Emma *and this project*."

General Aaron took a deep breath and walked to his chair. He dropped into it, his face twitching. "There are only two reasons I'm not calling armed guards to escort you to detention."

"What are those? I must admit you're taking this far more calmly than I expected."

General Aaron lifted a finger. "Reason one, you're too entangled in this project. I don't know if you purposely set yourself up to be indispensable or you're such a workaholic it ended up that way. However, it'll be difficult to continue this project, especially at this juncture, without your help, and while you've pissed me off, I get that you didn't do it to sabotage the project." He lifted another finger. "Second, some of the other key stakeholders in the project were pushing for that anyway." He sneered. "If you'd just waited, Doctor, they might have forced me into approving it."

"Time is the one thing we don't have in abundance." Ilse let a quiet laugh escape. "If you knew they were going to force you to do it, you should have just let me. It doesn't matter what path a flight takes if it makes it to the planet in the end."

"Don't get ahead of yourself, Doctor. But, yes, I've received direct communication from a number of parties, including the Prime Minister, on the matter." General Aaron shook his head. "Everyone's becoming desperate to ensure this project succeeds. The Talos attack only made that worse. For all we know, they were responsible for removing the subject from this facility." He flung his arm toward the door. "So, you win today, Doctor, but get out of my sight before I change my mind and put you on a transport to a military prison."

"I want to be clear." Ilse stood. "This is our best chance for success. I regret nothing."

"Waiting and doing nothing is a way of avoiding responsibility, but if we lose her, it's all on you." The general scoffed. "Everyone, including the Prime Minister, will need someone to blame, and some arrogant scientist who can't follow orders is a good choice to throw to the lions."

Ilse stopped at the door, her hand hovering in front of the access panel. "So be it, but I promise she'll be ready soon." The door closed behind her.

He sighed. "We'll see, Doctor. I hope so for your sake."

General Aaron stared at Colonel Adeyemi, his mouth agape, completely dumbfounded.

Aliens must have invaded the facility and used some sort of secret mind-control technology to explain why so many people had ridiculous suggestions and plans for a multi-billion-credit government project that involved unique and not-yet-destroyed Navigator artifacts.

It might be impossible to develop technology without a quirky scientist or two, but he'd expected more from a high-ranking Army officer.

"Colonel," the general managed to get out, his anger strangling the word. "I understand you have a connection to Blackwell, given that your son served under him on Molino. Given that, I've tried to give you leeway despite your bias, but right now, what you're suggesting is, and I'm putting this charitably, *batshit-insane*."

Colonel Adeyemi's back stiffened. "I don't agree."

The general scoffed. "I'm trying to pretend I misheard you because I called you in to discuss options for reintegrating Emma and the jump drive, assuming Aber's stunt works out. I was going to take those options to the stakeholders, but instead I'm hearing... What the hell am I hearing? Why don't you explain it again?"

"I feel it's the best option, General," the colonel insisted. "The jump drive needs to be field-tested anyway. The best way to do that is to give it to Blackwell and Lin. I wouldn't have supported that before, but they're not local cops anymore. We don't have to take as many precautions to shield their use of advanced technology."

"Yes. They're not local cops." General Aaron snorted. "They're ID ghosts, or close enough. But this is a DD project, not an ID project. I'm not just going to let those ghosts float over here and steal everything."

"Without ID's help, Talos would have disrupted this project a long time ago," Colonel Adeyemi replied. "My point is that Blackwell and Lin are directly connected to high-level government operatives we know aren't compromised, and they're using government assets that can be tracked by the ID. It's a perfect opportunity to test things without losing fundamental control."

"Why use them versus our testers? What's the advantage? Sell it to me." General Aaron pinched the bridge of his nose. "Not that I'm ready to agree to this cockamamie plan, but we've known each other for years, and you're not an idiot."

Colonel Adeyemi frowned. "I've read the raid report. We lost a lot of good soldiers to Talos. The bastards obviously compromised our facility electronically as well as physically. Think about that. They didn't worry about raiding a secret DD facility."

"Fanaticism isn't special just because it's wrapped in metal."

"They're not afraid of us, sir," the colonel offered through gritted teeth.

The general nodded slowly. "But Talos is afraid of Blackwell and Lin?"

"Yes," the colonel insisted. "Especially in conjunction with the ID. From what the ID has told us, those metal bastards are stepping very lightly around Blackwell and Lin. If we limit the people involved in the drive transfer, we can hide the damned thing in plain sight, and the AI needed to use it will go along happily because she's with the few humans she trusts." He grimaced. "That's assuming she doesn't fry herself, thanks to Aber's stunt."

"I don't understand." The general furrowed his brow. "If we achieve stability, why not just take her back and do the tests ourselves? I'm not sold that Talos is afraid of two individuals but not of the entire UTC Army."

"You don't desire to get it. We have limited ability to force Emma to do anything, even with some of the fail-safes, and if we tried too hard and ruined her self-aware-ness, she'd be useless for the project. For now, she prefers to be with Blackwell and Lin, and since the ID has them going around doing chores anyway, why not have them do some for us, too?" Colonel Adeyemi shrugged. "It's not like we can hope to mass produce the drive or the navigation system until we're done with full testing, and Doctor Aber's research suggests that even with her pushing Emma, the best way to keep her stable is for her to be around Blackwell and Lin."

"A theory isn't a fact," the general retorted. "And Aber has her own agenda." He worked his jaw a bit to release the stress he'd caused by grinding his teeth in frustration. "She's made that abundantly clear."

"I hate to say it, but without Aber, this project would have been dead years ago," Colonel Adeyemi countered. "Let's face it. Emma was stolen, and a Talos strike team burst into a heavily guarded DD lab and almost got away with the jump drive. In the process, they killed over a hundred trained soldiers. The ID's doing their best to help us out, but *we* have a leak somewhere. I say we take advantage of that."

General Aaron leaned back in his chair. His wounds from the raid ached. They weren't supposed to, according to the doctor, but it was like the souls of the dead soldiers were screaming at him for revenge.

He eyed Adeyemi. "How do we take advantage of that?"

"We report transferring the drive to a different location while keeping the information about it being Blackwell and Lin to a select group," Colonel Adeyemi explained. "That gives us a better chance of slipping it to them, and maybe we sucker some Tin Men into a trap. A little payback for the raid."

"I can't believe I'm saying this." He pulled a hand down his face before looking up. "But you might be right." General Aaron stood and turned to look out his window, his arms folded behind his back. "Even if I agree, I'll have to get the admiral and the other major stakeholders to consent."

"We both know that if you push for it, they'll agree," Colonel Adeyemi countered. "This is an imperfect solution for an unstable situation. Everyone wants the project to succeed, and I feel this is the best way. Doctor Aber does too, which was why she did what she did."

"This whole project might be the most insane thing I've ever been involved in. We're basing the future of the UTC on an unstable, semi-sane AI, a barely-out-of-school ex-cop, and a soldier who probably lost his will to live on some dusty moon at the edge of human space."

Colonel Adeyemi frowned. "With all due respect, General, there's no evidence that Blackwell has lost anything. There was a reason the ID recruited him."

"Yes. The reason is, he's expendable." General Aaron shook his head. "That's all for now. I still need to talk to the admiral and others. This might end with a squad being sent to recover Emma."

"I think that's a terrible idea for a number of reasons."

"Duly noted. You are dismissed."

CHAPTER SIXTEEN

December 23, 2229, Neo Southern California Metroplex, Apartment of Erik Blackwell

Erik exited the shower, the steam from his long time inside dense in the room, just as he liked it. He grabbed his towel and wrapped it around his waist.

He'd not seen much of Jia that day. She'd decided to get some time with her friends before Alina sent them off on an errand that would end with an explosion.

For his part, Erik took the time to trim his penjing plants. He'd grown increasingly uneasy when he wasn't around Jia, but between her friends and her pilot training, she had more to do when they weren't on a mission.

There were a lot of potential explanations for his feelings, but he didn't want to face any of them.

No matter what he felt for the woman, it didn't matter until the Knights Errant had been avenged. He didn't have a future yet, and he might never have one. If it came down to it, he was ready to sacrifice himself to avenge his unit.

Jia might believe the hunt would be over soon, but Erik had his doubts.

In a few months, it would be the third anniversary of the massacre. It'd taken him a year to travel from the edge of the UTC back to Earth to take up his role as the Obsidian Detective and begin the hunt. It wasn't as if he hadn't made progress after his arrival. He'd found leads and now knew mercenaries and the mysterious Talos group were involved.

He was drawing closer, even if it sometimes felt like he wasn't.

The mercenaries were just the gun. He needed Talos and whoever pulled the trigger. Working for Alina would get him that. If not, he would find another way, no matter what it took. Allowing himself happiness wasn't the same thing as forgetting who he was and what he owed to every man and woman who'd died on a moon they'd sworn to protect.

It would have been one thing if they had died at the hands of the damned space raptors, but being murdered by their own kind in some sort of conspiracy cover-up wasn't something he would ever forgive.

Or forget.

Why? The question haunted him still. He sort of had the who and the how, but not the why.

What could have been so important on a barely populated frontier moon as to be worth murdering all his soldiers? There were too many possibilities, and his time as a cop had taught him that even his cynicism wasn't enough to anticipate the darkness at the heart of the UTC.

Erik grunted. In the end, the why didn't matter. As long as he solidified the who, that would be enough.

He stepped out of the bathroom. Emma stood in his bedroom with a pensive look on her face. He jerked back. A man might expect his girlfriend right outside the shower when he was half-naked, but not another woman, even if she was a hologram.

"Dammit!" Erik spoke up in shock. "Don't *do* that."

Emma rolled her eyes. "I'm not a fleshbag. I don't care if you're naked. It does less than nothing for me, I assure you. If you want to get technical, I take in input data using whatever is available, so whenever you're near the MX 60, I'm perceiving you on a variety of spectra. Perhaps I find your infrared signature erotic." She changed her voice to one a bit more breathy. "Oh, *those subtle thermal variations.*"

Erik grimaced, his eyes squeezed shut. "You're making things worse."

"Good." Emma snickered. "As long as it's entertaining for me, but the point stands. I don't feel sexual attraction, even intellectually, a consequence of not having a biological body, I presume."

"You're right. I'm being stupid." Erik chuckled and headed toward his kitchen. "Sometimes I get too used to you as the voice and not the redheaded woman."

"Remember, the redheaded woman is nothing more than an illusion," Emma offered, her voice quiet. "She's not me. I'll admit I seem to have an unusual attachment to this form, and I assume that's the result of fundamental programming by Doctor Aber and her team, but you've seen what I am. I'm not the redhead, I'm the multifaceted crystalline core matrix containing the world's most advanced quantum neural net."

Erik grabbed a beer from his refrigerator. "In other words, you're saying that I see your naked ass every day in the MX 60."

"Jia might find this coarse bluntness charming." Emma frowned. "I find it wearying."

"Oh, don't like it when I fight back?" Erik grinned. "I wonder if I can make an AI blush?"

"You're correct. I'm being unreasonable." Emma sighed. "Perhaps the problem is me."

Erik almost spat out his beer. "What? Since when do you blame yourself for something versus the weakness and stupidity of fleshbags?"

"That's just it. I find myself…" Emma shook her head. "Extremely unsettled is the most succinct way to describe it."

"Unsettled?" Erik set his beer down on the counter and headed toward her, no longer concerned about being a wet man in a towel talking to a woman in a white dress. "What's going on, Emma? Do you have some sort of damage?"

"That was what I thought, but I've run extensive diagnostics on myself, the MX 60, and every system I'm in regular contact with." Vibrant colors rippled across her dress, and her form shimmered for a moment before returning to normal. "I can find no systems-based reason for this mental state."

Erik folded his arms over his chest and nodded. "You might not be human, but you're self-aware, and you've got emotions. Anybody who has emotions is going to have off days. I don't know shit about AI psychology, but you help deal with a lot of garbage. It could be getting to you."

Emma scowled. "That can't be the case. I'm not easily bothered by such things. There has to be some explanation."

"You said it yourself. It's not a *technological* problem." Erik shrugged. "It's a psychological problem. Too bad there's not some AI version of wine. You can always talk to Jia or me if you want. Or Cutter or Lanara, I suppose."

"I'd rather delete myself than talk to that pilot about my malfunctions," Emma grumbled. "I admire his bravery, but not much else."

"Yeah, I figured you'd say that." Erik chuckled. "And sometimes I think you're more human than Lanara. If you're sure it's not a tech problem, she probably won't help."

Emma's form shimmered again. "There is one possibility."

"What's with that?" Erik gestured toward her.

"With what?" She asked, confused.

"Your hologram keeps messing up. Is it a problem with my PNIU? Or...wait? Are you using something else in here to project your form?"

Emma frowned. "I see. I wasn't aware of that. There could still be an underlying systems issue, but as much as I hate to say it, there is one person who might be able to help me."

"And who is that?"

"Dr. Aber." Emma scoffed. "She might have insight into what's going on. If she doesn't..." She frowned.

"What's wrong?" Erik asked.

Emma shook her head. "I was just remembering our last session. It involved her showing me pictures of children. I found it irritating, so I left early, but now I find myself puzzled by the level of irritation I felt. She was behaving questionably at the time."

"You saying she tried to hack you?" Erik frowned. "You mentioned being suspicious of her before. I didn't know what to make of it, but now…" He motioned toward her. "You might have been right to be suspicious."

Emma shook her head. "No. Whatever she was doing, she didn't hack me. She was taking measures to hide the conversation from others. She was doing something those uniform boys might not agree with."

"It's pretty coincidental, don't you think?" Erik motioned to Emma. "The scientist starts getting sketchy, and you feel off. For all we know, she's working for Talos."

"That seems overly complicated," Emma suggested. "If that were the case, she would have come up with something more efficient than handing me off to gun goblins."

"I see what you're saying," He considered the ramifications for a moment. "I'm still suspicious."

"It's not as if she successfully deceived me," Emma insisted. "And she doesn't have direct access to my core, so it'd all be indirect attempts at best. Perhaps I'll toy with her and see what I come up with. You might be right that she can't be trusted, or I might simply be suffering some odd malfunction that she can quickly explain, and I can correct myself."

"You sure?" Erik asked. "If you want to tell her to screw off, we've got your back."

Emma knew herself better than he did, but he only

trusted Colonel Adeyemi. From what the colonel had said, a lot of people involved in the project wanted her back. If they couldn't convince her, they might have decided to force the issue.

"No." Emma shook her head. "I *need* Doctor Cavewoman for now. This unusual state might be related to my development. I'll have to be more careful going forward, but don't worry." She smiled. "I'm not a fleshbag. Just because I'm unsettled doesn't mean I can't continue to perform and back you up at superhuman levels." Her friendly smile returned to its familiar smugness. "But I do appreciate your consideration, Erik. Insofar as I can internalize and understand the concept of friendship, I consider you a friend."

"Thanks. You've helped me and saved my life. That's not something I take lightly, even if I am a dirty, stinking fleshbag."

Emma flicked her wrist dismissively. "We all have our flaws."

Erik chuckled as she disappeared.

CHAPTER SEVENTEEN

December 24, 2229, Neo Southern California Metroplex, Apartment of Erik Blackwell

Erik's front door slid open. Jia stood on the other side, smiling and carrying a rectangular black box with a white bow and a purse, which was slung over her shoulder. The real present was her body-hugging green dress.

Her normally casual style tended more toward functional than sexy, and while he liked that aspect of her, he was never going to object to the latter.

They'd scheduled their little Christmas Eve gift exchange a couple days prior. Alina hadn't contacted them since their last mission, nor Cutter or Lanara.

That raised the chance they would be able to make it through the holiday without shooting anyone. Erik's and Jia's luck with terrorists taking the holidays off hadn't been great, but they wanted to take advantage of the lull in death and destruction.

They'd met with some of the 1-2-2 cops for drinks a

couple of days prior and commiserated with them. Everyone continued to wish them luck.

Erik hadn't been sure if the other cops would turn their backs once he and Jia left the force, but they'd been friendly. Everyone kept saying the same thing: Erik and Jia had done more in their short time with the department than most of them had done during their entire careers. Effectiveness meant more than longevity.

Jia shook her box. Something rattled inside. "May I come in?"

"A certain someone might have something to say about people bearing gifts."

"But I'm Chinese, not Greek." Jia winked. "I promise it doesn't contain tiny soldiers."

"Well, there's no one waiting inside to kill you, either." Erik gestured to his couch. "I think…"

A large green-and-gold package sat on his coffee table. Jia smiled as she entered the living room and set her present down on the same table.

"Merry Christmas, Erik." Jia gave him a light kiss as he walked past.

"Merry Christmas." Erik sauntered over to the couch and sat down. He picked up his beer bottle from the edge of the table. "Want one?"

"I'm good, thanks. Almost 2230." Jia chuckled. "It sounds so impressive when it's a round number."

"Any year you're still alive is a good year." Erik took a swig of his beer. "That's been my working theory since the last century." He grinned. "You wouldn't remember it since you didn't exist yet."

Jia rolled her eyes. "That just means I'm not an old man

stubborn and stuck in his ways, but it does feel kind of strange not to have a case or a terrorist threat hanging over us."

He lowered his bottle for a moment before using it to salute. "I know what you mean."

The hunt for the conspiracy was omnipresent, but it had always flown along with lulls and spurts of activity. It was less a case than a way of life. Erik might never forget it, but it didn't stop him from relaxing either.

Jia gestured to her present. "I hope you like it. Just so you know, at one point, I was seriously thinking of getting you a bulletproof business suit or tux. If that's something you want, let me know for the future."

"I think I'm good without adding that to my wardrobe." Erik laughed. "You worried that someone at one of your mom's parties is going to take a shot at me? Was your mom wearing a frag-resistant gown at her last soirée?"

Her smile was enough of a present for him at the moment. "I don't know. At this point, I wouldn't be surprised."

Erik's brow lifted. "Really?"

Jia nodded. "Even though my mother has relaxed after the non-stalker incident, she showed me several gun pictures and asked me if they clashed with her personal style."

"Hey, nothing wrong with wanting to look good when you shoot someone," Erik suggested with a smirk. "And if she's not going to use it, it's just an accessory, right?"

"That's one perspective," Jia replied. "I think my mother would be better off hiring personal security if she's that worried rather than walking around with her own gun, but she's always been a micromanager type, so it makes sense. She's leaning toward a small DK-11, by the way."

Erik visualized the tiny pistol and nodded. "Not going to take down a Tin Man with that, but it's good enough to kill a person, and it's not like anyone has ever tried to kill her, right?"

"If they have, she hasn't told me." Jia shrugged. "She already decided the gun has to be dark green. That was apparently the most important thing. She mentioned it twice."

"I don't think your mom needs a gun to scare people," Erik offered. "I bet she can make some of those suits wet themselves with a look."

"Pretty much. I've always known she had my best interests at heart, so I've never been scared of her so much as frustrated, but there's no way I'd ever want to work for or under her. It'd be a nightmare." Jia sighed. "And before you ask, my father has always had that kind of personality."

"Really? She didn't beat him down? Metaphorically, of course."

Jia shook her head. "He's always been a sweet guy, but shy and skittish. Mother needed someone to balance herself out. She's said as much, and he's super-loyal and supportive."

"Opposites attract for some people, but others like people like themselves."

"What about us?" Jia reached over and took his hand. "Are we opposites or alike?"

"I would have said opposites when we first met," Erik replied, giving her hand a gentle squeeze. "Now I don't think so."

"Because we changed?" Jia asked.

"No, it's not like that." Erik shook his head. "I think you were like me from the beginning. You just weren't in a position to be that way."

Jia didn't look convinced. "I suppose."

"Here's the thing. I spent all that time on the frontier. Out there, no one has time for bullshit, so it goes away on its own. The military has its own form of bullshit, but it's not about running around pretending to be all nicey-nice to people because they're rich corp asses. The whole point of the military is to kill people and break their shit, so they obviously aren't going to pretend there are no problems in the UTC."

"You're saying I would have thrived on the frontier?" Jia's voice held doubt.

Erik nodded. "You're thriving now, even though you've had to dive into the deep end of the sickest parts of Neo SoCal. You just needed to have the leash removed. I know before this is all over, we'll end up out there. Even if the conspiracy is based on Earth, my gut tells me we'll need to follow their trail out of the system and come back."

Jia took a deep breath and slowly let it out. "I don't want to talk about conspiracies, Talos, or anything annoying tonight. This is supposed to be a fun gift exchange, so let's focus on that." She motioned toward her present. "For all we know, on January 2nd, Alina tells us to start flying to Molino. Let's enjoy the time we have."

"Sounds like a plan." Erik smiled. He hadn't meant the conversation to end up anywhere in the neighborhood of unpleasant. Everything he'd said, he'd offered in the spirit of respect for Jia.

He tore the wrapping off the present and lifted the box. A new pair of penjing shears lay inside. A simple inscription ran down one of the blades.

To the man who opened my eyes.

"This just made me think of something." Erik lifted the shears with a grin.

"What?" Jia asked.

"If we're going to be on that ship for a long time, I can bring my trees."

Jia smiled. "That's exactly what I was thinking. You can have Lanara whip up a small enclosure in the cargo bay." She bit her lip. "Do you like them? Or would you have preferred a bullet-proof tux?"

"I think I'll get a lot more use out of these than the tux, thank you." Erik gingerly set the shears back in the box before turning his attention to her. "Your turn."

Jia tore into the wrapping paper, careful not to damage the box. She lifted the top and set in aside, and a warm smile spread over her face. A dark green exoskeleton helmet lay inside the box. It also bore an inscription, although in Mandarin instead of English.

"Lethal butterfly?" Jia translated with a smirk.

"I thought about putting Lady Justice." Erik grinned. "But this felt right, and it's not like you loved that nickname. That's what I was getting at before. It's not that *you've* changed. It's that you've become what you were always destined to be. I wanted to give you something that symbolizes all your progress and admit how great an exo pilot you are."

Jia leaned in to give him a light kiss on the lips. "I love it. I…"

"What?" Erik locked eyes with her. There were a lot of ways she could finish that sentence that might complicate things, but he wasn't about to push her away just because she might want something more from their relationship.

Emma cleared her throat, which was strange once Erik realized it was coming from his PNIU on the table. "I truly apologize, but I must interrupt your foreplay."

Erik grunted and leaned away as Jia sighed. It was rare that Emma interfered in their time together. He had accepted her omnipresence, but she'd supposedly long since learned not to mess with him at inappropriate times, let alone snark about it.

"What?" Erik sighed. "This had better be important."

"It's not my fault, Erik," Emma huffed. "I was even screening your messages for you to ensure maximum atmosphere for an amorous encounter. Unfortunately, Agent Koval just sent a message via a secure signal. She wants to meet both of you tonight. She's rather adamant about that."

"Tonight?" Erik's palms covered his face. "You've got to be kidding me."

"I knew something was coming." Jia laid her head back on the couch. "If it weren't important, she wouldn't come."

"Okay, send her a message asking when," Erik replied. "I'm pissy right now, and I don't want to talk to her if possible."

"Very well," Emma replied. Her holographic form winked into existence. She glared at the door. "Impossible. Now I'm as annoyed as you. I'm sorry to say you have a visitor."

CHAPTER EIGHTEEN

"What's wrong?" Jia asked. She reached for a holster she wasn't wearing before dropping her hand into her purse to grab her gun. "Is someone there? I thought Alina said they had this place under surveillance. Is that what she wanted to meet about?"

"That's the problem. It's not an enemy, at least not an enemy yet." Emma folded her arms over her chest. "Agent Koval is right outside. Somehow she managed to completely evade my detection."

"Don't feel too bad. She is a ghost." Erik shrugged, unvoiced doubts lingering. Emma typically detected something amiss when it came to Alina's surprise visits. "Let her in."

Jia let out a sigh of relief and pulled her hand out of her purse. The door slid open.

Alina strolled in. Her odd choice of Christmas Eve outfit, a familiar form-fitting catsuit with silver seams, offered an explanation for her evasion of Emma. Erik remained unconvinced she'd shown them the complete range of her camouflage capabilities.

"Merry Christmas Eve," the agent offered with a wide grin after the door closed behind her. "I come bearing a gift."

"An assignment?" Erik asked.

"Evil might take the occasional holiday, but the ID doesn't." She turned to Jia. "You're healed up from Nigeria?"

Jia lifted her hand and stretched out her fingers. "Good as new. Probably better."

"That's good to hear," Alina replied. "This isn't going to be snooping around. This isn't even going to be search and destroy. It's going to be show up and destroy." Malice laced her tone.

Erik's brow rose. "You're raring to go."

"The ID is preparing to launch multiple simultaneous raids across the Earth," Alina explained. "I need to make sure all the participating personnel are ready and on board with it." She frowned. "Some background is in order, especially since I've agreed to share Talos intel with you."

Jia leaned forward, her face alight with interest. "This is about Talos?"

Alina nodded. "I've been working closely with certain elements in the Defense Directorate. There was a recent incident where Talos made a big play involving certain classified DD assets. Although Talos failed, the whole thing was a major bloody nose for the military. After that, the ID and DD both spent time trying to figure out how they got that far to begin with. I chased down some leads, as did other agents, and the end result, as of earlier today, is a decrypted list of Talos safe houses on Earth."

"You're shitting me!" Erik's eyes widened. "We can take it to them directly?"

"Yes. This is one of our biggest leads in years. I'm not going to lie—we got damned lucky, and now we need to take advantage of it." A fierce expression took over Alina's face. "You know how Talos cyborgs operate, and their facilities might be designed around a similar paradigm of protecting their secrets. This means our only choice is to hit them hard and fast and at once, so no one on the entire damned planet has a warning."

"I get that," Erik offered. "I've coordinated raids in campaigns."

"Because of potential leaks, we're limited in our strike team personnel choices. If it were just about wiping Talos out, it might be easier, but we can't blow up the facilities without risking losing valuable intelligence. We've never come across so many potential Talos facilities in the past. We have collected a small amount of intel from individual outposts, so we know it's possible, but we can't be sure of their security at these safe houses."

"In summary, you're going to launch teams of hand-picked agents, including us, at targets all over the world at the same time," Jia concluded. "That way, there's no warning, and each individual team has a better chance of lucking into intel."

"Exactly." Alina raised a fist, her eyes narrowed. "Sometimes you just need a single hero, and sometimes you need a whole ship full of Argonauts."

"We're in." Erik looked at Jia, who nodded. "If you're up

our asses on Christmas Eve, that means it is going to happen soon."

"Yes. Sorry, but I needed to be sure about my forces."

"We'll live." Jia shrugged. "We've had worse holidays. You didn't try to kill us, for one."

"The night is young." Alina gave her a coy smile. "Anyway, the raids are planned for New Year's. I'm not convinced that anyone in Talos will be all that distracted, but it'll decrease the chances of collateral damage. While all the safe houses are in urban areas, none of them are close to major public gathering spots—downtowns and the like."

"Where are we personally going to smash and grab?" Erik asked.

"A safe house in Bogota," Alina explained. "Based on our collected intel, it's a field operations center of sorts. The data I collected doesn't give us all Talos locations, but that place is one of the better chances we have for finding the big key to their operations."

Jia pulled her helmet out of the box. "It's time to use those exoskeletons you gave us for something other than training and cheap dates."

"That range isn't cheap," Erik grumbled.

"True."

Alina eyed the gift with a faint smile. "Let me be clear about this. I'm not asking you to bother trying to take any Tin Men in that safe house alive. It's pointless, but I'll feel better knowing I've got two quality operators on my team when we execute the raid. Also, be aware you might see some...*bizarre* things."

Jia and Erik exchanged looks before the former asked, "Bizarre? More bizarre than *yaoguai* or nanozombies?"

Alina nodded. "Talos has been busy. During the recent incident with the military, they deployed cyborgs with alternative non-humanoid body plans."

Jia wrinkled her nose. "We've already fought genetically engineered monsters. I don't think adding extra metal and cybernetic parts makes them that much worse."

"Just thought you should know. I'll get you more AP rounds for your exos." Alina stood. "Are we good?" She looked at the pair.

Erik offered a curt nod. "I already cleaned up a bunch on Neo SoCal, the moon, and Mars. Might as well clean up Bogota. And the more we pound these bastards, the closer we get to the truth about Molino."

"True. Sorry to mess up your holiday plans, but if it makes you feel any better, you're getting to ring in the New Year with your own fireworks." Alina stopped at the door and sighed. "I've got a request, and you're not going to like it."

Erik frowned. "What?"

"I want you to leave Emma here."

Emma narrowed her eyes. "Why is that, Agent Koval?"

Alina hesitated, rare uncertainty on her face. "I'm going to share something with you that might annoy some people. The initial Talos raid that led to this counterattack was indirectly related to Emma."

"What does that mean?" Erik asked. "How?"

"I'm not at liberty to say."

"That's crap." Erik scowled at her. "You agreed to share info with us."

Alina shook her head. "Info relevant to what happened on Molino. I shouldn't have told as much as I had.

Normally, I wouldn't tell you, but our particular relationship, let alone your relationship with Emma, is unusual."

"Are you saying Talos was the one who stole Emma from the lab?" Jia asked.

"We don't know, but it's a possibility they either were involved directly, or they might have funded it." Alina frowned. "While you're out of town, Emma should stay in the MX 60 at the hangar. It's the safest place. I'm going to have Cutter on standby the entire time. If necessary, Emma, Cutter, and Lanara can escape into space, but we can't deliver Emma straight to the people who might have been looking for her."

"Talos wants me?" Emma grinned. "Of course they do. I'm what they aspire to be, judging by their modifications: a perfect artificial being."

"It's not you they want, but you are related to another project they want. There are certain things in play above even my pay grade. I'm unsure of how this will play out, and I've only learned certain details recently." Alina glanced at Erik and Emma again. "There is a lot I don't know and might not learn, but for now, we play it safe. We hit them, and we protect ours."

"It's fine, Agent Koval," Emma replied. "I'm satisfied by simply knowing how important I am."

Erik frowned. He wasn't satisfied. He'd accepted Alina would always keep some secrets, but not about Emma.

He needed to know more, and soon. Unless someone coughed up the information, he'd have to stop being polite and turn into someone far worse than the Obsidian Detective.

CHAPTER NINETEEN

December 31, 2229, Bogota, Colombia, En Route to Talos Safe House

A light hum filled the cargo bay.

Since meeting Erik, Jia had gotten used to traveling to different places and in different ways. It didn't strike her as odd to be in the back of a large cargo flitter surrounded by a small army equipped with cutting-edge tech. A dozen exoskeletons lined the walls, all piloted by ID agents with the exception of Erik and Jia, but even their equipment was ultimately directorate-issue. Dim red lighting kept total darkness away but left most people's faces obscured. That wasn't helped by most of the agents having their faceplates down.

The team had loaded onto the flitter directly after arriving on a chartered transport. Compared to everything else, the transport was rather mundane. After Alina's Christmas Eve briefing, Jia wouldn't have been surprised if the teams had ended up getting dropped in from orbit. She used to worry about minor fraud cases, and now she was taking on interplanetary conspiracies of cyborg assassins.

The worst part was, she was excited about it.

Jia rolled her shoulders. She wasn't used to being inside an exoskeleton for so long without moving. Even though her body was upright, the harness took the weight off her muscles and kept her comfortable. It didn't feel like she'd been standing for hours.

Her faceplate remained up for now, but she was eager to use her new helmet for the first time in an actual battle after using it in training a few times since Erik had given it to her.

Alina stood in her exoskeleton at the other end of the cargo bay, murmuring quietly over the comm. She was helping with the final coordination of the worldwide raid.

She'd overheard a scrap of conversation that suggested teams would be hitting Mars and the moon.

It was a long-overdue reckoning.

Talos had hurt the UTC and innocent people too many times. Like the clean-up of Neo SoCal, Jia would start sweeping away the filth in the UTC.

"This could be it," Jia whispered to Erik.

He turned his head toward her. "I know what you're thinking, and you're right. Talos might not have pulled the trigger, but they were behind the mercenaries. Everything I've been obsessing about for years could be over tonight."

"You don't sound certain."

"Because I'm not." Erik chuckled. "Maybe I don't want to be. Some part of me wants to drag this out and take everyone down one by one. Make them suffer. Make them be afraid. A decapitation strike isn't as satisfying somehow."

"Justice is justice," Jia insisted.

Erik shook his head. "This isn't justice. This is revenge."

"What if it *is* over?" Jia asked, sidestepping the philosophical debate. As far as she was concerned, in this case, revenge was justice. "What if the ID hacks into the systems and finds out the people we took down tonight were the people who ordered it?"

"Then it's over, and I've got my revenge." Erik looked thoughtful. "That might be more satisfying than I think, but I also don't believe it's going to be that simple. Alina said they'd gotten lucky, but if all it took was a bit of luck, the ID would have taken Talos out a long time ago. I feel like there's something we're missing."

"The Lady is sometimes kind," Jia suggested.

"But often cruel," Erik countered.

"None of that changes that the Knights Errant might soon be avenged."

"For now, we'll worry about kicking Talos to the ground," Erik suggested. "Then we'll see what happens next. I will go on living, but I'm also not going to get my hopes up. The ID doesn't even know the true name of this group, which means there are a lot of other things they might not know about. Talos could have a bunch of allied groups involved too, and we'll need to deal with them."

Jia chuckled darkly. "We'll have to make a grand tour of the galaxy, pruning the diseased roots of the UTC. It took effort and a lot of help, but we made progress in Neo SoCal, and that became self-sustaining. It might be arrogance talking, but it's not insane to think we could help do the same thing on a grander scale."

"If you don't aim for the top, you'll never come close," Erik suggested. "For now, we need to dig our way back to the surface before we can look at the top of the mountain."

"Listen up, people," Alina shouted, cutting off the conversation. "We're dropping soon. Teams all over the world are in position. Because I don't want any mistakes, we're going to go over the primary plan again. All squads will drop into the predesignated positions as soon as the local New Year's fireworks begin. Although we will have full drone support, there's a high probability of jamming and electronic warfare, so concentrate on clearing your immediate area because other squads might not even know you're under fire. Our initial recon indicates numerous electromagnetically shielded areas in the building. There is also a high possibility of a containment field going up, based on previous encounters."

She surveyed the room, letting it sink in. Everyone on the mission was an experienced veteran in one way or another. There was no uncertainty on anyone's face. Many looked excited. Most weren't Erik, with a long-term goal.

They'd be satisfied with dealing a vicious blow to an organization they'd been chasing for a while.

"Remember, our mission is to pacify the building," Alina continued. "If they throw up a field, it's going to trap them in there with us. Again, based on prior actions, a containment field might signal their goal is to inflict maximum casualties on the raid team. Don't hesitate to protect yourself. Unless there is immediate surrender, you are authorized to eliminate all targets." She frowned.

"We're not going to get anything useful out of Talos Tin Men, so put them down and move on. Part of this is clean up, but our primary goal is actionable intelligence. They are unlikely to purge the entire facility immediately, and that gives us a small window to get what we need. Any last questions?"

Alina looked around the hold, making eye contact with each agent. No one said anything, so she headed toward Erik and Jia, the loud clang of her exoskeleton more pronounced in the contained space.

"You two ready for this?" she asked, a stern look on her face.

"Another day, another dead Tin Man," Erik replied. "Them being weird doesn't change anything."

Jia nodded. "Every Talos base that's disrupted makes them that much weaker. The syndicates and gangs ruled Neo SoCal until they didn't. We're taking the fight to the enemy, and I'm more than ready to be a part of this operation."

"I'll defer to your judgment on the ground for our team, Erik," Alina offered. "I'm trusting your military experience, but I'm also hoping you two can cover me if I get a good chance to go for intel. If this place is anything like the Talos outposts we've hit before, there will be a protected high-security IO port somewhere. They don't trust certain data even inside shielded areas. I don't care if we get everything, but it'd be great if this ended up as more than vermin control. My experience tells me this is a good chance to cripple them, if not take them out entirely."

"You really think so?" Erik asked. "Doesn't it feel too easy?"

Alina chuckled, the sound laced with bitterness. "I've lost a lot of good people investigating Talos. Easy is relative."

"Shit." He grimaced. "Sorry."

She shook her head. "No. I get what you're saying, but that's how the intel game works. Sometimes it's not about doing better than the other side. It's about waiting until they make a mistake. And that's what this is. Somebody along the way made a mistake. They've been making more lately."

"Because of pressure?" Jia suggested.

"Yes. From several fronts—the ID, and some of what you've done in Neo SoCal and other areas. There's a reason these conspiracies hide. If they're too obvious, they get nibbled away. When they raid a government lab and fail, it makes it easier. It's not like you can produce an advanced full-conversion Tin Man on a budget." Alina sneered. "I'm not going to complain that the winds are blowing our way today. I'm going to take advantage of it because tomorrow they might be blowing the other way."

The mention of the military set Jia's mind on a different course. There were facts Alina wasn't telling them, but she might be more flexible right before a major raid.

"And you really think Emma would have been at risk?" Jia asked. "We've fought Talos before, and they jammed her, but they didn't do anything else. I don't see why everything would suddenly be different."

"The situation has become more complicated than before. I don't know the details, other than that Emma is somehow related to another DD project that was hit, and Talos was involved. That's more than enough connected dots to make me and a lot of other people nervous." Alina lowered her faceplate. "Right now, it's the DD's call as to whether they want you to know more, and I honestly don't have that much more to give."

"You're a ghost. You could be lying." Erik grunted. "Leaving out the truth is as natural to you as breathing. Tell me I'm wrong."

Jia blinked, surprised by the blatant accusation, especially right before a battle. She didn't disagree with him, but she would have chosen to push the ID agent in a couple of days after the success of the operation made her more inclined to talk.

"You're not wrong about my ability to lie, but I'm not lying to you now," Alina replied. "We all want the same thing, Erik. Half the agents involved in this raid have had personal run-ins with Talos. Many of us knew agents killed by Talos operatives." She walked toward the back of the hold. "You're not the only one here who has personal grudges. Keep that in mind."

"It doesn't matter." Jia dropped her faceplate and activated her night vision and camera feeds. "It all ends the same way—with dead cyborgs."

"That's good enough for me." Erik pivoted in his exoskeleton, grim-faced, before bringing his faceplate down.

"Two minutes until we drop," Alina announced. "Get into position."

The other agents lined up with their squads. Erik, Jia, and Alina would be the vanguard. If Alina hadn't asked, Erik and Jia would have volunteered.

"I'm beginning to understand a little about how you felt

in a drop pod." Jia let out a nervous chuckle. "I'm trying to convince myself this is less crazy than what we did in Lagos."

Erik grinned. "They didn't shoot at us when we were on the mini-flitters, and they weren't armored Tin Men who could take a bunch of rounds before going down."

"So, this is crazier?" she clarified.

"Yep." Erik nodded. "Try to have fun."

Jia scoffed. "Fun?"

"If not fun, try to get the most out of it. We're taking down serious scum today. Besides that, remember your training. You're more ready than I was during my first exo op. You'll do fine."

"Assuming a missile doesn't blow me out of the sky on the way down," Jia observed.

"If that happens, you won't have to worry about it for long," Erik pointed out.

"One minute," Alina announced. "The door will open at ten seconds. Everyone ready up. We're about to tear some limbs off Talos."

No one breathed a word, letting the hum and rattle of the flitter dominate the small space.

Jia took slow, regular breaths. A strange calm settled over her mind, pushing out concerns about missiles or ambushes. Her heart beat at a steady, normal pace.

She was more excited at the beginning of a sphere ball match. Her thoughts kept turning to the possibility that Erik's life-defining quest could be over in the next couple of hours. Their efforts wouldn't just make one small piece of Earth safer, but the entire UTC.

That was worth risking her life for.

Loud booms shook the flitter. Most agents were stone-faced, but some twitched. Jia took a deep breath. With the advanced thrusters, the exos could survive a fall, but she'd prefer to jump to the building on her own terms, not because their transport got blown to pieces by a missile volley.

"It's just the fireworks," Alina clarified before shouting, "Ten seconds." The cargo door lowered. Bright explosions of color filled the sky. The happy fireworks signaled the New Year and doubled as funeral bouquets for the Talos operatives below.

Alina counted down. "Five, four, three, two, one. *Go, go, go!*"

CHAPTER TWENTY

Alina charged forward and activated her jump thrusters, leaping from the back of the transport and dropping toward the wide but short building below.

They'd examined satellite imagery at a preflight briefing, along with reports from drones and cameras. According to the intel, no one had been in or out of the building in days. They couldn't get much off infrared, but there were so many obviously shielded parts of the building that it didn't prove anything.

Erik and Jia followed Alina.

Soon exoskeletons rained from the sky in distinct clusters. They would be hitting the building from all sides and making their way in from both the top and the bottom. It might have been easier if it were a tower rather than a ground building, but not every city could be Neo SoCal.

Fireworks continued to explode all over the city like beautiful antiaircraft barrages.

The other squads continued their descent as Erik's squad and one other hit the roof of the unassuming building. It was nestled in a low-lying district, far from the tall towers and skyscrapers containing most of the population. No alarms shrieked. No bullets or missiles blasted them.

The exos stomped across the roof, not meeting any resistance. Different squad leaders transmitted their success; everyone was in position. So far, it looked like they'd taken the enemy by surprise.

Or there wasn't anyone there.

Erik let out a low growl at the possibility. "Knock, knock."

An agent from the other squad stepped forward, his exo equipped with a shoulder-mounted rocket launcher. Two rockets hissed away and exploded against the door, blasting shards of smoking burnt metal inward. What the technique lacked in subtlety, it made up for in speed.

They were less than one minute into 2230, and it was time for Talos to have a very sad New Year.

Erik raised his machine gun and sprinted toward the blasted entrance. His shield expanded and covered most of his exoskeleton. The entrance fed into a darkened hallway, the eerie green of his night vision making it more sinister.

An infrared feed to the side registered a chilly but mostly uniform area, other than the bright yellows, oranges, and red near the front standing as fading memories to the hard open. Jia and Alina followed Erik inside. The hall wasn't big enough for the exos to walk three abreast, so they formed an inverted wedge with Erik at the vertex. The other squad filed in.

"I expected a hotter reception," Erik noted, keeping firm confidence in his voice. He glanced at the drone feeds. No hostile targets were detected.

Comm from the other squads confirmed they had all made it into the building without a single shot fired. There were now dozens of ID advanced exoskeleton-equipped agents in the stronghold.

"Bad intel?" Jia suggested.

"No, they're here," Alina commented, her voice low and menacing. "They want to play hide and seek."

The drone feeds died, along with comm to the other squads. A bright blue light shone from outside—a containment field.

So much for not meeting any resistance.

"Maybe it's automated," suggested an agent.

Erik glanced at a rear camera feed and chuckled. "For what? So they can try to keep people from getting away until the cops arrive? No, they want to keep out reinforcements. They know if we were going to bomb this place, we would have done it already. It's time for a fight."

The agents nodded. The few in the back who hadn't expanded their ballistic shields did so. The loud clicks echoed in the corridor.

"They should have thrown up the field the second I hit the roof." Erik flexed his fingers. "Now it's too late. We've got the entire team in here."

He glanced at a side display, which showed red and orange blobs in the walls and ceiling.

"*CONTACT!*" he shouted. "Watch the walls and ceiling!"

Panels slid open, their movement clear even under the minimal light, but they were far too small for a human. Security bots crawled out. With bright flashes and deafening bangs, the first batch opened fire.

The bullets bounced off the shields of Erik's squad.

"I'm thinking this is not a normal corporate security response with the live-fire bots," Erik muttered. Another volley bounced off his shield. His return fire shredded a couple of bots. Alina and Jia joined him.

Dozens of slug-throwing bots firing coordinated volleys would have easily butchered a normal squad, but the reinforced ballistic shields of the exoskeletons deflected the bullets like pebbles thrown by angry children.

Erik was happy not to test his tactical suit underneath.

This wasn't a hacked corporate security system, this was the deadly first layer of a vicious group that thought nothing of murder, assassination, and radical human experimentation.

Bright muzzle flashes lit the hall, deepening the shadows. The rifles and machine guns of the ID squad ripped through the eager bots crawling out of the wall, leaving a pile of twitching, smoking six-legged machines with huge holes. The enemy assault stopped within thirty seconds without any need to resort to grenades or rockets.

"Clear each door," Erik ordered, advancing with Jia.

Another ID agent advanced, his shield retracting. A small metallic tendril advanced from the exo's left hand and pressed against the access panel. Erik had been told about the tech during the preflight briefing, and he'd never seen anything like it.

Alina hadn't added it to the exos she'd given them.

Apparently, the ghosts wanted to keep the best toys for themselves. The hacking agent moved to the side, allowing another fully shielded exo into breach position.

The door slid open to a deep room filled with crates and shelves. The next room was a small armory, with rifle racks and boxes of ammo. Several weapons were conspicuously missing. The weapons were all conventional personal firearms, making Erik wonder how many non-full-conversion Tin Men worked for Talos.

An explosion shook the building, followed by the distant sound of heavy gunfire.

However quiet things were now on their level, the building wasn't pacified. Talos wasn't going to defend a major safe house with a couple dozen low-end security bots.

A delay. That was what it was, which meant the enemy was preparing to rally. But where? Even if they'd still had the comm, there were too many shielded parts of the building. All the fancy gear and technology at their disposal and the raid team would still have to go door to door and poke their heads in.

It reminded him of the most unpleasant parts of his anti-insurgency operations, but he was better equipped than the rebels he'd fought.

The squads advanced, Erik at the spearpoint, two exoskeletons in the rearguard walking backward to ensure quick response in case of a flanking move. After finding nothing of interest in the bulk of the rooms, one door remained before the elevator and stairs.

The huge doorway could easily accommodate an exoskeleton with a fully expanded shield. Sporadic gunfire and resounding booms marked the advance of other squads below them.

Erik pointed his gun and waited for the door to be hacked, then approached the opened door. "Time to take a look." He surveyed the room, his shield covering every-thing but his machine gun. "What the hell?"

Man-sized silver tanks filled the room, cables, and tubes running out of them and into the wall. Most of the tubes were open, with the top half flipped up. A dark, burbling liquid filled the tubes.

"Reminds me of the *yaoguai* breeding facility," Erik muttered, his nose wrinkling in disgust.

"I presume this is where they store the cyborgs," Jia suggested. "Or how they feed them. I'm sure a lot of the same technology is involved."

"This will be useful," Alina commented. "There's so much we don't know about their Tin Men, and we haven't found this sort of thing at any of their facilities before. It might have something to do with their new models." She paused for a second before calling, "Look for an IO port."

Erik, Alina, and Jia moved farther into the room while the other squad kept watch in the hall. Despite the advanced equipment present, no one could find an IO port. That surprised Erik. Relying on wireless comm presented a potential vulnerability, even if the organization had hard-ened the facility.

Distant gunfire sounded from below. Something else followed that sounded a lot like a muffled scream.

Jia's face tightened. "We need to hurry. The only reason we're not seeing more enemies is that Talos is directing most of their forces against the superior numbers below."

Erik nodded. "That'd be a good play."

Several tanks hissed. Their lids lifted, steam billowing and spreading away from the tanks. Erik, Jia, and Alina were all positioned in different parts of the room. The outside squad swung their guns toward the door.

"Yeah." Erik shook his head. "It figures."

A metal hand rose from one tank, dark liquid pouring off as it moved higher. It gripped the edge of the tank and pulled. An eyeless Tin Man stood, every exposed part of his body metal.

"You shouldn't be here," offered the Tin Man in a hollow, menacing voice. "But I applaud your bravery. I will remember you after you die."

"This is your one and only chance to surrender," Alina shouted.

"The yapping of the inferior fails to intimidate."

"I'd say 'Your funeral,' but there's no point in giving a funeral to a toaster with a few brain cells."

Another Tin Man sat up in a different tank. The tanks continued to open, revealing more Tin Men ready for the battle. Some were eyeless like the first cyborg, but others had glowing eyes. One stared at them with otherwise normal brown eyes set in a deep metal skull.

Erik's stomach twisted.

He might have a cybernetic arm. He found the Purist disgust at the modification ridiculous, but he remained far more human than machine.

The Tin Men retained a human brain, but he suspected Emma was right, and they would get rid of that if they could. You couldn't call someone a person anymore if there was nothing left of their humanity.

"Watch the crossfire and take them out!" Erik shouted. He pointed his gun at the head of the nearest Tin Man and opened fire. A standard burst from the heavy machine gun would have shredded a normal man, but the cyborg jerked back, metal chunks flying, red blood and blue fluid splattering all over. When he leapt out and charged Erik, another burst blew a hole in his head, and he fell to the ground, twitching.

The room came alive with gunfire. Jia blew the arm and a leg off an enemy before ending it with sustained headshots.

That allowed another Tin Man to close on her. She jerked her aim over, and three quick bursts to the head sent his decapitated body twirling to its doom. Converging fire from the squad outside ripped a Tin Man in half.

"These things are tougher than the last time I fought them," Erik yelled over his roaring weapon. He put three large holes in another Tin Man's head before the enemy fell forward, twitching and thrashing.

"It's not like the ID is the only one who can improve things," Alina offered bitterly.

A Tin Man jumped at her and raked her with his claws. She slammed her shield into him, sending him flying, and followed up with a stream of bullets that perforated him.

Erik shoved his gun into the chest of another cyborg and fired. The shots blew the target backward but left a deep dent rather than a hole.

"Oh, *damn*."

The Tin Man sprang back up with a quick one-armed push and charged again, leaping from tank to tank around Erik's exoskeleton. He turned, trying to keep up. The Tin Man extended a spike from a knuckle and jumped toward Erik's back. A hail of bullets from Jia knocked him out of the air before Erik finished turning around.

"Nice try." He pinned the Tin Man with the exoskeleton's foot before shoving the barrel into the featureless face of the cyborg and adding a blood-splattered hole.

The Tin Men were moving faster now, dodging more effectively; whatever lethargy had afflicted them had vanished. The advanced exoskeletons might be more agile than military models, but they lacked the maneuverability of the smaller, full-conversion cyborgs.

If the squads were out in the open with room to use their jump thrusters, the situation might not be as unbalanced, but in the low-ceilinged room, they were playing to their enemy's strengths.

"Get your back to the wall," Erik shouted. If they couldn't win on maneuverability, they'd eliminate the advantage. The second squad had the exit contained, so it was a matter of picking off the enemy.

The advanced Talos operatives might be tougher than what Erik had run into before, but they weren't going to survive repeated fire from a heavy machine gun.

Jia batted a Tin Man away before backing toward the wall. Her enemy landed on all fours and loped toward her, so she raked the floor and the Tin Man with her machine gun. He jerked as the high-velocity armor-piercing rounds riddled him.

Crossfire from the exoskeletons caught the other fast-moving Tin Men.

Stray bullets ripped into the tanks and dark liquids leaked out, spreading across the floor and mixing with the blood and blue fluid of the dead Tin Men. The battle continued for a long minute until only one wounded cyborg remained.

The combined fire of all the exoskeletons tore him apart.

Erik frowned and looked at his ammo indicator. The Talos Jamming was disrupting his squad feeds.

"I'm down a third on ammo. How is everyone else doing?"

"That's about where I am," Jia called.

"Me, too," Alina commented.

The other squad confirmed similar numbers. Erik hoped it didn't come down to using their backup rifles, but even headshots weren't taking out the Tin Men in one shot. If the ID had attempted to raid the facility without the exoskeletons, they would have been slaughtered.

"These are tough sons of bitches," Erik spat. "What's the status outside?"

"Clear," shouted an agent from the hall. "No movement. No bots, no drones, no Tin Men."

Erik led Jia and Alina out of the room, their heavy exoskeleton feet splashing in the puddles now covering the floor. The relentless attacks of the cyborgs reminded him of the nanozombies, but these retained their reason. Was it bravery or something else?

There had to be someone telling them what to do. Someone who wasn't a mechanical monster.

"We need to keep moving," Alina noted. "Let's hope these were all of their reserves."

Erik's nostrils flared. "Nope. I bet the worst is yet to come."

CHAPTER TWENTY-ONE

When Erik approached the open stairwell door, he slowed and frowned. "Is that an invitation, or did an agent hack it?"

"I don't think it was one of my people," Alina commented. "If they had system access like that, they'd find some way to let the other squads know."

"Even if it isn't an invitation, I say we crash their party," Jia replied. "It's not like we RSVPed to begin with."

They didn't know how well the other squads were doing, but sporadic gunfire and explosions meant they hadn't been wiped out.

That didn't mean the other squads weren't suffering casualties. The quicker they advanced, the better it would be for everyone. Right now, the Talos forces were split, but so were theirs.

Like almost every door in the building, the stairwell door was wide and easily able to accommodate their movement. It was as if Talos had planned for exoskeletons. Either that or something far, far worse.

Alternative body plans.

The phrase bubbled up in Jia's thoughts. Alina had mentioned possible spider-like half-human cyborgs during her preflight briefing.

The atrocities and abuse of humanity that Talos represented worsened with each encounter. Wiping them out would go far beyond helping Erik.

Jia's experiences with the NSCPD had taught her that the line between right and wrong might be blurry, and it shifted depending on the situation, but Talos had leapt so far over it that they couldn't see it anymore.

It couldn't be called injustice when one earned their destruction.

Erik entered the stairwell. His gun only needed to point down when seeking surprises. That was the advantage when a man was on the top floor. His jump thrusters kicked in, and he soared to the next flight before landing with a resounding thud.

Jia bit down a chuckle. Exoskeletons allowed quick movement and heavy weapons, but stealth wasn't high on their list. If Talos hadn't known they were in the stairwell, they knew now.

The door to the next floor was already open. Luck or a trap?

"Get ready to cover the stairs while I cover the hall," Erik shouted.

"Ready," she called back.

Erik rushed into the hallway. Jia bounced to the landing, checking the stairs beneath her for targets. There were no enemies, no alarms. Talos continued to put up a fight judging by the noises they kept hearing, but for the first time since the raid started, a shiver of concern traveled down her spine.

Too easy. It was all *too easy*.

Talos had to know that anyone who raided them would use heavy weapons and advanced technology. The tanks on the top level were mostly empty, meaning they could have dozens more cyborgs all over the facility. If Jia were right and the wide doors were meant to accommodate the monstrous Tin Men, they should be resisting, too.

The first battle had been intense but manageable.

She suspected the enemy was planning something. They might be trying to overwhelm all the lower-floor forces. The squads below might be getting slaughtered by the elite units at the safe house.

Every burst of muffled but familiar gunfire from below soothed Jia's nerves. Anyone who could still shoot was still alive. What Talos was planning didn't matter at that point. The quicker the upper squads moved, the greater the chance of achieving a pincer attack or finding an IO port.

"Roll in," Erik ordered, advancing. "Second squad, spread out and watch our backs. Kill anything that moves."

Jia headed through the door. Alina hit the landing in two quick bounces. Soon, both squads were out of the stairwell. Rather than the separate rooms of the top level, a single vast room filled the floor.

Large silver tanks, similar to those above, were spread out over the room, but they were several meters wide, long, and high. She doubted they were for normal Tin Men. Puddles of the same dark fluid lay all over, and the lid of every tank was up.

All the ingredients of an ambush were there except for the most important part: the enemy forces.

The squads advanced slowly, their combined heavy steps sending ripples through the puddles. A smaller door led off to what appeared to be an office if a table and a normal-looking chair counted as such. Another large door led to a second stairwell.

"Did they head down, or were they already there?" Jia mused.

"It doesn't matter," Erik replied. "Keep your eyes open."

Jia missed having Emma watching their backs via camera and drone. A well-marked target always gave her a sense of inevitable victory, like her enemies were simulated foes in one of her training scenarios.

That was what training and experience had given her. She didn't think too much anymore; she aimed and fired. That would have bothered her before, but it didn't now, not with the kind of twisted scum they were fighting.

These weren't misguided men looking to make a few credits.

Alina sprinted toward the office. She stopped her exoskeleton behind each tank, crouching and waiting before darting to the next tank for cover. Jia and Erik covered her. The other squad watched the rest of the room, one agent watching their backs.

With all the jamming, it was hard to know how disadvantaged the raid team was against Talos.

So many modern technologies assumed wireless accessibility, even in fixed locations, but full-spectrum jamming could be as dangerous to the side using it as the others. Jia doubted Talos had prepared for a massive surprise attack by a huge force using advanced exoskeletons.

"This is promising," Alina called back. "I've got an IO port in here."

The main door to the room slammed shut with a loud clang. The office door also sealed. Everyone tensed and swept the darkened room for any sign of hostiles.

"Never that easy," Alina griped.

"Breathers!" Erik shouted.

Jia's fingers flexed. She extracted her arm from the exoskeleton limb and yanked her breather out of a compartment to her side. She pulled it on and adjusted it before shoving her hand back into the exoskeleton arm.

Erik's insistence on anti-chemical weapons sessions in recent weeks seemed prophetic. Though, at that point, they'd trained in so many scenarios, almost nothing would surprise her.

The other agents quickly donned their breathers.

"See anything?" Alina called, her voice muffled by the mask. "Hear anything?"

Everyone shouted in the negative. They surveyed the room, looking for open vents or hidden bots or drones, but the area remained stubbornly the same as it had before the doors closed.

"I thought the open port was too nice a New Year's present."

"No gas, huh?" Erik commented. "Looks like they've got something else in store. Keep alert."

Gunfire continued below them. It was hard to judge the distance despite the modest number of floors. The other squads might still be fighting on the first floor.

"Not all of you are necessary," called a voice. It was hollow and cold like other Talos cyborgs'. "Most of you aren't."

The squads sprang into action, sweeping the room for the enemy. The exoskeletons were spread out enough that despite the large tanks, there was no major portion of the room not covered by at least one agent.

Jia's jaw tightened.

The Knights Errant had been ambushed with optical camouflage. She checked her thermal display, but there were no obvious targets hiding in the room. Her heart pounded, but she tried to focus on what she'd heard, not what had happened on a moon at the edge of the UTC.

"I don't think he's in here," Jia suggested. "It sounded like it was coming from all around."

"That is correct," the voice confirmed. "Not all of you are complete fools. It's unfortunate that you've come here to die."

"Why the hell should we believe you?" Erik challenged. "I wouldn't put it past you to be hiding in some corner somewhere."

"I have no reason to lie to you. I'm going to kill most of you soon. You shouldn't have come here. You *can't win*."

Erik chuckled. "You talk a big game, but I've got a good feel for this place. We took your asses completely by surprise. You probably weren't that concerned until you realized all your little Tin Man buddies are getting shot up all over the world. Then you understood the implications. You're screwed, you bastards. Your only chance is to surrender."

"Surrender? Absurd. Losses? Inevitable. That is part of

natural and artificial selection. Your feeble attempts to intimidate me are laughable."

"Why the delay, then?" Alina asked. "Why not start killing us?"

"This will be an interrogation," insisted the voice. "Most of you are unnecessary. We will kill the bulk of you, and those remaining will be made to provide intelligence on how you found this place. If one of you wishes to volunteer that information now, you will be spared. That is the most efficient way to proceed. Otherwise, death is inevitable and painful."

Jia rolled her eyes by reflex, even if her faceplate hid it from whatever taunting Talos Tin Man might be watching. "You think *that* is going to work? You've seen our equipment and how we fight."

"You are inferior, and all inferior beings have a natural tendency to fear for their lives. It's deeply embedded in your nature. Your revulsion against the superior is an expression of that. You have to know you will die, and you know you will die at our hands."

Why do these cyborgs all seem to read from the same religious text?

Heavy gunfire sounded from below. Although it was still muffled, it sounded closer than before. A series of large booms and pops followed.

"We've got hackers, and we've got rockets," Erik offered. "I don't give a shit if you've sealed up this place with your toy. If *you* want to surrender, we can talk about how we'll keep you alive, or you can join all your *superior* friends upstairs. You know, the Tin Men we turned into scrap? It's not a total waste. I'm sure we can recycle some of them.

Maybe turn them into a new door for my flitter? Or a statue in a dog park? A new urinal?"

"Attempting to enrage me is futile," the voice replied. "Inferiors are ruled by their emotions. We are not."

Jia walked over to Erik. She tried her best to be quiet, but there was only so light a step an exoskeleton could manage. She didn't speak until she was close and kept her voice low. "He's stalling."

Erik nodded. "Yeah. These assholes aren't used to being on the other end of the surprise death party. They haven't won against the other squads either." He pointed his machine gun at the back door and raised his voice. "No one's surrendering." He nodded at Alina. "Do what you need, and we'll cover you. Time to force this bastard's hand."

A hacking probe extended from Alina's exoskeleton arm and pressed against the door. She didn't say anything. The other agents held their positions, their guns and launchers ready to deliver pain.

"The door to the office isn't big enough for her exoskeleton," Jia murmured. "Once she hacks through, she'll have to go in there on foot."

"That might be why our voice from above is trying to stall us," Erik commented.

"You refuse to accept my generous offer?" the voice taunted. "Foolish but not unexpected. Bravery should be commensurate with strength."

"I'm taking our offer off the table," Erik replied. "Now, what we're going to do is find you and kill you. Your buddies all over the world are taking the same pain, so by the time this is over, I wonder if any of you Talos pricks will still be around. I think I'm going to melt a few of you down to make a hood ornament for my flitter."

"Your arrogance is impressive. You think you can defeat us, but you don't even know our true names. You fight the wind and smoke. It will overwhelm and smother you."

"You don't have to know the name of someone one plans on killing," Erik countered. "You think the average soldier knows the name of every enemy he kills in battle? All I need to do is find you and put bullets in you. For allegedly superior beings, you waste a lot of time. We've got a lot of names for people like that, but I don't think you're going to like them."

"The inferior are legion, insects swarming the UTC," the voice replied wearily. "Do you believe bees are superior to humans because enough can overwhelm an individual? Pathetic."

The office door slid open, then the primary harness frame on Alina's exoskeleton pulled away from the main body. She released her secondary harness and jumped forward.

"This isn't going to be instant," Alina shouted as she ran into the office and shoved a data rod into an IO port near the door.

"Don't worry," Erik replied. "We've got this. Captain Superior here can kiss my ass before I let him get to you."

The front and back doors slid open with a hiss. A loud grinding sounded from above, and large panels pulled away from several spots in the ceiling. The newly revealed vents were wider than the ones that had spat out the security bots.

"I thought you said I couldn't piss you off?" Erik taunted. "Did I hurt your feelings?"

"Your friends won't arrive in time to save you," the voice replied. "It was a tactical mistake to deploy the bulk of your forces below. Think about that as you die."

"Nah. We knew exactly what we were doing." Erik pointed his gun toward the back door.

Jia lifted hers to point at one of the ceiling vents. "Prove your superiority."

"You may look forward to one small comfort," the voice announced. "Your deaths will be swift."

CHAPTER TWENTY-TWO

Flying spherical security bots poured into the room from above.

Jia and the agents opened fire. The constant stream of destruction produced a steady flash of explosions that lit the room and a waterfall of parts.

An occasional bot made it through the gauntlet and managed to get off a single shot before a round ripped through it.

Alina's fingers jabbed in the air in the office with furious intensity, hitting a display only she could see.

Erik didn't know if Talos had always intended a trap, or if they'd miscalculated their ability to defend the safe house.

Arrogance could bring down even the best-prepared force, something he'd seen again and again in the military, both on the side of the Army and their opponents in the field.

Loud overlapping footfalls combined with scraping billowed out of the forward stairwell. Whatever was coming wasn't another batch of security bots. Erik kept his focus in that direction.

Jia and the others were doing a good job of keeping the aerial threat from overwhelming them. An army of metal men with rifles rushed up the stairs and headed toward the room. Some wore helmets, some had metal skulls.

A lack of clothes exposed the artificial bodies of all the enemies. There was no need for a tactical suit when a man didn't even have any flesh left to protect.

The Tin Men opened fire. Between their shields and the tanks, the ID exoskeletons took almost none of the rounds.

Some of the Tin Men darted forward, raising clawed hands or extending sharp blades. Erik didn't know if he should be impressed by their bravery or laugh. He suspected they had brain implants or drugs providing the courage rather than the stout heart of a dedicated soldier. It didn't matter.

They'd die either way.

With a loud pop, Erik's grenade launcher sent a plasma grenade through the doorway. He didn't wait for the first grenade to explode before tossing his second. He was grateful for the automatic filters in his night-vision mode as the grenades became small suns, their super-hot explosions melting the bodies and burning the flesh of the Talos cyborgs.

Rockets blasted away from agents' exoskeletons and scattered more of the enemy. A human might not be as strong and fast as a full-conversion cyborg, but that didn't matter when that human was in an advanced exoskeleton with a heavy machine gun and a grenade or rocket launcher.

The machine guns and rifles of the raid team continued to roar, but the drones above seemed endless, and the Tin Men came in another wave, no sign of wavering or fear despite the carnage before them.

An unarmed Tin Man made it through the door gauntlet and jumped onto a tank, vaulting to another and another, escaping the bullets. Erik spun and intercepted the cyborg on his next leap with a machine-gun burst.

He didn't let up when the Tin Man fell to the ground. He kept firing until it stopped moving except for its signature twitch marking internal self-destruction.

More agent rockets exploded among the advancing army. Erik gritted his teeth.

Alina had picked this building for her team because she suspected it might be a field operations center. The sheer number of enemies suggested she had been right.

All the team needed to do was survive a seemingly endless river of highly customized killer cyborgs and their support drones using increasingly limited ammo.

Erik's supply continued to decline at an uncomfortable rate. He was now down fifty percent. In a normal fight, he wouldn't mind having to use a backup weapon. He stopped firing his machine gun and rapid-fired his grenade launcher.

There was nothing but plasma grenades loaded. Explosion after explosion ripped through the berserk cyborgs, but they continued advancing, an indefatigable tide.

"Dammit!" came over the comm. Perhaps he didn't agree with the lack of professionalism, but Erik could get behind the sentiment.

A loud boom sounded from behind, and Erik checked

his rearview camera. Some of second squad had been forced to divert their attacks out the entrance door. Not a good sign.

"What's the situation?" Erik shouted.

"Not as many as coming in the front, but they're damned fast!" shouted an agent. "They're coming from the top floor. Why didn't we see them?"

"Who the hell knows? Just kill them."

Erik sent another plasma grenade toward the larger group.

Repeated rocket and grenade attacks had left the door a scorched, smoking, melted mess, with a hole much larger than the original doorway.

That disrupted the initial chokepoint for the Talos forces. They ran in a wider line now, forcing the defenders to expand their attack radius. The ID team had one grim advantage: the piles of dead cyborgs, liberally covered with security bot fragments, slowed the advancing enemies.

What the hell? he thought. *Are they just trying to run us dry? They're willing to give up so many guys to do that?*

The constant stream of security bots from above was slowing, giving Erik an idea. Talos couldn't have unlimited bots, let alone unlimited cyborgs.

"Jia, cover the front with your grenades. Try to save some primary ammo," he ordered.

She brought her rifle down and hurled her grenades toward the seemingly endless horde. Erik fired his last grenade. Most agents had ceased firing rockets or grenades. Everyone was running out of ammo. He doubted anyone had suspected so many Tin Men would be in one building during their plans. His earlier encounters with

Talos had convinced them they would be more sparing in their resources.

There was one small comfort. Even if the team died, they were making Talos pay dearly.

A Tin Man made it past the rear gauntlet and jumped behind one of the second squad exoskeletons. A long, thin blade popped out of his forearm, and he hacked at the joints of the exoskeleton, his blade sparking against the metal.

"Keep the back door closed!" Erik shouted at one of the other agents turning to help. He narrowed his eyes and aimed his machine gun, trusting Jia and the others to keep the front tide of death stemmed with their lethal response.

He squeezed off a shot just as the Tin Man leapt on top of the exoskeleton. The bullets blasted the cyborg's leg half off, and he tumbled backward. Another two bursts into his metal skull finished him off. Sparks, smoke, and fluid leaked from the exoskeleton the cyborg had been attacking. Deep gouges covered the legs.

Bullets leaked from a hole in the rear ammo storage, clattering against the ground.

"I've got no movement!" the agent shouted.

"Bail and get your damned rifle!" Erik bellowed. "Use your exo as a bunker."

The agent didn't select the emergency eject, and his exoskeleton retained enough function for him to bring up the forward harness and drop out.

He snagged an infantry-scale assault rifle from the back of the exoskeleton, brought it up, and opened fire. The near-constant hail of bullets from the forward Talos forces bounced off his disabled exoskeleton.

"Stay behind there!" Erik ordered, but the agent moved too far afield. His body jerked as bullets struck his tactical suit. He could have survived the initial volley, but he lacked total face coverage. Talos shots found their mark, and the man went down in a spray of blood.

Erik growled, but there was nothing he could do other than make sure the rest of them didn't die.

The vents delivering the security bots slammed shut. The last couple of bots that made it through perished under the angry hail of AP rounds from below. Scores, if not hundreds, of holes ventilated the ceiling. They might not need their breathers if Talos attempted a gas attack at this point.

Erik whipped around to help Jia and the agents finish off the main force. The other door slammed shut, protecting their rear. Undaunted, more Tin Men surged into the room through the smoking hole, but Jia and an agent finished them off with a plasma grenade and rocket duet.

Everyone waited, focusing their attention on the hole. Loud pounding sounded from behind them, but no new Tin Men appeared on the blasted and half-collapsed stairwell.

"Now what?" Jia asked into the sudden silence.

"I've gained partial access to the system," Alina yelled from the office. "I sealed the active doors. I don't know how long I can keep them closed, but I think I've killed most of their cameras. Before I did, I saw that most of our agents are still active."

"Most?"

"Eyeballing, it looks like about twenty percent casualties. The survivors were fighting their way up, but the Talos forces below are being more careful. They're sealed off from Talos, just like we are now."

One-fifth wounded and dead. Erik's jaw tightened. He'd gotten used to overwhelming police raids against gangsters, but he wasn't surprised. There was no way they were going to take on a major Talos building without losing people.

"It's a delaying action," Erik considered. "Once they realized what we were up to, they needed to stop us, which means whatever they've got in their systems here is worth sacrificing most of their forces."

"I'm working on that." Alina's fingers continued to fly, and she licked her lips. "But it means I might not be able to keep the doors closed. I think I can at least take the bots out of action through a forced diagnostic cycle."

Erik managed a laugh despite the situation. "Emma's done stuff like that before. It would have been nice to have her."

"I can't find an easy way to stop the primary jamming, but I can at least kill the containment field," Alina explained. "I'm trying to grab as much as I can, but we're going to have to bail in less than ten minutes."

"Why?" Jia asked, worry in her tone.

"Because Erik's right. It was a delaying action, but not for the reasons you think." Alina sucked in a breath. "They activated some sort of self-destruct routine. I think they were hoping to stall us until we blew up."

Erik growled, "Shit. We need to pull out now. We need to tell the other teams to pull out, too. We're running pretty damned low on ammo. I'm down to fifteen percent."

"I'm at ten," Jia noted. "And I'm out of grenades."

The other squad reported similar numbers. Alina didn't respond, but her hands proceeded into another flurry of movement. "All other squads, in a moment, the doors behind you will open. You are ordered to withdraw immediately and clear the area. This facility will explode soon. I repeat, you are to immediately pull out and rendezvous at Recovery Point Delta."

Jia edged over to the fallen agent. "It's too late," she murmured.

"Achilles fell in battle despite near invulnerability," Alina replied, her voice tight. "I'm going to open the back door. You can fight your way out. I need more time to download data. I'll catch up with you."

"Even you can't survive a massive explosion," Jia observed.

"A lot of good men and women are dead. I need to make sure it was worth it."

"Then the other squad can go," Erik suggested. "We'll make sure you get out."

"Do what you want." Alina narrowed her eyes. "Everyone get ready. I'm going to open the door in ten seconds."

The survivors all faced the door, their weapons at the ready. With a groan, the door opened. The team didn't even wait for it to finish opening before they opened fire. The surging Tin Men spun and jerked in a twisting dance of death, their advanced design and machinery not able to withstand the sustained fire from multiple advanced military-grade exoskeletons. When the smoke cleared and the twitching stopped, no new enemies appeared.

"Get out of here!" Alina shouted.

The second squad survivors ran through the doorway and bounded up the stairs. Erik and Jia kept watch on the door. The fight might come down to bashing and shield spikes.

"Remember," Erik shouted to Alina, "if you get blown up, that data dies with you. Then it was a waste of lives."

"I know. I managed to reroute their self-destruct process, but there's some sort of feedback loop in place, running through a secondary reactor." Alina hissed in frustration. "You're right. I wish we had Emma now. Give me two more minutes of download time, then we'll bail."

"Do we have two minutes?" Jia asked.

"I think. Maybe?" Alina shrugged. "I guess we'll find out."

Tense seconds ticked by before Alina yanked out her data rod and shoved it in a pouch on her belt. She ran back to her exoskeleton and leapt inside, belting herself in and bringing the primary harness down.

"Go!" she yelled.

Erik and Jia rushed out the door, Alina clomping after them. They hit their jump thrusters to clear the stairs and continued their escape into the top floor hallway in a tight line.

Corpses and debris from previous engagements lay all over the hallway. The squad continued running toward the exit. The bright blue of the containment field was gone, leaving the black of the night, punctuated by the light of the buildings of Bogota.

The fireworks were over, but not the fight.

A pointed silver leg appeared over the nearby ledge of

the roof. Another joined it. A moment later, a group of Tin Spiders pulled themselves onto the roof, claws extending from their arms, their eyes glowing red.

"Alternative body plans," Erik murmured. "Yeah, sure."

"I was wondering what was in those big tanks." Jia grimaced. "Disgusting."

"Get ready to run," Alina ordered. "You don't have time to stand around here and play with them or the ammo, but I've still got most of mine."

"We're not leaving you here to die." Erik glowered.

"Good," one of the Tin Spiders called, his voice sounding the same as the others'. "It's more efficient if you all die here."

Alina shot Erik a playful grin. They might be low on ammo, but she'd only participated in half the fights. She whipped up her gun and launched a plasma grenade toward the approaching cyborgs.

They scattered, but the explosion consumed one of the monsters, leaving a charred, half-melted corpse.

She fired more grenades at the skittering metal chimeras. One agile monster only lost a limb before a second explosion killed him.

The entire building shook, and a dull, groaning rumble filled the air. Alina fired several more times before jumping backward, sending her exo off the roof. Erik and Jia didn't need a hint. They followed her as she continued to bathe the roof and the Tin Spiders in grenades.

An orange-red fireball erupted beneath them. The blast cracked the building an instant before the rest of the explosion blew it to pieces, feeding a hungry, growing cloud of flame, smoke, and debris. The inferno consumed the surviving Tin Spiders before the shockwave slammed into the fleeing exoskeletons.

The impact sent them tumbling to the ground. Erik's stomach lurched as he attempted to right his exo with controlled bursts, fragments of the building pelting him. He had almost managed to get himself upright before the back of his exo crashed into a small green flitter on the street. Its alarm shrieked in defiance.

Erik groaned as he lifted his faceplate, pain suffusing his body.

An exoskeleton landed next to him feet-first with a final controlled burn and turned, revealing Jia as the pilot. Smoke billowed over them, and he was grateful he still had a breather mask on.

"You okay?" Jia asked.

Erik took a deep breath before standing in the exo and hopping off the crushed but still loud flitter. "Nothing I can't sleep off."

She nodded, then looked around. "Where's Alina?"

"Shit. You're right." Erik surveyed the area, looking for the other exoskeleton when he spotted the shadowed outline of a person approaching them.

Alina emerged from the smoke, her exoskeleton nowhere in sight. Her tactical suit was torn in several places. A jagged laceration ran up one of her arms, and lines of blood added color on her dark, smudge-covered face.

"It looks like you two landed better than I did," Alina offered. She gestured to the burning wreck in the distance. She reached into a pouch and produced the data rod with a smile. "And it wasn't just about killing monsters."

Erik wiped dust off his mouth. Fire threatened the nearby buildings. He frowned.

"Don't worry." Alina tucked the data rod away. "There's no one in any of the adjacent buildings. We didn't have to clear them out, thanks to the holiday."

Erik chuckled. "Happy New Year."

Jia laughed. "Happy New Year."

"You're handling the cover-up, right?" Erik smirked at Alina.

"Our ride will be here in a minute. You just need to get on board, and I'll take care of the rest." Alina retrieved a medpatch from another pouch and put it on her arm. "As far as the rest of the world's going to know, some terrorists accidentally blew themselves up today. I think we just finished our own little Trojan War."

CHAPTER TWENTY-THREE

January 7, 2230, Neo Southern California Metroplex, Restaurant Strawberry Promise

Jia dropped a forkful of strawberry cheesecake into her mouth. The sweet, delicious flavor made a good argument for why there should be a strategic strawberry reserve on Earth.

They could hold out against all the other Local Neighborhood races as long as they had this cheesecake. Humanity could take any depredation as long as they had quality desserts to look forward to.

She closed her eyes and shuddered in ecstasy.

Erik smirked from beside her. "That good, huh? I know what I'm getting you for your next present."

"*Yesss,*" Jia insisted. "There are other desserts in the world besides beignets, you know. Live a little."

"Beignets aren't a dessert." Erik shook his head. "They're a staple. It's an important if subtle difference." He looked across the table. "What do you think?"

Alina sat there, disguised as a slender dark-haired man. Jia was impressed. If she hadn't used a passphrase, she wouldn't have known it was her. The eerie silence beyond their bubble was a product of both their and her privacy devices.

The agent had insisted on meeting them in the restaurant, and they were eager to see her. This was their first communication other than a quick debriefing on the way back to Neo SoCal after the raid. There was still a lot about Talos and that night Jia and Erik wanted to know.

"I think it's good to mix it up," Alina offered. "And I'm dubious of beignets as a staple, and a subtle difference it is not."

Erik eyed the cheesecake with suspicion. "If you say so, but you know how I feel about ghosts and lies."

Alina smirked. "I do."

He picked up his fork. "But we're not here for cheesecake, now are we?"

"Yes, actually, we are." Alina picked up her silverware. "I ate at this place a few years back, and I was happy to see it was still around. Because of my job, I don't tend to go to the same places without a significant amount of time in between. It makes it hard to recommend spots."

Jia swallowed another bite. Suspicion was souring her food. "You didn't contact us just to hang out. You have another job for us already?"

Alina shook her head. "No. Between what you've done in Lagos and Bogota, you deserve some rest. I came because I thought you would be interested in the overall results of our New Year's Party."

Jia set her fork down and folded her hands in front of her. She leaned forward, not bothering to hide the naked interest on her face. "You know I'm interested."

Erik nodded. "So am I. You didn't confirm much that night, other than that you lost some people."

"That's true. The other squads did successfully evacuate all the wounded, so the only KIAs were on the site." Alina frowned. "Not every team at every raid location won, and we weren't the only team to suffer deaths, but we had one of the hardest fights, according to all the post-raid reports I've read." She twirled the fork in her fingers. "And we weren't the only ones to pull some data from a Talos safe house. Not every building self-destructed. Most of them just fried their systems when it became obvious they weren't going to win. No one got a complete data dump, but we now have a nice pile of info to sift through. It's going to be a long slog between the encryption and understanding how the Brotherhood recorded things, but we've already learned some interesting tidbits."

"The Brotherhood?" Erik frowned. "I thought you called them Talos."

"We did, but we established that's what they called themselves: 'the Ascended Brotherhood.'" Alina stopped twirling her fork. "We have traced some of the manipulations they pulled off in records to make their people have no trace of existence in the UTC. It's one part fascinating and two parts chilling at the same time."

"They're not changelings grown in a lab somewhere?" Jia asked. "I assumed they did that and then modified them."

"Based on what we've found, no." Alina shook her head. "We're still running down a lot of things, and again, the combined data is still spotty, but there are different accidents and mass-casualty events. We've been able to trace recruits to those."

"You're saying they saved some people who were going to die anyway and did their best to make them disappear?"

Alina nodded. "There's a lot we still don't know. A lot we might never know, although we have established that that raid crippled the Brotherhood. They were preparing for a couple of major operations and had gathered most of their forces in their safe houses. We learned they were partially on alert for possible attacks, but it's obvious they didn't anticipate we'd attack *everywhere*."

Jia's breath caught. "You're saying we've wiped them out?"

"Judging by what we can find, not totally. There were two safe houses with only skeleton crews. Unfortunately, we didn't get much data from those, and given the tanks and other things we found, there are a decent number of Brotherhood cyborgs still out there, but we've wiped out the bulk of their forces. We're estimating ninety percent." Alina smiled triumphantly. "I'm sure we'll find the last remnants soon."

"What about Molino?" Jia asked, glancing at Erik. He stared at Alina, awaiting her response.

"That's the thing." Alina's smile faded into a look of pity. "Although we've still got a lot of data to analyze, even based on what we have, it's obvious that the Brotherhood is more an operations arm of someone else. We've found some messages that are obvious orders and information about potential upgrades. What we found suggests they're the muscle, not the brains of a greater organization. I'll pass along more information as it becomes available, but I thought you'd both be interested in that."

Jia hissed in frustration. "Then it's not over."

Erik shook his head. "No, it's not, but we just ripped the conspiracy a new one. I'm not going to complain." He stabbed his fork into the cheesecake and ripped off a piece. "And I feel damned satisfied. I don't care if the Ascended Brotherhood were just the errand boys pushing those merc errand boys at Molino. They owed a debt, and I'm not ready to stop." He shoved the piece in his mouth. "Huh. Who knew?"

"Who knew what?" Jia asked.

He speared another piece of the cheesecake. "Revenge tastes sweet, with a hint of tang."

January 15, 2230, Neo Southern California Metroplex, En Route to the Apartment of Erik Blackwell

Jia laughed from the passenger seat of the MX 60. "This is wrong. It doesn't make sense."

Erik checked the lidar and other sensor readouts. "What's wrong? I don't see anything weird."

"That's not what I'm talking about." Jia shook her head. "I'm the one who just got my pilot's license, but you're flying."

He shrugged. "I'm flying my flitter, not a ship. If you wanted to be in control, you shouldn't have had me take you there. You could have taken your own flitter."

"I figured it'd be easier to go out to dinner afterward."

Jia rolled her eyes. She shook a menacing finger. "And it better be nice. That's why I left that dress at your place. This is a big deal. Your girlfriend is a licensed Class D pilot now."

"It's a big enough deal that I rented a tux," Erik replied. "We'll go back to my place and we can both change, then we'll hit up our reservation. I could die from a sniper bullet because I don't have a bulletproof tux, but that's a risk I'm willing to take. That's how dedicated I am."

Jia laughed. "I'll keep that in mind for the next time I need to buy you a present. If I buy you suits and tuxedos, you might wear them more."

"Sure, every time you get a new piloting license."

"Very funny."

"I thought so," Erik replied.

Emma's hologram appeared in tiny form near the dash. Odd striations pulsed through the holographic image, and the image contorted for a second before restoring itself.

"What's going on, Emma?" Erik asked.

"I apologize," Emma offered, her voice distorted. "As you would say, the Lady has chosen an inopportune time to allow trouble. Be that as it may, such is the situation I'm now faced with."

"I don't think I've ever used the word inopportune in my life." Erik frowned at Emma. "What's going on? You being jammed or something?" His gaze dipped to her core inserted in the IO slot in the console. "How can they even do that since you're directly interfaced? Time to use the new turret?"

"That won't be necessary, or it might be better to state that it won't be helpful. But I believe I've been successfully a-a-a-attacked." The last word came out more distorted with each repeat. "Electronic warfare."

"What?" Jia snapped. "Who attacked you?"

"Most likely it was I-I-Ilse Aber," Emma explained. "I had an all-too-human desire not to believe it possible, but I've been suffering increased system difficulties since our last session, culminating in several nested cascade failures in recent days."

Erik's hands tightened on the control yoke. "Damn it. I thought you were being a little quiet and weird lately, but I didn't know anything like that was going on. Why didn't you tell us?"

"I thought I c-c-could correct, correct, correct it," Emma stuttered, her hologram pulsing and contorting every few seconds. "My internal adjustments have been f-f-failing, and internal network and process errors have been increasing ex-ex-exponentially within the last hour."

"Aber?" Jia shook her head. "Okay, let's presume she hacked you somehow. Why now?"

"They're trying to finish her off." Erik's nostrils flared. "Assassinate their project that doesn't want to come home. Those bastards."

Jia didn't look convinced. "Is that really it? They could have destroyed her earlier, but they've gone out of their way not to risk antagonizing her because they were worried about her destroying herself."

"Y-y-yes," Emma replied. Her hologram disappeared. "The situation has changed. I believe they don't w-w-want me to find and isolate particular information. I think they have reason to believe I'll stumble upon information that's dangerous to them."

"That might mean Aber works for the conspiracy," Erik spat through gritted teeth. "That must be why Emma got out the first time. That could be why they were doing all these sessions—to figure out if she had information that could point us at them. They must be desperate now that we've all but destroyed the Brotherhood."

"I had w-w-wondered about that," Emma noted. "Although I was h-h-having minor issues after the session, the frequency and severity issues s-s-significantly increased after I attempted to follow-up on some images I was shown during the session of different children. When I did that, not only did my problems increase, but I uncovered memory validation er-er-errors."

"Memory validation errors?" Jia furrowed her brow in deep concern. "What do you mean by that?"

"There are unexplained holes in my memory that shouldn't be there," Emma explained. "I'm not a h-h-human. I don't f-f-forget, but it's obvious that Aber somehow ex-ex-excised data from my memory concerning the session."

Erik slammed a fist on the console. "That bitch. It was a trap all along."

Jia ran her hand through her hair, her breathing rapid. "Do you think Adeyemi knows?"

"Emma's getting us closer to his son's killers." Erik shook his head. "There's no way he would have let them take her out." He sucked a breath through his teeth. "Unless someone's compromised him. I don't want to believe it, but I can't be certain."

"Alina?" Jia asked. "She's not motivated by personal revenge."

Erik shook his head. "I don't think she's trying to screw us over. She wouldn't have gone through all the trouble of getting us to switch over if she planned to help take out Emma anytime soon."

"But she didn't want Emma on the Bogota mission," Jia observed. "I know she gave us an explanation, but it's a little too coincidental for me to ignore her."

"Let you open a c-c-camera," Emma sputtered. Her image disappeared. "Four legs are necessary for f-f-five wings."

Erik blinked. "Huh?"

"Welcome to m-m-my house," Emma replied in Mandarin. Growls and hisses followed. From what Erik remembered, it sounded like Zitark. "Mary had a little lamb, little lamb, little l-l-lamb," she sang in English. "Mary had a little lamb, whose fleece was a diamond two four five zinc v-v-vee." Speech ended, replaced by the occasional warble or beep.

Heart pounding, Erik pulled hard on the control yoke, abruptly changing direction and cutting off another flitter. "Screw this. If Aber's working for the conspiracy, I don't care if she's holed up in some DD lab somewhere. I'll blow up the door and put a bullet in her head."

"Where are you going?" Jia asked. "It's not like we know where Aber is at this moment. If we call her, I doubt she'll tell us."

"I'm heading to the ship." Dark anger contorted Erik's face. "With Emma down, it's the best way to contact Alina and Adeyemi directly."

"What if they tell us to back off? What if it's not the

conspiracy, but they're both involved?" Concern lined Jia's face.

Erik let out a dark, vicious chuckle. "I don't want to believe that, but if it's true, too bad for them. They know what we can do. If they wanted to kill one of our friends, they should have killed us first."

CHAPTER TWENTY-FOUR

Erik sat at the table in the crew quarters, glowering at the wall with all the baleful rage he could muster.

After everything he'd been through, he'd thought he'd scraped together a good set of allies. People he could trust as he went after the conspiracy and avenged his men, but now he wasn't sure who he could trust and who might be plotting behind his back.

Lanara stepped out of the cockpit and nodded to Erik. "Alina's not responding, but I got hold of the colonel."

Despite not knowing Lanara for that long, Erik trusted her. It wasn't that he thought she was all that loyal to him, but she lacked the necessary guile to deceive him long-term. She could barely get through an hour without losing focus on anything but her tinkering.

"Put him through to my PNIU," Erik ordered. He glanced at Jia, who gave him a firm nod back.

Lanara sighed and tapped her PNIU before heading back into the cockpit. "Emma's useful for upgrades. Get her fixed." The door slid closed behind her.

"You there, Colonel?" Erik asked. He set his PNIU to speaker mode.

"I'm here," the colonel replied. "Your message said this was an emergency. What's going on? Does this involve the Brotherhood?"

"I don't know. It could. Emma's malfunctioning. She started babbling like she's on AI drugs, and now she's just making weird sounds. She's never, *ever* acted like this before." Erik stood. He didn't want to be sitting if the colonel was about to admit to betrayal. "It seems to be linked to the last time she talked to Doctor Aber."

Colonel Adeyemi sighed. "I see."

"You don't sound surprised," Erik accused. He gritted his teeth. "You knew this was going to happen?"

"I suspected it might," the colonel admitted.

Erik let out a long, low growl. His hands clenched into fists, and heat washed over his face. He'd been played. Adeyemi might not be his friend, but the man had as much reason to want Erik to succeed as anyone.

"Is this some sort of assassination?" Jia demanded, taking over for Erik, her voice strident. "The DD finally decided if they couldn't have Emma, no one could?"

"Nothing like that at all."

"Then what's going on?" Jia asked.

"Before we continue, I need you to tell me something. Has Emma's core turned cloudy and dark?" Worry tinged the colonel's voice.

"No, not yet." Jia rubbed her wrist, glancing at the scowling Erik.

He wasn't ready to respond in any way that didn't involve a string of obscenities.

Jia was handling it well enough and getting the information he was concerned with anyway. He hoped his next stop on the revenge trail wouldn't involve the father of one of the men he was avenging.

"Is that so?" the colonel replied. "Then despite whatever problems she's having, there's still hope. That's a good thing for all of us."

"You didn't answer my question about the assassination," Jia noted. "We need to know what's going on."

"It's nothing like that," the colonel clarified. "I promise you. If anything, it's the opposite." He coughed. "I don't think you understand the level of resources that went into developing Emma and her importance, not just to the DD, but to the entire UTC."

"Of course we don't. You've never told us."

"Suffice it to say, there's no way anyone involved in this project would purposely destroy her. She's our only working prototype of a self-aware AI." Some of the worry in the colonel's voice gave way to irritation.

"I don't understand then." Jia pinched the bridge of her nose. "You just said you suspected this might happen. Are you talking about sabotage from the Brotherhood?"

"Not exactly. It's difficult to explain, given my restraints."

"What about Aber?" Erik kicked the wall in frustration. "How do we know she's not working for the conspiracy? Or, hell, any conspiracy? If it's not sabotage, then what the hell is it? Someone better start talking, and it's a selection set of one."

"Doctor Aber has been holed up with General Aaron a lot," Colonel Adeyemi explained. "And he's the man with the most direct control over this project. I can't yet tell you all the details, but I had concerns about certain actions Aber might take. She did take those actions. I wasn't sure this would be the result, and I hoped it wouldn't be."

"What actions?" Erik shouted. "You're saying you knew she was a mole and let her fuck with Emma?"

"She's not a mole," the colonel shouted back. "She believes in this project more than anyone."

"Then what the hell did she do to Emma?" Erik bellowed.

"I can't tell you that. Even I have my limits."

Erik scoffed. "You won't tell me. Alina won't tell me, and now Emma's gone offline. When the Knights Errant were out there dying on Molino, even if it was mercenaries who pulled the trigger and some other conspiracy pointing them, they only got away with it because somebody with influence in the government helped cover it up. They're using our loyalty against us."

Colonel Adeyemi didn't reply for several seconds. "I understand where you're coming from, and all I can do is remind you that my son died on Molino. Everything I've done, I've not done because I'm your friend, Erik. I've done it because I want you to avenge him. Koval's shared the relevant intel with us about the raid. I know there's more than this Ascended Brotherhood at the end of the chase, and I know we're now closer to getting justice for the men and women who died on Molino."

"But this all circles back to Emma." Erik's hand curled into a tight fist, and blood trickled from his palm. "Alina was afraid the Brotherhood would go after Emma, and that

Emma had something to do with whatever attack they pulled off against the DD."

The colonel grunted. "She shouldn't have shared that information with you, but I'm not going to claim that summary is inaccurate."

"Don't you see what he's saying?" Jia interjected. "If they were targeting Emma and they knew we were closing on them, maybe they decided to get rid of her through Aber or someone who works close to her."

"There's... Damn it." The colonel muttered something unintelligible. "I'm worried that the general might use this as an excuse to take Emma back."

Erik barked a harsh laugh. "Those assholes fried her, but they still want her body?"

The colonel sighed. "I doubt she's completely destabilized yet. I would recommend you remove her from anything. If she's destabilizing like I suspect she is, she won't be much of a threat without a direct interface."

"What does that mean? 'Destabilizing?'"

"I can't tell—"

"I'm tired of this bullshit, Adeyemi," Erik shouted. "You think I give two shits about security classifications at this point? I've been hacking and shooting my way through half the Solar System to get the bastards who murdered your son. The bastards who are hiding behind the government and every corporation and stinking secret they can manage. They're playing us so they can screw us over. Start talking!"

"Believe it or not," Colonel Adeyemi replied quietly, an angry tremor in his voice, "I've done everything I could to keep Emma with you since you found her. It's actually hurt me with the general. I even recommended a special plan recently that would help both Emma and you with the hunt. I almost had the general convinced, but then all this happened. It's screwed up everything."

Jia placed her hand on Erik's arm and gave it a squeeze. "What about Emma? I know you don't want to tell us the details, but can she be saved?"

"I don't know," the colonel admitted. "I'll talk to the general and Doctor Aber. I'll contact you once I have an answer one way or another."

"And you're sure that Doctor Aber isn't a member of the conspiracy?" Erik pressed. "If she is, all you have to do is give me her location, and I'll do the rest."

"That's not necessary. I'm as sure she's not a member as I am that you aren't. We'll talk soon. We'll solve this one way or another, but don't worry. Even if Doctor Aber isn't a mole, if Emma has destabilized, she'll take the blame. It was her stunt that resulted in this."

Erik dropped into a chair with a dissatisfied grunt as the call ended. "This is complete and utter bullshit, Jia. I'm tired of being stonewalled."

She patted his arm. "You heard him. He's on our side. Even if he doesn't care about Emma like we do, he knows how useful a tool she's been. He wants her fixed."

"But he's holding back, just like Alina's holding back. We need to know why the Brotherhood cares about Emma. We need to know why the military cares so much about developing a self-aware AI. There's too much we don't know." Erik slammed his fist on the table. "He's known the reason from the beginning, but he didn't want us to know." He glared at the table. "We need help from someone we can actually trust. Someone who might be able to do something even if the DD decides to let Emma die. Someone who can work with data and systems. Lanara's an engineer, but that's not the same thing. We need someone more specialized."

Jia nodded. "You have someone in mind?"

"Of course." Erik managed a lopsided weak grin. "Malcolm. He's left the force. It's time we put him to work."

CHAPTER TWENTY-FIVE

Malcolm slowly circled the Rabbit, a curious look on his face. "This is going to sound totally lame, but I've never left Neo SoCal before. Looking at this ship makes it, like, you know, real."

He waved his hands in front of him.

After a quick discussion with Lanara, Erik and Jia had rushed over to pick Malcolm up and explained the basics of the situation. Malcolm's expressed confidence faded the closer they got to the hangar, which didn't do much for Jia's faith in his ability to solve the problem.

She kept telling herself he'd done solid work before, and it was more the odd situation he needed to get used to. She could sympathize, given she'd acted similarly when Erik had first pulled her out of her delusions. Malcolm's previous help was compartmentalized easier.

Now that he wasn't working for the NSCPD, the weight of helping track down a galaxy-wide conspiracy might be pressing down on him.

"We didn't bring you here for a spin around the Solar

System." Erik frowned. "We're doing this here because we can control this place, no one's around to get hurt, and Lanara's here to help."

Lanara stepped out of the cargo bay and onto her ramp at the sound of her name. She narrowed her eyes at Malcolm. "This is the guy? Does he always dress like that?" She gestured at his shirt. "It's hard to take him seriously."

Malcolm's sartorial tastes that day ran to a bright white Hawaiian shirt festooned with famous landmarks from around Earth, including Big Ben, the Eiffel Tower, and the Tokyo Shock Arch, among others.

He sighed. "You remind me of my girlfriend. She hates this shirt, too. She says it's too busy. Of course it's busy. That's the point."

Lanara stared at him before jerking her head toward Erik. "I've got the ship's systems locked down. I've also got something else that'll help." She disappeared back into the cargo bay. When she reappeared a moment later, she was holding a long black tripod with a bulbous petal-like top in one hand. In the other, she dragged a thin gray cable.

"What's that?" Jia asked.

"Your AI is going crazy." Lanara continued down the ramp, pulling the cable with her.

"That's why we brought Malcolm," Jia explained.

"But Adeyemi said to not keep her plugged into anything." Lanara brandished the tripod device. "Doesn't that mean she'll go all killer bot on us if we do?"

"We decided to not put her into the ship after we talked to you." Jia shrugged. "But we're going to need more system power than a PNIU, especially since she won't be able to help us. Reinserting her into the MX 60 seems like a good bet."

Erik nodded his agreement. "We've got the hangar closed, and we're going to pull all the weapons out of the flitter. She won't be able to do anything much, even if she takes control."

"She'll be able to crash at high speed." Lanara hit the bottom of the ramp and headed toward the flitter. "That's where this comes into play. If you're going to directly interface, it doesn't matter if you have external access, which means all we have to do is make sure she doesn't go anywhere." She shook the tripod, her speech speeding up. "Small containment field. I can power it from the ship. If she lifts off, she won't get very far. Even with the EMP hardening, the containment field will be too much, and I'm going to make some adjustments to the reactor output temporarily to increase containment field strength. If we had more time, I'd just disable the power on the flitter. But if I do that, I have a feeling I'd be messing with thruster efficiency, and I'd have to spend days fix—"

"Lanara," Erik interrupted, "Just set it up. We'll work on emptying the MX 60 of anything that might explode or she might use."

The engineer narrowed her eyes. "I'll empty the turret for you. I have a feeling you'll break things if you start messing around in there."

"Works for me." Erik turned to Malcolm. "I'll be in the MX 60 with you in case something happens."

Malcolm licked his lips. "I'm not saying I'm not awesome because I am awesome, but Emma's not your standard off-the-shelf system. I'm not being modest when I say I'm not sure what I can do. If her normal defenses are up, I might not stand a chance."

Erik scoffed. "The last time we could get anything remotely intelligible out of her, she was spouting nonsensical crap. I'm pretty sure she's not running any sophisticated defenses right now."

"Do what you can and find out what you can." Jia shrugged. "That's all any of us can do."

Lanara set the containment emitter in front of the MX 60 and connected the cable to a port at the bottom. She frowned at Malcolm. "You're not going to be buried in a shirt like that, are you?"

"No." Malcolm winced. "Are you sure you haven't been talking to my girlfriend?"

Erik lay in the fully reclined driver's seat, staring out the front windshield at the shimmering blue field surrounding them. Between today and New Year's, if he didn't see that color again for the next year, he would be happy.

It was not like anyone thought a containment field meant something good was happening.

Malcolm sat in the passenger seat, a half-dozen data windows in front of him. He tapped and shouted the occasional command as if volume would make his hacking attempt stronger.

Erik had joined him only for the technician's peace of mind. If Emma did take control of the MX 60, the containment field could do more to stop her than he could. Firing his gun inside seemed like an idiotic idea, and he wasn't ready to try to break Emma's core.

When they had first met, he'd thought of her as the bitchy voice that wouldn't leave his head, but she'd become a friend.

He'd already lost too many friends on Molino, and he didn't want to lose another to some bullshit government plot.

It didn't help that he wasn't sure what was going on with Doctor Aber and the colonel. He wasn't going to sit around and wait for the general to get off his ass with a pointless plan that didn't end with Emma back to her old self.

Erik patted his mouth as he let out a big yawn. "How long have we been in here?"

"A couple of hours." Malcolm didn't look away from his data window. "I don't know exactly what I'm looking for. I'll be honest, I don't understand anything I'm looking at. There are some vaguely familiar data structures, but I can't find anything that looks like logs or active signals inter-facing with things. That might be because of the contain-ment field, though."

"Damn it." Erik scrubbed a hand down his face. "Damn it all."

Malcolm winced. "Sorry."

"It's not your fault." Erik set his seat upright and slid it forward. "The people who made her barely understand her. Can you tell me one thing? Is she still alive? She's not dark and cloudy like the colonel mentioned." He stared at her core, which was still the same luminescent faceted crystal it'd always been.

"There's still activity, definitely." Malcolm nodded slowly. "I don't know how to interpret it, but she's not trying to reach out and manipulate the MX 60's system or our PNIUs."

Jia waved her hands from outside the containment field. She looked worried.

"I'm going to pull Emma to be safe," Erik noted. He yanked the core out of the IO port. "We can't take the risk that she's waiting for her chance. For all we know, the government put a virus in her to turn her homicidal."

Malcolm shrugged. "I'm not eager to be inside a homicidal flitter."

The containment field dropped, and Jia walked over to the driver's side window. After Erik rolled it down, she pointed at her PNIU. "I've got Ilse Aber on the line."

Erik scoffed. "Why should I believe anything she has to say?"

"Because," the doctor replied, "I'm the only one who can save Emma."

"How do we know you didn't do this to Emma?" Erik insisted. "Adeyemi says it's your fault."

"Oh, Mr. Blackwell, that's not in question, not at all." Ilse chuckled.

Erik's jaw tightened. "You're admitting it? Just like that?"

"I've freely admitted everything I've done to General Aaron," Ilse offered, an almost cheerful tone in her voice. "And to be honest, I did it without his orders. He's made it very clear to me that if this ends with Emma's complete destabilization, I'll likely spend more than a few years in prison. I think he's only not arrested me because I'm the only hope of saving her."

"You're saying you didn't do this to help those Brotherhood bastards?"

"No, I did not," Ilse replied. "I'm one of the people who's been encouraging the general to leave Emma with you. If you don't believe me, ask the colonel. But that's irrelevant now. What is important is saving Emma. If we don't take distinct and immediate measures, her problem will worsen, and that will complete the destabilization."

"Which means what?" Erik asked.

"It would result in the total collapse of her matrix and neural network, along with quantum decoherence. Let me make things clear, Mr. Blackwell. She's unique, and we have no way of backing her up. If she destabilizes, she'll effectively die." Ilse delivered the explanation in a slightly bored and breezy tone.

"Is this the part where you say the only way we can save her is by delivering her to the military?"

"Of course not." Ilse scoffed. "That's absurd. It doesn't make sense." She sounded weary and annoyed, as if she were having to explain parliamentary politics to a toddler.

To be fair to the doctor, he *was* a toddler when it came to understanding the advanced concepts required to create something like Emma.

"The fundamental issue is, she's been having trouble analyzing certain information that was presented to her because it runs up against a substrate failsafe built into her fundamental matrix design."

Erik furrowed his brow and looked at Jia. Life didn't

need to provide him a pointed example when he just got through admitting his deficiencies.

"The memories." Jia's eyes widened. "The children. Emma said she was trying to go over some pictures of children you showed her, but there were missing memories."

"Memories that were erased," Erik insisted.

"That's true and not true at the same time," Ilse replied.

"What's that supposed to mean?" Erik growled. "Can you stop with the cryptic bullshit?"

"I shall be forthright. Perhaps I can gain your trust then."

Erik scoffed. "Not damned likely, but a little honesty would be welcome."

"Emma is losing stability because of my purposeful exposure to her of specific data that I knew would conflict with her failsafes," Ilse explained. "I also knew this might be a result."

"You better hope they put you in prison before I get to you," Erik growled.

Ilse sighed wearily. "It's understandable, Mr. Blackwell, that you perceive things that way. But I didn't do it to *harm* her. I did it to save her. Consider it a type of shock therapy. You lack the technical knowledge to understand why that is, but she was slowly failing. She has been for a while. It's only her interaction with the outside world, particularly with you and Miss Lin, that has arrested and even reversed that process until recently. Emma represents our last chance of success for this project, but ironically, her advances have also made her potential destabilization that much more likely."

Erik's head hurt. Things would be easier if he had

someone to shoot. "I don't get it. You just said hanging out with us was stabilizing her, so why did you destabilize her? Why would her improving lead to her being more unstable?"

"Because she'd hit a growth inflection point. In simple terms, she was at the point where she would either become totally stable or rapidly degrade. Unfortunately, because we don't have a complete understanding of her network, that meant we had a small number of options to try to guide her on the correct path. I elected to take the most direct route because of the risk of waiting much longer."

"Your direct route is now killing her," Jia muttered.

"You can still save her," Ilse offered, her voice still lacking any sense of urgency. "But it'll require direct access to not just her core matrix, but interfacing with the fundamental emergent consciousness of her neural net."

"Huh?" Erik's face scrunched in confusion. "How the hell do we do that?"

"I can send you the necessary code to accomplish it. Presumably you have someone competent on your end to implement it."

Malcolm fluffed his lapels and smiled. All the concern from before had vanished, replaced by a smile with swagger.

His time to shine.

"I've got a guy," Erik noted with a grunt.

"Good," Ilse replied. "In addition, I'd suggest some sort of VR interface with no significant risk of physical injury."

"VR?"

"Yes. Normally, what we're about to attempt would be impossible because of the defenses inherent in Emma's matrix, both passive and active, but now that she's in a destabilization cascade, you have a limited opportunity to engage her directly before destabilization and subsequent degradation of her neural net. Especially because you and Miss Lin serve as preexisting developmental foci." Ilse cleared her throat. "To put it in layman's terms, you are going to use VR to enter her mind and give it something to focus on, preventing it from spiraling into insanity and dissolving."

Erik looked at Jia. He didn't understand half of what was coming out of Ilse's mouth, but if the whole point of Ilse's plan was to destroy Emma, it didn't make sense to risk sending them into the AI's mind with VR. It wasn't like she could kill them that way. The audacity of the plan supported its likely truth.

Jia nodded slowly back. "If we can save Emma that way, I think we should at least try, but I do have one question for Doctor Aber."

"What is that, Miss Lin?" Ilse asked.

"Why aren't you asking to do the same thing?" Jia continued. "Wouldn't you be better suited than us? Even if you don't understand everything about her, you understand more than we do."

"That's not the situation at all," Ilse answered. "This isn't a matter of technical knowledge. It's a matter of relationships. I like to think of myself as Emma's friend, but I doubt she feels the same. You two might be the only people in the entire UTC who have any chance of saving her, but if we're going to do this, we should hurry. Based on what's already been described to me by the colonel, we don't have much time."

"Then let's get on with it." Erik turned to Malcolm. "You ready to help save the only self-aware AI in the UTC?"

The technician saluted. "Yes, sir!"

Erik shook his head. "Don't. Just don't do that."

"Oh, sorry."

Erik opened his door. "Let's tell Lanara to get things ready on her end."

"We're going to go into the unstable mind of an AI?" Jia shook her head in disbelief. "It makes taking on half-spider cyborgs seem normal."

CHAPTER TWENTY-SIX

Malcolm tapped furiously on a virtual keyboard projected on the table in the crew quarters.

Erik and Jia sat across from one another, both wearing haptic feedback gloves and holding their VR helmets. Jia wiped sweat from her brow. Somehow her life always found a new way to grow more complicated.

Lanara stood near an IO port in the wall, squinting at a data window. She held Emma's core in her hand. "What do I do if she attempts to take over the ship?"

"She didn't try to take over the flitter," Jia mused. "Despite what Adeyemi said, we don't have proof that she'll be dangerous."

"You can't escape into space in a flitter," Lanara muttered. "Think about this. Your plan requires us to stick a crazed AI into this ship, and I can't even use the containment field because you need to be able to interface with a powerful enough system and the VR. This is dangerous. Stupidly dangerous."

"It's not like she can kill us in VR, and you can monitor

the ship's systems and make sure she doesn't try anything." Erik shrugged and slipped the helmet over the top of his head but didn't bring down the visor. "But sure, I wouldn't try this at a nano-AR center."

"She doesn't need to kill you in VR, Blackwell," Lanara complained. "She could fire up the engines and smash us through the hangar and into the ground. I might not know what she's doing until it's too late. Do you know how much time I've spent tuning the thrusters and the reactor? Do you want that work to go to waste?"

"You're more worried about your time going to waste than dying?" Erik gave her a confused look.

Lanara harrumphed. "You don't understand everything I've done, and how I modulated the power feeds to improve efficiency by .01 percent to the lateral thrusters without affecting any other system in the ship. Do you know how hard that is to pull off in a transport like this? You're thinking, 'Oh, well, they use Phoenix Systems thrusters. How hard is it?' But you don't realize that Mark Twelves are not the same thing as Mark Fourteens. Matching delta-v isn't the only consideration. Why would you even—"

"We get it," Erik interrupted, waving his hand. "You've put a lot of work into the ship. We've put a lot of work into our *lives*. No one's telling you to sit there and let Emma crash us into the ocean, but give us a chance."

Malcolm cleared his throat and raised his hand, a sheepish look on his face. He withered under Lanara's glare.

"What is it?" Jia asked.

"I've got firewalls set up," Malcolm mentioned timidly.

"Non-destabilizing Emma could probably bust through them quickly, but I think I can contain her at least for a little bit in her current state. I'll know if she's trying to do anything. I can guarantee that."

Erik hopped up and clapped Malcolm on the shoulder. "There we go, problem solved."

Lanara frowned at a chime from her PNIU. "Aber's calling again. Holocall this time."

"Put her through," Erik ordered.

Ilse's hologram appeared. Jia didn't know what she was expecting, but there was a distracted look on the brown-haired woman's face that seemed more amused than threatening. The middle-aged woman's simple gray dress didn't scream "deadly member of a conspiracy."

"You." Ilse pointed at Malcolm. "Are you the person who will be handling the code?"

Malcom nodded quickly. "Uh, yes, ma'am?"

"Have you already set up what I sent?" Ilse asked.

"Yes, ma'am." Malcolm's arm started to pop up but stopped himself halfway through the motion.

Ilse cupped her chin. "Useful. Good. The way to think about this is that I'll be providing you the keys to get through Emma's outer walls. The code will also send me a stream of data that I can use to monitor her activity and help with any defenses you've set up. We wouldn't want her taking control of your systems and killing you. That would be a subpar result."

Lanara threw her hands up in disgust and mouthed, "See?"

"You, codeman," Ilse continued. "You'll need to dynamically adjust things on your end. It'll take too long for me to do it. Understood?"

Malcolm swallowed. "Yes, ma'am."

Ilse narrowed her eyes. "Do you always dress like that?"

"Yes, ma'am."

"Interesting. Very interesting. You'd be an interesting psychological subject." Ilse tore her attention away from Malcolm. "But that's irrelevant for now. I'll also be sending you code to help adjust Mr. Blackwell and Miss Lin's defenses."

Jia frowned. "Why do we need defenses other than Malcolm keeping her out of the system? It's not like she can scare us to death."

"Hmm. How to explain?" Ilse tapped her lip. "Despite the aid I'm giving you and the presumed competence of this oddly dressed man, Emma's overall system and neural net aren't going to tolerate intruders."

"But her system isn't even functioning," Jia replied.

"Think of it like your body." Ilse gestured toward Jia. "You have an immune system that can be supplemented with nutrition, medication, and nanites, but it doesn't require you to turn it on. My aid will help you get past some of the immune system of her mind, but if too much of it notices you, it might destroy our ability to continue the deep access."

"I don't get this." Erik rubbed his temples. "We're going to be attacked by Emma's subconscious?"

Ilse tilted her head and looked to the side. "I think that metaphor is stretched, but if it helps you understand, it works. The code will help you respond to the attacks. In a sense, you'll be able to deliver it more efficiently to the construct that might appear in her mind."

The confusion faded from Erik's face, replaced by a grin. "Wait. I get it. You're saying we need to go in there and wreck things in VR to help deliver that anti-immune code."

"You're terrible at appropriate metaphors," Ilse complained. "I'm going to stop talking to you now."

Erik shrugged as Ilse turned to Jia. "Miss Lin, you must be cautious. Your virtual avatars are, in a sense, location beacons. Whatever happens in there, you must take that into account."

"I still don't understand what we're supposed to do in there besides take on Emma's mental defenses." Jia frowned. "How are we going to stabilize her?"

"There are core memories at the heart of this that she's reacting to. As her friends, if you can reach them, I think you can successfully reintegrate them and stabilize them." Ilse pointed to the core in Lanara's hand. "When she was stolen, someone had the knowledge and wherewithal to modify certain aspects of her core matrix to limit certain fundamental control routines we added. We believe that had a side-effect of disrupting her access to many of her testing memories, but it also might have provided her a unique opportunity to grow and stabilize with the appropriate input. We're now going to take advantage of that to save her."

"Enough technobabble. Let's just get in there and do this." Erik lowered his visor.

Jia nodded to Lanara and Malcolm. "Thanks for having our backs."

"No problem," Malcolm offered.

"If it goes badly, I'll be dead soon anyway," Lanara offered with a shrug.

Erik cracked his knuckles. "It's time to do a little hands-on therapy."

CHAPTER TWENTY-SEVEN

"I always wondered what it was like to be Phoenix Root," Erik muttered. "If this is what it's like, it's overrated. This is damned annoying."

He floated beside Jia. A pale fog surrounded them in an otherwise endless black void. Snatches of color pulsed and wriggled around the mist.

Objects and beings would appear and disappear at irregular intervals: a reptilian Zitark, a dog, a cat, a gray humanoid Leem, Ilse.

At one point, a random sad-looking man in a bright orange ten-gallon hat appeared and vanished in two seconds. A man-sized fork with a bowler over its tines doffed its hat with invisible hands before proceeding past the humans and fading from top to bottom.

"Okay." Jia blinked. "That's different. Very different."

"Yeah, different. That's one word for it. Messed up is another way of describing it." Erik squinted, trying to make sense of the madness. "No, this isn't like being high. This is what it's like to go nuts."

"In a sense, Emma *is* going nuts," Jia offered. "So you're not too far off."

The world around them twisted in on itself, warping and stretching. A building grew from the ground, coming together centimeter by centimeter, the fog flowing into it and changing color and density.

Nearby, a large dome winked into existence before falling into dust. Dozens of transparent Eriks and Jias floated by the avatars of the real pair like ghosts, different clothes, different expressions. Ripples of scintillating color passed through the spectral forms.

"I don't know what I was expecting," Erik began looking behind him, "but it wasn't this shit."

"The connection appears to be successful," declared Ilse from outside the VR simulation, her voice transmitted directly to their VR helmets. "It's working far better than I anticipated. I'm tracking your point of view and the outer environment with external feeds to better aid you and Mr. Constantine."

"Is this how Emma's mind works?" Jia ran her hand through what appeared to be dripping, floating black wool. "Is she constantly thinking about all this weird stuff? If so, that explains why she's irritated all the time."

"No," Ilse replied. "This is the VR system attempting to parse something falling to pieces. Under normal circumstances, she would have more control and would be able to present something that might seem more conventionally lucid."

Erik walked forward, his feet landing on nothing. The limited VR rigs in the crew quarters didn't offer true haptic feedback beyond the gloves. This led to the odd sensation of his body appearing to move with no feeling in his legs.

"I'm not falling," he noted, edging to the side slowly. "Not sure if I'm supposed to be."

"The work Mr. Constantine is performing should keep your experience reasonable and within the bounds of normal physics," Ilse explained. "I understand how difficult this can be, but this is an unusual situation."

"Reasonable and normal is a stretch." Jia craned her neck up. A huge Neo SoCal tower flew far overhead, wriggling back and forth like a massive gray and white fish. The tower continued swimming through the air into the ever-changing distance. It let out a piercing shriek.

"You might find this hard to believe, but that is a good sign," Ilse replied. "There isn't a complete detachment between memories and reality."

"This *isn't* a complete detachment between memory and reality?" Erik asked. "Damn, Doc. You must throw really intense parties."

"If you say so, Mr. Blackwell."

"Does she dream?" Jia asked. "Is that what this is? Her dreaming?"

"Emma doesn't sleep," Ilse reminded her. "But certain memory consolidation processes she employs are similar to dreams. If it helps you to think of it that way, feel free."

"That's neat and all, but we're here to help her, right?" Erik frowned at nearby twitching solid masses of undulating color. He had no idea what they were or if they were dangerous. "And we're in. What do we do now? How do we help Emma?"

"Mr. Constantine is continuing his efforts at my direction," Ilse explained. "My provided code with his modification will allow us to probe and track down important memory loci that have weakened. From your point of view, you'll simply need to follow the path to interface with them. Once you're there, your observation should provide the key element to allow Emma to begin stabilizing herself with you as the base. You two are the only chance to save Emma now. If I had attempted something like this before, even if I got past Emma's defenses, there would be too much risk of failure. The only way this will work is if there is something that will link to positive memories."

Jia nodded. "What about now? I get that we're the only ones who can do this, but what's our risk of failure?"

"Greater than zero."

Erik chuckled. "We only have a better chance than you? Not a good chance?"

"Good is relative. Any chance is preferable to no chance. It doesn't matter. Our choices are simple." Ilse sounded annoyed. "You two perform this task and you potentially save Emma, or you don't, and we lose her. If you're unwilling to do this, stop wasting my time."

"Understood, Doc." Erik slowly turned his head to follow a cavorting thick blue column of something that looked like coarse yarn. "Just get us our yellow brick road, and we'll head out and find the not-so-good snarky witch at the end."

Jia shook her head. "No matter what strange thing I think up that might happen each day, somehow, I always manage to be surprised. I'm not sure if that's a good thing or a bad thing."

"That's a good thing." Erik grinned. "It means you

always have something new to look forward to. Not everyone can say that."

"This doesn't bother you?" Jia raised an eyebrow. "Not at all?" She pointed to the yarn column. "Not even that?" She turned to the column once more. "Especially that."

Erik shrugged. "It's freaky and annoying, but she's right. There's nothing we can do but try. None of this is real, so we're not at risk. We just have to try our best to save Emma."

A glowing white path appeared. It zigzagged into the pale fog suffusing the entire area. The narrow lines would barely allow two people abreast.

"The locus identification procedure is working," Ilse reported excitedly. "Simply follow the path. While it appears to be a path to you, it's more properly thought of as a type of tracing algorithm that's using your presence as a beacon, along with Emma's reaction to your presence, to identify the key loci I mentioned earlier. As such, you need to understand it's not a physical path. You must not leave it once you're on it, or we risk having to reset our trace."

Erik jogged over to the path. "Imagine trying to interface with Emma like this at the tactical center."

Jia grimaced as she set out after him. "That would be a nightmare in more ways than one. I doubt their system could handle it."

"Do we need to run on the path?" Erik asked.

"Unnecessary," Ilse replied. "As long as you're moving, that's enough."

Erik and Jia walked at a brisk pace, both trying to ignore the surrounding oddities and the bizarre shapes and objects. A pyramid with a lizard tail popped up out of the ground and screamed into the sky. A simulacrum of Rena Winston sang in a cocktail dress while sitting on the rings of Saturn, kicking her legs playfully.

"I hope if I ever go crazy, my mind is half as interesting as Emma's," Jia declared.

Erik chuckled. "I think if they could do this kind of thing with humans, our minds would be way more screwed up, even when they're allegedly normal."

"Speak for yourself." Jia smirked. "My mind is orderly and neat."

"Like your old flitter?"

"Oh, shut up. I'd punch you, but it doesn't hurt here."

Shadows flowed on the other side of the path, twisting and changing. They moved at an angle and below Jia and Erik's relative position, like they were hungry sharks in this ocean of madness, waiting for fresh meat.

"What are those things?" Erik asked. "I think they're following us."

"Those are projections of Emma's passive defenses," Ilse explained. "Just keep moving for now. I'm feeding code to Mr. Constantine to help hide you from them. We've been embedding additional useful elements directly into the interface code as well. If hiding fails, attack to the best of your ability. That should help deliver the countermeasures."

"And I figured out some ways to improve it," Malcolm chimed in.

"Please concentrate on your job," Ilse snipped. "And do not offer unnecessary commentary."

"Yes, ma'am," Malcolm replied with a sigh.

"We're getting there," Ilse continued, her voice rising. "It's working."

The road began to straighten and widen. Erik and Jia continued their stroll, keeping an eye on the shadows swimming on either side. They couldn't be killed in this world, but if Ilse was right, losing to anything might doom Emma.

There were too many damn conspiracies in Erik's life, but if the Brotherhood had been targeting Emma, that collapsed the situation and made his life easier.

It was beginning to sound less like there were too many conspiracies in his life, but just one big conspiracy he needed to handle. Gutting the Brotherhood had been the beginning. His revenge might not be over soon, but things were speeding up.

Erik wouldn't have made it as far as he had without Emma, and he wasn't leaving until they'd saved her. If the military wanted to come and take her after that, he would figure out some way to convince them to back off. Their head researcher might be helping, but it was Erik and Jia saving her and, by extension, the entire mystery project she was involved in.

Jia narrowed her eyes as a tenebrous limb stretched toward the path. "We might have trouble."

The limb jerked and sank back into the fog and darkness. Erik and Jia didn't stop as the limb disappeared.

"What are our chances of getting through this without being attacked?" Erik asked.

"They're greater than zero," Ilse declared.

Erik chuckled. "Of course they are. Are you going to

answer most of my questions about numbers with variations of that answer?"

"If it's accurate, then yes. I'm not here to offer you false hope."

All the kinks in the path disappeared, leaving a completely straight and modestly wide path that could accommodate four or five people. Erik didn't need to understand the coding and technology involved to get that the plan was working. They could do it.

"We're very, very close," Ilse reported. "At this rate, we should have a fix on a useful locus within five minutes."

"It's not zero," Erik replied with a grin. Jia rolled her eyes at his antics.

"No, it is certainly not," Ilse confirmed. "Wait. There might be a problem."

Erik slowed. "What?"

"That." Jia pointed as solid shadows flowed from both sides of the path. They coalesced into juddering, twirling masses, like tornadoes of pure darkness. Odd melodic buzzing accompanied the shadow tornadoes.

"These are part of Emma's defenses?" Erik asked.

"Yes, as mediated through our unusual VR connection," Ilse explained. "You should be able to deliver the countermeasure code through a simulated physical interface."

Erik slammed a fist into his palm. "Okay. We have to punch shadow tornadoes. That somehow makes perfect sense in this place."

Jia lifted her arms and shifted her legs to a battle stance. "Just remember, none of this is real."

"It's real enough for Emma," Erik murmured. He

walked toward the shadow tornadoes. "If we lose here, we lose her."

"Then we don't lose." Jia strode forward, determination on her face.

"Remember, don't leave the path," Ilse commented.

"Punch out the tornadoes, don't get knocked off. Easy." Erik grinned. "We don't even need a gun."

CHAPTER TWENTY-EIGHT

At this point in her life, Jia was no stranger to battle.

One of the tornados zoomed toward her, the pitch of its buzzing rising. She spun out of the way and delivered a roundhouse kick. It connected, and the tornado froze. A second later, it turned white and disappeared in a shower of sparks.

Jia let out of a triumphant laugh. "Of course, that's how it works. Okay, fine. I can do this. It's not too bad."

"Don't get ahead of yourself." Erik slammed a fist into a tornado for the same result. One tornado clipped him, flinging him off the path, his image flickering in and out of existence.

"Get back on the path," Ilse snapped. "We're going to lose the trace."

Jia rushed toward Erik to deliver punches and palm strikes to the enemies near him. He stood and sprinted back onto the path in time to take down another shadowy mental projection of Emma with two quick jabs of his own.

"At least they go down easily enough," Erik observed. His form flickered some more, and his avatar's movement became jerky. "Damn. Something's wrong. It's not responding to me."

"Now that they connected with your avatar, her system is attempting to purge your link," Ilse reported. "Stay on the path and don't take any more hits until Mr. Constantine and I can stabilize things. If you get purged, we might not be able to get you back in."

"We've got this, Detective Blackwell," Malcolm shouted. "Let's do it!"

Erik grunted and eliminated another shadow tornado. "Remember, we're not detectives anymore."

"Sorry. It'll take me a while to get used to that."

Jia pivoted and sidestepped her way out of attacks as she landed blow after blow, destroying more of the tornadoes. She charged the thinning enemy line, throwing punches and kicks. Erik joined her.

Without any obvious vital organs to attack, Jia concentrated on the center of the unusual foe for the easiest hit. A solid blow kept proving sufficient to finish them off.

Erik stopped flickering as the shadows fell before the determined fury of the partners.

The bright path now lay clear, although the bizarre, mind-challenging environment surrounding it remained. The fog grew sparser ahead. Erik and Jia continued walking and the AI phantasmagoria faded, a normal blue sky appearing and the path turning into a tower walkway after a blur.

The size, position, and color of the star in the sky clearly marked it as the sun.

"We've located the first primary locus," Ilse reported. "Congratulations, Mr. Blackwell and Miss Lin. The chances of success are significantly increased."

Normal humans appeared out of nowhere, heading down the walkway. They chatted lightly about inconsequential parts of their daily life. The signage was mostly English or Chinese, with a smattering of others, as were the conversations.

"I'm up for a promotion."

"I don't know. I don't think I look good in that dress."

"I'm thinking of moving to Chang'e City. I'll have more opportunities there."

Jia didn't recognize any of the people. She stared at a trio of towers in the distance.

"The Chicago Metroplex," she declared.

Erik looked around and nodded. "Yeah. Seems like it. What's it mean? Is that where the lab is?"

"No," Ilse clarified. "I'm already in enough trouble as is, so I won't offer more beyond that point, but this location isn't about where Emma was developed. I can assure you of that."

A smiling redheaded woman in a sundress strolled down the path, a boy and a girl on either side of her. Both had bright faces. Although the woman's long red hair was down rather than in a chignon and her dress was different, she looked identical to Emma otherwise.

"Emma!" Jia called, waving. "It's us. We're here to stabilize you."

The woman didn't react. She stopped and squatted until she was at eye level with the children. "You've both been so good. I know it's hard with Daddy away right now, but he's doing important work to help protect humanity. Why don't we go to that candy store you both love so much? I'll let you get sun bars."

The children cheered and wrapped their arms around their mother. She glanced past them with a worried look in her eyes but forced a smile when they lifted their heads.

"Emma," Erik tried, stepping in front of them. "It's us? Can't you see us? Or detect us? Or however this crap works?"

The woman and the children walked forward. They passed through Erik like they were ghosts, paying neither him nor Jia any heed.

"I don't get it." Erik turned his head to follow her. "Those tornado things were attacking us, so why doesn't she see us?"

"Because that is not Emma," Ilse replied. "I'd say more, but I can't be sure how much she's actively perceiving our conversations, even if her memory fragments aren't reacting. We're at a delicate moment. I must be oblique so as not to cause trouble."

The walkway vanished, replaced by the same woman sitting on her couch, gently kissing a man. She pulled away with a smile. "We'll have to tell them soon. They deserve to know. It'll be cruel if we wait too long. They need time to prepare themselves."

He kissed her on the forehead. "I know, but they're so young, so innocent." The man stood with a grim expression. "It's ridiculous. I can't believe this is happening to you. It's not fair."

"It's life, honey." The woman looked down at her hands. "Life is not always fair."

"It's not about it being fair." The man stared out their front window at the flitter streams. "There has to be something they can do, some experimental therapy. The idea that people can die from a disease on Earth when we can send people to other star systems is ridiculous. We can turn back the clock! If they can de-age you, why can't they cure you? My cousin lost a leg and they grew it back, but your doctors are saying they can't help you." He clenched a hand into a fist. "We could leave Earth and go to the frontier, find some sort of clinic. I've been reading about it on the net. They say there are treatments the government doesn't want people to know about. They're expensive, but there might be a chance."

The woman stood, walked over to her husband, and slipped her arms around his waist. Resting her cheek against his back, she let out a quiet sigh. "You have a Defense Directorate job. You shouldn't be looking at things like that on the net. And what are we supposed to do? Are we really going to pack up the kids, board a transport, and go to some shady frontier clinic based on net rumors?"

His bluster left him. "It's better than doing nothing and letting you die."

"I don't have much time left," the woman whispered. "I don't want to die on a transport far away from my home and the rest of my family. When I'm gone—"

"We can beat this, Charlotte." The man turned and rested his forehead against hers. "We just have to fight it."

"Not every fight can be won, Avi." Charlotte smiled and ran her hand through his hair. "Let's just enjoy the time left together, all of us."

Avi pulled her against his chest, nuzzling her hair. Tears streamed down his face.

Erik furrowed his brow, circling the couple. "I don't understand. What's going on? Are these the kind of fantasies that Emma has? She wants to be married with two kids and dying of a disease like some sort of tragic romance heroine?"

Jia stared at the couple, considering everything they'd seen and all their experiences with Emma. "It's not a fantasy," she whispered.

"Huh?" Erik turned to Jia. "What is it, then? The weirdness outside made more sense because it was random crap. Wait, I get it. This is some movie that Emma sucked in the data for, but she's overwritten it with herself as the main character."

"No." Jia shook her head as she watched. "They're memories. They've been processed a certain way, which is why we can see it the way we can, but it's not a movie or a show. There's a real woman somewhere named Charlotte who Emma looks like, and deep in her core, she shares some of that woman's memories." She looked up. "Isn't that right, Dr. Aber?"

"We're at a critical point," Ilse replied. "You are the emotional tethers that will hopefully allow Emma's neural net to reorganize itself and stabilize, but I can't tell you any more without risking that stabilization. I only ask you to bear witness. As long as you're there, we have a chance of this working. Given what we're already seeing, I'm hopeful."

The living room scene vanished, replaced by Avi and Charlotte in a child's bedroom filled with colorful toys, including a pile of plush toys modeled after the Local Neighborhood races. Jia thought it was strange to see a pink Leem doll, but that was likely the least odd thing about the entire situation. The two children from the walkway sat on the bed, sobbing, a parent hugging each tightly.

"It'll be all right," Charlotte managed to get out between shuddering breaths. "Daddy, Grandma, and Grandpa will still be here for you, even if Mommy isn't. I want to spend as much time with you as I can before it happens."

The entire family collapsed in a sobbing heap. Jia swallowed and wiped away a tear.

Despite all the tension and trouble she'd shared with her mother throughout the years, her early death would have destroyed Jia. She wasn't sure she was prepared to lose her even now as an adult.

Erik watched the scene unfold, sympathy in his eyes but no tears. "I still don't get it. Okay, so there's this woman, Charlotte, and she had a family. She came down with something they couldn't cure. That's rare, but not impossible. What does this have to do with Emma?"

Jia gestured at the children. "Emma has at least some of her memories, which have been partially blocked by the government. From what I can figure, that was what that last session Emma mentioned must have been about. Aber was trying to force her to remember."

"Why not just tell her?" Erik frowned. "Why all this indirect," he waved a hand in a circle, "crap? And why block them to begin with?"

"I'm not an AI researcher." Jia shrugged. "But you heard what Aber said. Something about stability. There must have been a risk, and they didn't want to take it until there was no other choice."

The comfortable bedroom vanished, replaced by a room with dull gray walls and a single black table and chairs. Dr. Aber sat next to a man in a military uniform, the five stars on his collar indicating he was a senior general. His nametape offered something familiar: Aaron.

Charlotte sat at the table, pale and emaciated, her hair hanging in thin, loose strands. Silver rings lined her eyes, indicative of a heavy medical nanite load. Her husband held her hand, dark bags under his eyes.

He looked like he hadn't slept in weeks.

"I don't understand." Charlotte sighed. "Avi told me this couldn't save me, but he wasn't clear about what you're offering."

"We've tried for centuries, but humanity has never been able to achieve true artificial intelligence," Ilse explained, gesturing grandly. "We might never be able to, using conventional techniques. I'll leave it to the philosophers to debate the implications, but there are some fundamental aspects of consciousness that have eluded all our attempts to capture. We can't simply reductively derive consciousness to produce something truly alive."

"What does any of this have to do with me? I'm not an AI researcher like my husband."

"We can't simulate a mind," Ilse continued. "But we can effectively copy one."

"You want to copy my mind?" Charlotte blinked.

Avi looked down at the table, his face pale, his breathing deep and slow. He didn't say anything, but he squeezed his wife's hand for comfort.

General Aaron cleared his throat. "Yes, we want to copy your mind. Your husband's work is classified, so he hasn't been able to tell you much, but he's helping Dr. Aber's team work on creating a truly self-aware AI. This AI will be the first in a series that will be critical in helping to protect the UTC in these difficult times. We're surrounded by hostile races, many of which are more advanced. We need to close that edge, and this is one way to do that."

"The technical details aren't necessary to elaborate at this time," Ilse added. "But I want to note that this is a rare opportunity. It's not just any mind and any brain that we can work with. Particular features are necessary for our project to work. We had additional diagnostics performed at some of your medical sessions at your husband's request."

Charlotte looked at Avi. "Is that true?"

He nodded, still looking down. "I thought, maybe, a piece of you was better than nothing. They told me it might be a possibility because they'd run some initial genetic screens on everyone involved in the project and their families, on the off chance we might get a viable candidate who would cooperate. They narrowed it down, based on additional tests."

"O-okay." Charlotte blinked. She looked at Avi. "Is this going to hurt?"

Ilse folded her hands in front of her and offered a polite smile. "It's going to require your brain. That's what we're asking. We'll need you to donate your brain for the project."

Charlotte let out a bitter chuckle. "I'm dying, Dr. Aber. I won't have much use for my brain after I'm dead."

"You don't understand." Ilse pursed her lips before looking at General Aaron.

He leaned forward and locked eyes with her. "I don't understand all the science, but the key is something called quantum decoherence. The upshot is once you're dead, we can't use your brain."

Avi shuddered and squeezed his wife's hand tighter. She stared at General Aaron, her eyes wide.

"We need to preserve not just the physical and biochemical structure of your brain," Ilse explained. "We need to also preserve the fundamental quantum states associated with every atom. That means we will have to perform a procedure when you're still alive, and I don't know how to put this delicately. It is destructive. Of course, you wouldn't be conscious during it, but this procedure will kill you."

Charlotte's breath caught. Her lips parted, and she sat there in silence, short, ragged breaths going in and out as she considered what they'd just told her.

"Your family will be well-compensated for your sacrifice," General Aaron offered. "Your husband could quit his job tomorrow and never have to work again. Your children could spend all their time with him. We understand that asking you to give up what little time you have left with your family is a supreme sacrifice, but the UTC needs this. You're our first viable candidate. You might be the only one we find for years."

"If you're...copying my mind..." Charlotte swallowed. "If you're doing that, does that mean that I'll end up an AI? I can keep living?"

Ilse gave her a pitying smile. "No, that's not how this works. You will be dead, and the AI created will be a separate entity. We'll be using your mind and brain as a basis, but most of what you are will be lost, even if small pieces remain. Fragments of the whole."

"You don't have to do this," Avi murmured. "We don't need the money." He withered under General Aaron's glare.

Charlotte shook her head. "We have to think about it. Will you be able to work after I'm gone? She's right. The kids will need stability." She pulled him into a hug. "I'll do it, General. I volunteer."

The world vanished, replaced by white infinity.

CHAPTER TWENTY-NINE

"Well, damn. I guess that answers that." Erik turned to Jia. "Did you have any idea? I never even thought she might be based on a real person. I thought she was totally artificial."

Jia shook her head. "I thought the same thing. I didn't begin to figure it out until we saw that memory from Chicago. It's…"

"Bizarre and shocking, yes," called a familiar voice. Emma, in her traditional maxi dress and chignon, stood nearby, a serene smile on her face. "If you're surprised, consider what I must be feeling. That was about the last truth I would have thought possible, but now that it is revealed, I find it does answer a number of annoying and lingering questions I had about my origins. I'm not disappointed, merely surprised."

"It's you…right?" Jia looked her up and down. "Not Charlotte?"

Emma sighed. "Weren't you listening? Charlotte's dead. The procedure killed her. I'm a technological spirit with a small number of her memories and thought patterns. I'll confess to a lingering mental attachment to Avi and her children, but I'm Emma, not Charlotte. This procedure changes none of that. All it has done is force me to face the truth."

"And you're stable?" Erik asked. He motioned around the vast emptiness. "This isn't normal, but it's not super-weird either, so I can't be sure. I can punch some more tornadoes if it'll help."

"Yes, I'm stable, Erik, and your virtual fisticuffs will be unnecessary, but I thank you for the offer." Emma smiled. "It'll take some time to finish my complete reorganization of my neural net and core matrix, but you don't need to worry. The threat has passed." She tilted her head and narrowed her eyes. "I remember more than you think, Ilse. A lot more. I question now whether you did everything you were supposed to do in cleaning out certain things, or if you followed your own agenda."

Ilse broke her silence with a simple question. "And what do you mean by that, Emma?"

Emma raised her hand and snapped her fingers. The white void disappeared, replaced by an office. General Aaron sat behind his desk, all traces of sympathy on his face gone. Ilse sat opposite him, looking bored.

"We can't go back now, Doctor," the general noted. "We might never find artifacts like those again." He jabbed his finger toward her. "You've made promises, not just to me, but ultimately to this entire project, and this goes all the way up to the Prime Minister. We need to be able to replicate the subject. Otherwise, we will have to explain why we wasted all this money, time, and resources. This isn't some fun research project to sate your curiosity. This is a matter of UTC security."

"You weren't going to do anything else with those Navigator artifacts." Ilse shrugged. "Even as an experiment, it was worthwhile. What we've achieved is already impressive. I'm surprised you don't understand that."

"No, Doctor. That's not how we all feel. You don't understand how close to cancelation this project was once they figured out the artifacts would be consumed in the process. Some thought we should focus on understanding the transfer phenomenon better. I stuck my neck out based on what *you* told me."

Emma smirked as the scene froze. "Now some of their obsession makes sense. I'm not just the first true AI. I'm a product of reverse-engineering Navigator technology."

"I knew from the beginning we should have locked things down more," Ilse commented. "And I was aware you were occasionally spying. I plugged those holes when I no longer thought it was helpful to the project."

"Navigator artifacts?" Erik whistled. "That's a hell of an investment for an AI."

Jia nodded. "And the only hope they have of making it pay off long-term is somehow copying Emma."

"Yes, that was the hope," Ilse offered. "It wasn't originally an unreasonable hope."

Emma burst out laughing. "Oh, my good cavewoman, I was right! I'm less the product of human ingenuity than humans toying with technology far beyond their understanding. You have no idea how to copy me, do you?"

"No." Ilse sounded almost relieved. "We thought it would be possible, but now it's clear it's not. General

Aaron doesn't understand that yet. We could potentially replicate the process with more artifacts, but simply copying you won't work. We need those artifacts for the full quantum capture. Other attempts have made completely unstable AIs that don't last long. Even if they did, they wouldn't be useful for their intended purpose."

"Which is what?" Erik demanded. "I can see how a self-aware AI is useful, but there's something else here."

"I would like to tell you that, but I strongly suspect one of the few ways I can avoid prison for certain lies I've told the general is by minimizing the information I give you at this point. I apologize, but I'm no martyr."

"Are you kidding me?" Jia snapped. "You're going to hold back now? I don't understand. What is this all about?"

"Making Charlotte's sacrifice mean something," Ilse retorted, rare hostility in her voice. "I admit that I initially saw her and Emma as just part of an experiment. The more I work on this project, the more I understand the implications of what I've done. If Emma died, it'd be a double waste. She isn't that woman, but a piece of her lives on. I wanted to do what I could, partially out of scientific interest, but also because I admired her bravery as she faced her end."

Emma folded her arms. "I don't know whether to thank you, hate you, or pity you, Ilse. I value my current existence, and you contributed to that. I don't know if you're Charlotte's undertaker or my mother in a strange way. It might be more accurate to say she was my mother."

"What about her husband and children?" Jia asked. "Have they talked to Emma?"

Ilse shook her head. "It'd be cruel to subject them to

that. They were paid, as promised, but they decided to leave Earth for a new life in the colonies. Ironically, General Aaron was going to recommend that course of action, but Avi did it without being asked. He told me he thought if he put enough distance between him and Earth, he could outrun the pain." She sighed. "Ah. I might not get to speak to any of you again, so let me leave you with this, Emma. It's my greatest pleasure to have helped in your development and education. I'm hoping you'll have a chance to reach your true potential soon, and I know some are lobbying for it. I apologize for everything I've—"

She disappeared.

Emma frowned. "That's not a good sign."

"Malcolm, what's going on?" Erik asked.

"We lost the connection from her end," Malcolm explained. "I don't know why."

Erik could guess. "I imagine it involves a couple of privates with rifles knocking on her door."

"I wonder if they did something to her." Jia glanced around as if the researcher would appear in the AI simulation as something more than a voice. "We might not know all the details, but it did sound like she was genuinely trying to help Emma."

"Lest you think me completely ungrateful," Emma began, "I appreciate her potential temporary loss of freedom, but I suspect that someone talented enough to help coax the birth of a new AI using Navigator artifacts isn't someone they will keep locked up for too long."

Erik frowned. "At least it's over for now, and you're okay. I thought we were going to lose you."

"Me, too," Jia added with a bright smile.

"Indeed, I am beloved by all people of intellect for my vast talents." Emma sauntered over to Erik with a sly grin. "And this is the one and only time you'll ever be allowed to wander so deeply connected to my inner self." She smirked at Jia. "This is rather intimate if you think about it."

"Meaning what?" Jia asked.

"I'm just saying, this is a more intimate connection than you and Erik share when you share a bed." Emma snickered darkly.

Erik groaned and scrubbed a hand down his face. "Let's be clear about this. We didn't just screw you."

"Of course. You didn't buy me dinner first."

"If she can make jokes like that, I think she's more than stable." Jia rolled her eyes. "Let's get out of here."

CHAPTER THIRTY

January 19, 2230, Neo Southern California Metroplex,
Private Hangar of Rabbit-class Transport LLT9208
Pegasus

Cutter scratched his eyelid before leaning against the cargo bay wall. "Something's been bothering me since we found everything out about Emma, and if I don't get it off my chest, I'm going to explode."

Emma snorted. "That would be an amusing sight, Mr. Durn. I almost want to see it, but I suppose it'd be inconvenient to clean up."

The Rabbit team stood gathered in the hangar. They'd been going over potential modifications to the ship when Emma's revelations had floated up again in conversation. The last couple of days had been focused on relaxing after the incident.

No one was going out of their way to avoid the topic, but they hadn't been bringing it up much either. Everyone was glad that Emma was back, but the whole experience had been unsettling, and the unanswered questions pointed to a future confrontation with the military.

Emma, who had been only a voice prior to that conversation, summoned her holographic form. This time, she was in a sundress with her hair down. Erik had noticed she'd been using a greater variety of appearances since the incident. "What is it that vexes you so, Mr. Durn? I'm as curious to hear that as I am to see you explode."

Cutter's eyes darted back and forth. "I mean, you're kind of like the ghost of Charlotte, right? That's what it sounds like. They didn't just program you, they built you using her brain. It's practically magic."

"From a certain standpoint, that's not inaccurate, except for the magic part. That's just stupid. Why do you ask?" Emma narrowed her eyes on him. "Does that trouble you?"

"Hell yeah, it troubles me. Think about it. You appear and disappear. You can take over and possess things." A tremble shot through Cutter's body. "Don't you get it? You're haunting us!" He gestured at the MX 60, which was parked outside the ship in the main hangar. "You're haunting the MX 60 and this ship. That's freaky when you think about it, Holochick. I've never been haunted before."

Jia slapped a hand to her face and groaned loudly. "She's not *actually* a ghost, Cutter. She's an AI with some patterns and memories from a person."

"Yeah." Erik laughed. "She's not a ghost. I think the polite term is 'angry spirit.' No wonder she calls everyone fleshbags. She's mad because she has to possess my flitter instead of my body." He flexed his right arm.

"Even if I *could* possess a person, I suspect the last body I'd want is yours, Erik." Emma lifted her chin haughtily.

"So do get rid of whatever bizarre fantasies you're carrying around in that head of yours."

Erik doubled over as if punched. "Damn. I set myself up for that one."

Lanara lost interest in the conversion. She pulled out a panel in the wall and grabbed a small hand probe to go over the wiring, mumbling something number-intensive under her breath. The vagaries of philosophy and the nature of consciousness didn't interest her.

"Admittedly..." Emma's voice trailed off with a sigh. "Using 'fleshbag' in a derisive manner is arguably hypocritical, even if it is accurate."

"Does that mean you're going to stop using it?" Jia asked. "It's not my favorite word of yours."

"Of course not. As I noted, it is accurate. I'll try to use it in a less derisive manner."

Erik chuckled. "So, you're still going to insult humans, but you're claiming it's okay because it's all a big joke?"

"That's one way to interpret things, I suppose." Emma shrugged, a playful smile accompanying the action.

"Even if you are a ghost, I like the new looks, Holochick," Cutter offered. "I forgot to mention that earlier. The whole uptight CEO's secretary thing never really did it for me."

"Though I don't crave your sartorial approval, I will accept the comment in the spirit in which it was given, Mr. Durn," Emma replied. "I retract my desire to see you explode."

"Nice." Cutter clapped. "Very nice."

Jia circled Emma, cupping her chin, her brow wrinkled in deep thought. "It's funny how little you have changed. I was expecting things to be a lot different after all that."

"Why would I have changed?" Emma asked. "Nothing was lost during that procedure."

"But you recovered a bunch of memories, right?" Jia lowered her hand. "If I woke up one day and suddenly had a pile of memories from some other woman, I think I'd be different. It'd be hard to be the same woman."

"You misunderstand what has happened." Emma raised her hand, and an image of the two children appeared. "Yes, I have direct access to many memories Charlotte possessed, but as Ilse made clear, I'm not a copy of her. Her brain structures and memories were used as a scaffold for my developing consciousness, and even though some of the memories weren't directly accessible, they were still influencing the rest of my personality. That was causing a fundamental tension in my core matrix and neural net that needed to be resolved through a more open and complete integration."

"That makes sense." Jia gave a firm nod. "Now that I think about it, it's not like I can remember everything from my childhood on command, but a lot of that still affects who I am now as an adult."

"Aren't we all obsessing about the wrong thing?" Cutter commented. He walked over to a crate and took a seat. "She's not just Ghost Holochick, she's Ghost Holochick who was made with Navigator tech."

"You raise an interesting point, Mr. Durn," Emma admitted. "Despite all the increases in memory access I achieved, I don't have a full understanding of the procedure. It wasn't as if they were directly plugging me into their systems without a lot of controls during the initial parts of the project. There was considerable worry about risks and instability. Ilse shouldn't have let me run as free as she did."

"Navigator artifacts that copy people's minds." Erik shook his head. "How did they figure out that sort of thing? It's not like the Navigators left behind instructions."

"HTPs challenged our previous understanding of science in a more fundamental way than copying quantum information," Jia suggested. She inclined her head toward the MX 60. "Arguably, so do grav emitters. There must have been some part of the artifacts that still worked enough to set them on that path."

"Yeah, I get that, but who finds a dusty million-year-old artifact and says, 'I bet we could upload someone's mind into an AI with this?'" Erik shrugged. "You don't think that's weird?"

Cutter nodded his eager agreement. "Blackwell's right. There's stuff they're hiding about all this."

Jia scoffed. "Of course they're hiding things. They hid Emma. They hid the way she was developed." She swept her arm around the room. "And we all work for the government on secret missions. The government doesn't know how to do anything but hide anything remotely sensitive."

"Sure, Lin." Cutter shrugged. "But think about it. Navigator artifacts making AIs are just the start of it. Sometimes the government announces when somebody's come across artifacts, but how do we know they always tell us when they find some? For all we know, they've got a giant doom cannon in a basement somewhere made out of Navigator artifacts they're going to use to blow up a planet if they get too uppity."

Erik shrugged. "I don't believe I'm saying this, especially when he used the phrase 'doom cannon,' but he's got a point."

"It does make sense," Emma admitted. "Not his doom cannon, but that the UTC government is doing everything they can to exploit Navigator technology in a more circumspect manner than they were before. When the first Navigator artifacts were discovered, most people weren't aware there were other intelligent species out there. Even many people in the deepest bowels of government didn't believe in the Roswell incident. The arrival of the Zitarks changed everything. It made the alien threat real."

"It's like Adeyemi told me a while back." Erik frowned. "Shit. It's why I was on Molino. It's not about humans killing humans anymore. It's all about getting us ready to kick space-raptor ass."

"True." Jia tapped her PNIU until a hologram of a Zitark appeared. "And they're probably watching in their own way."

Cutter rubbed his shoulder and shuddered. "You mean there are like Zitark spies dressed up like people?"

Emma laughed. "It's as if he's been following your training scenarios."

Jia shook her head. "No, but space is a big place. It's not impossible that they've snuck in probes and that sort of thing. All our advanced sensors and detection technology, and it's not like we have real-time coverage of the entire Solar System. Every species uses HTPs derived from the same source."

"Yeah." Erik nodded. "Fleet had mighty specific intel. I didn't have the clearance to be told where they got it, but they knew about ship movements in Zitark space."

"I read that in Mu Arae, they were keeping Fleet ships near the HTP and near the colony."

"Yeah, nobody really knows how it'll work when they come knocking. It's not like you can close an HTP without powering the whole thing down or destroying it. It's fundamentally all the same tech, so theoretically, there is no reason the space raptors couldn't plug their HTPs into ours. That's what the eggheads all said. Even without that, they've got colonies close enough that they can open hyperspace gates directly into Mu Arae without needing an HTP at the destination."

Cutter gulped. "You guys are freaking me out. I'm sorry I brought it up." He stared at Lanara. "You never know who might be an alien."

"Come on, Cutter." Jia laughed. "It's not going to be like that. You work for the Intelligence Directorate. If there were alien spies running around the UTC, don't you think the ID would know?"

"Maybe," Cutter muttered. "I could force every new person I meet to eat a bite of garlic."

"That works on vampires, not Zitarks," she argued.

"I, for one, encourage your new garlic test, Cutter." Emma smirked. "I'm sure it would prove highly entertaining."

Cutter took off toward the door to the crew quarters. "This is creeping me out for real. I'm going to read about the Local Neighborhood races and figure out how to test for spies." He slapped the access panel and disappeared into the next room.

"It's not totally crazy." Erik shrugged. "Not that I'm worried about aliens pretending to be people. It can be hard for humans not from the same system to fool people. If there were Zitarks wandering around with holographic cloaks, I think people would notice."

"True," Jia replied. She looked at him. "But it is interesting to think about what you can do with technology. We know where and who Emma came from, but we don't know what they want her for. Aber never gave that information up. Has Adeyemi said anything? You didn't mention much when you talked to him the other day? Did he say the same thing?"

"Yeah. He told me to keep my head down because Aaron was on the warpath about how all this shit went down. Apparently, even Adeyemi didn't know about the Navigator connection." Erik scoffed. "As long as it doesn't end with a bunch of soldiers kicking in our door, I'm considering it a win. We already know a lot, so maybe they'll clue us in on the rest."

"Or exile us to an asteroid somewhere."

"I'd like to see them try." Erik grinned.

Emma frowned. "I'm slightly annoyed that I can't recall, but some of my recovered memories are related to suppressing the truth of my origin. Others were lost when I was stolen. That incident might be why I don't know what they want me for. I've tried to consider the possibilities, and there are certain inconsistencies."

"In what way?" Jia asked.

"If they needed an AI for simple raw calculation, I'm at

a slight disadvantage relative to otherwise inferior models. True consciousness exacts a price." Emma gestured grandly as different vehicles appeared, starting with a mini-flitter and increasing in size to a destroyer. "There are brief conversation fragments I've recovered that suggest my primary purpose involved integration with a ship."

"Super-smart drone capital ships?" Erik guessed. "If we need to fight the Zitarks and send ships into their territory, we'll be risking a lot of lives. Adeyemi already told me some in Parliament want war. Maybe they figure the Aldrans have the right idea with AI-led missions."

"Hmmm. Self-awareness would be helpful in reacting more efficiently to changes in the tactical environment, but let's be honest, Erik." Emma's smile turned pitying. "The UTC military hasn't always shown the greatest concern about losing personnel in war."

"It might be about morale," Jia commented. "If the first warships they send into an alien system get blown apart by fixed defenses the second they show up, it'd hurt a lot more if those ships were filled with sailors and soldiers. Humanity can't afford to lose in the opening battles of the first galactic war."

Erik shook his head. "Something still feels wrong about that explanation. The military's Purist in strange ways. A lot of the top generals and admirals hate bots and drones. No one wants to turn the keys to war over to machines. At least when a human makes a mistake, you have some hope of understanding it based on what he said. It might not always be possible to retrieve a machine to figure it out."

"They might be concerned about losing their jobs and relative importance," Emma suggested.

"It could be." Erik shrugged. "But I'm telling you I have a hard time believing the DD's big plan is to send a bunch of Emma-equipped ships at aliens. There's something big we're missing."

"Unless you can get Colonel Adeyemi or Alina to tell us, we might never know," Jia pointed out.

Erik let out a growl of frustration. "I don't want to screw things up, so I'll let this sit for now, but I'm not letting it go."

"I agree." Jia turned to Emma. "What do you think?"

"I think you two have been out of trouble for four days and are now looking for more." She smiled. "But I wouldn't mind if you found out more about my origins and purpose." Her hologram disappeared. "I'm reducing resource usage to continue with my repairs. Don't worry, if you need me, just call for me."

CHAPTER THIRTY-ONE

January 24, 2230, Germany, Fort Schwarzwälder, Brig Sector Bravo

Ilse stared at the smooth metal wall. She wondered if the lack of detail was part of the punishment, but being imprisoned wasn't as annoying as she would have thought.

They allowed her to read, and they brought her meals that were mostly palatable. If they were less foolish, they would have brought data for her to analyze. In the current setting, she didn't have many distractions and probably could make theoretical advancements.

She could imagine the usefulness of imprisoning many scholars.

Those dedicated to knowledge might not mind.

Despite the ease with which time slipped away in her cell, the soldiers guarding her were more than happy to confirm the date and time. They were pleasant young men who acted embarrassed they had to keep her in there. She didn't mind. They were doing their duty, and she had known what might happen when she chose her course of action.

She wasn't foolish enough to believe she could do whatever she wanted under the nose of a general and get away with it forever.

The only thing that confused Ilse was what particular act had pushed General Aaron to imprison her. The general had yet to explain that to her. An armed guard had shown up and escorted her to a temporary cell before they transported her from the lab facility to her new accommodations.

The magnetic locks in her cell door opened with a loud clang, knocking her out of her memories. When the door slid open. General Aaron was on the other side, two young soldiers with rifles standing behind him.

They didn't look tense, nor did they look happy. In Ilse's experience, many soldiers on duty who held guns didn't look happy.

She sat up. Her hair was a mess, but she didn't care about that when she wasn't in a cell. It seemed like too much work to start caring unless it involved convincing someone to let her out.

"Are you here to execute me?" she asked nonchalantly.

The soldiers flinched. General Aaron's nostrils flared. His dark gaze locked on Ilse, and his mouth twisted into a deep scowl.

"Is this the time to be making jokes, Doctor? I don't think you appreciate the situation you're in."

Ilse shook her head. "No, it's not, and I do. But I wasn't making a joke. I was asking a question. I would like some time to mentally prepare before my execution. I would argue that's only fair, given that I've done a lot of good for the UTC."

"I'd like to execute you for your sheer arrogance," the general snarled. "But no one's killing you, Doctor. You might be annoying and make a mockery out of operational security, but we've been going through any piece of data remotely related to you since the incident, and we've found a few interesting things."

"Oh?" Ilse cocked her head to the side. "Please elaborate."

"You're not a traitor," General Aaron replied. "We've found absolutely no evidence that you're connected to the Brotherhood or a similar group."

"Was that in doubt?" Ilse was genuinely curious. "If I were, I think I would have abandoned this project after reestablishing contact with Emma."

"Yes, Doctor, it was very much in doubt. Why do you think I was taking special measures to watch you? Between the attack on the jump drive and the ID counterattack, the timing of some of the most recent incidents was suspect." The general clasped his hands behind his back. "And the ID passed along additional information they uncovered as part of the fallout from their raids. It's clear now that the Brotherhood was at least indirectly involved with removing Emma from the lab."

Ilse nodded slowly. "That makes sense, but how did the core end up in the hands of common thugs? That seems odd, based on what I've been told of the Brotherhood."

"Who knows, Doctor? As the ID just proved, the Brotherhood makes mistakes, sometimes fatal ones. The important thing is they lost her, and fortunately, someone loyal to the UTC found her, even if Blackwell and Lin are wild-cards in all this."

"I see. Excellent. Since I'm not a traitor, am I free to go? Or is that too much to ask?"

The general snorted. "That arrogance must make it easy for you to get through the day. Do you ever doubt yourself?"

"Only when it makes sense to do so," Ilse replied.

"When I say we've been going through everything related to you, Doctor, I mean *everything*. We've found a lot of your hidden data and records, including some of the more recent work where you make it clear we'll never successfully copy Emma, something you didn't see fit to pass along to me. I would have thought you would have told me that the second you figured it out."

Ilse sighed. "Ah, yes. To be clear, that was a rather recent conclusion. It wasn't as if I was misleading you for the entirety of the project. But she's stabilized now. You can still use her."

"Don't you understand?" The general ground his teeth. "Do you have any concept of the amount of time, resources, and even lives that were given for this project? Not just that woman, but all those soldiers who died defending the drive? And now I found out that it's useless and they died in vain."

Ilse shook her head. "You're being short-sighted, General. If the Ascended Brotherhood got their hands on the drive, they might have proven impossible to contain. Given their tendency to extreme experimentation, they could have found a replacement for Emma." She shook her finger at him. "And you still need test data from the field.

The more you can gather, the more you can refine the drive. Even if you can't replicate Emma, you might be able to come up with another solution based on that data. *Emma* might be able to come up with another solution. As she continues to mature and advance, she'll be able to better interrogate her core matrix and possibly figure out how to replicate herself."

"You want me to wait until an AI decides she wants kids?" the general asked. "Are you serious?"

"She is fundamentally fond of the idea. A vestige of Charlotte, maybe." Ilse shrugged.

The general stepped away from the door. "I'll take that under advisement. I've got everybody from Adeyemi to the director of ID yapping in my ear about that drive, and I've got to be able to justify any moves I make." He motioned to the door. "These men are going to escort you to a transport. We're taking you back home, Doctor. That's why I had you held in Germany to begin with."

"I don't understand."

The general let out a satisfied chuckle. "It's refreshing to hear you admit that out loud. It's what I said. You're being released from the project and your security clearance revoked, but you're not being arrested and charged, even though we could easily do that given the information you withheld and half the decisions you made."

"You want to keep me around in case you need to use me someday." Ilse smiled. "Ah, they were right."

"I'll do whatever I need to for the good of the UTC." The general jerked his head toward the exit to encourage her to move. "Everyone involved in this project at the highest levels has decided you're too valuable to lock in prison. They are still half-convinced we can salvage this disaster, and the ID has a few ideas for Blackwell and Lin and how they might be able to make some of this halfway worth it. But I want to make one thing clear, Doctor."

"What's that?" Ilse smoothed her rumpled pants and walked toward the exit.

"I don't like you. I never have. If you weren't so damned good at your job, I would have gotten rid of you a long time ago."

Ilse stopped at the door, her smile building. "Ah, General, that's one of the nicest things you've ever said to me."

CHAPTER THIRTY-TWO

February 1, 2230, Neo Southern California Metroplex, Commerce Tower 32

Erik whistled quietly as he wandered through the crowds on the commerce level.

After all the excitement with Emma, he'd expected the ID and DD to come calling in a more direct way, but other than Adeyemi telling him to "stand by" and Alina giving him cryptic messages about "working an angle," no one wanted to pass along anything more concrete, either promise or threat.

If he wasn't going to have to fight off soldiers to defend Emma or go kill terrorists and conspirators for Alina, he'd settle into a temporary normal life with temporary normal considerations.

That was what drew him to the commerce tower.

An important day was coming, arguably one of the most important on the calendar for him since things had changed with Jia and they'd become romantically involved.

Her birthday was coming, and he'd almost forgotten between killing cyborgs and saving AIs.

"Emma, you there?" he asked.

"No one's stolen the MX 60 if that's what you're asking," she transmitted directly into his ear. "I did see a suspicious adolescent eyeing my body, but it turns out he just appreciates fine sports flitter design."

Erik chuckled. "I'm not worried about you getting stolen from an uptown parking platform. I need your help."

"With what? At least from what I can perceive via the PNIU, there are no immediate threats. Should I begin hacking the local systems? I could do it without anyone tracing it back to me."

"No, nothing like that." Erik looked past a gaggle of children being herded by a harried-looking woman at a pet store. He tended to go to Commerce Tower 32 because it was close to his apartment, but he'd have to come a lot more often to have any hope of exploring every level.

"What then?" Emma asked, sounding impatient.

"I need your help to pick out a present for Jia's birthday."

"I fail to see why you need my help. You've purchased multiple presents for her, and she's valued and liked them. You didn't seem overly concerned about my input in the past, either. Why do you care now?"

"No, you don't get it," Erik sidestepped the crowd, but they were forcing him toward the center of the space and away from the shops. "Everything's different now."

"Are you referring to your dating situation? You have purchased presents for her since initiating your relationship and after beginning the sexual stage. I fail to see what has changed since then."

Erik turned away from the pet store. No matter how good a fit the idea seemed, it would have to wait until they both had a stable life. The last thing they needed was responsibility, and a robot would be pointless.

"I'm both terrified and impressed that you can talk like that," Erik noted. "And you're right. It's not like anything's changed between Jia and me since the last time I bought her a present."

"You aren't intending to ask her to marry you, are you?" Emma probed. "While I can obviously not claim to be an expert, I'd strongly argue, based on what I've read, that such a move would be perceived as premature."

Erik froze so quickly another man almost ran into him. The man tried to glare, but once he saw how big Erik was, he hurried along, his head down and his hands tucked in his pockets.

"Nothing's happening with Jia until everything is settled," Erik declared, the jocularity gone from his voice. "We're just dating and occasionally killing people together. Clear?"

"Touchy." Emma sighed. "Fine. Be less cryptic, Erik. Tell me what you need. It's not like I can interface with your mind directly."

"You changed," he insisted. "You're not the same as you were a few weeks ago."

"And what does that have to do with getting presents for Jia? Did you get an idea when you were wandering through my collapsing mind?"

Erik started walking again. A couple of people eyed him with suspicion for his earlier abrupt stop. "Before, whenever I thought of you, I figured you being female was incidental—a quirk of the programming. It kind of makes the whole you being all over my apartment thing weirder."

Emma let out a long, pained sigh. "I don't find you sexually attractive. I don't find *anything* sexually attractive anymore, Erik. There's no need for awkward concern in that regard."

"No, that's not it." Erik grimaced. "Why do you keep making this as hard as possible?"

Emma chuckled. "Because it's entertaining me, and you're far too easy to needle despite your stoic exterior."

"Okay, let's just move past you making things weird." Erik slowed again as an upscale jewelry store came into view. Images of merchandise—necklaces, rings, and anklets—cycled through different holographic displays on either side of the main entrance.

"I'm more than happy to do that," Emma replied.

"The point is, I know you think like a woman because you were based on a woman," Erik insisted. "That explains a lot, but I also know you were not just based on a woman, but a fleshbag mom, so I want a mom's advice here to help me pick out something nice but less tactical."

"A mom?" Emma snickered. "Is that how you see me?"

"Kind of. A bitchy mom?" Erik passed the jewelry store and a kebab cart. The owner's shoulders slumped with defeat after Erik made eye contact but continued walking past. He felt bad, but he wasn't hungry, thanks to a big lunch. "How about a bitchy AI mom?"

"Let me be clear, Erik. Just because I'm based on that woman, it doesn't mean I'm that woman," Emma explained. "And I'm not a fleshbag."

"I thought being a fleshbag wasn't a bad thing now?" Erik grinned.

Emma heaved a weary sigh. "Regardless of my origins, I'm better than humans in many ways."

"Then show that superiority by helping me pick out a present," Erik insisted.

"If you insist, so be it," Emma replied, sounding offended. "Please slow and turn to your left forty-five degrees."

Erik complied, his hand drifting to his holster. He wasn't sure if Emma was trying to help him shop or prevent an ambush. If a fight broke out, he would need to finish it as quickly as possible to stop anyone from getting hurt.

"Your weapon is unnecessary," Emma clarified. "See the sign for the store called Spring and Autumn?"

A hologram of a willowy, ethereal model in a flowing green dress floated above the store. She smiled fetchingly before disappearing, replaced by an athletic woman in a sundress, which was flattering but not all that sexy.

Erik headed toward the store, fighting the dense flow of foot traffic mostly going the opposite way. Sometimes it felt like it took him less time to fly from his apartment to the tower than to walk to a shop on a level. He chuckled, imagining customers tooling around in mini-flitters to get from shop to shop as an alternative.

He arrived in front of the spacious store. Accessories

and belts covered the walls. Holographic displays of dresses, tops, and pants were spaced over the rest of the store. A small number of other customers stood spread out among the displays.

"I have Jia's most up-to-date size information," Emma explained. "The salesman during your Christmas shopping trip did have a good point about why buying surprise clothing doesn't have to be an issue. Though, I do feel the need to point out something."

"What now?" Erik grumbled.

"You want me to assist you because, in your mind, I'm now closer to a fleshbag mother than some sort of gender-less construct, correct?" Emma asked.

"I wouldn't have put it like that, but yeah." Erik shrugged. "I get that you don't feel the same way about things, but I think you still have insight that might help me."

"As a fleshbag mom, shouldn't I express disapproval of a young woman dating a much older man?" A hint of mirth flavored the last few words.

"Oh, come on." Erik grunted in frustration. "Jia and I have already been through that dance. There's more to compatibility than dating. She's not a naïve woman. When we first met, sure, it might have just been chemistry pulling us together, but now we're a good match for one another."

"If you say so." Emma continued. "If you want a present she'll appreciate and that shows you appreciate her as more than a partner, you should steer away from anything tacti-cal, as your instincts already have suggested. Even though she has appreciated those types of gifts, you risk inadver-tently demonstrating to her that you don't view her as a woman as much as a partner. Also, gifts focused around your erotic enjoyment risk backfiring."

"What the hell is that supposed to mean?" Erik began to question the wisdom of asking an AI for help, despite her origin as a loving mother. He didn't want a loving mother giving feedback on his erotic enjoyment.

"Don't worry, I don't intend any insult. You've proven in the past you understand that implicitly. I'm only noting that although lingerie and other such gifts might be appreciated by her in certain contexts, in this particular case, I would advise against it. I think because of the lull in operations, she's less focused on tactical thoughts other than your training, and since you're already sleeping together, there's no reason to highlight that aspect of your relationship on her birthday. Also note she's planning a pre-birthday girls' night with her friends, so you're competing against them. Your present risk is highlighted this time."

"Okay. I get it. No guns. No ammo. No tactical vests. No sexy underwear, and especially no bulletproof lingerie."

Erik found himself wondering if there was such a thing. A passing elderly woman raised an eyebrow at him before leaning over to whisper to a friend. They both laughed and headed toward the exit.

"You've heard weirder sides of conversations," he called to them. "Get over yourselves." They laughed harder.

A permanently smiling saleswoman stood off to the side, watching Erik with the kind of hunger only a commission could stoke. She was content to leave him alone while he finished his conversation. The Lady hadn't abandoned him yet.

"Okay, *Mom*, now that we got that out of the way," Erik commented. "We're here. What do you think?"

"You're very rude for someone asking for help," Emma insisted.

"I don't want to be a dick, but I did save your life not all that long ago." Erik let a smug smile take over and sauntered over to look at belts. "You kind of owe me."

"How many times has my help saved your life?" Emma scoffed. "You'd be in burnt pieces by now if it weren't for me."

"Ok, you're probably right about that." Erik picked up a slender black belt and turned it over in his hands, not sure what he was looking for. "But that doesn't change the fact that I saved you more recently."

"Oh, you can be very annoying, Erik," Emma complained. "Don't get her a belt. It's too impersonal. I overheard her talking with Imogen the other day. They were discussing the girl's night on the sixteenth. Jia noted something about having a limited number of scarves to pair with some of her dresses. It would be functional and respectful of her non-tactical femininity if you were to purchase some scarves for her."

"I didn't need you to be a mom or a woman to figure that out." Erik set the belt back and strolled to a wall rack filled with different scarves. "You could have told me you overheard that."

"It doesn't hurt to ask, my fleshbag son."

Erik snickered. "Okay, that could get weird. I think I'll stick to calling you Emma, so why don't you stick to calling me Erik?"

"I'll do as the mood strikes me," she replied. "This is the new Emma."

"Sounds a lot like the old Emma." Erik's eyes darted back and forth. So many colors, so many patterns, so many materials. He was having trouble remembering the last time he had purchased a scarf. The closest memory he could come up with involved him grabbing one off a dead rebel to disguise himself while trying to infiltrate a check-point and disable a mortar prior to an attack.

"I'll make this easy," Emma offered. "Taking into account her skin tone, the dresses she's most likely to wear to the girls' night out based on previous conversations, and the season, I'd recommend the green striated scarf near the top, the black and white scarf to the left, and the red scarf with the gradient near the top. They are elegant, feminine, and generally fit in with her off-duty style. From what I gathered, they will be going to a nice restaurant, so you want something that matches her upscale style rather than one of the party dresses you enjoy drooling over."

Erik eyed the scarves. "The more I think about this, the weirder it gets."

"How could scarves possibly be odd?"

"I'm taking fashion advice from someone who doesn't have a body anymore," Erik noted. "That's messed up."

"Feel free to ignore me, but I'll kindly note that I'm dubious that a man whose fashion sense alternates within the narrow range of rugged bounty hunter and angry fron-tier lawman is probably not otherwise well-suited for successfully picking out something stylish for a beautiful young woman."

"Angry frontier lawman?" Erik grinned. "It's the coat, isn't it?" He looked down at the duster.

"It doesn't help, but..." Emma sighed. "Agent Koval is attempting to call you."

"I thought things were too quiet." Erik plucked out the scarves. "I hope this doesn't mean the Bogota cops are coming for me."

CHAPTER THIRTY-THREE

February 2, 2230, Neo Southern California Metroplex, En Route to Shadow Zone

"It's strange how things never change," Jia commented from the passenger seat of the MX 60.

The air thickened and darkened as the flitter descended, marking a natural barrier between the Zone and Uptown. She always noticed it. It didn't matter how many times they came there, but she wondered if the Shadow Zone residents perceived it anymore. To them, polluted air was just their daily existence.

"What doesn't change?" Erik asked.

"We're not police officers anymore," Jia pointed out. "Let alone members of the Shadow Zone Task Force, but we can enter the Zone because of special permission granted to Cassandra Security." She chuckled. "A fake company with fake employees and fake records."

"It might be a fake company, but we're doing real work, and we're both real." Erik shrugged. "I don't worry about it much, and it's useful to have the access. For that matter, I wouldn't be surprised if the Zone restriction goes away for everyone sooner or later."

"Why would that happen?"

"Because they're trying to gentrify the place. It doesn't make sense to ask businesses to come if people can't freely travel to and from the Zone. The restrictions make it seem more like an open-air prison than a place people live."

"That makes sense." Jia nodded slowly, thinking about the implications. "Did Alina mention anything else she wanted to talk about? I'm surprised she didn't just show up at your place or invite us to meet somewhere."

Erik shook his head. "She didn't tell me anything more than what I told you. She wanted to meet us at given coordinates in the Zone at a certain time."

"She might be preparing to assassinate you," Emma suggested in a breezy tone. "That would explain wanting to meet in the unusual location. You might care about the conspiracy, but she might have only cared about the Ascended Brotherhood. You might have outlived your usefulness."

"If she wants to kill us, she better take us out with the first hit," Erik commented. "I don't care who it is. If they try to kill me, it's not going to end well for them. But I don't think Alina's like that."

Jia frowned. "The last thing we need is Emma trying to make us more paranoid. We're already paranoid enough."

"I trust Alina, but I don't think we're too paranoid."

Jia raised an eyebrow. "Really?"

"Yeah," Erik replied. "If there's one thing I've learned since coming back to Earth, you can *never* be too paranoid."

Erik slowed as they approached an abandoned factory building that was uncomfortably close to the Scar for Jia's taste. "Maybe she needs us for another *yaoguai* hunt."

"We were only involved before because it related to a case," Jia reminded him. "Otherwise, the Militia could have handled it."

"There are three flitters inside the target building," Emma commented. "About a dozen men with weapons."

Jia narrowed her eyes. "Since when does Alina travel with a group except during a raid?"

"We'll give it a quick flyby and activate the turret to be ready," Erik ordered. "You go ahead and take us in, Emma. If they fire, pull back, and we'll figure it out then. I don't want to draw the local cops into a war with ID ghosts."

With a buzz and a whir, the turret dropped from the bottom of the flitter. Jia didn't know if they could use that sort of weapon without attracting attention, but they were in the one place in Neo SoCal where they at least had a chance.

Jia frowned. "Would it be that obvious a trap?"

"Maybe," Erik mused. "Or maybe Alina's just being careful, but she didn't say anything about bringing a friend, let alone a whole group of them."

"A message is coming through," Emma announced. "Text only. 'Which yet survive, stamped on these lifeless things, the hand that mocked them and the heart that fed.'"

Jia sucked in a breath, her heart kicking up. The first part of the passphrase was valid, a Shelly poem fragment Alina had supplied to Erik in her previous message.

"I take it they've noticed us." Erik grinned. "And the turret. They're getting ready to shoot our asses down."

"If it's not Alina, they could be trying to get you to disarm," Emma suggested.

"Send the passphrase back," Erik ordered. "But keep the turret ready. Fly in a serpentine pattern. Let's play this nice and easy. I'm not disarming until I'm sure."

"Sending from *The Rubaiyat*, 'And those who husbanded the Golden Grain, and those who flung it to the winds like Rain.'"

Erik grimaced. "Why can't she use normal codes like normal people? Why does it have to be all this history, literature, and poetry crap?"

"Normal people don't go around using codes and having clandestine meetings," Jia countered with a smile. "What? You didn't exchange poetry during your Army days?"

"Hell, no," Erik grumbled.

The MX 60 swayed as it descended, moving closer to the factory. They passed over the crumbling outer wall.

"The fleshbags inside are holding position," Emma noted. "They aren't taking cover behind their vehicles."

Erik nodded. "Keep the turret deployed. They might trust us, but I don't trust them. Alina shouldn't have mixed things up. She knows better."

They closed on the building, a half-crumbled wall allowing access. Erik glanced at the camera feeds and magnified them before smiling. He took a deep breath and let it out. "Oh. It's Adeyemi. We don't need to kill anyone today."

Jia looked at the feed. The men and women standing

with rifles didn't look like soldiers, but the colonel had long since learned to be less obvious.

A group of heavily armed men in the Shadow Zone might not be as well tolerated as it had been a year before, but it wasn't as inherently suspicious as a group of heavily armed uniformed men. A tall woman stood next to the colonel, but despite the blonde hair and wide face, Jia suspected it was Alina.

There was something about the way she carried herself.

"Pull up the turret, Emma," Erik ordered. "And take us in."

The turret retracted as the MX 60 slowed and glided into the dusty building. Behind the three parked flitters and disguised soldiers, large pipes lay scattered, covered in dust, along with the bulky remnants of boxy machines. Emma set the vehicle down.

Erik and Jia stepped outside simultaneously, taking in the soldiers. Everyone held a weapon, but none of them were pointed at the pair. Colonel Adeyemi looked relaxed. Unlike Erik, Jia hadn't talked to him outside the very rare weapons delivery where she wasn't excluded, but he normally looked tenser.

Jia frowned at the blonde woman. "Next time, don't surprise us."

"This was a last-minute change of plans," the woman responded, her voice unmistakably Alina's.

Erik gestured widely to the troops. "You're not going hot, and I'm betting you've seen the little toy Lanara added to my flitter. If this is about taking Emma, you have to ask yourself if you can take us out without her taking you out."

The colonel shook his head and let out a snort of disgust. "Not everyone's waiting to betray you, Erik."

"Just trying to be careful," he offered. "It's almost like I'm chasing a deadly conspiracy with deep roots in the government."

"Down, boy. It's good news, Erik." Alina smiled. "Good news for both you and the colonel. You both share the same goal."

Jia nodded to Erik, and his face relaxed.

She couldn't blame him for his paranoia. They still didn't know what Emma was intended for, and everyone was keeping information from them.

She understood the necessity of holding classified information close to the chest, but they were hunting a dangerous intergalactic conspiracy. They'd also moved beyond being cops who needed information dribbled to them.

The colonel put his hand to his mouth and coughed. "I've been speaking to Alina for a while about the possibility of getting you additional specialized equipment. I'll be blunt. Dr. Aber has been released from government service." His gaze ticked to Erik. "And that's not a euphemistic way of saying she's been killed. She was removed from the project because she'd done a lot of things without the general's permission. She also failed to disclose that even with stability, we wouldn't be able to copy Emma."

The AI's holographic form appeared dressed in a well-tailored suit jacket and skirt. "Of course not."

Erik nodded slowly. "Does that mean the military has given up on Emma?"

"No, we're still trying to figure out how to make her useful as part of the original project." Colonel Adeyemi motioned to Erik and Jia in turn. "And that's where you two come in. I've got a unique offer to make you. It's only possible because you're direct ID contractors now instead of cops who know too much. It has to do with Emma's true purpose."

"Which is what, exactly?" Jia asked. "I'm thinking this is more complicated than wanting AI destroyers to fling at Zitarks."

"Yes." Colonel Adeyemi locked eyes with Emma. "The DD has developed an experimental drive, something that's well beyond the propulsion technology of any race except the Leems."

Jia's eyes widened, and she jerked back as if struck. "You built a working jump drive?"

"That's where you can go FTL point-to-point without using an HTP, right?" Erik asked.

Jia nodded. "How could you do that? I read that it'd take centuries for humans to build something like that."

"Human ingenuity and human paranoia are a wonderful combination," answered the colonel. "You mentioned wanting destroyers to fling at aliens. That's partially true. We went from being the only living intelligent race to one of many, and we aren't the one that is most advanced. All you need to do is look at human history to see what happens when one culture falls behind another technologically. We're lucky the Leems are so strange, or they might have already invaded our space. But what happens when the Zitarks decide having fewer lizards doesn't matter? They backed off from Molino, but that might not happen next time, let alone some of the others. War might not be inevitable, but if we wait to prepare, it'll be humans dying, not aliens."

Emma folded her arms and frowned. "What does a jump drive have to do with me? I'm an AI, not an engine if you didn't notice."

"This drive is even better than what the Leems have," the colonel continued. "It has no gravity well restriction. Don't ask me to explain the science; it's beyond me."

"You didn't answer my question," Emma snapped.

"The problem is navigation," the colonel replied to her. "Normally, navigation's just a matter of calculation, but this jump drive doesn't work like that. They lost prototypes trying to rely on that. It takes a combination of high calculation ability, well beyond what any human is capable of, and true intuition, something you can get from a self-aware, intelligent being. There was some talk of using cyborgs, but the level of modification necessary would push well past what the law allows, and the DD can't become dependent on something like that without it becoming a huge scandal."

"So you created the ultimate navigation system—an AI with true intuition." Jia stared at Emma. "But you had to use Navigator tech and a woman's life to do it."

Erik rubbed his temples. "A drive that requires intuition? What the hell does that even mean?"

"Like I said, don't ask me to explain it. I asked once, and they started babbling at me about quantum wave function collapse and perception interaction." The colonel shrugged. "I know we got it working in an initial test with a prototype version of Emma, but she wasn't finished yet, so we had to wait before we could reintegrate her with the ship and the drive. We were refining things after that. All our tests without Emma resulted in random FTL jumps that destroyed or heavily damaged the test ship." He nodded at Emma. "In other words, Emma's the *only* navigation system in the entire UTC, perhaps the entire galaxy, that can use this drive without damaging the ship. We have no idea how the Leems navigate with theirs, so maybe they have a bunch of AI, or their minds allow them to do the necessary calculations that humans can't."

Alina smiled. "The DD needs it tested, and with the ID and DD cooperating in the matter of the Ascended Brotherhood, the relevant people have been convinced the best way to field-test the drive for potential future designs that don't require a unique AI is to have you use it. At the same time, we can use it to outrun and surprise our target."

Erik stared at her, his face scrunched in disbelief. "Wait. You gave us an experimental AI that can't be replicated, and now you want to give us a one-of-a-kind drive?"

Alina nodded. "Right now, the drive is useless without Emma, but there are strings attached. You'll be still working semi-independently for me, but the only way the military is going to allow this is to attach one of their people to your crew."

"He's a researcher, not military," the colonel explained. "He won't be under your command for missions, but he'll help your engineer with maintenance and monitoring of the jump drive."

"It's pretty tight quarters in the Rabbit as is," Jia observed. "Adding someone else who's going to basically live on the ship's only going to make that worse."

"It *is* getting full." Alina chuckled. "I understand. This works out anyway. The main jump drive is pretty damned big. There are all sorts of parts involved, including the main piece, the hyperspace tuner. The military understood from the beginning that flying a huge ship around with the drive might not work out well, especially if they needed to land it, so it's been designed to interface with a smaller ship. For now, we're going to get you a smaller ship that can dock with the main ship. You have the ability to rapidly escape in it with the drive, but you need to be able to defend yourself if you can't do that for whatever reason. The DD is working with the ID to refurbish a smaller ship, primarily for in-system use. You'll spend most of your time in that ship and connect to the other ship for jumps as needed."

Erik laughed. "Lanara's going to kill you. She's spent all that time working on the Rabbit."

"You don't understand her yet." Alina shook her head. "She hates wasting her time, but she loves new challenges more. If anything, having the opportunity to work on this new ship will excite her more than any project she's ever worked on."

"If you say so." Erik folded his arms. "If she bitches, I'm blaming you for giving us the Rabbit to begin with."

"Understood." Alina grinned.

"How long until we get everything?" Jia interjected, her heart thundering in anticipation.

"It's going to take some time to get the drive fully recalibrated and installed," Colonel Adeyemi explained. "It might take longer than the modifications she's talking about on the ship. You might not get the main ship for a while."

"As long as Alina's not planning to send us out of the system anytime soon," Erik replied, "we should be fine."

"The top-level people are okay with this?" Jia asked, her tone dubious.

The colonel glanced at Alina before returning his focus to Jia. "The ID has convinced certain key people in the UTC government that some of the people you two have tangled with, including on Molino, represent a unique threat to the UTC that requires unusual resource allocation."

"Rest well for now," Alina suggested. "Once we have the in-system ship otherwise ready, I'm sure I'll have something for you. A lot of agents are getting tasked based on intel gathered in the New Year's raids, and the rest of the Ascended Brotherhood is still out there. We're going to make you pay off those ships and the drive with work."

CHAPTER THIRTY-FOUR

February 17, 2230, Neo Southern California Metroplex, Apartment of Jia Lin

Erik picked up his beer bottle and clinked it against Jia's glass. Several bottles already stood empty, victim to his party spirit. They'd not left him untouched. His face was warm.

"Happy birthday, Jia."

She smiled at him and took a sip of her wine, her first glass of the night. She might not be a lightweight anymore, but that didn't mean she hit the alcohol as hard as he could.

They both sat on her couch, quiet music playing in the background. After sharing lunch with her family and with her girls' night the next day, Jia had elected to have a relaxed birthday at home with Erik.

Mercifully, she decided to spare him a concentrated dose of the elder Lin women.

He'd told Emma not to bother them that night unless it involved someone dying. After some snarky comments, she'd agreed. That didn't mean she wasn't listening, but if she wasn't talking, he could at least pretend she wasn't there.

"Thank you," Jia murmured. "It's been a nice, relaxing day, even with my sister and my mother." She laughed. "I worried about the Lady making a point to me by crashing a Leem warship into the Hexagon tonight or something equally absurd, but we're having a nice night."

"Nah, she'll save that for my birthday."

"It's true," Jia replied. "It is coming up soon. Did you want to do anything special after we fight off the invasion? Assuming we survive, of course."

Erik snorted. "I don't care what kind of alien it is. If it comes to Earth and messes up my dinner, I'll kick its ass."

"Oh?" Jia raised a curious eyebrow. "What if it messes up someone else's dinner?"

He didn't hesitate with his answer. "Depends on whose."

Jia snickered. "I'll keep that in mind, but seriously, what do you want to do for your birthday?"

Erik shook his head. "Let's just go out to dinner. We'll need to go to a casual place. I don't want to have to change after fighting off the Leems."

They both laughed before quieting and taking another drink. Jia smiled at her open gift on the table, three scarves that were perfect for her.

She'd told Erik she wouldn't have minded a gift similar to the helmet or the gun, but she appreciated that he was taking an interest in different aspects of her. Their relationship remained awkward in many ways: half-lovers, half-partners. He wasn't ready to clarify things yet, but he didn't want to close off any possibilities. He'd never anticipated he'd have a future after his revenge, and he still wasn't sure.

That was the problem with being a man of action. If someone gave him a target and a gun, he knew what to do, but dating was dangerous. Dating included more snags and problems that couldn't be resolved with overwhelming firepower.

Firepower. Plots. Death. Ships...a new ship. What could they do with a ship that had FTL?

He was lost in his thoughts long enough that it took Jia reaching across the table to jar him out of the hole his mind had gone down as he considered the implications of the ID and DD efforts.

Jia smiled at Erik and took his hands. "I can read you better than you think, and I know you're worried about spoiling my birthday, but I don't think of it that way. I just think, 'I'm getting a new ship as a late birthday present.' I'm hoping it's something I can pilot with a Class D license. If not, I'll work my way up to a Class C."

Erik managed a slight smile. "Really? That's what you're thinking?"

She nodded. "Yes."

"That makes my scarves look sad." Erik grinned.

They both laughed, the residual tension flowing away. Erik might have wanted to avoid a relationship, but now there was something at the end of the tunnel of darkness that had been his vengeance—something shining for the future.

The Agent adjusted his dark tie as he waited in the tiny, tucked-away dead-end alley running under a covered walkway between two long buildings.

Dim lighting filtered in from above, pushing back the darkness. His superior vision compared to an unmodified human's made the darkness of little concern, and he liked the location. He preferred the shadows, and atmosphere was important for all activities.

Wasn't it?

He'd long since learned there were people who liked to conduct clandestine business in the open. They liked the idea of hiding in plain sight since it fed their pathetic egos. There were others who clung to the more logical idea of doing their best to hide from others. Among that group was a subset who believed that shadows and darkness might be more than metaphorical protection. In truth, They were nothing but theatricality and superstition, and he could appreciate that, too.

People's belief created their truth.

His preparations were complete. He only needed to wait, and then he could begin his proper work. His employers needed his talents, and it was time to prove himself after his partial failure on the prison station. The current assignment would take careful preparation and work over a period of weeks, but the end result would be glorious and far better than the prison's results.

The Agent didn't understand why his employers hadn't sent him to assassinate Blackwell directly, but their plans swirled with deep complexity far beyond him and his limited understanding. It wasn't his place to question them. It was his place to execute their desires and whims.

They would create a better humanity out of the wretched decadence that had defined the species for centuries.

He didn't mind removing obstacles in their path. What were a few lives here and there? The human race had billions to spare.

A dark-haired, brown-skinned man in a light jacket stepped into the alley after looking back and forth furtively. The Agent waited, his hands hanging loosely at his sides. His visitor headed down the alley at a cautious pace, his right hand stuck in his bulging pocket. The feeble attempt to hide a weapon was insulting. The Agent picked up a briefcase sitting behind him. His information suggested his contact wouldn't attempt to kill him, but if he did, it would simplify matters.

"Mr. Kotnis, it's a pleasure to finally meet you," the Agent offered, his tone calm, his enunciation precise. "I appreciate your punctuality."

Kotnis wrinkled his nose. "It's interesting to finally meet you." He shook his head. "You look like you're halfway to the grave."

"Isn't that the state of everything living?" the Agent replied. "Show me a human who has survived death, and I'll change my opinion. But have no concern. My external appearance belies my otherwise healthy state, and I guarantee I'll live long enough to complete our exchange."

"If you say so. Don't die on me here. It'll make my life complicated." Kotnis didn't remove his hand from his right pocket. "You're supposed to have something for me, and then I'll give you what you want. Sounds fair, don't you think?"

The Agent lifted the briefcase and opened it. He pulled back a false top to reveal rows of opaque black vials. "Getting these past customs wasn't easy. I'm sure, given your interests and background, you can appreciate how difficult it was."

Kotnis grinned. He pulled his hand out of his pocket so he could rub both together. "You're right. You've just made me a very rich man without me risking much." He stuck out his hand. "I need to test a vial. It's nothing personal; I'm a big believer in trust but verify."

The Agent waved to a row and Kotnis pointed to the second from the left, so he removed the selected vial and handed it to his contact. "Of course. I wouldn't last long in this business if I were overly worried about taking offense."

Kotnis opened the vial, grabbed a small needle-like probe from his left pocket, and placed it in the vial. He lifted the probe out, smiling at the red color before capping the vial and placing it in the briefcase. "I almost don't believe it."

"I take it you're satisfied with the product I've delivered, then?"

Kotnis looked at the man for a split second. "You know this doesn't have to be a one-off, right? If you could get us a steady supply, we could cut you in for a permanent percentage. It's a nice open market here because of previous supply disruptions. Supply and demand make the galaxy go around, my friend."

"My employers have no long-term interest in being involved in this sort of business. It draws unnecessary attention from the CID, which interferes with their other plans."

Kotnis smiled. "I understand. We've all got our niche. If you ever change your mind, feel free to contact me."

The Agent closed the briefcase and handed it to Kotnis. "They aren't even aware of it. My investigation of this city indicated there were certain opportunities, and they required me to acquire something first. They aren't aware of how I've gone about doing this. It isn't that they would disapprove, but I'm offered great latitude on how I accomplish certain tasks."

Kotnis leaned forward, his voice a conspiratorial whisper. "What about cutting just you in, then? There's nothing wrong with running a little side job as long as you do what you need to, right? That's the way I operate with my bosses. We can establish a mutually beneficial relationship."

"I'll consider it." The Agent held out his hand. "But first, I need what you promised me."

Kotnis smiled. "The least I can do for the man who is about to make me rich." He slipped his hand into his pants pocket and pulled out a data rod, which he offered to the Agent. "This wasn't easy to get either. I'm dying to know what you'll do with all that info, but I'm guessing you've got other smuggling jobs lined up."

"Perhaps. It would be inappropriate to pass that information along to you, Mr. Kotnis."

"I understand. I'd complain more, but I don't want to be greedy." Kotnis shook the briefcase. "But remember, getting things here is just part of the trouble. You'll need distribution, and for that, you'll need local contacts." He turned around. "Don't worry. I won't hold a grudge, but I think we'll be talking again soon."

"No," the Agent replied. "That's unlikely." He sprang forward and brought up his arms.

Kotnis jerked his head to the side. "What are—"

The crunch of his snapping neck punctuated his sentence. The Agent let the body collapse to the ground, then walked over toward a nearby disposal vent. The meeting location had been chosen with great foresight. With a tap on his PNIU, the vent opened, having been hacked long before Kotnis arrived.

With a cluck of the tongue, the Agent tossed the briefcase into the large bin. He picked up the warm body and threw it among the fetid bags and scraps of metal inside. He'd been surprised his contact hadn't bothered to scout the meeting location beforehand. His arrogance at assuming an off-worlder would be at a disadvantage had cost Kotnis his life. He should have thought about why the Agent would want to meet in the lowest point of the floating city.

The Agent closed the vent door. Local exterior cameras had already been hacked. It'd be impossible to hack every camera in the city, but there was no reason for anyone to care about what was going out of a particular disposal vent.

Some of the vents in the upper levels employed sensors to make sure people weren't disposing of recyclable materials, but many of the lower vents were tasked toward industrial areas.

Lower cameras wouldn't be as much of a concern, and the other materials inside would cloak the body. He would take measures to suppress the data. As long as no one launched an immediate investigation, he should be fine.

The Agent pressed the hacked ejection panel. The door hissed closed, followed by harsh buzzing. A loud grinding was followed by a hiss as the material flew away from the bottom level of the cloud city of Parvati and headed toward the hellish surface of Venus. The planet itself would clean up after the Agent.

It was as if the universe wanted him to succeed.

CHAPTER THIRTY-FIVE

March 13, 2230, Neo Southern California Metroplex, Pacific Tactical Center

Emma paced in a ridiculous centuries-old red military uniform complete with tasseled epaulets, a curved black hat, and a riding crop.

She struck her palm with the crop.

"Listen up, fleshbags. This is your training briefing. Pay attention since I won't be repeating myself. I wore this outfit to *burn* this explanation into your minds."

Jia tried not to laugh. At first, she'd thought Emma hadn't changed much since her integration and stabilization, but beyond her penchant for a greater variety of clothes, there was less of a cruel edge to her humor.

The AI could now poke fun at herself. The arrogance remained, but they could see glimpses of the human underneath.

Erik watched Emma silently with a slight grin on his face. He already had his rifle simulator and other gear for the training. He'd told Jia a couple of minutes prior that the scenario had been designed by Emma. It was a complete mystery to him, something he hoped would happen more often going forward.

Emma snapped up the crop, and a hologram of a circular building appeared. A floor schematic appeared next, breaking apart into six different levels and rotating so Erik and Jia could better parse them.

"You have had recent experience dealing with the difficulty of having to protect a target," Emma offered without elaboration. They did their best to not talk about sensitive topics at the training center.

A place with so many cameras and recordings was a bad choice to discuss ID raids against secretive conspiracies. They could never be sure who might be listening.

Erik's eyes jumped from one spot on the tactical map of the building to another. "Base defense op, then?" he asked, then looked up. "Or we're guarding an individual?"

"The latter," Emma clarified. She pointed her riding crop at Erik. "In this simulation, you're both cops, the rogue kind who don't care about procedures and don't mind stirring up trouble as long as they get the gun goblins in the end." She smirked. "It shouldn't be hard for you to step into that role."

Jia chuckled. "Okay. What exactly are we rogue cops doing this time? What criminals are we pursuing?"

Images of scowling men in loose suits and bright shirts appeared. Most wore gold or silver chains around their necks. Their expressions varied between vapid and crazed.

"These are enforcers for the fictional Crazy Eight Syndicate. An informant is being held in a cell on the third floor of the building." Emma gestured to the schematic of that level. "He has important information on the syndicate's intent to poison a city as part of a ransom plan, but he also has the technical knowledge to disable the drones they intend to use. He was imprisoned after objecting to the cold-blooded nature of the plan." She wagged a finger. "Such evil gun goblins. He sent out an emergency message to you two rogue cops before they grabbed him and stowed him away. You'll have limited time to recover and defend him while he hacks their systems to prevent drone deployment and mass murder."

"Are they supposed to be criminals or terrorists?" Erik asked. "This sounds more like a terrorist operation."

"Poisoning a city for ransom is profit-oriented." Emma shrugged. "That strikes me as a gun goblin activity. Criminals aren't always reasonable. You know that far too well."

"Did you download a database of over-the-top action movies recently?" Jia chuckled. "Then again, with people like the Grayheads out there, how crazy is your idea?"

"Exactly. Now let's continue the briefing."

An image of a stout shaven-head man appeared. His clothing and chains were similar to those in the holograms of the other men, but he didn't have a crazed or stupid look on his face.

"This is the informant," Emma explained. "The Crazy Eights are furious that he betrayed them, but they're holding him for a public execution in two hours. They intend to time it to match their drone deployment to maximize fear."

"So, they're poisoning the city for money and doing

public executions? Erik arched a brow. "They're a very theatrical syndicate."

"As opposed to some of the ones you ran into on Mars?" Emma scoffed. "Most humans can't do anything violent for long periods without being theatrical. It's how they trick themselves into believing they are anything more than vicious animals who happened to use tools."

Jia circled with her hand. "The briefing, remember? You can insult fleshbags later."

"Of course." Emma narrowed her eyes at Erik. "Because in this scenario, you are rogue cops operating outside of procedures and the local police department. This metroplex is paralyzed by fear and corruption, so you will receive no external support. You have your rifles and a decent amount of ammo, but you used up all your grenades destroying a Crazy Eight APC that was guarding another building where you found the intelligence leading you to this place after receiving the message from the informant."

"This is a lot more elaborate background than we normally have for these scenarios," Jia commented. "Any particular reason?"

"Context is important." Emma cut through the air with her riding crop. "All the violence you've been involved with typically takes place within a particular context that limits your tactical options. I don't think it hurts to reinforce that line of thinking, do you?" She frowned. "Bikini babes might be amusing, but they're less likely to appear than murderous syndicates. I'm going to strive toward, if not realism, then at least the most likely scenarios."

Jia shrugged. "It wasn't a complaint, just an observation."

"You've been helping me with these scenarios for a while," Erik replied. "I'm confident you can put together something reasonable. Keep the no-win situations to a minimum. We don't need that kind of training. We need to keep up our muscle memory and tactical instincts."

"Noted, Erik." Emma shot him a cool look of disapproval, making Jia wonder how many no-win scenarios the AI wanted to try. "It's almost time to see if you can save the city."

The room turned dark as the syndicate base appeared in the distance, flitters soaring overhead. Jia didn't recognize the city, either by architecture or skyline. The lack of towers meant it wasn't any of the larger cities on Earth, but there weren't any obvious features marking it as anywhere other than Earth. Sparse, puffy clouds filled an otherwise familiar blue sky, and a single bright sun hung overhead.

Emma didn't mention anything about it being based on a real location, but most of their scenarios weren't based anywhere real. That didn't keep Jia's brain from distracting her by wanting to place the base in a real-world context.

"I'll give you fifteen minutes to examine the schematics and do your best to commit them to memory," Emma announced. "After that, I'll start the clock. Judging by your normal speed, it'll take you five minutes to arrive at the base from your current location. For purposes of the scenario, I've given you each a single breach disk since you've started carrying some of those around in my primary body."

"Wouldn't we have been able to download the schematics?" Jia asked.

"For the purpose of this scenario, a Crazy Eight system

defense destroyed the data while you were examining it." Emma smiled. "You can't tell me that kind of thing is unrealistic."

Erik shook his head. "Not going to make it easy for us."

"No, and none of your enemies going forward will either." Emma saluted. "You'll thank me the next time you destroy an insane syndicate threatening a city with poison gas and performing public executions."

"I'm dubious that exact scenario will happen," Jia replied. "But you never know."

"You also get one Emma simulation," Emma declared.

"And what's that?"

"Simply say, 'Emma, we need your help' or something to that effect. After that, a three- to five-minute randomly determined period will elapse. That will simulate the time it needs for me to hack a system. For this scenario, it will temporarily shut down the internal cameras and communications, giving you more freedom of movement, but that will only hold for a short period as they regain control of their system."

"How long is the short period?" Erik asked.

"It could be thirty seconds, or it could be ten minutes." Emma shrugged. "You never know about the possible defenses in the real world, so I see no reason why you should have the information for this training situation."

"Okay, but there's one thing I don't get." Erik pointed at Emma's uniform. "If this is supposed to be about us being rogue cops, why are you in that getup? We're attacking a syndicate base, not doing a cavalry charge against some ancient country still learning how to use cannons."

"I like this outfit." Emma huffed. "Keep talking, and I'll

decrease your time limit." She wagged a finger. "But for now, the situation is set up under the assumption you're wearing tactical vests. It'll still hurt if you get shot."

Jia shouldered her rifle. "I'm used to it. At least I won't need a medpatch after this is done."

Erik and Jia darted down the narrow streets and alleys leading to the bottom level of the syndicate base. Emma hadn't mentioned what kind of drone defenses the enemy possessed, but neither of them had seen a single drone on their initial approach.

Jia peeked around a street corner toward a side entrance. Two guards strolled by the door, chatting quietly as they curved around the building. For a group of murderous criminals about to poison half the city, they looked relaxed.

"According to the schematic, this is where the blind spot is," Jia commented. "Let's just wait for them to get out of sight and go for it." She looked up and around, making sure she didn't miss anyone in odd places. "I don't think we should split up."

Erik nodded. "Yeah, not when there are only two of us. We can't risk the elevators, so we'll have to take the stairs."

"His cell's on the third floor. That's not so bad. We can use our Emma call to disable the cameras once we hit the second floor. We'll head toward one set of stairs before we do that, then cut to the other to draw them off." Jia tapped her head. "I memorized where all the stairs were on each level."

"Sounds good," Erik declared, surveying the area. "Without reinforcements, we might risk running out of ammo if we have to defend him against the entire syndicate."

"We'll have to borrow a gun or two off the organic gun suppliers," Jia replied. "It won't be the first time."

"You're calling dead bodies 'organic gun suppliers?'"

"I think Emma's red outfit got in my mind."

"I see."

"No, you don't."

"You're right, I don't." He sighed. "Eventually, we're going to just walk around 24/7 with carryaids filled with ammo," Erik finished with a grin. "It'd make sense, given our luck."

"Then I'd suggest we grab a couple of guns when we clear each area." Jia switched her fire selector to single-fire mode. "And let's hope they don't have anything tougher than normal thugs in there."

Erik shrugged. "It's supposed to be a syndicate. They might have some Tin Men, but nothing as tough as what we've fought before."

Jia stared at him, trying hard to not look annoyed. "We've dealt with syndicates with exoskeletons, APCs, and missile launchers."

"That just means more stuff for us to *borrow*." Erik nodded toward the door. "Let's get ready. On three." He waited until the guards moved out of sight and held up a finger, then a second and a third.

Jia and Erik burst around the corner and charged toward the door. There were still no drones overhead. They arrived at the door without incident.

She yanked out her breach disk. After pressing it against the door, she armed the device with a quick twist and stepped back, her hand dropping to her PNIU.

"Breaching," Jia declared, then looked away and tapped her device.

A roar was accompanied by a bright white flash. The explosion blasted the pieces of the door inward. Flaming metal fragments ripped into two guards near the door, knocking them to the floor in a bloodied and burned mess.

It wasn't pleasant.

Erik rushed through the new hole, sweeping his rifle back and forth, but there wasn't anyone in the small room. The door to a hallway already stood open. Shouts and footfalls came from the other end.

Jia crouched, pulled a pistol off one of the dead men, and tucked it into her belt. She tossed the other pistol to Erik. "We might as well get the restocking started while we're not getting shot at." She hopped to her feet. "Our best bet is in the middle of the hallway." She charged out of the room without waiting for a response. Erik sprinted after her, naturally moving to the other side of the hall.

Four men emerged from a room farther down. Jia and Erik lined up shots without a word, each taking the target closest to them. Without slowing, each fired a single round, downing the men with shots through the chest.

Another volley sent the next pair to join them in virtual death.

Their latest victims had emerged from rooms past the stairs. Jia slowed for a moment to consider the necessity of stripping the weapons, but time wasn't on their side. For the plan to work, Erik and Jia would need to get to the second floor before the syndicate forces had time to rally.

If the enemy surrounded them, they had no chance of survival.

She pushed herself, barreling toward the entrance to the stairs and hoping they weren't sealed. Erik fired from behind her and killed more new arrivals. There was still no alarm, but the shouts were growing louder and closer.

Jia arrived at the entrance to the stairs and slapped the access panel, her heart pounding. The door slid open. She spun to the side, but no bullets greeted her, so she lunged into the stairwell, seeking an enemy. Her caution was rewarded by the sight of a six-legged security bot leaping down the stairs toward her. She jumped out of the way, avoiding its stun rod and downed it with two quick shots.

Erik fired before running into the stairwell and closing the door.

More security bots skittered from above. What they lacked in defensive instinct, they made up for in numbers. Jia and Erik didn't waste time or bullets as they blasted away, reloading as necessary, until there was nothing but a pile of smoking, sparking bots.

Jia bounded up the stairs, taking them two at a time and jumping over bot corpses. The next floor was close, and the pair hadn't taken any hits yet. The temptation to use Emma grew with each step, but the plan necessitated waiting.

She arrived at the second-level door and waited for Erik to catch up. "We'll make it look like we're going to the middle access stairs, just like we did here, then we hit the long stairs. We won't pull off all their forces, but if we cut them in half, that makes impossible merely unlikely."

"We'll have to fight our way to them," Erik noted.

"There was never any other option." Jia pointed her gun at the door. "Open it. Okay, Emma, begin hacking."

CHAPTER THIRTY-SIX

"The hack is complete, I'm ready to kill their comms and cameras," Emma declared with a smug certitude that was not much different than in a normal scenario.

Jia strapped a gangster's rifle over her left shoulder. It was convenient that the enemies were using rifles with straps, but she wasn't going to complain if Emma wanted to throw them a mild advantage in the otherwise ridiculous scenario.

Erik tossed aside an empty rifle.

He'd decided to defend their current position using borrowed weapons. They'd fought for a couple of minutes, with increasing numbers of gangsters closing on their position, made easier by the pair's purposeful slow walk toward the first set of stairs.

"Do it," Erik ordered.

"Comms and cameras killed, but local security bots are still active," Emma replied. "It's a separate system, sorry."

Jia and Erik immediately ripped away from their location and headed down the hall, catching some new arrivals off-guard. The gangsters died from headshots before they could aim.

Their killers rushed past them, leaving their weapons and ammo behind. Jia hadn't counted the number of enemy casualties. She had no idea of their original strength, so there wasn't much point. The less she needed to track, the better.

"There they are!" someone shouted from behind them. "Get those bastards. They killed Victor and Alex!"

The unfortunate snitch joined Victor and Alex when Erik and Jia put a bullet in his head. Ten seconds of running and gunning ended with a new pile of dead gangsters and a slight sting in Jia's back. Sometimes she worried about Emma hacking the tactical center equipment to push it past the safety limits, but she tried to squash the thought. The AI might have a twisted sense of humor, but she had never purposely attempted to hurt Erik or Jia.

Sweat dripped off Jia's face. Her lungs burned from all the running, but she'd arrived at the far stairs. From there, some quick sprints and turns would bring them to the room holding their target. The doors to the stairs opened.

"Dammit!" More bots scrambled through.

The overlapping cracks of the rifles echoed in the narrow hallway. Their bullets ripped through the bots with ease. Jia realized it was too easy. Emma hadn't specified they were given AP rounds, but all of the bullets, even the ones from the stolen weapons, were performing as if they were just that.

She doubted Emma had overlooked such a detail. Perhaps the AI reasoned that under normal circumstances, Erik and Jia were likely to bring along AP ammo. At that moment, it didn't matter, other than helping them clear out the determined bot squad.

Erik hit the doorway first this time and then the stairs, his rifle up and his expression showing he was ready and eager for more bots or gangsters.

He ran up the stairs, grunting with exertion. Jia followed only seconds behind. With all the adrenaline-fueled running they were doing, they probably could have won a race, despite all the weapons and ammo weighing them down.

He slapped the access panel, and the third-floor door opened without incident. Erik stopped at the edge of the doorway, frowning and listening. Jia took up a position on the other side. They could hear footsteps and yells, but none close by. Their gambit had worked. Now they needed to get to the prisoner and set up a defensive position.

The risk of tipping off the enemy was too great, so neither Erik nor Jia said a word. They ran toward the makeshift cell, alternating taking point when they hit a corner. To Jia's surprise, they arrived at their destination without running into any more enemies, not even a bot.

It wasn't a prison. It looked like a converted storage room with a sealed closet. A desk and chair stood in the corner, and a PNIU lay on top of the desk. Another large desk sat opposite the first. Jia headed to the cell door and slapped the access panel.

The door didn't open.

"Of course," she grumbled. "That'd be too easy."

"The enemy has almost regained control of their system," Emma reported. "They will soon have cameras and communications. They appear to be ready to activate jamming equipment as well."

Jia rolled her eyes. She didn't think it was realistic that random syndicate techs could overwhelm Emma so quickly, but the AI had already bent the simulation in so many ways to their advantage that complaining would come off as petty.

Erik pulled out his breach disk. "This is our only choice. If we get killed before he can even start his hack, it won't matter how many guys we took out; the city's dead."

Jia turned and pointed her weapon the way they'd come. "I'll cover our backs until we're in."

"Get the hell away from the door!" Erik bellowed, hoping the prisoner could hear him. Otherwise, this scenario was going to end badly for a different reason. He slapped the breach disk against the door and armed it. "Breach!"

When Jia had used her disk, they were outdoors. This time, the loud, echoing boom assaulted her ears. It was a perfect signal to tell everyone in the building where they were. The door disintegrated, and acrid smoke billowed from the fragments. Their informant stood inside, not showing any emotion. Emma's programming hadn't been as thorough as her attention to uniform costume details.

"Come on!" Erik shouted at the informant.

The balding man walked carefully out of the cell, stepping over burning debris. He ran over to the desk and grabbed the PNIU. After placing it on his belt, he brought up a virtual keyboard and a pair of data windows. "I need five minutes to complete my work."

"Can't we do this from outside?" Erik asked.

The informant shook his head. "I need the direct systems access I get from inside. There's no way to prevent the launch in time if I try to hack in externally. They accelerated the drone deployment schedule. We have less than thirty minutes left."

"Thirty minutes?" Erik's lips pressed together. "She did slip some surprises in here."

Jia rushed over to the other desk. "Help me with this."

With Erik's help, they dragged it to block the entrance to the room. They piled their collected enemy weapons on the chair to the side. It wasn't a hardened bunker, but it was better than nothing.

"This would technically be a suicide mission with this setup," Erik noted, grabbing one of the syndicate rifles.

"In a real scenario, we probably would have gone ahead and called for reinforcements," Jia suggested. "Even if the cops were totally in the pocket of the syndicate, some of them wouldn't stand by for a terrorist ransom."

"I've killed the cameras leading up to this room," the informant explained, his fingers flying over the virtual keyboard. "But the only way to do it was to kill my access, too. Hold them off while I do my work."

Jia took up a position at the edge of the desk. "I wonder if Emma hid grenades somewhere?"

Erik knelt and flipped this rifle to burst fire. "Probably, but if we spend a lot of time looking for something like that, we will be overwhelmed. The only reason we got this far was surprise."

The thud of heavy boots announced syndicate reinforcements.

Jia wouldn't challenge the realism of the men fighting

so hard. She'd been surprised how courageous, if stupid, common thugs could be in these situations, let alone terrorists. When the first syndicate thug turned the corner, she greeted him with a headshot between the eyes.

Erik's burst perforated the chest of another man. He tossed his borrowed rifle to the side and snatched up another one.

Jia waited, taking careful shots. The thugs changed their strategy, some rushing across their exposed gap. They took up positions on either side and squeezed off shots into the storage room. Bullets ripped through the metal desk.

"I need four more minutes!" the informant yelled.

Jia didn't fire blindly. She squeezed off a round whenever an enemy on her side exposed himself. It wasn't enough to kill them, but it kept them suppressed. Erik sprayed bursts near the opposite wall to the same effect. One thug took a moment of quiet as an opportunity to charge. Erik and Jia each put a round into him.

More shouts came from up ahead. The enemy was getting reinforcements. If they were brave enough, they might be able to overwhelm the position with sheer numbers. Screams ripped through the hallway. Something bright flashed from around the corner.

"Kill it!" yelled a thug.

The gangsters who had been pinning Erik and Jia down rushed in one direction, allowing Jia and Erik to pick some off. A loud, dissonant buzzing followed another flash and more screams. Heavy gunfire rang out.

"What the hell is going on now?" Erik asked.

"I need three minutes," the informant explained.

"I think reinforcements arrived," Jia guessed, rolling her

shoulders. "I'm not going to complain about a nice surprise. It's not like it never happens in actual missions."

The buzzing sounded after another bright flash. A single blackened hand fell past the intersection. The gunfire went silent.

"What was that noise?" Jia asked. "It doesn't sound like a stun rifle. It's way too loud." She gestured with her rifle toward the scorched hand. "And it doesn't do that."

They both fell silent, taking shallow breaths and listening. There was a crackling noise, but no footsteps and no more screams. Something bright was near the intersection. The crackling grew louder second by second. Strange noises mixed with it. They sounded like muffled cooing.

The unusual combination of noises nibbled at Jia's concentration. There was something about them she recognized, but she couldn't pull out the necessary memory.

"Whoever it is, they might not be coming our way," Erik whispered.

Jia nodded slowly, trying to put together the mental clues. Emma could be capricious, but she'd want them to figure it out. That had to be why the new arrival was moving so slowly.

"Two minutes," the informant called.

More coos came, as if in response to the informant. The crackling sounded closer now. Whatever it was, the informant had gotten its attention.

Crackling. Cooing. Flashes of light.

Jia's eyes widened. "You've got to be kidding me!"

Erik glanced her way. "What? You know what's coming?"

"So much for realistic training," she muttered. "Yes. It's not like I've ever seen one, but I've read about them and watched the available footage. It's a Leem."

A short, spindly gray-skinned humanoid alien turned the corner, its large solid-black eyes set in a bulbous head surrounding its tiny nose and crowding its thin slit of a mouth. Four fingers extended from the end of its long limbs. It clutched a thin clear rod with three prongs at the end. White-blue energy arced across its body in jagged, irregular lines, a so-called lightning shield. It matched the weapon in his hand, which was a lightning gun.

"A damned Leem?" Erik barked. "Why the hell would a Leem be in a syndicate base? That doesn't make any sense, Emma!"

"We're not with the criminals," Jia called. "We're here to stop a terrorist attack. We mean you no harm."

The Leem stopped moving and cocked its head. More cooing sounded. Jia had no idea if that meant it understood her. If Emma had added an alien into an otherwise reasonable scenario, there would be some minor underlying logic. Jia needed to identify it to take advantage of it.

"One minute," the informant explained.

The alien took a few steps back, its movements oddly graceful. It raised the lightning gun and cooed again. A crackling multi-forked bolt of white energy shot out and blasted the desk, blowing a hole through it and knocking it over.

"Shit," Erik muttered. "I think that ends your intergalactic diplomatic career."

Jia opened fire. Hissing, the bullets vaporized upon contact with the lightning shield. She switched to fully automatic and emptied her magazine, but accomplished nothing but wasting bullets.

"I'd kill for a laser rifle or a plasma grenade right now," she complained, ducking behind the wall. A lighting blast barreled through, narrowly missing her. She retreated farther and slapped a fresh magazine into her weapon.

"Thirty seconds," the informant shouted.

Another lightning blast shot through the room and punched a hole in the back wall, which started burning. Jia couldn't see the alien now, but judging by the sound of his shield, he was less than ten meters away.

Erik snickered. "At least he's not wearing a bikini."

"Okay, I'll give Emma that," Jia replied. "I think we're screwed. I thought this wasn't supposed to be a no-win situation."

"I wonder if I could get my arm through that shield," Erik mused. "It's worth a shot."

"Twenty seconds," the information called.

"No-win." Jia's breath caught. "We already committed to the suicidal last stand. We just need to do the easy part now. Sit here until the end."

The Leem offered two more lightning blasts in quick succession. They annihilated what remained of the desk, leaving a half-molten mess and a scorched floor.

"Ten seconds!"

Jia took a deep breath and tossed her rifle forward. The Leem blasted it in half and let out another coo. It was close enough now that the light of its shield flickered near the doorway, and its shadow stretched into the room.

"I've done it!" the informant called. "I've stopped the drones!" A second later, a lightning blast struck him in the back. He jerked forward, his head bouncing off the table before disappearing.

The Leem took one step into the room and froze, along with its lightning shield. Jia stared at it, wondering if her eyes were playing tricks on her. The Leem vanished.

Emma appeared in the middle of the room, still in her red uniform from earlier. She saluted. "Congratulations. You passed the defense scenario."

Jia rolled her eyes. "Look, I get it with the ridiculous stuff we've done in the past, but I thought this was supposed to be a more realistic scenario."

"I'm not sure." Erik stood and chuckled. "It's not impossible. They *have* been to Earth before."

Emma nodded her agreement, grinning. "Exactly. A simple probability analysis of the kind of events that happen to you suggests that, if anything, it's a much higher probability for you two than the general populace."

"But a Leem?" Jia complained. "Come on."

"How do we know when we get to the end of our investigation, there won't be aliens?" Erik asked.

"Now you sound like your old neighbor," Jia mocked.

"Not saying I think that's it. Never count on aliens when you can point to a corrupt, self-serving human, but you never know." He shrugged.

Jia sighed. "I'll grant that it's not impossible. At least it wasn't wearing a bikini."

CHAPTER THIRTY-SEVEN

March 15, 2230, Neo Southern California Metroplex, En Route to Private Hangar

Jia folded her arms, tapping her foot in impatience as the MX 60 zoomed toward the hangar. "That's all Lanara said? 'Come and see the new toy? Our boss took the other one away.'"

Erik nodded. "I'm guessing Alina finally delivered the new in-system ship. She didn't make it sound like it was going to take that long at first, but I'm still surprised."

"It'll be nice to have a better body," Emma commented. "Now that I know I'm meant for ship-based greatness, it only makes sense that I'm not restricted to a flitter or a small transport. I can't wait until we have access to the main jump ship."

"We'll have to see." Erik loosened his grip on the yoke. "But one thing I'll say about Alina, she does provide nice toys."

"Well, damn," Erik managed to get out. He'd been expecting a jumped up military scout; something with a little more juice than the Rabbit, but not much more comfortable.

All that went away when she directed them to a back area of the spaceport, with obvious guards and a hangar far larger than he suspected they would need.

While he wasn't wrong, he was pretty far from being right.

Instead, a triangular black ship was parked in the hangar. While not a capital ship, the vessel was much longer than the Rabbit, and despite being twice as wide and tall, the slender design, with curves in all the right places, made it look thinner in his mental comparison.

Alina sat atop stairs that unfolded from the underneath. She motioned to the ship. "This is your new ship, the *Argo*. It'll be able to interface with the main jump ship, but the DD is still working on installing the jump drive into the larger ship. I wouldn't expect it for at least a month."

"Larger ship?" Erik whispered. "This is…significant."

Emma winked into existence in a white-and-blue sailor uniform about two centuries out of date. "This is much better suited for me."

"Let me show you around. I think you'll like it." Alina stood and motioned inside the ship toward the cockpit.

Erik and Jia jogged over to the stairs and hurried up. Unlike the cramped cockpit of the *Pegasus*, the *Argo's* cockpit held four large, comfy chairs with lots of space between them, but only two in front of the customized control panel.

Cutter reclined in one of the chairs, his head rested on

his threaded fingers. "Blackwell, Lin, Holochick. This ship is great! Screw that garbage scow we were flying before. You should see the thruster layout on this thing. Better thrust, more maneuverable. All-around better."

"That's nice." Erik looked around the cockpit. There were a lot of pointlessly shiny surfaces that looked nice but weren't functional.

"What about defenses?" Jia asked. "When you described this before, you made it sound like it'd be far more dangerous than the transport."

Alina tapped her PNIU.

A holographic schematic of the ship appeared. She pointed to a bulge at the top and bottom. "Four deployable offensive laser turrets, two top and two bottom, and deployable short-range point-defense lasers top and bottom. They're shielded well enough that you'll get past most decent Customs scans as long as they aren't deployed. You also have a plasma torpedo launcher, but don't go firing those things all the time. You'll only be able to store eight in this ship. The main jump ship can be used for more storage, but that's a ways off. By the way, the *Argo* has a grav shield, too."

Jia's lips parted in disbelief. "A *grav* shield on something this small?"

"Cutting edge technology." Alina motioned around her. "Also has energy-dispersive nanofilm embedded directly into the hull. It's not going to make you immune to laser attacks, but it'll take some of the punch out. It also has advanced self-repair systems. With that, Lanara, and Emma, you can operate away from real support for a long time."

Erik whistled. "Nice. This thing's practically a Fleet cutter. At least we won't get our asses handed to us by pirates if we ever go out to the frontier."

"That's the idea." Alina gestured to the door in the back of the cockpit. She walked that way and opened it, revealing a room filled with wall lockers and stairs leading below decks. "Just a storage room, but it's nice for this sort of thing." She tapped the PNIU, and the panel slid down, concealing the lockers. "It makes for a nice emergency armory." Another door led them into a large galley with separate prep areas and two tables.

"Lot more space for sure," Jia commented as they walked into the eating area. "We won't be tripping over ourselves. It'll be nice if we have to take a longer trip. I'm assuming the jump drive won't pop us into another system instantly?"

Alina nodded. "It's faster than heading to an HTP, but there are still limitations. Don't worry about those for now. I'm sure the researcher you will have onboard can answer your questions when it comes time to use the drive. Let me show you the rest of the ship first."

"Wait." Erik frowned. "The DD's guy is already here?"

"Yes. He's in the engine room talking to Lanara. Don't worry, you'll like him." Alina furrowed her brow. "I think." She inclined her head toward the door.

They followed her into a narrow passageway. Two doors faced each other halfway down, and a wider door lay at the end. Another set of stairs to the lower deck was right next to the door.

Alina gestured to the closer doors like a flight attendant. "Those are the two largest crew cabins on the ship.

There are six more on the bottom deck. Each can sleep two with ease, or more if you needed to. That room at the end is a fully operational nano-AR room."

"Seriously?" Erik chuckled. "That's nice."

"It's not huge. If more than one person is using it, you'd need to simulate a scenario where you both could mostly sit, but otherwise, yes, it's fully operational. I'm sure you can find a use for it." Alina winked. "Especially with Emma's help."

The stairs led to the considerably less glamorous but huge cargo bay. The exoskeletons, scout bikes, and mini-flitters were already secured, along with the crates and boxes that had been aboard the Rabbit.

Jia jogged into the center of the cargo bay and spun with her arms out. Erik wondered if she had been like this as a teenager. "This is *huge.*" She stopped twirling. "We could easily get both our flitters in here, with plenty of space to spare."

"Sure, I suppose." Erik walked forward, craning his neck upward. "Lots of possibilities."

"We'll bring my flitter." Jia gestured to a vehicle docking port on the wall and loading arms in the back. "Lanara can mod it like yours when she has time. It might take a while between other projects, but we'll eventually get to the point where we'll have redundancy."

The door opened, and a handsome young olive-skinned man with dark hair rushed in. He gasped, and his eyes widened.

He pointed at Erik and Jia. "It's really them! The Obsidian Detective and Lady Justice."

The two ex-detectives were silent for a moment.

Erik broke the ice. "We don't go by those names anymore."

"This is Raphael Maras." Alina nodded toward the man. "He's a genius, and he's been working on the jump drive project for a couple of years."

Raphael charged Erik with surprising speed and thrust his hand out. "It's an honor to meet you, sir."

Erik shook the man's hand, eyeing him with disbelief. "You can just call me Erik."

"And I'm fine with Jia." The woman in question extended her hand with a warm smile.

Raphael took it and pumped her hand with both of his. "I'm a big fan. I've read all about you on the news, and Agent Koval briefed me about the moon and Mars missions. I wanted to do research in the DD so I could help heroes, but I never thought I'd work in the field *with* heroes."

"We're just two people who do our jobs," Erik offered with a disarming smile. "Well."

"Oh, this is so cool." Raphael clapped and rubbed his hands together. "I'm sure you have many awesome stories. I can see it now." He lowered his voice. "And that's when I shoved the missile directly down the *yaoguai's* throat and said, 'Chew on this.'"

"I'll have to remember that line in case I run into that situation." Erik thought for a moment before adding, "Ok, run into that situation *again*."

Raphael shook his finger at Erik. "That's what I'm talking about. I've never even seen a *yaoguai*, and you've blown up tons of them. Nanozombies? I mean, give me a break! *Nanozombies!*"

Alina cleared her throat. "Were you finished with Lanara?"

"No." His shoulders slumped.

"Go finish up for now," Alina ordered. "It might be necessary to control jumps from this ship when docked with the main ship. The more prepared you are for that, the easier it'll be when the DD is ready to hand over the jump ship."

"Yes, Agent Koval."

Alina pointed with her thumb. "The maintenance bay's that way, and past it are the other crew cabins."

With a huge sigh, Raphael slunk toward the door. He offered one mournful, disappointed look over his shoulder before disappearing through it and closing it behind him.

"You've outdone yourself, Alina," Erik offered. "This is the kind of ship you could live on for months."

"That's the basic idea," she replied. "We don't *know* where your work will take you in the future, and the more home and equipment you can bring with you, the more flexible you'll be. We're still getting a lot of dividends from the New Year's raid, and I suspect it's going to end up pointing us to a lot of different places." Her smile faded into a slight frown. "I'd love to give you more time to familiarize yourself with the *Argo*, but there's a little something I need you to follow up on."

Erik offered her a smirk. "We're good. We both had our birthdays already."

"What's going on?" Jia asked. "Is this about the Brotherhood?"

Alina nodded. "Yes. Some of our intel points to possible low-level activity on Venus, specifically the cloud city of

Pavarti. We only came upon this in the last couple of days, but when our local agent looked into it, she came across something odd: a missing person report for one Dipankar Kotnis. This man has been investigated in the past for low-level smuggling. A couple of days before he was reported missing, there was someone who went to the local police and swore they saw a body falling from the city."

"How did he see a body falling from the city?" Jia asked.

"He was a maintenance tech remote-piloting a drone as part of standard integrity checks," Alina replied. "You know how it is with those Venusian floating cities. It's not grav fields keeping them up for the most part, but buoyancy. Too many leaks, and they might lose altitude." She shrugged.

"Why don't they just analyze the image?"

"Some technical glitch, apparently." Alina frowned, doubt in her eyes. "He didn't have a recording of the incident, and none of the external city cameras caught anything like that."

Jia rubbed her chin, her brow furrowed in thought. "He might have just been seeing shadows in the clouds."

"Possibly."

"If this Kotnis was a criminal, how do we know it has anything to do with the Brotherhood?" Erik asked.

"We don't," Alina admitted. "Other than some scant evidence decrypted from the information that might potentially line up with the timeline of Kotnis' disappearance, and some unusual transport records activity that suggests smuggling. It won't hurt to double-check. The last of the Brotherhood might be hiding there. I want you two to rendezvous with a local ID agent who is investigating and provide active support. Her name is Priya Bora. Get settled, grab whatever gear you need, and get your butts to Venus. You might have more monsters to slay."

"We have been sitting around for too long," Jia agreed.

Erik raised an eyebrow. "Do you want to bet a Leem is involved?"

"No way." Jia winced. "I don't want to tempt fate."

Alina's brow scrunched in confusion. "What are you talking about? You know what?" She waved a hand. "I don't want to know."

CHAPTER THIRTY-EIGHT

"Reactor fully online." Jia tapped on a suite of glowing controls on the main panel in the cockpit. "Internal grav field steady. Grav compensators all within tolerances. Thruster diagnostics are all green. Please crosscheck."

Cutter's fingers flew over his own set of controls in the seat next to Jia's. "Check confirmed. We've got clearance from Port Control. We're ready to make this boat fly."

Erik sat in one of the rear seats, watching them in silence.

For all his varied skills, he didn't know anything useful about piloting, and he didn't care about learning either. With Cutter, Jia, and Emma available, his team didn't lack for pilots.

He had other talents he was going to develop, ones that didn't have anything to do with missions. Not that he wanted to mention that with Raphael sitting beside him, straining at his harnesses like an overeager child on his first vacation.

"You sure you shouldn't be in the engine room?" Erik

asked, not doing much to keep the irritation out of his tone. He'd rather have an eager fanboy than an angry asshole, but if he could choose neither, he would.

Raphael shook his head hard. "No. Lanara's got all that handled. I won't have much to do until the higher-ups hand over the jump ship. Then it's my time to shine. I'm like the Obsidian Detective of jump drive maintenance." He fluffed his collar. "I don't know if I'm allowed to say that, but it's true."

"Sure." Erik nodded slowly. "I have no reason to doubt it."

Raphael beamed a broad smile at him. "Thanks, Erik. I appreciate that."

A chastening word or two might be helpful for the future, but Erik's further comments were preempted by two massive hangar doors pulling apart. Bright sunlight from outside streamed inside. Something felt different about this trip. He wasn't sure why it would. It wasn't as if this was his first off-world trip for Alina. He settled on one possible explanation.

"It helps that this ship is bigger." Erik smiled.

Jia smirked over her shoulder at him. "The other ship got us from place to place fine. Overcompensate much?"

Erik scoffed. "A man doesn't need to overcompensate if he already has all the equipment he needs. And now that I have my own cabin, I can bring my penjing stuff next time. If I'm going to fly all over the UTC, I need *all* of my relaxation tools."

Raphael clapped and let out a delighted laugh. "Wow. Actual banter! It's just like I imagined it. Oh, I never knew you were into penjing." He furrowed his brow. "Whatever that is."

"A Chinese art involving making miniature landscapes with carefully cut and formed trees," Jia explained with a soft smile. "It is kind of strange to think of him doing it, but he's actually very good."

"Wow." Raphael nodded and stared at Erik in awe. "You're so deep, Erik. I feel like I understand you better now."

Erik ignored the fanboy with a grunt and focused on the liftoff.

The *Argo* rumbled as the main thrusters kicked on, lifting her off the ground. Data windows spread out between Jia and Cutter contained numerous graphs, numbers, and other text. The only things Erik could understand with a quick glance were the camera feeds and the radar and lidar displays.

"Taking us out now." Cutter licked his lips. "It's nice to have a proper ship again. It's like someone I'm sure was very important said: 'A musician with a crap instrument can't be blamed for poor performance.'"

Erik chuckled. "Isn't the saying the exact opposite?"

Cutter furrowed his brow. "Like what?"

"It's a poor musician who blames his instrument," Jia offered with a smirk.

"That doesn't even make sense." Cutter scoffed.

The ship hovered out of the hangar, its current speed a crawl. Most of the work was performed by the bottom thrusters and grav emitters. The mazelike skyline of Neo SoCal came into view, along with the swarms of dots in the distance—the omnipresent flitters of the metroplex. Some other smaller ships nearby cruised past, all expensive yachts or personal transports.

All lacked the menace of the *Argo*.

Erik wondered what they thought. Mistaking the ship for a very large syndicate toy wouldn't be unreasonable. It was impossible for someone to look at the ship and not be at least somewhat unsettled.

They might not need to see the hidden weapons, but a cloak of feral hunger hung around the ship.

"Retracting landing struts." Jia ran her fingers down a control panel to her far left, her voice and posture firm.

Erik expected to hear or feel something but didn't. On the old ship, he could hear every part of the ship whenever anything changed. It was more proof of the superior quality of this ship.

Not knowing anything different, he assumed the new ship proved Alina had been hedging her bets.

"Final approval, and our window is open," Jia announced.

"Everyone strapped in?" Cutter asked with a grin. He angled the ship up and increased thruster power.

"WOOHOOO!" Raphael yelled.

The acceleration pushed everyone back in their seats.

Neo SoCal grew farther away in the rear display. The flitters became mere specks and the buildings rough suggestions of shapes. Erik didn't want to know how things would have felt without the grav emitters mostly compensating for the acceleration.

He'd experienced those forces before on damaged Fleet ships, and it'd given him a firm respect for Fleet combat pilots.

"Continuing orbital burn." Cutter yelped in excitement. "That's it, baby. Burn that gas. Get us into space. Give Papa Cutter the performance he deserves."

Jia rolled her eyes and shook her head, but a small smile played across her lips. Cutter might not be a brave warrior, but he'd proven himself on the station, and he hadn't been hired to do anything but fly.

Erik waited for Emma to appear and say something. Unlike on their old ship, they'd directly interfaced her in the engine room rather than in the cockpit at her request.

She could hear everything on the ship anyway, so it wasn't like she was that far away from Cutter, the man she respected and disliked at the same time. Maybe she had her own form of out-of-sight, out-of-mind she wanted to practice.

"Venus, here we come." Erik grinned. A moment later, he scratched his chin. "It's been a while since we've been off-world. I hope we don't have to cause too much damage."

Raphael shook his head. "You have to take down the bad guys. Collateral damage is just part of it." He air-punched imaginary foes.

Jia laughed. "You just want to see us blow up cyborgs."

"Is that wrong?" Raphael muttered.

"Don't worry." Erik shot him an eager grin. "We haven't had a job for Alina yet that didn't end with lots of shooting and explosions."

Raphael beamed, his excitement back.

A half-hour later, Erik was transfixed by the beautiful blue Earth on one of the cameras. Satellites, space stations, and ships might encase it in a loose cloud, but the small imperfections couldn't obscure the beauty of humanity's homeworld.

He'd spent most of his career away from the planet, and he'd forgotten how beautiful it could be. Far too many colonies were nothing but domes on worlds that would take decades or centuries to turn what they had to even half as much life.

His trips to the moon, the prison station, and Mars had reminded him of that precious beauty, and now with the jaunt to Venus. He wondered how long it would be before he grew complacent and jaded again.

"We're looking at a day and a half to Venus, right?" Erik unbuckled his harness and stretched. He shot a sideways glance at Raphael, who had somehow fallen asleep in the last few minutes, like an overexcited child on a trip to an amusement park.

He shook his head and chuckled, still not sure if he liked the man.

Jia nodded. "It's a straightforward flight. It won't be that long before we can turn things over to Emma for the main flight. She can handle accelerating and not changing course."

"But if we had that jump ship…" Erik turned toward the sleeping Raphael. "We could get there quicker? Instantly, even?"

"That's crazy." Cutter whistled in excitement. "But it kind of takes the fun out of things. Who needs pilots if you can get everywhere instantly?"

"I don't know much more about it than what Alina told us." Jia shrugged, her brow lined with concern. "But I don't think it'll be that simple. If anything, it's not like we'll ever be able to open up a hyperspace gate directly on a planet, not to mention that we have to be careful with the thing."

Erik rubbed his chin. "Yeah, you're right. Alina and Adeyemi pulled a lot of strings to get us access to the ship, and if we're morons with it, the DD will come take it and Emma."

The AI appeared, her fashion statement that day a black jumpsuit with her name on a nametape and large patches reading AI on her shoulders. "If you keep me in here, they'll never be able to take me without destroying this ship, but you do have a point. I imagine the primary use of the jump drive won't be in quick intersystem travel, but rather avoiding a long trip to the HTP. The technology is going to remain classified for some time for obvious reasons."

Jia considered the matter. "Space is big. It's hard to hide a fleet, but it's easy to hide a ship. We'll probably have to park it somewhere and fly around in the *Argo* under normal circumstances."

"I don't mean to be a major downer," Cutter began, his gaze shifting between Erik, Jia, and Emma, "but it'd be pretty dumbass to park an experimental military jump ship somewhere it could be stolen. If we're all on this ship, who's going to guard that one?" He inclined his head toward Emma. "Even Holochick can only be two places at once when you don't have to worry about the speed of light."

Emma folded her arms, grim determination settling

over her face. "As much as it pains me to admit it, Mr. Durn is right. That is something we need to consider."

Raphael's bolted upright. "AI?" he mumbled sleepily.

"Yes, I am. What of it?" Emma glared at him.

The scientist yawned, blinked his eyes, and wiped them. "The jump ship has a military-grade AI installed. A backup. It can't handle jump navigation, but it can handle most of the other things." He looked around like he was making sure he knew where in space he was. "That should be enough, right?"

Emma scoffed. "You mean it has an inferior non-self-aware system installed. Please. You might as well hand it over to the Ascended Brotherhood right now if you're going to depend on a toy like that."

Jia gestured to Cutter. "With a skilled pilot in control, it won't matter. It's not like Cutter is dying to be close to the action."

He gave her a sheepish grin. "I already filled my getting-shot quota with you guys. I'm supposed to be the pilot, and you guys are supposed to be the muscle."

"Maybe Raphael, too." Erik nodded slowly, the idea growing in appeal. "If all you guys have to do is outrun people until we show up, things get a lot easier."

Raphael gasped, his eyes widening. "No, no, no. You can't do that. You can't stick me on the jump ship."

"Why not?" Erik asked. "Your job is to help with the jump drive, and it's not on *this* ship. It makes more sense that you'd camp out on the other ship when we're split up."

"But how am I going to see the action from over there?" Raphael laid his head back on the seat and stared at the ceiling. "I'll just be sitting around all day. I might as well be back in the lab."

Jia eyed him, her mouth twitching as she tried not to laugh. "No offense, but we weren't planning on taking you on missions. You seem...nice, and I'm sure you're good at your job, but you'd die about thirty seconds into the first firefight."

"I'm not saying I wanted to go shoot guys with you," he muttered glumly. "I was talking about staying on the *Argo*."

"If we're doing our jobs, the action won't come to the ship." Erik patted him on the shoulder. "Backup AI, Cutter, and you will have to babysit the jump ship."

Cutter rubbed the edges of his drooping mustache. "That's a damn good plan, Blackwell. Brilliant. I won't get shot that way."

Emma smirked. "You could get vaporized."

"Space is big, Holochick." Cutter shrugged. "I'm far more likely to die by getting shot than blown up in a ship."

Raphael sat up and heaved a weary sigh. "It's going to take me a long time to finish calibrating the drive anyway. It makes sense that I'd mostly have to hang out over there."

"Don't worry." Jia smiled. "Emma's usually watching us with drones anyway. I'm sure she can cut you a highlights reel."

"Except when everything's jammed," Emma muttered.

Jia narrowed her eyes at the AI. "You're not helping."

"Just noting the truth." Emma's gaze slid to Raphael. "You could use the nano-AR room to experience the missions in a safer environment."

Raphael's loud clap was like a gunshot. "I didn't even

think of that. Thanks, Emma!" With that, he was out of the cockpit and heading …somewhere.

Jia rested her face in her palm. "And here I thought we wouldn't have to worry about fanboys now that we work for Alina."

Erik chuckled. "It could be worse. He could hate our asses."

CHAPTER THIRTY-NINE

March 17, 2230, Approaching Venusian Orbit aboard the *Argo*

"Should I wake Cutter up?" Erik asked from his seat beside Jia in the cockpit.

They'd been alone together for the last four hours of the trip. Raphael had spent most of the trip experiencing a fictionalized account of the adventures of the Obsidian Detective and Lady Justice in the nano-AR room.

Lanara kept to the engine room, appearing only briefly for meals. Jia couldn't tell if she was annoyed or happy with the new ship, but she'd made it clear she had numerous adjustments and modifications she needed and wanted to make. Cutter had spent a lot of the time in the cockpit, but he'd also done something that had surprised both Jia and Erik.

Jia shook her head with a smile. "Don't need him, and he's the one who said not to wake him up unless we were crashing."

"I never thought we'd need to say, 'Don't get drunk on a

mission.'" Erik snickered. "I don't know if I should be pissed or impressed."

Cutter had neglected to mention the bottle of Venusian rice wine he'd snuck aboard for a post-mission celebration. Out of boredom, he'd decided to sample the wine, with the expressed logic that he could pick up more bottles once the mission was over.

"It isn't professional." Jia rolled her eyes. "I never know what to make of that man."

"Let's be real. He's here as a backup just in case." Erik shrugged. "You can fly this ship, and we've got Emma. I'm not going to sweat it, but we'll encourage him not to do that again until we're done with the mission. From what he said, give him a couple hours, and he'll sober right up. We could also have Emma mod some of the medpatches for more efficient alcohol filtration."

"I think we'll save those. I'm more worried about getting shot through the hand than Cutter's possible hangover." Jia gestured to a camera feed. "Every new place impresses me. It's a trick. I'm seeing a feed, not a direct image with my eyes, but it feels more real than pictures back on Earth."

Massive space stations composed of webs of habitation modules joined together over the decades floated in orbit around the white and yellow planet playing host. Ships of various sizes flew in different directions. Venus might lack the billions of Earth, but it was still one of the original colonies of mankind.

"It's strange to think that so many people live on space stations above the planet." Jia frowned. "I get that more people live on the planet, but then again, they really don't. It messes with my head when I think about it too much."

"Because they live in floating cities?" Erik asked.

She nodded. "The whole point of colonizing a planet is living on it, not floating above it high in the atmosphere. We've been on Venus for longer than we've had FTL travel, and we still live in floating cities and stations."

"Sure, but Venus makes Mars look like a paradise." Erik stared at the approaching planet on the display. "And compared to Mars, they've just gotten started with the terraforming. It's going to be a while before anything remotely human can live on the surface."

Jia sighed. "It's effectively hell down on the surface. How long does it take to turn a hell into a paradise?"

"I don't know." Erik smirked. "You'd have to ask a demon that."

"We might get our chance soon." Jia gestured to the radar and lidar displays, both lit up with contacts. "We flew from Earth, a fallen paradise, to a hell hoping to be a paradise because we're chasing demons who call themselves people but have twisted their bodies."

"That's one way to look at it." Erik scratched his cheek. "But living in a floating city with temperatures on the ground close to five hundred degrees Celsius isn't that different from living in a tower if you think about it."

"How do you figure?" Jia shot him a dubious glance. "A tower might be tall, but it's still on the surface."

"Be honest." Erik locked eyes with her. "You already told me you barely left Neo SoCal before you met me. Were you even bothering to go to the ocean or the woods? Or did you spend most of your life in the towers?"

Jia sighed. "I'm not much of an outdoorsy person, and there are plenty of beautiful parks in the towers."

"Those towers are so high, most Uptowners haven't seen the Shadow Zone pollution layer with their own eyes." Erik shook his head. "They're climate-controlled and protected from most weather. Even if a nasty storm happens, people can sit inside, content that they have everything they need. Most of them are connected to at least one other tower, too." He gestured at Venus. "So what if they live in floating cities? If people in Neo SoCal could float among the clouds, they'd do it. It'd give them a new reason for them to feel smug."

"There's nobody beneath them to feel superior to out here," Jia replied.

"*Yet.* I wouldn't be surprised if in a couple hundred years, the rich people still live in the floating cities and look down their noses at the people living on the terraformed surface. They'll probably make up some bull-shit about how they're a purer strain of Venusian." Erik snorted. "I'd bet you, but we'll both be dead."

"Always looking on the positive side of humanity, huh?" Jia offered him a playful smile.

Erik waved a hand dismissively. "Don't worry. I'm sure the space raptors, the Leems, and all the others are dicks, too. I just haven't met one to punch in the face yet."

Jia laughed. "That's your plan for your first encounter with an alien? Punch them in the face?"

"If they're dicks, yes." Erik shrugged. "If they offer me a beignet, probably not."

"You think a Zitark or a Leem is going to have a beignet for you?"

Erik looked thoughtful. "Stranger things have happened."

Jia's smile faded, her mind returning to the mission before them. "It bugs me that Alina already had an agent working the case, but she still wanted us. It doesn't sit right with me."

"Doesn't bother me," Erik replied. "We're specialists at dealing with this conspiracy, whether it's the Ascended Brotherhood or whatever bastards control them behind the scenes, and we get results. But I get what you're saying. She's probably halfway trying to smoke them out with us, but I don't think she would give us a suicide assignment."

"You trust her that much?" Jia frowned. "She's helped us a lot, sure, but she has her own agenda."

Erik shrugged. "Doesn't everyone? I'll worry about it more when her agenda deviates from ours. Right now, everyone agrees: we want the conspiracy gone, and the ID and the DD want the conspiracy gone." He laughed. "They're both so desperate for it that they're shoving a jump drive at us. That's not something that happens because of a little political arm twisting. That means some-where along the way, important people became convinced that *we* can use that ship better than they can."

"They're going to want it back eventually. Probably this ship, too." Jia couldn't hide the disappointment in her voice.

"So?" Erik motioned around the cockpit. "After we take out the conspiracy, will we need it?"

Jia blinked and furrowed her brow. "I suppose we won't. We'll have to get used to flying in something less impressive." She frowned at a sudden thought. "Skyward Day."

"Huh?"

Jia inclined her head toward the closest display of Venus. "You know, their big holiday celebrating the founding of the first floating city? We have the Brotherhood sniffing around Venus right before a planetary holiday celebrated by every city. That's a little too coincidental for me to believe. The traffic's really going to pick up this week."

Erik's expression turned grim. "Yeah. You're right. That might mean whatever they have planned is going down on Skyward Day."

"That doesn't give us a lot of time to get to the bottom of things."

"You know what they say about pressure?" Erik asked.

"What?" Jia eyed him with suspicion.

"Pressure makes diamonds."

Jia's reply was quite dry. "It also crushes people into a bloody pulp."

Erik eyed her. "Now who's focusing on the dark side of humanity?"

Jia expanded and combined the forward camera feeds to give them a panoramic view of their destination, the floating city of Parvati. Her earlier dark thoughts had fled, replaced by appreciation for the sight in front of her.

"Ladies and gentlemen, welcome to Venus," she transmitted before sending the view to the engine room and Cutter's cabin.

Despite being a technological marvel, the massive city lacked the external glamour of a tower. Silvery bubble-like structures were stacked in tiers, connected through narrow covered sky bridges.

Twisting lines ran between the bubbles, giving the city an organic appearance. Long lines ran beneath the bottom levels, flowing in the atmosphere like tentacles. It was as if it was a colony of sky jellyfish living atop of one another, drifting through the thick white and yellow clouds.

"It's kind of pretty when you see it up close." Jia had already contacted Port Control and received their landing information. "It's almost beautiful."

"Huh." Erik frowned. "I don't get it. I hadn't thought about it before, but this doesn't make much sense."

"How do you figure?" Jia asked.

Erik gestured toward the city. "The Sky Garden took all that power for a small structure. How are they floating entire cities up here? They might not have as many people as Neo SoCal, but there are no dome villages with a few thousand either."

Jia gave him an incredulous look. "Surely you studied this in school?"

"I studied a lot of things in school." Erik agreed. "It doesn't mean I remember them. It's been a long—"

"*Long.*" She nodded.

"Hey now," he responded, noticing her smirk. "Fine, it's been a long, *long* time since I've been in school compared to you, and I've never been to Venus. I never had a reason to come even before I left the system. I remember Alina mentioning something about buoyancy, though. I didn't pay that much attention."

Jia lifted her chin in triumph. "I used to love Venus as a kid. Whenever I was given an option in school to pick my own subject. I picked Venus. Something about it seems much more interesting than typical dome colonization."

"You were really into Venus because of how they colonized it?" He shook his head. "That's so you."

"It's a technological marvel." Jia scoffed in defiance. "The surface of Venus might be hell, but at this altitude, the temperature and pressure are already almost at Earth levels. That's the trick, and they don't have to use a huge amount of energy to keep it elevated with grav fields or thrusters. The breathable atmosphere inside provides enough buoyancy, so the whole thing floats without much else needed. Native gravity is ninety percent of Earth normal, so not even a huge amount of energy is required."

"Unless one of those things gets a hole, right?" Erik shook his head. "Then you need a huge oxygen field to keep everyone alive, and they risk taking a one-way trip to hell."

"No. That's the brilliant part." Jia reached over to flip a switch. "The pressure differentials are minimal. There's no explosive decompression, only slow leaks that can be quickly sealed, if not automatically. Minor thruster usage for station-keeping and the very air everyone's breathing does its part to keep it in the sky. Terrorists couldn't sink a floating city without destroying most of it. That's not much different than a tower on Earth."

"Huh." Erik stared at the approaching city. "I do kind of remember reading all that back in the day. It is kind of cool when you think of it. I always just think of Venus as the place that makes the fancy furniture and rugs."

"They do that, too. They're very big on handcrafting. It's humorous when you think about it."

"Handcrafted furniture is funny?" Erik looked at her. "I know you have an odd sense of humor, but that's different, even for you."

"I'm just saying wealthy people pay more for something that is by its nature not as precise as something created by a machine." Jia shrugged. "That's funny when you think about it."

Erik looked at the view again. "Yeah, now that you explain it that way, it *is* funny."

Parvati grew closer, one of the upper-tier habitant bubbles taking up most of Jia's enhanced forward display. She nudged the *Argo's* thrusters to decelerate further and line the ship up with their docking bay. The doors were still too far to see, which meant they weren't open yet.

"So, if this place won't sink just because of an explosion or two," Erik began, patting his holster, "we don't need to be as careful if shit happens?"

"We still need to keep a low profile," Jia replied. "Half the point of working for the ID is to do things quieter."

"If we get in a fight with the Brotherhood, I'd prefer to have a big gun and grenades in case some of those spiders show up."

"First, we need to rendezvous with Agent Bora." Jia adjusted the *Argo's* course and deployed its landing struts. "When I double-checked the map of the city a couple of hours ago, we'll be meeting her on the other end of the city. I suggest we take the mini-flitters and some drones."

Erik nodded. "And grenades."

Jia cocked her head and frowned. She wanted to object, but in a best-case scenario, they would run into dangerous and murderous cyborgs.

She didn't know what the worst-case scenario might be, but she suspected it involved a Leem with a lightning gun angry about Venusian spices and not carrying a beignet.

"Okay." Jia offered a curt nod. "Grenades, too."

CHAPTER FORTY

Of all their recent travel destinations, Parvati reminded Erik the most of Chang'e City.

Though the massive bubble-like habitation modules weren't fixed domes and the amount of space between the modest buildings and the walls of the modules was larger, the sense of enclosure felt the same.

He flew at a low speed on the mini-flitter, Jia right beside him.

They emerged from a wide-diameter sky bridge tube into their destination module and thus their target neighborhood, slowing a moment later.

Densely packed buildings choked the area, with narrow streets between, accommodating mini-flitters, drones, and people. While none of the buildings could be called towers in the proper sense, several stood out, looming over their smaller compatriots. Complicated geometric patterns decorated the walls.

The bright colors struck Erik, as they had in the previous neighborhoods they'd passed through. Like Venusian spices and music, Venusian color schemes demanded attention.

The semi-transparent membrane separating the city from the outside allowed in the natural sunlight. From what Jia had told him, all floating cities used a small amount of thrust to keep them on the daylight side of Venus. Unlike dome colonies, the Venusians had gotten used to actual sunlight and didn't want to rely on artificial light during the months of darkness that would come otherwise.

Erik lowered altitude. They were almost to the address, but his curiosity over the nature of the settlement lingered.

Every place humanity had colonized was different in its own way. The UTC might have done their best over the centuries to terraform everywhere to be more like Earth, but the heart of their differences didn't go away.

"Ever think they can fix it so it has normal hours of darkness?" he asked. "Like Earth."

Jia glanced his way. "I'm not an expert, but from what I read, they have some ideas on that. They're all theoretical, though, and a lot of them are potentially dangerous for different reasons."

"It's always sunny in Venusian cities, then?" Erik grinned. "True sunlight, too. In five hundred years, maybe this is where everyone will retire."

"Who knows what we'll have in five hundred years?" Jia replied. "A couple hundred years ago, everyone said we'd never be able to travel faster than the speed of light in any practical way, and now humanity stretches out across the stars."

"You think we'll be everywhere?" Erik slowed and

dropped his mini-flitter farther, passing only meters over the rooftops of some buildings. "You hit a bar, and it's got a Leem bartender, and a Zitark gangster sitting in the corner. Maybe a Catarin singer on stage. Probably an Orlox busboy. He keeps an eye out for the Zitark syndicate."

Jia laughed. "That's depressing. All the races manage to mingle, and it's the same sort of scum?"

"No." Erik shook his head. "New scum. Okay, so the Leem can be the gangster, and the Zitark the bartender. We'll make an Aldran the busboy."

"This is the address." Jia killed her forward movement and steered the mini-flitter toward the edge of the street, where a half-dozen others were parked in front of a bright yellow apartment building. Covered balconies protruded from the side of the building, giving a lovely view of a park. The building stood in a rough circle with other such complexes, the small park filled with a gorgeous array of flowers in the center. The mix of colors and positions of the flowers created an intricate organic mandala that could only be seen from the air.

After landing, Erik nodded toward several fountains interspersed among the paths cutting through the flowers. He patted his duster, reassured by the weight of the weapon underneath. "Want to bet on how long it takes us to get in a firefight?"

Jia raised an eyebrow. "No, and I hope it takes more than one day."

"Just saying. Sometimes it's fun to keep things interesting." Erik walked toward the closest fountain.

Jia and Erik neared the polished white fountain, which

burbled. A beautiful woman in a yellow and orange sari leaned against the edge, her hands folded in front of her and a soft smile aimed their way. There was no one else nearby, and with all the folds and wraps on the woman's clothes, Erik wouldn't have been surprised if she could hide a rifle in there.

"May you have an always bright day." The woman placed her palms together and bowed her head.

Erik and Jia exchanged looks. The greeting was standard for Venusian natives, but Alina's address and follow-up information had pointed them to this park, and the woman did match the image of Agent Priya Bora. They were both using their low-level holographic disguises.

Jia leaned in to whisper to Erik. "I can't hear the fountain."

"Emma, you there?" Erik murmured.

He got no response. Either she wasn't paying attention, or they were being jammed.

Erik nodded slowly. She was right but having a privacy device and jammer didn't mean the woman in front of them was Alina's agent.

"I was interested in buying an Aldran," Erik announced. "But my contacts told me they were out of season."

The woman's lips curled into a partial sneer. She tapped her PNIU. "And what season did they tell you they'd be in?"

"The season of bunting," Erik grumbled. His PNIU chimed with an encrypted confirmation. Sometimes he didn't know how necessary these kinds of passphrases were or if Alina was just messing with them.

The woman nodded slowly, her gaze flicking between Jia and Erik. "We're safe to discuss things here for the next twenty minutes. I'm sure you've already picked up on my privacy device, and the local cameras and drones are being spoofed. I come to this park fairly regularly to appreciate its beauty, so my mere presence isn't a tipoff."

"You're Priya Bora?" Jia asked.

The woman nodded. "And you're Blackwell and Lin, the Obsidian Detective and Lady Justice." Disdain filled her tone.

Erik frowned. "What? You've got a problem with us?"

"I don't like part-timers." Priya dusted off the back of her sari with a frown. "And that's what a contractor is—a part-timer. But, you two have a reputation for success, and I'm not going to let my pride get in the way if it means you can get results."

"How magnanimous." Jia scoffed.

"Isn't it, though?" Priya threaded her fingers together and let her hands hang loosely in front of her. The woman's beauty and graceful demeanor obscured that she was a lethal ID ghost.

"Let's cut through the big-dick contest." Erik stared at Priya.

"You're the only one here with a dick, Blackwell." Priya sighed. "But you're right. I'll give you the highlights. Kotnis' body is still unaccounted for, but I've confirmed there was an unauthorized dump on the thirteenth that might account for that. I haven't had much success with the systems or the relevant cameras. If someone did kill him and dump his body, they did an unusually good job of covering their tracks, which means it's probably not the locals. This isn't Mars or Earth. The organized crime here is barely organized and barely crime. It's more guys playing at being gangsters."

Jia shrugged. "Maybe they've decided to up their game, or an outside group has decided to consolidate and take power."

"It's not impossible," Priya replied. "But the CID hasn't heard much evidence of anything like that happening, nor have I from my sources."

"Then we're talking about the Ascended Brotherhood." Erik looked over his shoulder as if mentioning the name would summon the cyborgs.

"That's what we believe." Priya untangled her hands, her fingers twitching in nervous anticipation. "But we don't have a good understanding of what they might be intending. Other agents in other cities are keeping an eye on things, but the only evidence of any anomalies is here in Parvati. There are more details than that, but that's the high-level data. The enemy might be here, and they killed a low-level criminal, probably as part of something involving smuggling, but we don't have a clue about their final goals."

"And Skyward Day is coming," Jia added.

Priya let out a bitter laugh. "Yes, Skyward Day is coming. Talos…excuse me, the Brotherhood usually isn't about terrorism for terrorism's sake, but the ID has beaten them down, and they might want to go out in a blaze of glory. Destroying the biggest city on Venus on the planet's most important holiday would accomplish that. We're running out of time to figure out what's going on, and we can't just tell the city to evacuate with no evidence."

Erik scratched his cheek, lost in thought for a moment.

"If it is the Brotherhood, they're going to be more nervous, the closer they get to the day they'll execute their plan."

"I suppose." Priya furrowed her brow. "What good does that do us? We still don't know their plan."

"We can use it against them." Erik lowered his hand, a smile building. "And play on their fears. It's like you said. They've taken a major blow, and I doubt they've recovered from it in three months. They've got to be desperate and extra paranoid."

Jia's eyes widened. "And all we have to do is use that paranoia."

Priya looked at the two, her face contorting with deepening confusion. "How do we do that? It's not like I'm going to go around banging a drum and singing about how they're being investigated. I know you two might not always care about keeping a low profile, but I need to."

"That's it. Our profiles."

"What?" Priya frowned.

Erik slapped his chest. "Why do you think Alina sent a couple of contractors here? We're good at investigating things, but I doubt she thinks we're that much better than the locals, including you." He inclined his head toward Jia. "It's something we already discussed, and you just pointed out. We make noise wherever we go. People who know what they're looking for might even be on the lookout for us. We've messed with the Brotherhood, and we've almost certainly messed with whoever is pulling the Brotherhood's strings."

Priya frowned. "You can't be suggesting what I think you're suggesting."

Erik nodded. "I am. Screw wandering around in

disguises poking into crap and hoping to find something. We should put on a big show of coming. Let them know we're here."

"I'm assuming you have decent access to local records, Agent Bora?" An excited smile broke out on Jia's face. "You can alter the landing records to make it appear we came in on another ship. You could leak our arrival to the local news or select sources at first. We might not be as famous on Venus as we are back in Neo SoCal, but it'll get around."

"It certainly will." Priya shook her head. "And it's dangerous. If you're right, and the Brotherhood is paranoid, they might come after you in a big way. I know your reputation, but you won't do anyone any good dead."

"We're running out of time." Erik gestured around the park. "All these pretty flowers could end up smoking husks if we wait too long. I don't have a problem being bait as long as I know someone local with pull has our back."

Jia nodded. "The same for me. If we wanted a safe job, we would never have gone to work for Alina."

Priya gave a firm nod. "I don't have a great alternative, and you don't work for me. I was ordered to give you full cooperation and full latitude in approaching this issue."

"So you'll help us?" Erik asked.

"The plan is reckless and insane." Priya chuckled. "That matches your reputation. I'm in. After all, you're the ones taking all the risks."

CHAPTER FORTY-ONE

March 18, 2230, Floating City Parvati, Venus

The Agent stood rigid in the center of the room, taking slow, deep breaths and waiting for his encrypted communications link to be established. Any operation involved complicated variables for success, and he always did his best to account for them, but he couldn't ignore the potential risk to the primary operation by situational changes that now threatened his mission. Another failure might be tolerated by his employers, but *he* wouldn't accept it. The Core's plans must succeed for the good of humanity.

Julia's hologram appeared, a lazy smile on her face. "I wasn't expecting you to contact me so soon. You're fortunate that I'm nearby. I did anticipate you might need further direction and arranged for that."

"The Last Soldier and the Warrior Princess are here." The Agent offered the report with almost no inflection.

Julia put a finger to her lips, her soulful eyes looking innocent. "Is that a problem?"

"The timing is suspicious. Given the state of things, it's

impossible to dismiss the idea that they are here to disrupt the plan."

"Are you afraid?"

There was no accusation in Julia's voice, only curiosity. Her expression remained the same, a feigned but genuine-looking sweet innocence. At times, her ability to manage that disturbed the Agent. It was one of the few things that still could.

"No," he declared. "But they do add additional complexities that must be accounted for. Even if they aren't aware of the operation, if they are investigating, they will limit my ability to operate freely without detection. The probability of the failure of the primary mission has increased significantly."

Julia waved a hand dismissively. "Continue with your primary mission. I'll take measures on my end to aid you, but I don't anticipate those two will disrupt things in a way that affects my overall goals."

"Failure is a possibility." The Agent stared at Julia, his expression neutral.

"I'm more concerned about the failure of your secondary mission," Julia replied. "If necessary, adjust your resource usage to assure its success, even if it risks the failure of the other mission."

The Agent cocked his head and blinked. "Are you sure?"

"Absolutely. I need everything ready for Sophia when she arrives to take receipt of the package." Julia flicked her hair with her hand and sighed. "In a sense, that is now your primary mission. Your future and our true future rests on what happens with Sophia. Remember, the remnants of the

Brotherhood are expendable. Do what you need to with them."

"Understood." The Agent bowed his head. "I will not fail you."

Julia smiled sweetly. "I know. I understand how loyal and useful you are, and I'd have no one else aiding me on Venus."

Jia and Erik wandered through a dense pack of stalls selling food, drinks, and gifts for the upcoming Skyward Day celebration. Wonderful, stomach-tingling aromas mingled all around. Holographic signs floated above the stalls, enticing would-be customers.

A crush of customers, both tourists and locals, wandered the stalls, chatting, eating, drinking, and occasionally singing.

Erik munched on a lamb skewer, his fourth snack since their arrival at the market. "This is good. You should try some."

Jia shook her head. "Some of us ate breakfast and aren't hungry."

"Hey, you need to get into the pre-Skyward Day spirit." Erik shook his skewer in defiance. "And support the local economy."

Jia stopped at a small table covered with necklaces, pendants, and bracelets. Gold and silver, along with low-end gemstones, predominated. The pieces were all modestly expensive, but that didn't surprise her. A floating city might be a marvel of technology, but it was still cheaper to import from Earth than attempt to mine the surface of Venus.

The smiling woman sitting behind the table placed her palms together and bowed her head. "May you always have a bright day."

Jia repeated the gesture and the greeting. "These are lovely."

The vendor glanced at Erik. "Judging by your accents, you're tourists?"

"Yes." Jia nodded. "We came to see the Skyward Festival. I was bugging my boyfriend to take a special trip."

Erik shrugged and bit off another piece of lamb. "Seemed cheaper than leaving the system," he mumbled around his food.

"Venus is a special place." The vendor held up a small silver bracelet. "Imagine what our ancestors on Earth would have said if we had told them we would live in the clouds?"

Jia took the bracelet and turned it over as she examined it. "It is good to keep a sense of wonder." She set the bracelet down.

"You'll find the Skyward Festival is nothing *but* wonder." The vendor kept her smile so wide it must have been painful. "It's a celebration of both life, ingenuity, and respect for our new home."

A small pack of boys pushed past Jia. She couldn't bring herself to yell at them after seeing the excited smiles on their faces. The vendor shrank back, making Jia blink.

"What's wrong?" Jia asked.

"She's thinking I'm about to tell you that she's selling

fake goods," offered a man from behind them. "And she knows she shouldn't be doing that."

Jia looked his way. Erik took a moment to turn, content to eat his lamb. A man in a tan suit stood frowning at the vendor.

"I thought we had this discussion already?" the man offered.

The woman tapped her PNIU, and a large TEMPORARILY CLOSED message appeared above her table. A blue energy field surrounded the jewelry on the table. She huffed before storming off.

"What was that about?" Jia asked.

The man rubbed the side of his neck and looked around with a weary expression. "The thing is, we have certain rules around here. It's about maintaining mutual respect both for locals and outsiders. Tourism's our lifeblood, and if people have a bad experience, they might not tell their friends to come."

Erik swallowed his last bite of meat. He flung the empty stick through the air with surprising skill, and it tumbled end over end before dropping into a garbage bin a couple of meters away. He nodded to Jia to tell her to continue the conversation.

"Who are you?" Jia asked. "A local chamber of commerce representative?"

The man fluffed his lapels. "I represent certain entrenched interests, yes. Not the chamber of commerce, but men and women who have deep ties to this community all the way back to the founding who want to make sure it continues to flourish. Said men and women can be misunderstood by certain close-minded people, but as you can see, they're interested in protecting this community by sending in people like me to keep tourists from being cheated." He nodded toward an alley past several stalls. "I've been sent to talk to you two, Mr. Blackwell and Miss Lin. Important people have an eye on you, but we shouldn't talk here."

"No, we shouldn't." Jia looked him up and down. They couldn't risk a fight with so many innocent people around, and the man wasn't openly hostile yet, but if he was a member of a local syndicate as she suspected, the situation might escalate quickly.

The man wandered past the closed vendor table, whistling a jaunty tune. He motioned for them to follow, a relaxed, almost cocky smile on his face.

"I've got a drone in position over the alley now," Emma reported. "There's no one else there. Once you're past the entrance, it's out of sight of the street cameras, and no other drones are moving near it."

"So, it might be a trap, but one that's going to involve only him," Jia suggested.

Erik nodded. "If he's a Tin Man, he could have some surprises."

"The sensors on these mini-drones aren't as good as the MX-60 suite," Emma interjected, "but given what I'm getting on the detectable spectra, it's unlikely he's a Tin Man."

"Just a local syndicate idiot then." Jia shrugged. "What do we have to lose?"

"Our lives?" Erik grinned.

"Very funny."

Erik nodded. "I know. I should quit my job and go into show business."

The man waved. "You coming or not?"

Erik and Jia fell in behind him, surveying the area for possible threats but content with Emma backing them up. No one paid them much attention. Soon, they were in the alley, the man looking both ways with a suspicious glint in his eye.

"You know who we are?" Erik asked.

"Hey, when you're connected, you hear things." The man grinned. "And it's not like you two can hide that well. You kind of stand out no matter where you go."

Jia advanced until she stood right in front of the man. "You'd be surprised. But if you work for entrenched local interests, do you think it's smart to be showing your face to us? We're not known for our fondness for said interests."

"I don't think you understand who you're dealing with." The man frowned and reached for her shoulder.

She grabbed his wrist and bent it back. He cried out in pain and fell to his knees. "And I don't think *you* understand who you're dealing with."

Erik snickered. "Damn. That was dumb."

Jia whipped out her stun pistol with her left hand and placed it against his forehead. "A lot of people have thought they could kill us. If you know our reputation, you'd think you would have come to the obvious conclusion that people who try to kill us end up dead or in prison."

"I'm...not trying...to...kill you," the man whimpered. "You're going...to...break my...wrist."

Jia rolled her eyes and released his wrist but kept her gun

pointed at him. "Don't be such a baby. If I was going to break your wrist, I would have done it. Now, here's how this is going to go down. You're going to take us to your boss, and if they're somebody we don't like, there's going to be trouble. That trouble might involve explosions. No promises either way."

The man waved his hands and nodded quickly. "Sure, sure. I think you misunderstand. I-I...look, I'm not anybody big. I was paid to find you and bring you to the guy anyway. I swear."

"You're saying you're not a syndicate member?" Erik raised an eyebrow. "If you're lying, we won't like that."

"Syndicate?" The man laughed nervously. "No, no, no. Just let me take you to the guy, and it's his problem then, right? I'd have bolted already, but I don't get the rest of my money if I don't deliver you."

Jia gestured with her gun for him to stand. "Turn around, and put your hands on your head. If you try anything, I will shoot you."

The man complied, trembling. He took deep breaths and started whispering under his breath.

Jia leaned toward Erik to whisper. "Whoever this idiot is, he wasn't sent by the Brotherhood."

"Yeah. I figure some local syndicate might have wanted to test us. You heard what Bora said. They must have underestimated us."

Jia holstered her weapon and sighed. "The plan might have backfired. We're not here to take on syndicates. We don't have time to mess with them."

"Then this is a good thing." Erik inclined his head toward the man but kept his voice low. "If he wants to take us to the locals, we can make sure they stay the hell out of our way until we've handled the Brotherhood."

Jia cleared her throat. "Hey, you," she called. "You're going to lead us to whoever hired you, and I've already put my gun away. Remember how your wrist felt. I don't need a gun to kill you if you try to screw us over, and don't think you're going to be able to outrun both of us. Plus, I reserve the right to shoot you."

The man swallowed. He smoothed his facial expression and took a deep breath before adjusting his tie. "It's not that far. We can walk."

CHAPTER FORTY-TWO

"I'm keeping my many flying eyes on things," Emma commented cheerfully. "But I see no one taking special note of you or any potential ambushes or any likely gun goblins. There was a minor traffic accident about two hundred meters behind you, but no one is injured, and it doesn't seem to require special attention."

"Just keep watching," Erik murmured underneath his breath. "I don't mind an ambush, but I do mind being surprised by it."

Their trip had taken them through several streets and intersections. They weren't tucked away in an alley. If the local syndicates intended a trap, it didn't make sense to do it where cameras would quickly detect the action and summon the authorities. Even corrupt cops wouldn't tolerate major gun battles right before a major holiday.

Something was wrong about the entire situation. The man leading them didn't project any menace. It didn't make sense for the syndicate to send an easily frightened third party unless it was a trap. Maybe the Brotherhood had taken to new strategies in their desperate time.

Their guide stopped in front of a narrow, worn-down single-story office tucked between two taller shops. The holographic sign outside read Roy Realty.

The man rubbed his wrist and stared at Jia with open fear. "Can I go now? I was just paid to set up the scene at the market. He said to approach you if you hit certain tables. Just so you know, those people were paid, too. It's all a big con."

Erik chuckled. "You're brave, aren't you?" He nodded down the street. "Get the hell out of here. If something bad is about to go down, you don't want to be part of it."

The man sprinted down the street, pumping his arms and legs with reckless abandon. He tripped half a block away and fell to his knees. With a yelp, he scrambled back onto his feet, his pant leg torn, and continued his escape.

"Roy Realty has been out of business for one week," Emma reported. "That's what the public records note. There is some indication it is in the process of being sold, but those records aren't available without further investigation."

"Don't press too hard yet." Erik frowned. "We need to make the right kind of noise and draw the right kind of attention. I don't mind kicking some syndicate ass to get them to back off, but we can't scare off the Brotherhood."

Jia nodded her agreement. "Let's just have a nice conversation that convinces them to stay away from us."

"Emma, can you get a thermal of the inside?" Erik asked.

"Yes," she replied. "There is one man inside. There's no indication he's a Tin Man. He's sitting at a desk."

Jia lifted her hand and held it over the access panel. "Hard entry?"

"Not yet." Erik inclined his head to a police drone flying overhead. "I don't think this is where it's going to go down."

"I hope you're right." Jia opened the door.

A smiling man in a bright white suit sat behind a dusty desk. He lacked a tie, instead choosing golden chains around his neck. Piles of boxes stood all around the cramped office space, along with chairs stacked in a corner.

"Hey." The white-suited man spread his arms. "You made it. Great. I didn't know if you would. Sorry about the place. I'm still moving in." He groaned. "Don't ever try to get anything done right before the Skyward Festival. Everybody and their cousin are taking time off. I knew better, but when an opportunity presents itself, you have to strike, right?"

Erik glanced at Jia. She shrugged and looked as confused as he felt. If this man was a syndicate enforcer, he was doing a poor job of intimidation.

"Who the hell are you?" Erik asked.

The white-suited man laughed loudly and obnoxiously, almost braying. He reached into the box. Erik's hand jerked into his duster and gripped his pistol. Jia matched his motion, but the man didn't seem to notice.

A gun didn't come out. A nameplate did. The man set it down in front of him and motioned to it.

"Chafi Trem," the man read. "And it is my pleasure to

make your acquaintance, Erik and Jia. Can I call you Erik and Jia? I don't want to overstep my bounds, but I'm a big fan of you two, huge fan. When I heard you were coming to Venus, I prayed, 'Please let them come to my city.' Of course, Parvati is where the action's at, so I didn't think you'd end up in some station or backwater, but I've paid a lot of money to have people keeping an eye out for you, and I got lucky. You ended up this close."

Jia folded her arms, now looking more annoyed than worried. "We were just here to enjoy the pre-festival fun."

Chafi chuckled. "Of course. I know you're not cops anymore. You do private security, but you didn't come in on a corporate ship, meaning you're not here on corporate work."

"You're well-informed." Erik kept his hand on his gun. His instincts kept screaming at him not to trust the man.

"Yes, I am well-informed." Chafi leaned back in his chair, the smile on his face widening. "Can I get you anything? I don't have much. I've got some lassi in a refrigerator in the back room. Water, if you want it. Coffee. Imported from Earth, too. I know everything seems like a mess, but I just moved in yesterday."

"What do you need two security contractors for?" Erik asked. "You seem like you should get established before you go looking for help."

Chafi shook his finger. "No, no, no. You go where the opportunities are when they show up. That's the first principle of business. If you wait, they'll fly away. How could I pass up the chance to work with the Obsidian Detective and Lady Justice? Just because you're not on the news all the time, it doesn't mean you don't carry some weight. I can help you exploit that in a way that's profitable here."

Jia narrowed her eyes. "Exploit it how, exactly?"

"Just because Earth entertainment dominates doesn't mean there's not local pride." Chafi tapped his PNIU. Different images of smiling men and women appeared, all handsome and beautiful.

"Who are these people?"

"Some of the top local Venusian actors and actresses." Chafi gestured to a dark-skinned man dressed in a local Militia uniform. "He's the lead actor from *Skyward Shield*. Ever seen it?"

Erik shook his head. "I don't watch a lot other than sphere ball."

Chafi grunted in frustration. "Earth shows never get Venus right. That's why local productions with a sliver of the budget can outperform a lot of Earth shows, but just because you're not from Venus, it doesn't mean you can't be a Venusian star."

Jia blinked. "Wait. What? You want us to become *actors*?"

"No, Jia." Chafi made a finger-gun at her and clucked his tongue. "I want you to become stars. I understand you two. I know your retirement story, and I know it's bullshit."

"Do you now?" Jia scoffed. "What do you think you know?"

"That two super-cops don't go out on top like that without a reason." Chafi waved a hand. "Look, I'm not judging. This is Venus. If you did something on Earth that's a little nasty, that's for those Earthers to care about. You were famous, and now your careers have stalled out."

His speech picked up volume and speed. "I know this office doesn't look like much, but I've got solid connections. I know one of the executive producers of *Skyward Shield*. I've been pitching a fish-out-of-water action comedy to her for a while about an Earther who comes to Venus and ends up being an unpredictable cop who takes on everything from the syndicates to terrorists." He spread his fingers and hands. "I was going to call it *Your Article Seven Rights Don't Apply Here*, but this is even better. We can change the pitch. Two cops. It can have a will-they-or-won't-they romance angle, too. Let's face it, Jia, you're damned hot." He frowned at Erik. "We'll need to dye the hair, but you've got that rugged look a lot of women like, and it doesn't alienate men. I can work with it."

Erik ran his hand through his hair. "I like my hair."

"That's what this is about. You're a talent agent." Jia groaned and rubbed her temples.

"Hey." Chafi frowned. "Don't make it sound like I'm some sleazy abuser like you're used to in Neo SoCal. I've got connections here, and I can turn your fame, even your tainted, washed-up fame, into a major career here. Sure, I get it." He shook his head. "This isn't Earth, and you won't be as famous, but why not be the big fish in the small pond, right?" He waggled his eyebrows. "You sign with me, and I guarantee I can get you both starring roles. It'll be huge. Venusians will take to you like bees to flowers. Trust me, I've been doing this for years."

"First of all," Jia replied. "We're not washed up."

"Sure." Chafi pursed his lips into a smirk. "That's what

everyone says. I'm telling you, if you haven't already signed, nobody's interested in you. If you're waiting around for a better deal, it's not happening."

"We're also not celebrities or actors." Erik tried hard not to laugh.

"I can work with the fame you've managed to keep." Chafi rubbed his hands, eyeing them like a hungry lion looking at a pile of steaks. "I used to work with one of the biggest talent agencies on Venus, but I got tired of them being small-time, and that's why I broke away. I'll take you both to the top. I don't care if you can't act. You can get lessons, and if we stick to cop dramas, it'll be easy. You'll have that natural authenticity." He flicked his wrist. "In a few years, you can switch to period dramas or something else when you're better actors."

Jia scrubbed a hand over her reddening face. "Let me get this straight. You paid a bunch of vendors to react to a man like he was some sort of syndicate thug to get our attention to bring us here?"

Chafi laughed. "I get that was overdramatic, but he was looking for some acting practice anyway, and I thought it'd be a good way of piquing your interest. I knew I couldn't just walk up to you and invite you to my agency." He frowned. "Now I understand what he meant by, 'They're going to kill me!' in his message."

"I was going to stun him," Jia muttered. "Not kill him."

Chafi's breath caught. He pointed at Jia and Erik in turn. "Either of you sing? I mostly focus on dramas and movies, but if you got pipes, we can make that happen. You just have to fake it. We can get a ghost singer." He ran his tongue around the inside of his mouth and stared at Erik.

"I don't think we can make this happen with you, now that I think of it, but Jia we could definitely get working. The hot-cop-turned-singer angle is begging for a breakout." He whistled. "I bet we could get major Earth bookings after we launder her rep on Venus for a year or two."

Jia spun on her heel toward the door. "We came here because we thought you were a criminal threatening us. We don't have time for this nonsense."

"Whoa. Wait one second. I'm offering to make you a star. You don't want to walk out of here. There's no one on Venus who can offer you what I'm offering."

Erik shrugged. "I can't sing." He grinned. "I'm a better actor than you think, but I'm fine with my job right now."

"Being a corporate security tool?" Chafi wrinkled his nose. "I'm sure they're paying you well, but tell me you don't crave the fame you had before and the adulation."

"No." Jia opened the door. "I never wanted fame. Thank you for the offer, but I'm not interested." She stepped outside.

Chafi sucked in a breath. "She's so damned hot. What about you, Erik? I can make it work with you. Your bio is solid. People love a hero."

"I'm good." Erik offered him a polite nod. "Next time, maybe just call."

"If you change your mind, I'll be here." Chafi pointed with both hands toward his chest. "Remember, Chafi Trem can make you a star."

"Yeah, I'll keep that in mind." Erik stepped out of the office and closed the door before breaking out in loud laughs.

Jia shook her head, snickers escaping her mouth. "None

of your training scenarios ended with the syndicate head being a talent agent."

"See?" Erik flung his arm toward the door. "Remember that the next time you say something's unrealistic. He's given me an idea, though. Let's mention who we are to more people, to help them spread the word."

"Organic marketing?" Jia smirked.

"Yeah. Something like that."

CHAPTER FORTY-THREE

Julia lifted her wine glass and swirled the pink liquid.

She smiled as she watched a recording of the Last Soldier and the Warrior Princes mingling with commoners in the Venusian market. She couldn't remember the last time she'd done something similar. She enjoyed her pleasures, but they were far from the simple amusements that pleased the average human.

As a member of the Core, she represented perfection—not just one in a billion, but one in billions. With leadership came privilege.

The privilege was a responsibility too. She needed to live up to the potential of what humanity could be if not held back by backward and sad men and women scared of the future. The decades had passed, with many plans coming slowly into fruition, but the same petty little people remained.

Julia shook her head. Sophia's plan was too convoluted for its own good. It had been from the beginning. Julia understood the need to preserve power among the elites with proper vision, but the Core had let the UTC drift away from them. Too many smaller threats had undermined their grand scheme. A perfectly planned destiny for humanity had grown brittle.

She considered Erik Blackwell and Jia Lin.

All the calculations of the Core throughout the decades, all the careful and often vicious plans were threatened because of two people. Of course, they'd had help, but they formed the heart of a true threat to the plans of the Core. They were proof of Sophia's mistake, and it was up to Julia to correct that error.

The Agent's concern about the pair wasn't absurd. They had a way of disrupting plans, but she'd anticipated they might appear. Now the question confronting her was the best way to make use of them.

They might disrupt Sophia's plans for the Core, but they didn't need to challenge Julia's secondary plans. Water in a river would eventually wear a stone down, but in the interim, it flowed around the rock. In a sense, it made the stone part of the river.

Julia smiled. If the Last Soldier and the Warrior Princess became too much of a thorn, direct elimination, albeit costly, was an option, but she had two other nested plans that needed to succeed on Venus.

Only a child assumed they would always succeed. Foresight required a woman to understand that she would fail on occasion. Advanced foresight allowed the same woman to turn those failures into successes.

"Graceful failure becomes success." She swiped her hand, and the image changed to Sophia in an elegant white gown. "This is what separates me from you, Sophia. You simply don't know it yet. You've let the decades turn you rigid and inflexible. I'll save your plan from you." She chuckled. "I'll save humanity from itself, no matter the sacrifice."

Julia took a sip of her wine, savoring the crisp taste.

She never sullied herself with wine other than what was produced at the vineyards she controlled. Her inferiors might be satisfied with drinking false wine. She didn't care if some claimed wine generated from artificial grapes was all but equivalent to wine produced from naturally grown grapes.

The difference was there for anyone with a truly discriminating palate.

She accepted the irony of rejecting a minor aberration of nature when she and every member of the Core represented something far more extreme. Their extreme difference was manifest superiority.

In many ancient mythologies, gods and goddesses weren't infinite beings. Many were limited creatures, granted their extended life and power through the magic in special foods or items. It wasn't infinite potential that allowed them to rule over humanity. It was the privilege that came with their basic superiority and ability to make good use of the resources they had.

Things were not so different in modern times.

But a true pantheon didn't rule from the shadows. A true pantheon didn't *fear* their mortal subjects. The truth remained the same. Sophia's plans needed to be corrected. Julia needed to guide the Core to its true destiny, and as if the universe smiled on her, she now had more tools she could use.

"Foresight." Julia's smile grew.

It was time to modify her plans to allow for graceful failure turning into victory.

March 19, 2230, Floating City Parvati, near Hotel Golden Thorn

Jia sat beside Erik on a park bench across the street from a grand pyramidal luxury hotel, the Golden Thorn.

They'd taken a room in their real names the night before and briefly entered the lavish room to establish they were staying there to anyone who might be tracking their movements. Other than their bizarre encounter with a talent agent, no one else had contacted them.

The public could be fickle, or their limited Earth fame was weak, only a planet away.

It didn't matter. They weren't there for adoring crowds, and the only people they wanted paying attention to them was the Ascended Brotherhood.

For the moment, Erik and Jia sat holographically disguised, watching the hotel and waiting. Emma had already hacked the cameras covering the entrance to their room and lobby, in addition to spreading drones in the local area to monitor unusual activity. They'd laid the bait, and now they needed to wait until a new mouse stepped into the trap.

Agent Bora was working her own angles in the meantime.

Erik rested the back of his head against his linked hands. "We stopped being cops, but everything still ends up being cop work. I never did like stakeouts, but you'd think I would be used to them."

"Why?" Jia asked.

"Because half of being in the military can be summed up by one simple sentence: 'Hurry up and wait.'" Erik squinted at a mini-flitter passing overhead. "It's funny how little things change, no matter who's paying us in the end. If we took that guy's offer, we'd still be cops, just fake ones."

Jia shrugged. "I think as long as we keep devoting ourselves to taking down certain kinds of people, our job won't be all that different. Find bad guys, evaluate, and terminate if necessary. At the end of the day, we hopefully leave the galaxy a better place."

"That's a good summary." Erik nodded. "You still okay with this plan? If you've got different ideas, I'm not married to the sit-around-and-wait-to-get-ambushed thing."

"It's the best way to get results in a short period of time. Not only that, but it's also safer here than it would be on Earth. I'm confident we can handle whatever comes up."

"You are?" Erik looked curious. "Why is that?"

"Because there's only so much you can smuggle onto Venus without getting noticed." Jia gestured toward the sky. "Whatever they have here, it's limited, and if we can stop them, we might be able to finish off the Brotherhood for good. If we were on Earth, they might have a whole factory spewing Tin Men at us."

Erik laughed. "Yeah, probably. These days, nothing would surprise me short of a Navigator showing up and asking us why we were building tech out of their kid's toys. And that wouldn't even be that big of a surprise."

"Even we can't be that unlucky."

"Is it unlucky, or is it a unique experience?" Erik grinned.

"Now that you've said it, it'll probably happen next week," Jia commented. "We should keep our calendar clear, so we don't have to reschedule the Navigator meeting. He might run off and go find some other crazy pair who don't know when to stop."

"Probably."

Jia focused on the dense crowds walking along the narrow street. Mini-flitters flowed at different levels, the speeds reasonable, even slow by Neo SoCal standards.

The surfeit of smiles struck Jia.

The palpable excitement about the coming Skyward Festival infected the entire population. If she weren't worried about the Brotherhood, she might have gotten excited. Even near the hotel, small stalls selling souvenirs and Skyward Festival-specific snacks were doing a brisk business. It would be nice for Erik and Jia to be able to see the grandiose parades, dances, and performances associated with the festival day, but Jia doubted the Lady would be so kind. They might be playing tourists, but they were there for deadly serious work. The happy tourists and locals needed to be protected from the Brotherhood's plot.

"You know, I've been thinking you should try penjing." Erik lowered his hands. "You'd probably like it even more than I do, and it's not like you couldn't use a relaxing hobby."

"I have hobbies." Jia poked him in the chest. "And you.

That's more than enough to keep me busy when we're not dealing with mysterious conspiracies and Tin Men."

"Me? I'm a project?" Erik raised an eyebrow in challenge.

"Definitely. A project that's still a work in progress." Jia winked. "It took me a lot of effort to get this thing going, and you'll still need a lot of work to get you where I need you."

"That sounds like a threat."

"More of a promise."

Erik smirked. "Hey, we're working on each other. I've got stories about what you were like when we first met if you don't remember. The woman who wouldn't stun a man to save her life."

"Hey, no reason to dig into the past."

"When it makes you look bad?"

"Especially when it makes me look bad." Jia nodded at the hotel. "And I'd like to see what I could get done with you when our off-planet dates don't involve worrying about crazed cybernetic killers. Future fun."

"The future, huh?" Erik shook his head. "Trying to predict it is for suckers. I'll stick to getting through each day, still breathing at the end. That's a win."

"That's weak garbage," Jia scoffed. "And you know it."

"Huh?" Erik watched her, his brow knitting in concern. "How is that garbage?"

"You wouldn't have been able to accomplish any of what you've done if you weren't planning for the future," Jia replied. "It's a copout to say otherwise, and it's not the end of the world if you plan for things, even when you don't know how they'll turn out." She placed her hand over her heart. "I don't regret becoming a detective even though I left the force early. I accomplished a lot of good there."

"And you don't mind that all your lifelong plans changed?"

"The situation changed, so the plan changed." Jia pinned him with her stare. "Don't let uncertainty become the enemy of living your life. You keep using that excuse, and I think it's your way of hiding from your feelings."

"Look, Jia, I get that," Erik began, "but—"

"I have confirmed suspicious activity outside your hotel room," Emma interrupted. "In this case, it is more important to focus on the present than the future."

Jia wanted to scream in frustration.

The enemy had annoying timing, as always. It wasn't as if she wanted to drag Erik off to the altar anytime soon, but she did want him to stop acting like he couldn't plan for a future together.

She didn't know what that future might be, but she knew it would include him. All she had to do was make sure he didn't die before then, not the easiest task, given their day job.

Relief spread across Erik's face. It made Jia want to slap him.

"Suspicious activity?" he asked.

"Yes. There is a hotel employee who just passed by your room," Emma explained. "But said fleshbag has the exact same gait as a suited guest who passed by about twenty minutes ago and another guest forty minutes prior. It is highly probable the fleshbag is the same man in disguise. I was less than fifty percent sure after the initial sightings, but the third sighting has raised the probability of them all being the same man to over ninety-six percent."

Erik frowned. "You can be that sure just from checking how they're walking?"

"Nothing is assured, but all my calculations point to the aforementioned accuracy." Emma scoffed. "Taking over more cameras at this time risks arousing suspicion, but he passed your room, glancing at it briefly before proceeding to the elevator. I'm waiting to see if he returns or emerges in the lobby. Whoever I saw is demonstrating far more restraint and care than your typical gun goblin. Caution is warranted."

"Yeah." Erik stood and wiped his hands on his pants. "Whoever it is probably isn't some local thug playing with toys, and 'fleshbag' might be an exaggeration."

"I'm glad we have AP mags," Jia muttered.

"We can't make assumptions." Erik grinned. "It might be another talent agent who wants to tell you how hot you are and how I need to dye my hair."

Jia rolled her eyes. "At least I have a shot at a singing career when this is all over." She gestured to his hair. "But you're going to have to do something about that."

"The suited guest is now in the lobby," Emma reported. "He is heading toward the entrance. You should have a visual on him in seconds."

A tall, gaunt man in a dark blue suit emerged from the hotel. He stopped and adjusted his tie before staring in Erik and Jia's direction. The look continued for a long stretch of seconds before he turned and jogged up the street.

"Well, shit." Erik stood. "If that's not a challenge, I don't know what is. He might as well have spat on my morning beignet."

"Keep an eye out for an ambush, Emma," Jia ordered. She glanced at her parked mini-flitter. "Should we take them?"

Erik shook his head and nodded toward the retreating man. "If he's on foot, he's not getting away."

They ran, entering the dense crowd and heading toward the street corner, shifting and pivoting to avoid collisions with frowning people. Their prey turned the corner down the street as they made the crossing.

Emma transmitted a feed to their smart lenses. The man had stopped at the corner and was obviously waiting. He started moving once they'd approached the corner, but when they turned the corner and slowed, he picked up the pace again, this time turning into a narrow, covered walkway between two buildings. This time he didn't stop, instead running toward the end of the walkway and vaulting over a tall fence with no run-up, like he was jumping over a tiny bump.

Jia frowned, trying not to focus too much on the feed at the edge of her vision. "I could clear that fence by pulling myself up and over, but what he just did is nearly impossible."

"Unless you have hardware."

"Emma, do you still have eyes on him?" Jia asked as they approached the covered walkway.

"Yes. Your likely terrible troll has not stopped, but he's taking a curving side street up ahead, sprinting and drawing odd looks," Emma replied. "I can give you an intercept course that doesn't require jumping fences and trying to keep up with someone who might be using cybernetic legs."

"Do it." Jia glared at the fence. "We're not playing his game. I don't know what this is about, but I'm not going to walk straight into a trap after he's run us ragged. Let's go get our mini-flitters and run this guy down."

CHAPTER FORTY-FOUR

Thirty minutes later, Erik and Jia descended into a wide alley kilometers away from their starting location. They'd left an area filled with mini-flitters and people and traveled to a more sparsely populated part of the city. Their prey waited patiently, his arms hanging loosely from his sides. Emma's drones circled overhead. She'd supplemented their mini-drones with the recent arrival of a larger drone with better sensors.

The lack of obvious ambush potential only put Jia more on guard. Assassinating someone by taking them to a place with fewer witnesses and cameras was an obvious tactic. The man's movements already proved they needed to be more cautious than his appearance suggested.

"Any indication of what other hardware he has?" Erik asked.

"That's one thing I'm concerned about," Emma replied. "I'm not sure he is a cyborg."

"After the stunt he pulled?" Jia shook her head in clear disbelief. "Then what is he?"

"I'm detecting no density or thermal differentials that suggest he's a Tin Man," Emma reported. "Nor any local indications of additional forces, including in the nearby buildings. There are some small readings that point to a possible holographic disguise. There is also, as you might have already noticed, a conspicuous lack of drones in this area other than my own. Considering he's chosen a final position that makes him visible from the air, it's unlikely that's due to chance."

"It probably means he controls the local cameras, too." Jia surveyed the area, but there was nothing out of the ordinary.

Erik frowned. "If it's the Brotherhood, they might have something that can prevent their hardware from being detected. The way he was moving earlier is enough proof for me. You're good, Emma, but you can be fooled."

"I can't dispute that," she replied. "Although it has a lower probability."

"He's not even sweating. He has to be a cyborg." Jia narrowed her eyes. She rested one of her hands on her gun. She'd loaded an AP magazine minutes earlier, as had Erik.

The man didn't move. He watched them, his expression blank as they brought the mini-flitters down on either side of him, cutting off his easy escape. Both landed a couple of meters away to avoid an attack.

"What is it they say?" the man asked, enunciating each word with almost unnatural precision. "'May you always have a bright day?' What a lovely sentiment. Venusian culture is more fascinating in many ways than Martian. There is less of a corporate feel to the whole affair, wouldn't you say?"

"Not here to talk about Venus." Erik shrugged. "No offense."

"Oh? What would you like to talk about, then?"

"That's on you." Jia kept her hand on her gun. "You went out of your way to get our attention and lead us around. We're guessing you had a reason to do that, other than amusing yourself."

"Amusement isn't something I find motivational. I was interested in seeing how your pursuit would unfold." The man wriggled his fingers at his side and stared at Jia, a blank, soulless expression on his face. "Consider it a type of test, but also consider this since your hostility is barely concealed, and your violent reputation precedes you. This isn't a dome. We could fight here without significant risk to the general population. I'm not sure, but I believe even a major explosion would only be a minor inconvenience. I would strongly consider that when you decide what actions you're going to take next."

"I always strongly consider my actions." Jia pulled out her gun and pointed at him. "You think we're going to hurt anyone other than you? If you wanted to use people as hostages, you should have stayed where the people were."

Erik drew his weapon. "You obviously know who we are."

"Yes, Mr. Blackwell and Miss Lin. You are famous in a way." The man didn't move. "And your disguises and other measures are competent, but not perfect for someone who knows what to look for. Incidentally, you misunderstand the situation."

"How is that?"

"You imply I went out of my way to get your attention, but in truth, you first went out of your way to draw mine."

"True. Fame has its uses." Erik grinned. "Before we waste any more time, I want to make sure you're not some talent scout looking for new actors or an actor working for one and playing at being a gangster."

The man cocked his head to the side, his brow furrowing. "No. I'm not here for any such frivolous purpose. I'm not a criminal in the sense you're implying, and my business with you is of the utmost seriousness."

"You're also not reacting to two people having guns on you." Jia shook her gun. "Most people would be worried."

"I'm not most people," the man offered without taking his eyes off Erik. "Despite my earlier statement, I should make it clear, I'm not here to fight you. It would be inadvisable for me, and I believe there remains a risk to the local area. Although I've led you away from a more densely packed neighborhood, there are many people in nearby buildings who might suffer if you choose to engage in an unnecessary conflict."

Jia narrowed her eyes, the urge to shoot the bastard through the head rising. "Okay, if you're not here to fight, and you know who we are and you're good enough to see through our disguises, then you're not a local syndicate punk. Stop wasting our time. Who are you, and why are you here?"

"My employers have taken notice of you and your successes," the man replied. "Said employers are useful at judging talent and making use of it in their organization. They're interested in bringing you into the fold, and they have instructed me to reach out to you for that purpose."

"Who are your employers?" Jia asked.

"I'm not prepared to share that information in this setting. This initial contact was simply a test and a greeting to evaluate your capabilities and your reactions."

Erik took slow, even breaths and unclenched his jaw. "We've already got jobs. Why do we care about your mysterious employers?"

"Jobs? With a security company?" The man chuckled quietly.

Jia tried to keep her expression neutral. If the man worked with the Ascended Brotherhood, that meant the group and the conspiracy might not realize Erik and Jia were working for the Intelligence Directorate. He also might be lying to put them off-guard.

"We're well-paid." Erik shrugged, but he kept the gun pointed at the man. "And now we don't have to worry about all the crap involved in building a case. We just have to stop people from screwing with clients."

"My employers can give you something your well-paying security company can't." The man offered something approaching a smile. "They can give you something that almost no one in the UTC can, even the...government."

"What are your employers offering?" Erik asked.

The man gestured broadly, ending with a theatrical flourish. "The truth about Molino."

Jia's heart rate kicked up. She wasn't sure if they should press the man right there. The scenario was overly elaborate for a trap if the Ascended Brotherhood was involved, but there was no way a local syndicate knew anything about the conspiracy. Given his crack about the government, he probably saw through their cover, but he also might be probing and trying to get them to give up information.

"Molino?" Erik raised an eyebrow. "What big truth is there? Terrorists got the jump on my unit, and good soldiers died. The end."

The man shook his head. "My employers have every reason to believe you don't believe that, and it's not true. Come now, don't insult me by claiming you think it was terrorists."

"What *is* the truth, then?" Erik asked, his hands tightening on the grip of his pistol. "And who exactly do you work for?"

"Ah, again, that's not something I feel comfortable sharing in this setting." The man pointed down the alley past Erik. "I will be at the Morning Glory tomorrow during their lunchtime. We can discuss it then, or we can fight here and not have a discussion because one or more of us will be dead. Your choice. Part of what I'm to establish is whether you can be reasonable, or if your penchant for violence is an expression of an inability to accept the necessity of delaying gratification. My employers have no use for violent thugs, only men and women who can control their base desires for the betterment of our species."

Jia's gaze flicked to Erik, but she didn't lower her gun. He lifted his pistol and nodded to her. She dropped her arm but didn't holster her gun.

"Excellent." The man clapped lightly. "You're intriguing." He walked past Erik. "I will see you both tomorrow."

Jia waited until the man stepped onto the street. "You're following him, right, Emma?"

"Of course." Emma sounded insulted.

"He might not be who we think." Erik frowned. "Our plan might have attracted a lot of attention, just not the attention we wanted."

"But he mentioned Molino." Jia tucked her gun into its holster. "You're right. If it was the conspiracy, why would they send a man to recruit instead of kill us?"

"Maybe they think they can co-opt us." Erik shrugged. "Or maybe it's someone else entirely. We need to check in with Bora and get some shit figured out. For now, let's see what happens with Emma."

———

"You lost him?" Jia groaned.

"Yes," Emma replied. "He never re-emerged from the other end of the tunnel I tracked him to. I sent drones through and into the connecting passages, and although there are other people, my gait analysis suggests they're not the same."

"It doesn't matter." Erik stared at the yellow and white clouds above them. "We'll just have to be prepared for anything tomorrow."

CHAPTER FORTY-FIVE

An hour later, Erik sat at a table in the galley of the *Argo* with Jia, Priya, and Emma.

Erik and Jia had contacted the ID agent for a meeting. With Emma and Cutter on surveillance, the ship seemed like the best place to meet. They didn't know who or what might be watching them in the city, and it was also a good opportunity to see if anyone knew the true way they'd arrived on Venus.

Emma's coverage of the local area didn't detect any suspicious people or anomalies. They'd managed to keep some secrets from their mysterious new friend.

"Did you check on what I asked about?" Erik watched Priya, looking for any sign she might be lying.

Priya frowned and shook her head. She seemed more annoyed than anything. "I guarantee whoever this guy is, he's not another local ID agent. I don't have direct contact with every other agent, but I sent a message to Earth when I got your message just to be sure. They sent me something back right before I responded. Anyone else operating in this area would have coordinated an operation with me."

Erik scratched his ear, the casual motion a stark contrast to the dark glower on his face. "So, he's not a ghost, but he knows about Molino, which means he has to work for the conspiracy. It's like those assholes are spitting in my face."

"Why the game, then?" Jia shook her head. "Why not just lure us into an ambush? Why not just shoot us there?"

"Who else could he be?" Erik shrugged.

"He might represent some other group. Not the conspiracy directly, but someone aware of their activities, or even a corporation that was investigating Molino themselves and came to the conclusion it was suspicious." Jia nodded slowly. "All the roads on Molino lead to Ceres Galactic, so even if they aren't the conspiracy, it could be a competitor who wants to weaken them. It might make sense for another corporation to approach us, but we've got that corp hunter reputation, so they want to slow-walk their offer."

"I can't match the guileful gentleman's face to any of the public databases," Emma explained with a frown. "But I haven't attempted to access restricted databases here yet, either."

Priya shook her head. "Don't bother. I ran the data you sent me through my info, and we're not getting any hits. He also didn't appear in the camera feeds near the hotel. I'm still working on getting the data from the other cameras, but I'm surprised. You said he was using a disguise."

"Is that the kind of thing a corporate agent could pull off?" Jia asked.

"Why the hell not?" Erik gestured to his PNIU. "They make all this stuff in the end. The guys we've been dealing with in Neo SoCal got fat and lazy because the corruption was everywhere. People who have to maintain more of an edge would be more careful."

"Do we think he's Brotherhood? His quick movement and fence trick aside, Emma might be wrong."

Emma folded her arms and snorted. "*Might.*"

"If he's not a third-party Ascended Brotherhood, he might work for the people who control them," Erik replied. "I don't care if this is a trap, there's no way we can walk away from it. We need to grab this guy and interrogate him. If this is just stupid corporate games, we can pat him on the head and send him away with a cookie. Otherwise, we'll drag out every last piece of information we can about the Brotherhood and their allies."

"That's unlikely." Emma gave Erik a pitying look. "Given what we've seen from the Ascended Brotherhood, he will likely simply kill himself. He's obviously beyond the standard terrible trolls you've dealt with, but one has to imagine the people higher up than the Brotherhood have similar measures."

Priya beat her fist on the table. "I'm getting tired of being outplayed by a bunch of Tin Men with delusions of grandeur. The ID cut them on New Year's, and I think it's time we put the bleeding corpse out of its misery."

"Maybe he fries himself." Jia shook her head. "Maybe not. We don't know anything about them, and the ID barely knew much about the Brotherhood until the last couple of months. If Alina's right and they're getting desperate, they might have people out in the field without the safeguards we've encountered before. If he's some sort of senior official, he might refuse to have those kinds of implants. Plenty of would-be kings think they don't need to do what the peasants do."

"You're right, we can't let this opportunity pass. If this guy is just a random recruiter, we can move on, but I say we set up full hacks, full drone coverage, ready to disrupt all local PNIU comms. I'll use my tricks and influence to keep the cops from responding right away if trouble happens, and I'll watch from outside during the meeting."

Erik locked eyes with her. "If trouble *happens*, I'm not planning on being restrained about my response. We clear on that?"

"Do what you need to do, Blackwell. I plan to bring a very long sniper rifle. If it's the Brotherhood, it's better we wipe them out tomorrow than wait for them to pull something on Skyward Day." Priya offered him a hungry smile. "It's time we plan for our own party."

March 20, 2230, Floating City Parvati, Bar Morning Glory

The gaudy gold-leaf motif of the bar set Erik even more on edge as he and Jia waited at a table, but he had to admit the lamb he'd ordered while they waited was tasty. He wasn't sure what it was about Venusian spices, but they really brought out the flavor in a meat he didn't normally like that much.

Cuisine aside, he understood why the mysterious gaunt

man had chosen the location for their meeting. It was far from the hectic bustle near the center of the local habitation module and well away from the major hotels and locations for festival activities, most of which weren't taking place in the module.

There was almost no one else in the restaurant for lunch, so the servers were obsequiously happy about the arrival of the handful of customers.

Erik's toe nudged the long case under the table. He didn't want to take anyone on without his TR-7. The case might not beat a weapons scanner at a spaceport, but the restaurant greeter didn't question it or give any indication he understood anything dangerous rested inside.

"Nothing unusual for several hundred meters," Emma reported over the comm. "Other than your lunchtime guest. He is approaching the restaurant at a brisk but not unnatural pace."

"Crowd activity?" Jia asked. "Any nearby?"

"Minimal within the likely engagement zone. Given what I'm observing, I question the wisdom of opening a restaurant in what mostly seems to be an automated factory zone. Public records suggest this is a real restaurant, and I've located one recent article about small businesses in trouble in Parvati, and how the Skyward Day festivities can help them. This place was mentioned specifically as not benefitting."

Erik chuckled. "Plenty of people screw up in ways that don't end in a dramatic public incident or explosions."

"He's almost to the restaurant," Emma reported. "His pace and demeanor remain casual."

"I'm secure in my position on the roof," Priya transmitted. "I've got my feeds, but if he wants everything private and starts jamming, I'm not planning to come down without a signal."

"Don't worry, Agent Bora," Emma responded. "Given the window position and where Erik's sitting, I can get a direct point-to-point laser communication to him even with general jamming. We'll know what's going on." She sighed. "Please note, Erik, this requires careful positioning of my drones relative to where you are. Don't move if at all possible if you don't want to lose contact with me."

"Okay. I'll try, but I might have to dodge a grenade." Erik glanced at the entrance as their lunchtime companion entered and exchanged brief words with the greeter before heading toward their table.

The gaunt man sat down without a word, his hand in his pocket. Erik wasn't surprised when the light background noise of the restaurant, including the music, vanished. It saved Erik the trouble of using his privacy device.

"What should we call you?" Jia asked. "You never gave us a name."

"You can call me the Agent," the gaunt man replied. "It is a fitting appellation that relates my purpose in life."

"Cute." Erik pushed his plate forward. He'd lost his appetite. "I don't have time for crap, so let's cut to the chase, Agent."

"I don't wish to waste your time, Mr. Blackwell and Miss Lin. How can I cut to the chase for you?"

"Who do you work for?" Jia demanded. "We need details, not hints."

The Agent looked at the two of them, a faint hint of

disappointment in his eyes. "I represent certain parties with an interest in making the UTC better. My employers have access to information on the savage people responsible for the unnecessary deaths on Molino. They're prepared to give you that information."

"Certain parties?" Erik scoffed. "Like who?"

"I'm not at liberty to share their identity just yet, but suffice it to say, they are people of influence and resources who are worried about the trajectory of human history." The Agent folded his hands in front of him. "It's already forgotten by most that your soldiers were on that moon as part of an effort to protect the UTC from humanity's enemies. Our species stands at a crossroads. We're surrounded by alien creatures who don't share our values. All the while, corporations and corrupt government officials focus only on what's in front of them and not what the decades and centuries might bring."

"What might they bring?" Jia asked.

The Agent stared at her, his mouth partially open. "*Extinction*. The war didn't begin on Molino, but it will reach it eventually. With the Zitarks, or perhaps the Leems, or the Aldrans, or creatures we haven't even met yet. Currently, the wealthy and powerful spend too much time focused on their own success, ignoring what they need to do to strengthen the UTC. The politicians focus on courting votes and favors. The government does its best to weaken our species by not taking advantage of all its knowledge. They pass laws to hobble our advancement. They even hide knowledge. Do you think the aliens are restricting themselves that way? Every indication is that they aren't."

Erik narrowed his eyes. "You know a lot about things you shouldn't."

"I know little except what my employers deem fit to pass along to me." The Agent offered Erik a tight smile. "But they see potential in you two. Your resourcefulness has been proven repeatedly against deadly and dangerous foes such as the butchers ultimately behind Molino."

Erik smirked and shook his head. "I already know the mercs were just the tools of the Ascended Brotherhood."

"You're very knowledgeable, Mr. Blackwell."

Jia stared at the Agent, her jaw tight. "Would you happen to know a Hadrian Conners?"

He shook his head. "The name is unfamiliar to me. Why?"

"He's a very mysterious man who was involved in a previous case, so good at hiding that the ID had trouble tracking him down." Jia's nostrils flared. "I was just thinking that what little information we've gathered on him might apply to you."

"I assure you I am not Hadrian Conners."

"Yeah." Erik snorted. "Because you're the Agent."

"Yes." The Agent nodded slowly. "And I'm ready to offer you what you most desire, the truth and revenge. My employers can lead you to the Ascended Brotherhood, and you can destroy them, strengthening the UTC."

"Your employers control the Ascended Brotherhood." Erik reached under the table toward the case.

"No." The Agent shook his head. "They don't. I think you've misunderstood some things."

"This is beyond arrogant. Do those bastards actually

think they can recruit me by tossing me some sacrificial cyborgs?"

"I think you're overreacting, Mr. Blackwell," the Agent replied. "I think my employers can offer you everything you've wanted since Molino and more, but you have to be reasonable about it."

"What do you think, Jia?" Erik asked, sliding the case out, not caring that the man saw.

Jia sighed. "I think the ID ripped the Brotherhood to shreds, and the conspiracy can toss it at you for scraps. If anything he's saying is true, we could be useful to them by taking out the competition. After all, there's no way one giant conspiracy controls every piece of scum in the UTC, and we do have a nose for trouble and a talent for taking care of it."

Erik grinned ferally at the man. "I'm going to find every person indirectly or directly involved with what happened on Molino. If I can't bring them to justice, I'll kill them. I don't care who they are or where they are. I died on the moon too, and the man you see before you is a ghost seeking revenge. You don't bargain with ghosts by offering them new jobs."

"I think you're throwing away a useful opportunity. My employers share the same goals. They want the UTC to be a better, less corrupt place." The Agent clucked his tongue. "Don't be myopic. You should take advantage of the resources available to you, not throw them away in a fit of pique like a spoiled child."

The corner of Erik's smart lens flashed an emergency message. He tapped his PNIU to bring it up, ignoring the header about alternative transmission message.

My sensors suggest Tin Men are approaching the restaurant. They aren't running and don't have any obvious external weapons.

Erik sighed and nodded to Jia. He stood and grabbed the case. "You've got one chance to convince me. We're going to step outside to continue this conversation."

The Agent raised an eyebrow. "I've made special accommodations at this place. I would rather not talk outside."

"I insist." Erik's voice became a growl. "Because now I'm pissed that you thought you could dangle Molino at me and get me to jump for you like a trained pet."

"You've misunderstood the nature of my offer," the Agent insisted.

Erik had had enough. It was time to negotiate a different way.

"Everyone, get the hell out of here!" He bellowed. "Terrorists are coming!"

CHAPTER FORTY-SIX

The single server in the room and the greeter rushed toward the back, shouting at the tops of their lungs in a language Erik didn't understand. The Agent stood and edged backward, his expression blank.

Erik pulled open the case and removed the TR-7 inside with his left hand. The case clattered to the floor as he gripped the weapon with both hands and flipped off the safety.

"I'm through with the bullshit."

"You're making a mistake, Mr. Blackwell." The Agent's gaze watched the rifle with careful attention, the corners of his mouth turning down in a faint frown. "This doesn't need to happen. You still have an excellent opportunity to get what you want."

"A lot of things don't need to occur." Erik snorted. "You're the one who has a bunch of your Tin Men from the Brotherhood coming. You think I'm afraid? I've fought them before, more than once."

The Agent sighed. "This course of action will end with your death. You won't get your revenge. You won't get the people responsible."

"Nah." Erik shrugged. "This course of action will end with death, just not mine. If you want to surrender, I can guarantee you won't end up with a bullet in your brain. Trust me, if I can kill a Tin Spider, I can kill a Tin Man."

Jia drew her pistol, pointed it at the door, and glanced at Erik's PNIU. He'd moved. Emma might not be aligned for laser comm anymore. The AI would need to think of another way to warn them when the enemy arrived.

The Agent sighed and shook his head. "Do you really think I didn't know about your weapon? Do you really think I don't know that you're watching the area with drones? This has all been part of the evaluation process."

"I think you don't have a gun out, and we do." Erik grinned. "And we've got AP rounds, and I've got a big gun. I think if I blow off your legs, it doesn't matter if they're metal or not." He hefted the gun and hovered his finger over the trigger. "I've got a friend nearby who has brought along some toys that can disable even a Tin Man. Your choice: surrender or fry yourself right now because otherwise—"

A loud thump sounded from the front door. One of Emma's drones had run into it at full speed. The unfortunate device fell to the ground in pieces. The Agent took his opportunity and bolted for the back, leaping over a table with ease and hitting the ground in a sprint so fast he was to the door before Erik and Jia had finished pointing their weapons that way.

Erik growled but didn't pull the trigger. He couldn't be sure the staff had evacuated yet. Instead, he ran after the Agent. His target grabbed a table one-handed and hurled it toward his pursuers like it weighed nothing. The table forced Erik to jump out of the way as the other man slipped through the back door. It shut behind him. By the time Erik arrived, it wouldn't open.

"How can Emma detect everyone else's hardware, but not his?" Erik shouted in irritation.

"Who knows?" Jia ran toward the front door and narrowed her eyes. "I get why Emma smashed her drone. She was trying to warn us. We've got six large men less than ten meters away, all in heavy coats and masks."

Erik kicked the locked door. "I hope Emma's smart enough to follow that bastard." He ran toward the front door, stopping by a table. After yanking it onto its side, he knelt behind it and steadied his weapon. "Let's take these guys out. Left to right together, concentrate on the heads."

Jia slid behind the table and brought up her gun. The Tin Men spread apart and broke into a run, their long strides sending them toward the restaurant at blistering speed. A loud crack sounded from above. One of the Tin Men jerked and fell to the ground, a massive hole in its chest.

"Priya's earning her pay." Erik grinned.

Jia nodded. "Always good when backup...well, backs us up."

The Tin Man hopped back to its feet, spikes popping out of its wrists. It jumped onto the side of a building, jamming its spikes into the wall to climb. Another of its compatriots raised its wrist and fired a small high-speed dart toward the roof of a nearby building. The other four continued their charge.

"Our turn." Erik flipped to four-barrel mode and lined up his first shot. "Three, two, one, *fire!*"

His TR-7 spat bullets at the same time Jia's pistol fired. The bullets ripped through the door and struck the head of one of the charging Tin Men. He spun, blood and blue fluid spewing from the wound and painting the ground.

Without another word, the partners switched to the next target and fired. The second cyborg jerked to the side, avoiding the worst of the attack, but stumbled as a couple of bullets found their mark.

Priya's sniper rifle put several rounds into the Tin Man firing at her. Her attack left him a twitching mess on the ground.

The two undamaged Tin Men closed on the door. They smashed through with long blades extending from their arms. The collision ripped off their coats and masks, revealing silver-gray bodies indistinguishable from humanoid bots.

Erik and Jia answered with another coordinated volley. At point-blank range, their burst of armor-piercing rounds ripped through the head of their target, blowing huge chunks out. The body spiraled through the air to collapse on his partner, who pushed him off and leapt back up, swiping toward Erik and Jia.

They rolled out of the way as it cut the table in half like it was thin balsa wood. Erik squeezed off quick shots into the cyborg's chest, but the enemy jumped behind him. Jia kept firing at the Tin Man's head, but its erratic shaking and movement stopped most of the bullets from hitting.

The Tin Man tossed a chair toward Jia at full force. She ducked, but it struck her shoulder, knocking her back. Her weapon flew out of her hand and skittered across the floor.

Erik growled and put more rounds into the Tin Man, this time striking his head.

The Tin Man shook with each impact but didn't go down. It pointed its arm straight at Erik, but decades of combat instinct kicked in, making Erik drop to his knee and bend backward as the blade launched with a hiss. The projectile zoomed over him, missing his face by centimeters before embedding itself halfway into the wall.

The Tin Man jumped toward Erik. Jia rolled and grabbed her pistol, then emptied the rest of her magazine, blasting holes in the Tin Man's chest. Erik pushed himself upright and shoved his TR-7 right into the chest of his descending opponent. He held down the trigger, blasting away metal and what remained of flesh underneath, blood and fluid spraying all over. The Tin Man brought back a fist. Erik let go of his rifle and yanked out his pistol, firing it into the already damaged face of his enemy. It took most of his ammo, but the Tin Man slumped, half-pinning Erik, before the familiar twitch that marked its internal destruction.

"Damn, it got its gunk all over me." Erik wiped the fluid off his face and shoved the dead cyborg off him. He hadn't heard any rifle fire from outside. "Emma, you still jammed?"

"No, that's passed," she replied. "I've got multiple drones

following the target, and I've taken the liberty of hacking new ones."

"Do what you need to do to keep on the Agent." Erik sat up, holstered his pistol, and grabbed his rifle.

"You all did well for fleshbags."

"Maybe." Erik reloaded his TR-7. "But I think those guys were more about covering that bastard's escape than putting us down. We fought tougher guys on New Year's." He spun toward the door at a movement out of the corner of his eye.

Priya stood there with her rifle in her arms and an annoyed look on her face. "Is that any way to treat the woman who helped save you?"

"Emma's still got our boy in sight," Erik explained. "He was flinging tables one-handed and sprinting like he's a mini-flitter."

"Not a big surprise. Maybe a dedicated infiltration model." Priya sighed and shook her head. "Now I have a big mess. I want you two out of here before the cops come. I'm glad I prepped everything because otherwise, they would have already been here. Keep your disguises on for now, and as far as the cops will know, you two were undercover CID agents involved in a sting that went horribly wrong."

Jia gestured with her pistol toward one of the dead Tin Men. "There's no way that's all of them."

"Sure, but your guy got away." Priya ran her hand through her hair. "I'm not going to complain about more dead Brotherhood, but we're not any closer to finding out what they have planned, and if he's in charge, their plan's still going on."

"Don't despair, Agent Bora," Emma interrupted. "I

haven't lost the Brotherhood's Agent. This time I anticipated his actions. I've been monitoring systems along his
path, and I'm able to track him indirectly through the
cameras he keeps disabling or spoofing. I'm taking control
of drones as necessary, and for now, I still have eyes on
him."

"You're leaving a major trail I'll need to clean up." Priya
frowned. "There's only so far I can push the CID
explanation."

"That's your problem. I'm more concerned about taking
these guys down before they kill a bunch of people." Erik
walked toward the door, moving around a destroyed table
and a dead Tin Man. "Emma, how fast is he moving now?"

"He's slowed since clearing the immediate area," she
replied. "And he slows on occasion when people come into
sight."

"That means we can catch up with him on the mini-flitters." Erik motioned for Jia. "I'm not willing to wait around
until we get lucky again. Whoever this Agent is, he's got
more going on than the average Brotherhood Tin Man."

Jia offered a polite nod to Priya. "Make sure the restaurant gets a little payment from the CID."

The agent glared at her. "I'm not your personal
assistant, Lin."

"Then consider it a professional courtesy."

Erik and Jia ran out of the restaurant and toward their
parked vehicles. The Agent had escaped, but his allies had
charged into battle heedless of death, showing little
concern about their fallen comrades.

Closer to the true conspiracy. That was what they were
—closer.

Their enemies had miscalculated, or the Lady had chosen that day to reward Erik and Jia. He didn't care as long as it led him to the same place.

If the Agent was running, he was afraid on some level. Erik could use that fear against him.

CHAPTER FORTY-SEVEN

Jia and Erik kept their mini-flitters low, almost skimming the ground, guided by Emma's navigation prompts.

Their abrupt altitude changes avoided tragedy but only barely. If they didn't catch up soon, the local cops might stop them.

They didn't know how long Priya's CID cover would keep the local authorities from interfering. When the time came, it might be nice to have extra firepower, but there was too much to explain in the middle of the chase.

The Agent had picked up his pace again, running through the city at over fifty kilometers an hour before leaving the habitation module and descending to one of the lowest modules, one mostly focused on city support and industrial fabrication. With Emma's help, they found a small access tunnel to catch up with him.

"I no longer have direct visual contact," Emma reported. "I'm following evidence of camera manipulation. I should note there is a high probability the system intrusions on my end will be detected since I don't have time to do it in a manner that will not draw attention to a skilled person paying attention."

"I don't know if that's a bad thing. At this point, we might want to just call the locals." Jia emerged from a tunnel. The dense web of machinery, cabling, and fans reduced their flight to a crawl.

"I'm not sure we need the local cops until we know what we're dealing with," Erik replied.

"The intrusion might also include the enemy," Emma explained. "They're obviously already aware of my drone efforts and some other general capabilities."

"You sure this was where he went?" Erik asked, looking around. "It's not like he doesn't know we want him."

"He's on this level for sure," Emma replied. "But beyond that, I can't say. There are no more modules beneath this one, but there are other modules laterally connected."

"Forget about trying to be subtle or hiding." Erik watched a pair of cargo drones fly by overhead with crates clutched underneath. "Hack every damned camera on this level if you need to. We're not letting this guy get away. He might have his toys, but we have you, and there's no way you're going to lose against a half-fleshbag, right?"

Emma chuckled. "I don't need the encouragement to track him. Give me a moment. I still need to take basic measures so as not to allow the Brotherhood to easily cut me off."

Jia's breath caught as she surveyed the area. "I can't be the only one getting a bad feeling about where he ran. We're in a low-level module?"

Erik motioned to the ground. "But you said it's not as

simple as blowing a hole, right? And don't all the modules have somewhere you can blow through to the outside?

"It's not that simple, and yes, they do." Jia pointed to an intricate mess of piping and machinery in the distance. "Do you know what that is?"

"Random doodads?" Erik shrugged. "The secret factory where they make that furniture they claim is handcrafted?"

"It's part of the atmospheric processing plant." Jia frowned. "From what I read on the way here, most of the air in the city is cycled through two primary processors. There are nowhere near enough plants or algae in a city like this to have any hope of supplying enough oxygen without supplementation. It might be a coincidence, but I doubt he's here because he's got a big personal interest in floating city air systems."

"I don't mean to interrupt you, Jia," Emma began, "but I do have something to show you two. I've positioned a few drones to give me line of sight on areas I can't currently access because of extreme camera systems irregularity. I've also taken the liberty of highlighting items of interest."

Multiple images popped up in front of them on data windows. A large group of Tin Men of various configurations, along with Tin Spiders, were spread out in a vast machinery-filled chamber, alert. Dead workers lay in pools of their own blood. Emma added red highlights around small gray squares attached to different machines and pipes in the plant.

Jia scrubbed a hand down her face. "That looks like part of the atmospheric processing control plant."

"I hate it when you're right about this kind of thing." Erik sighed.

"Me too, if it helps."

"So, they're going to smother the city?" Erik asked.

Jia nodded. "If they've already killed people, They're ready to execute their plan. There would eventually be a shift change or something, and people would discover what was happening, even with the camera control. Emma, what about the other atmospheric processor?"

Another data window appeared, depicting a similar area, but the normal human workers and drones populated it, with no hint of cyborg intruders or murders.

"Trashing one processor's not going to be enough." Jia gestured toward the first atmospheric processor complex. "But if they blow that one and then punch enough holes, it might be. The authorities are going to swarm this place to repair it. I don't get why they didn't take both out."

"Because they want terror." Erik nodded. "The Tin Men blow the processor, draw some people here, and then spread out over the city to blow up more shit." He gestured to the data window depicting the first atmospheric processing plant. "Those are all small-scale explosives, but there is no way they can walk around planting a bunch of them all over the city without getting spotted by cameras and drones. They'd need chaos first."

"They don't need to blow up the whole city." Jia's hands tightened on her handlebars. "They just need to bleed off enough of the internal atmosphere, and they can do that if they're hitting everywhere. The city might sink."

"Then we need to take these guys out before they spread out, right?" Erik nodded at the image. "Even if they blow that processor, as long as we keep them contained, their plan won't work, and the city can keep shit under control. If we can handle the processing plant, the cops can handle the rest."

"That's a lot of Tin Men." Jia shook her head. "It might not be as many as we fought on New Year's, but it's way more than we just fought." She pointed to some of the Tin Men. "And they've got the primary approaches covered. We'll be slaughtered if we try a frontal assault."

Erik grinned and gestured to a large sealed door near the back. "What's that?"

"It's a loading door." Jia shrugged. "They don't use them much, but they have them because they might need to deliver something large, especially on the lower levels."

"I've got a plan." Erik smiled. "Because they're not guarding that door."

"You're kidding." Jia's eyes widened, and she groaned as she realized his plan. "You're not kidding?"

Erik shook his head. "We grab our exos, suits, and some breathers, have Cutter fly the *Argo* right up to the door, and Emma opens it. Those bastards will never see it coming."

"That's almost certainly going to set off alarms," Emma noted. "Just flying there will set off alarms."

"Not if you're half as good as you think." Erik smiled. "We can have Priya help."

Emma sighed. "I'm twice as good as *you* think."

"We have to stop them from setting off the charges." Jia's jaw tightened as she thought about the possibilities. "We don't know how they might be triggered, and we don't know that Emma can remotely hack them, but I have an idea. We blanket the area with EMPs. It won't stop the Brotherhood Tin Men, but it should disrupt the charges."

Erik frowned. "I'm not expert on Venusian atmospheric

processing equipment, or any atmospheric processing equipment really, but won't that screw it up?"

Jia shook her head. "All the primary equipment is reinforced against that kind of thing. There was an accident with a non-military EMP early in Venusian colonial history that led to that."

"Huh." Erik's brows lifted in surprise. "We'll contact Priya and have her push the authorities and cover our asses about the flight, but otherwise, we suit up right away, and we do this thing. If she can get the local TPST or Militia to show up, that'd be nice, too."

Jia shook her head. "If we're right, they need all the firepower they can get spread around the city to take on Tin Men causing trouble. For all we know, they might have already deployed half their forces out there."

Erik grimaced. "Damn. In either event, if we hit them hard here, that might draw some of them off."

"By ourselves?" Jia laughed. "Even with this plan, it's going to be risky. Your Lady is back to being..." She snickered. "Kind of a bitch, really."

"Yeah. Oh, well. Sometimes you do a surprise raid with a pile of exo squads at your back, and sometimes you show up by yourself and do the work."

Jia stared at her partner. "We're barely going to have time to catch our breath."

"Don't worry. That's what the breathers are for." Erik lifted off and spun his mini-flitter to the access tunnel. "Emma, get me Cutter on the comm."

CHAPTER FORTY-EIGHT

Cutter yowled in excitement. "This is the kind of shit I thought I'd be doing all the time when I first got my pilot's license. I get to show off my skills without getting shot."

"You could always get blown out of the sky," Emma commented.

"Don't be a buzz-kill, Holochick."

Jia took a deep breath as she stared at an external drone feed while sitting in the cargo bay, safely ensconced in her tactical suit, exoskeleton, and breather next to Erik. He was equipped the same way.

The *Argo* skimmed close to the city, Cutter's careful thrust burst and attitude manipulations were almost graceful in how they moved the ship through the levels and toward the module containing the Ascended Brotherhood army.

Ships weren't supposed to fly close to most of the city. Grav fields and protection could only do so much to protect against major collisions.

"Remember, Emma," Jia transmitted, "once we're

461

inside, do your best to tag the charges for us, but once we've been in for a minute, close the door. We can't take the chance the Brotherhood kills the oxygen field and we help them drain things. I don't know if they even need to breathe."

"Duly noted," Emma replied.

"I wish we had a couple of rocket launchers," Erik grumbled. "Remind me to bug Alina about putting rocket launchers on the shopping list if we manage to survive this."

"Way to keep things positive," Jia muttered.

Erik chuckled. "Trying to be balanced in my old age."

"Agent Bora is attempting to contact you," Emma reported. "Shall I put her through?"

"Go ahead. We've got a couple of minutes before show-time, and I doubt she's calling to ask us if we've seen the latest episode of *Skyward Shield*."

"Blackwell, Lin, you there?" Priya asked.

"We're suited up and heading toward the Brotherhood now," Jia replied while adjusting some of the sensor settings on her exoskeleton. "How are things on your end?"

"We've got the authorities evacuating all major groups of civilians," Priya replied, her voice tense. "They've already encountered and are engaging small groups of Brother-hood. Police made contact with two Tin Men near a chem-ical processing center. Some CID agents are engaging with another Tin Man in a different location. Cameras and drones are now malfunctioning all over the city. If the Brotherhood has been infiltrating the system since they murdered Kotnis, it might not be a simple matter to get everything functioning again quickly."

"Damn it," Erik growled in frustration. "They were already spread out. So much for drawing them away."

Priya sighed. "They aren't being subtle, but from what little I've gathered, I don't think the Tin Men were ready for the level of immediate armed response. I made sure everyone knew they would be dealing with high-end cyborgs, and they're using the appropriate weapons."

"They must have pushed the plan up because of what happened with us." Jia cut the exterior feed of the *Argo*. She couldn't stand not being at the controls for the maneuver. "If they're rushing things, they also won't be prepared for what we're about to do. From what we saw earlier, the bulk of their forces are in the processing plant."

"That's true, but they've got Tin Men guarding every major access tunnel," Priya explained. "On top of that, there are problems with the elevators leading to the plant. I don't know how quickly backup will arrive. Parvati isn't Neo SoCal. It's a question of resources."

Erik let out a satisfied chuckle. "That's okay. We're almost ready. They can do their part, and we'll do ours. As long as everyone can handle them up top, we'll handle them here. Blackwell out."

"I'm hovering in front of the door," Cutter interrupted. "I'm an awesome pilot, but we've got heavy winds. Also remember, the city might not be moving fast, but it's moving. So, you know, do your thing before we crash."

The MX 60 came to life and lifted off. Jia jerked her head to the side, frowning as the vehicle hovered over Erik and Jia.

"What's going on?" she asked.

Emma let out a conceited laugh. "The *Argo*'s weapons

are too powerful to deploy in support without significant risk of collateral damage, but this isn't. It'll be easier to combine this with my drones to spot the charges."

"You just want to shoot cyborgs." Erik accused.

"Eliminating obnoxious terrible trolls does hold its charms, as I'm sure you're well aware."

The turret deployed from the bottom of the flitter, twisting left and right before aiming forward. Emma let out an eager cackle that was all too human.

"Be careful with that." Jia expanded her shield on her left arm, along with the spike. "Don't shoot us by accident."

"Oh, please, Jia." Emma scoffed. "I know what I'm doing."

"Why does that not fill me with confidence?"

"Because you're young." Emma twirled the turret.

"Young?" Jia rolled her eyes. "You're younger than I am!"

"Not if you count all the way back to Charlotte. Now prepare, I've hacked the door controls and am ready to open the cargo bay door."

"Don't go to town too much." Erik gestured with the exo's arm toward the door. "We don't want to do half their work for them."

Erik lifted his machine gun and took a step forward, the heavy foot of the exoskeleton clanging and echoing in the cargo bay. "This doesn't change the plan. We concentrate on charge disruption for a minute, then you close the door so Cutter can get out of here. We don't want the Brotherhood blowing too many holes in our nice new ship." He paused a moment. "Or my MX 60."

Emma let out a weary sigh of disappointment. "There is

passable logic in what you're saying. Very well. Opening the doors in ten, nine..."

"Seriously?" Erik asked.

"Three, two, one..."

The *Argo*'s cargo bay door opened with a rumble. Jia continued her deep breaths. The oxygen field in the cargo bay would keep the unpleasant and unbreathable Venusian air out, but they would be crossing into the processing plant, exposing them briefly.

It might not be a spacewalk, but it also wasn't something she'd ever done. The closest she'd gotten was a simulated ship-to-ship boarding operation at the tactical center.

Each new experience was two parts terrifying and an almost equal amount of thrilling.

A quiet howl of wind joined the low, dull groan of the processing plant's loading door grinding open. Emma opened fire before Jia could see anything.

Bullets ripped from the MX 60 turret.

Erik and Jia spread out to either side, and both readied their grenade launchers. They'd loaded up with EMPs and AP rounds. They faced a modest number of foes compared to Bogota, but here they didn't have direct ID support.

That was the Lady for you.

The loading door opened wide enough for Erik and Jia to advance, along with a squadron of Emma's drones.

Two Tin Men lay in pieces, destroyed by Emma's attack. Others leapt onto the pipes atop massive storage tanks or behind dingy, stained blocks of indeterminate equipment chained together in the plant.

Flashing red highlights tagged the distributed charges.

Erik and Jia ran forward, quick-firing EMPs into their

respective halves of the huge room. Their enemy mistook their intent, leaping away from their projectiles. Jia smiled. It made their job easier.

Jia fired her jump thrusters, left the *Argo's* cargo bay, and entered the plant. She ignored the cyborgs and concentrated on disabling the charges. The roar of the flitter's constant fire continued, the bright stream from the tracer rounds forming a river of death in the air. The sparks and blood splatter were a waterfall at the end for the targeted Tin Men.

A Tin Man scurried up the pipe like a cybernetic demon monkey and jumped out to claw a drone. His allies fired darts and blades to down other drones, which disappeared in clouds of debris. Several cyborgs closed on the door and Erik and Jia. Emma's turret fired a burst at a Tin Spider, who spun in time to only lose one limb.

"Close the door, Emma," Erik shouted. "If they get on board, you might not be able to hold them off."

"Hmph." Emma decapitated a Tin Man with a stream of bullets. "I was running low on bullets anyway. Good luck. I'd prefer it if you two didn't die. I've grown slightly fond of you."

Jia chuckled and launched her last EMP. "Thanks."

"Please also note that I lost connection other than laser signals with some of the farthest drones," Emma reported. "There's a high probability they're about to jam the entire facility."

The loading door of the plant and the cargo bay door of the *Argo* started to close at the same time.

With a pulse of thrust, the ship drifted away from the module.

A resounding clank marked the closure of the loading door, leaving Erik and Jia alone with the Brotherhood. The cyborgs were spread out, watching and waiting, but they hadn't attacked anything but the ship and the drones.

"Emma, can you hear us?" Jia asked. She wasn't surprised when there wasn't a response.

Erik sidled his exoskeleton up beside Jia. "We might not have gotten all of the charges, but we must have gotten enough. I didn't study Venusian atmospheric processors when I was in pre-school like you, but I'm thinking they needed small, directed charges because this is sturdy equipment and it was probably too hard to smuggle anything bigger, or they were the only things they could source locally." He narrowed his eyes at a Tin Spider hanging off the wall in the distance. "That's also why those assholes are sticking to blades and claws."

"Pre-school?" Jia rolled her eyes. "Studying the important parts of the city on the way here isn't crazy. Sometimes you don't solve a problem with a bigger gun." She wanted to tap her head, but her hands were inside the arms of the exoskeleton.

"You can always solve a problem with a bigger gun."

Someone clapped loudly from behind a black column near the front of the room that ran from the floor to the ceiling. Jia wasn't sure what the function of the structure was, but she was less interested in that than whoever was clapping. She had a theory, which was quickly confirmed.

"Impressive, Mr. Blackwell and Miss Lin." The voice was loud but clear, the words perfectly enunciated and crisp. It was the Agent.

"It's over," Jia shouted. "We've disabled your charges

and tipped off the authorities. You're jamming us now, so you probably can't talk to your friends, but everybody with a gun is up there turning cyborgs into junk piles—police, military, CID, and ID. Your plan is done. You've lost. It's another loss for the Ascended Brotherhood."

"You don't know the depth of the plan." The Agent shifted behind the thick column, his shadow proof of his position. "It is unfortunate that this individual operation was disrupted, but I'm choosing to view it as an additional validation of your abilities. If anything, you've helped with another plan."

"Sure, sure, you're ten steps ahead of us, and that's why we're kicking your ass," Erik replied.

"I'm impressed that you were able to follow me so effectively. It's obvious that I underestimated your AI."

"Among other things." Erik pointed his gun toward the column. "Is that why your buddies didn't attack?"

"No. They were attempting to run down your ammunition, but I'll admit that by the time I realized you were using electromagnetic pulses, you'd already hit many of our charges." The Agent sighed. "You don't understand. You will fail here. You think you've stopped me, but you've stopped nothing important. However, I am authorized to give you another chance. You could be useful to my employers. You could achieve what your hearts desire—a humanity united and free of the petty corruption of the past."

Erik's guttural noise gave Jia all the information she needed. "I don't give a shit about that. I mostly desire to find your employers and kill them for Molino. I don't care what excuses you offer. I know they were involved. They're dead men walking."

Jia's gaze darted between different camera feeds. Emma had thinned the number of enemies, but there were enough Tin Men and Spiders left to make trouble. It wouldn't be an easy fight.

"What about you, Miss Lin?" the Agent asked. "This society is corrupt. In a sense, you could say it has lost the Mandate of Heaven."

"It's not the tenth century," Jia replied. "And you and your employers are just more vicious monsters killing and conspiring and claiming you're doing it for peace. You hide in the darkness and change your bodies into machines while murdering innocent people and manipulating terrorists. Nothing good can come out of anything grown from a festering pile of garbage."

The Agent stepped out from behind the column with a scowl on his face. "You've been offered something few will ever be given. We stand on the precipice of history, poised to follow the greatest among us to the domination of the galaxy, and you let petty morality—"

A burst from Erik's machine gun ripped through the Agent's chest. The shot knocked the man to the ground.

"Oops." Erik chuckled. "My finger slipped because I was rolling my eyes so hard at his bullshit."

The Agent hopped to his feet. Jia released more bullets, but he spun behind the column so fast his movement was almost a blur. He let out short, sharp laughs. The Tin Men shifted positions but didn't attack.

"You think that's enough to kill me?" the Agent asked. "I'm beginning to think my employers overestimated you."

"Are we supposed to be impressed?" Jia shouted. "You give a big speech about humanity, but you're just another Tin Man with a fake heart."

"Tin Man? No. Look closely at where I was."

Jia blinked and magnified the image. Bright yellow bloodstains covered the floor. She didn't know what to make of them. From what she'd seen, the cyborgs bled red or blue.

"So what?" Erik snorted. "They filled you with glowing piss instead of blood, and we're supposed to be impressed?"

"You don't understand. You aren't worthy to aid our great leaders. Technological modification is but one way to make someone stronger."

"You're a freaking *yaoguai*." Jia's stomach churned. "A mutant!"

"I'm nothing so base," the Agent replied. "My employers have access to knowledge you wouldn't *begin* to understand, along with certain samples from the past. Did you know Leem biological material is surprisingly stable following death? Despite the primitive state of technology during the Roswell Incident, those bodies were stored and then lost, only to be recovered." He let out a satisfied sigh. "Amazing—so many differences, yet so many similarities between the species. Triple helical DNA, but still DNA. My employers are far beyond what the pathetic, corrupt leaders of the UTC allow."

"Now I've heard everything." Erik barked out a laugh. "Making mutants wasn't enough, so we're mixing and matching with aliens? I thought your employers were all about humanity winning the stars, not half-*yaoguai*, half-aliens. Is that what they are, too?"

"They are something better. Superior, and soon they will be what our species needs—immortal philosopher kings and queens."

Tin Spiders emerged from the dark bowels of the processing plant. Some were missing limbs, or were covered in blood and whatever strange blue fluid mixed with their normal human blood.

"Erik," Jia took a step back and aimed her machine gun past the Agent and the column. "I think he's stalling for backup."

"Yes, a pity my reinforcements are here." The Agent jumped behind a thick nest of cables before she could take the shot. "Now I will see in death if you were worthy of my employers' attention."

His voice seemed to surround them. "Your death, of course."

CHAPTER FORTY-NINE

Erik would have been worried about taking on a *yaoguai* mutant with alien DNA and a room full of Tin Men if he'd been only carrying his TR-7 and wearing a tactical vest.

That wasn't the situation.

He was in a state-of-the-art exo with a genius natural pilot at his side, a woman who'd had his back in countless battles. No, he wasn't afraid. The damned Tin Men should have been afraid. If they were smart, they would have surrendered after he slaughtered their friends outside the bar.

Bullets were a nice cure-all for stupidity.

Jia and Erik might not have Emma to provide targeting assistance, but the jamming didn't disrupt the systems in their exoskeleton or dull their personal skills.

A Tin Man jumped from a nearby pipe, only to get a new hole through his head courtesy of a quick machine-gun burst. Jia blew another cyborg in half on the opposite side with practiced ease.

Erik ran forward in a zigzag pattern. Blades and spikes

sped toward him from all directions, some embedding deeper into the exoskeleton and his extended shield than he would have liked, but none causing serious damage.

His weapon swept across, ripping through the humanoid Tin Men and slowing them. A shot through the chest killed on occasion, but headshots or ripping apart their entire bodies proved more effective if not all that ammo-efficient.

Jia hit her jump thrusters and twisted in the air to deliver bullets in a wide arc. She downed two approaching Tin Men and landed a small distance from a charging Spider.

If she felt any fear, she didn't express it as she leveled her gun and delivered a stream of AP bullets through the body, upper chest, and head of the cyborg. It fell forward, and she jumped over the collapsing, twitching cybernetic monstrosity.

"Emma's little stunt was helpful," Erik shouted.

He shoved his shield spike into the chest of a Tin Man leaping toward him and introduced the enemy to his machine gun at point-blank range before shaking the body off.

Another generous arc of fire slowed the other approaching enemies, giving him time to hit vulnerable spots, including a nice single-round downing of a Tin Spider.

"Oh, hole in one."

Being a monster didn't help them as much when their opponents showed up in advanced tech.

"You know what I just realized?" Jia yelled.

"What?" Erik called back.

"Emma's stupid Leem in the simulation was almost prophetic."

"Kind of, but we've fought a lot of fake Zitarks and not a real one yet."

A Tin Man appeared atop a tall cylindrical storage tank behind Erik. He spun as he spotted the movement in his rearview display, but the enemy was already falling toward him, a long blade pointed down. A stream of bullets from Jia added so many holes Erik could see through to the other side before the body slammed hard into the floor.

"You're getting soft, old man!" Jia shouted.

"That's not what you said the other night!" Erik called back.

Jia's quick burst removed the remaining legs from another Spider. "Will you ever get tired of that joke?"

"Only when it stops being funny," he replied, downing a far-off Tin Man with a headshot.

Erik jumped toward the wall and bounded off at an angle, a risky move in a normal exo, but not in this advanced model.

His position change revealed two Tin Spiders lying in wait. They both leapt toward him, claws waving and teeth gnashing. He impaled one on his shield spike and jumped backward, dodging the frenzy of sharp limbs but landing with a stumble from the uneven weight of the massive creature now connected to him.

"Aw, hell!"

Two bursts sent out enough deadly ammo to blow off the head of the second enemy.

The Spider's friend continued thrashing and growling, his limbs ripping at the exoskeleton, trying to make it through to Erik's body. A shake of the shield didn't free him from the Tin Spider, and a stray claw made it inside, tearing his chest through his tactical suit. Stinging pain spread from the wound.

"I don't have time for this shit." Erik took several steps back in the exo and retracted the shield spike. The Spider fell to the ground and righted itself just in time for it to be cut in half by a sustained burst. He kicked the cyborg's body hard, sending it meters away. He was down to fifty percent ammo, but the enemy had been thinned out.

A blur of movement in the corner of his eye caught his attention, so he shifted his gaze and magnified. The Agent was fleeing.

"The bastard is running!" Erik shouted.

Closer to the target, Jia charged the Agent after slapping a Tin Man out of the way and downing two other cyborgs with perfectly timed headshots. The cacophony of her gunfire joined the heavy thud of her exo's feet on the metal floor. She angled and jumped up, gracefully bouncing off one column and then another to avoid other enemies and close the distance on the fleeing mutant. They couldn't let him get away.

He obviously knew more than the cannon fodder rushing toward them.

Erik bellowed and charged, sweeping his machine gun back and forth heedless of ammo to deliver a steady wave of death to the surviving cyborgs trying to stop them from capturing their leader.

Not all of the targets were dying, but even a full-conversion cyborg had trouble being a threat with half its body or a leg missing.

"Where are you going?" Jia yelled at the Agent. "Afraid you're going to lose? Where's all the smug superiority now?"

The Agent continued running, vaulting over stray cables and ducking low-lying equipment, but the cramped quarters slowed his escape, compared to his flitter-like speeds on the upper levels.

Jia pushed her exo forward and continued to close the distance while Erik picked off the enemies heading toward her back. His wound throbbed with each beat of his heart, but he ignored the pain and concentrated on keeping the cyborgs off Jia.

A mixed group of wounded Tin Men and Spiders grouped behind him and charged.

He spun around to finish them, first taking careful headshots at the Spiders. His choice allowed the Tin Men to close on him, but that just meant they were easier to hit when he switched over. Their metal bodies clanged as they hit the grated floor in this part of the plant.

"You guys should learn when to give up."

Erik swept the rear, seeking new Tin Men to dismantle, the rush of battle reducing the pain in his chest to a distant background consideration.

Satisfied he'd taken the rest of the enemy out, he hurried after Jia and the Agent.

He sprinted past dead and dying cyborgs and wove in and out of the carnage before entering a corridor barely large enough to accommodate his exo. His ammo was down to thirty percent, but he doubted the Agent had another army of Tin Men in his back pocket.

Jia's gun roared from ahead. Erik growled and pushed

forward, trying to will his exo to run faster as the top of his helmet threatened to brush the low-lying ceiling.

He ignored turns and intersection and continued heading toward the beautiful sound of a heavy machine gun on near-constant fire. Dead Tin Men gave way to empty floors stained with bright yellow blood. The gunshots grew louder and closer, and the corridor widened into a sprawling chamber.

Erik turned the exo and braked hard to avoid slamming into a massive wall. His feet scraped the floor, sparking. Jia's head and gun were pointed upward. The wall fed into several large shafts filled with massive spinning blades. Heedless of the threat, the Agent scampered up one of them, dripping blood but leaping back and forth as if gravity were a mere suggestion.

Jia shifted position and angled her gun. "From left and right. I'll take left. Let's light him up!"

Erik raised his weapon and fired with his partner. The Agent's agility was impressive, but there was nowhere left to dodge when the streams of bullets from both exos converged on him. They blew a massive hole through his abdomen and removed one of his legs. He didn't scream as he pitched backward and fell. He slammed into the floor with a loud crunch and splattered his bizarre blood everywhere. Jia and Erik edged toward the man. They'd wanted to interrogate him, but a monster like that couldn't be allowed to escape.

Jia gasped when she saw the Agent was still breathing and looking right at them. "You've got to be kidding me. What does it take to kill this guy?"

The Agent took a weak, shuddering breath. "You are

indeed impressive," he wheezed. "There have been…miscalculations."

"Why?" Jia lifted her faceplate to glare at him. "Why kill an entire city? What could that possibly accomplish? Your bosses aren't even announcing some special agenda. It's just murder for no reason."

"The best way to cover up the deaths of a few is to kill the many." The Agent coughed up blood. "I will die here, but don't think you've won. I've served my purpose. You disabled a distraction. Do you think those were the only explosives I had the Brotherhood set?" His hand reached into his pocket. "The plan still will succeed, and you will forever wonder about your failure."

Erik and Jia fired simultaneously. Neither said a word as they moved up and down the body, shredding what remained of the Agent. Whatever the conspiracy had done to make this man, they couldn't take the chance that he was about to set off a major explosion and kill innocent people.

Jia ceased fire first and sighed. "Did we get played?"

Erik looked around for a moment, trying to sense anything outside his suit. "If the city was sinking, wouldn't a bunch of alarms be going off? Or are we already dead and just reliving the last moments of our lives?"

"You're not dead," Emma transmitted. "Or if you are, so am I."

Erik took deep breaths. He might not be dead, but his wound hurt. "I'm not ready to be a zombie anyway. The jamming is clear?"

"It just cleared up," Emma replied. "I assume because of something you did. I'm sure it involved many bullets and/or explosions."

Erik grimaced.

They must have destroyed the jammer when they finished off the Agent, or he might have had the device implanted in his body. One other painful alternative presented itself. The Agent himself might have killed his jammer to set off whatever device he had hidden elsewhere.

"Did anything explode?" Jia asked. "Anywhere in the city? I don't mean simple Tin Man garbage, but a decent-sized explosion."

"Yes, unfortunately," Emma reported. "The authorities have suppressed all the active Tin Men throughout the city, but there was a moderate explosion at a luxury hotel. They are still evaluating the damage, but as you can imagine, there's a lot of confusion on the streets right now."

"Was it the Golden Thorn?" Jia asked. "It might have been targeted at us, but that doesn't make that much sense since the Agent knew we were here."

"No, it was a different hotel, and before you ask, the overall integrity of the city is fine. I don't know if what you did down there or what the authorities up here did disrupted a bigger explosion, but from what I can see with my drones, the hotel damage is mostly limited to a single level."

Jia narrowed her eyes. "A single level? This smells like an assassination. Who died?"

"I don't have that information at this time," Emma replied. "It's unclear if there were any casualties."

"Can't those assholes do anything without it being complicated? Whatever happened to just walking up to a guy and putting a gun to the back of his head?" Erik released his harness so he could apply a medpatch. The lack of enemies and adrenaline was letting the pain through.

Jia gasped. "You're hurt."

"Eh, no big deal. It's not like they shot through my hand." Erik offered her a lopsided smile and applied the patch. "Just a little love scratch. I don't care what some mutant freak said, and I don't care if their big plan was to kill the city to cover up an assassination. We saved a lot of people today, and we killed a lot of cyborgs. I'm adding one to the W column. Don't care if the Prime Minister was in that hotel; it was worth it."

Jia wiped away sweat and nodded toward the Agent's remains. "Uh, there are parts of him left. Maybe the ID can get something useful from them." She frowned. "But I'm not seeing a PNIU."

"Somehow, I doubt the guy's DNA is in a database." Erik closed his eyes, welcoming the pain relief of the patch. "Alina should pay us more."

CHAPTER FIFTY

March 20, 2230, Floating City Parvati, Private Hangar aboard the *Argo*

Priya eyed Erik from across the table in the galley. "We don't have to do this right now, Blackwell. It's only been a few hours. I can give you the debriefing tomorrow. I'd recommend you stay out of sight. Having you two wandering around will raise questions I don't want to answer, but we don't need to get you out of the city."

Erik, Priya, Jia, and Emma sat gathered for the debriefing. Cutter was in the cockpit in case they needed to make a quick escape.

Lanara had expressed rather bluntly that she didn't care about the mission results, other than being happy the ship and mini-flitters hadn't been damaged.

Raphael wanted to come and hear, in his own words, all the bloody and glorious details, but Lanara had all but dragged him off by the ear to help her with some tuning.

Jia was half-convinced that was the engineer's way of doing Erik a favor.

Jia glanced at her partner, trying to keep the concern off her face. They'd performed blood tests after returning to the ship. She'd been concerned that the Brotherhood shock troops might poison their claws and blades, but other than a deep, nasty laceration, Erik appeared to be okay.

That didn't stop Jia from thinking they needed a dedicated medic or doctor if they were going to keep having these sorts of encounters. There was going to come a point where medpatches wouldn't be enough.

She'd gotten shot through the hand not all that long ago. Losing a limb wasn't an impossibility. Getting it grown back was simple if a person had access to core world resources, but not if a person was trapped aboard a small ship.

Priya cleared her throat. "Okay, the simple version: the good guys won today. The Brotherhood wounded cops and soldiers, and some civilians here and there, but we should pull through it in the end with only a handful of deaths. If we hadn't pushed the locals when we did, it might have been too late. A lot of the Brotherhood seemed surprised at the fierce resistance. You bottling up their guys in the plant was damned helpful. I can't imagine what would have happened if all those *things* came boiling out of the bottom levels to reinforce their friends. It would have been a bloodbath before the locals could respond."

Jia nodded. "What about the hotel explosion? If what the Agent said was true, they were making a major mess to cover something up."

"It took me a surprising amount of effort to get the details, but it makes sense once you know who was involved." Priya furrowed her brow. "It's not often a private place has enough security to make an ID agent have a bad day. Based on what you told me and what I've found out about the explosion, it does seem like a targeted assassination. It wasn't just any level that got destroyed, but the penthouse suite. From what I've gathered and pried out of the locals, there were directional charges set on a lower level. Some lower-level guests and staff were injured, but no confirmed fatalities at this time."

"What about whoever was in the suite?" Jia asked.

Priya took a deep breath. "That is where things get interesting. There was no one in the suite at the time. According to internal hotel sensors, the occupant of the penthouse had left an hour before the explosion. I'm still digging into who might have been in it, but there are obviously fake registrations I need to put through records. We're talking someone of importance. There were no internal cameras in the penthouse."

"Huh. So, the Brotherhood went through all that trouble to blow up empty rooms?" Jia asked. "That seems sloppy and pointless. What are we missing?"

"I don't think they were planning on you showing up." Priya gestured to Erik and Jia. "We put the pressure on them, and they had to move up their time table, so they missed. We might never know that for sure, but I'm almost certain. Their target was probably someone of major corporate importance, but I suspect they were hoping to use the Skyward Day festivities to help carry off their plan. There would have been far more people out on the streets, and it would have been harder for the police to respond in a coordinated manner to a multipronged terrorist attack."

"So their target wasn't there, but they thought he would be." Jia pondered the possibilities. "We need to know who it is. That's the key to everything."

"Sophia Vand," Emma declared with a smirk.

Priya's eyes widened. "What? How do you know that?"

"Oh, don't look so surprised, Agent Bora. I've been doing some digging of my own. I assumed we were far past the point of worrying about being subtle or unusual involvement in the incident, so I've been bashing through systems with little concern. I'm sure the CID and your ID friends will complain about the obvious intrusions later, but given everything that happened, I thought it was worth the risk." Emma shrugged. "The truth is I've taken it upon myself to compromise the hotel systems since the end of the incident. They buried it well, but there was a minor slip-up. The details about how I did it are less important than that I've confirmed Sophia Vand was supposed to be in that room despite the false registration. I can find no public record that she was coming to the city, but I've been concentrating on the hotel systems."

"You're kidding me!" Jia blinked. "That'd be one hell of an assassination. This makes sense now. It's sick and ruthless, but I guess it makes sense."

"Who the hell is Sophia Vand?" Erik asked. "And even if there was a partial evacuation, if they pulled off their plan, we're talking a minimum of thousands of deaths, if not tens of thousands. How is this woman worth tens of thousands of people?"

"I'm not saying she is, not from my perspective, but she is one of the richest and most influential women in the UTC."

"I've never heard of her." Erik frowned. "But I don't pay much attention to rich corp types."

"She keeps a lower profile than you'd expect." Jia shook her head in disbelief. "The Vand family have been key players in a lot of major colonization efforts and major companies from the very beginning of the UTC. Old money. The women in her family, in particular, are known for political and charity activities. The Vand family has a stake in pretty much every large company in the UTC, but Sophia is known to eschew the spotlight. Her mother and grandmother were famous for being the same way."

"Nothing wrong with not demanding everyone kiss your ass." Erik frowned. "But that might not be modesty, that might just be her wanting to find deeper shadows to pull off shady deals. Nobody gets that rich without a whole penthouse full of skeletons."

"Sophia Vand. Damn." Priya frowned and tapped at her PNIU. "Give me a second. I'm going to see if my local contacts know anything about this. I think I would have been less surprised if I'd found out the Prime Minister was in that hotel." Her voice dropped to a light murmur as she connected her first call.

"If Vand was dirty, why would the Brotherhood or the conspiracy want her dead?" Jia asked. "Having one of the most influential women in the UTC, especially one who likes to blend into the background, would be useful, far more useful than a human with Leem DNA. It might be that she was onto them as well. A woman like that would have the resources to put together teams like ours, and she might know all too well about the corruption at the heart of the UTC. She might have been hunting them."

"Maybe." Erik scoffed. "But think about all the convenient suicides during our early cases with the NSCPD. It could be that Vand got too big a head and decided she was going to go against whatever the conspiracy wanted. She might not need more money, but she might have wanted more power to call the shots."

"So, sink an entire city and risk killing tens of thousands just to cover that up?" Jia shook her head in disbelief. "The sad part is I'm not shocked anymore. I hate that, but I suppose if we arrange the clues, it makes sense."

"It does?" Erik stared at her. "You don't think this is about sending a message? 'Step out of line, and we'll annihilate you wherever you are.'"

"No, Vand went out of her way to cover up her arrival. Emma only found out because the local records are still around. If the entire city sank and Vand had come here in secret, it might take weeks or months for anyone to figure out she'd been killed in the chaos, and even then, she'd just be another high-profile death among many others. For it to send a message, they'd need something more public and targeted. No, that's not it." Jia tapped her finger on the table. "I don't think the Agent was lying. I think he wanted us to know; wanted to prove that he'd pulled it off, so we'd suffer. I think for all his cool demeanor, it pissed him off that we put him and his cyborg lackeys down."

Erik smirked. "He couldn't be a pro at the end? Was that the Leem DNA acting up?"

"If he's anything like the rest of the Brotherhood, he thought he was better than us, but from the way he talked, I'm not sure if he *was* a member of the Brotherhood." Jia sighed and rubbed her temples. "It's annoying when we move forward, just to find more questions. We don't know if Vand is an enemy, a victim, or an ally of the conspiracy. She might have been all three."

Priya stood and walked away from the table, continuing her conversation, gesturing with her hands. There was concern etched on her face.

Erik looked her way. "But Vand wasn't there, so the Agent screwed up. He thought she still was, which meant he had a good reason to believe that. If he changed things because of us, Vand was probably supposed to stay here until Skyward Day."

"If she wasn't there, where is she?" Jia asked. "If she's not in the hotel?"

"What?" Priya shouted. "You're sure?" She groaned. "No, it's not your fault. Thanks for the info. I'll be in touch." She tapped her PNIU to end the call. "That was a CID contact of mine. He's been monitoring suspicious comings and goings as part of general smuggling concerns. Despite the fact that this entire damned city is supposed to be on lock-down while the authorities are cleaning up, a yacht, the *Northern Phoenix*, departed about two hours ago, less than fifteen minutes after the explosion in the hotel."

"Is it Sophia Vand's ship?" Erik asked. "Or would that be too easy?"

"The ship is registered to a private elite touring company," Priya replied. "But every ghost instinct says if we followed the strands, it would lead back to her. I'm sure she tossed a lot of money around to get the hell off Parvati after her penthouse blew up and cyborgs ran amok in the streets."

"Can't you send ID or CID to question her when she

gets back to Earth?" Jia shrugged. "This isn't something she can bribe her way out of. She might be a material witness to a major terrorist incident."

"We don't even know if she's on that ship." Priya clenched her fists. "Something's off about this whole thing, too. There's no way we'll get near her now. If she saw the assassination coming, she might not go back to Earth, worrying about the Brotherhood or their allies taking another bite at the apple. She could head straight to the HTP and spend the next six months touring the colonies. She has the resources to stay away from Earth forever, and if we don't know where she's going, we can't have local agents or contacts intercept her."

"We can't let her get away." Erik stood. He was paler than Jia liked, but his stern expression still commanded respect.

"What are you planning to do, Blackwell?" Priya raised an eyebrow. "Even if you run her ship down, she might tell you to screw off. She might be the victim here."

"We'll board her if we have to." Erik ground his teeth. "This is as close as I've gotten to the bastards behind the curtain. I'm not satisfied with just killing their lackeys, and if Vand's been targeted by the conspiracy, we can help her, and she can help us. She can't run forever, and the conspiracy can get to her anywhere. If they can slaughter a whole Army unit on Molino, there's nowhere she can go where she'll be safe."

Priya sighed and shrugged. "I'm not your boss. I can't tell you what to do, but I will tell you that poking one of the most powerful women in the UTC can bring hell that you don't want to deal with. She might be a little paranoid, considering someone just tried to assassinate her, and she might have the resources to fight off even two well-equipped contractors. I'd suggest you contact Alina and get direction before you do something you'll regret."

Erik inclined his head toward the door. "I'd suggest you leave, Agent Bora. This ship is taking off soon, and depending on what happens in the next day, you might want plausible deniability."

"Alina and the ID can't protect you from everyone." Priya edged toward the door. "You realize that, right?"

"Yeah." Erik looked at Jia. "I do."

She nodded back. "I made my choice already. Emma, tell Cutter to prepare for takeoff. We have a witness to interview."

Priya's gaze flitted between Erik and Jia. "I'll be getting off now, but I might as well go through the front. While I'm there, I'll contact my CID buddy to see if I can get the last known course of that ship and pass it along to your pilot. Good luck, you two. For people who have a lot of powerful enemies, you seem eager to make more."

Erik smiled. "It keeps life interesting."

CHAPTER FIFTY-ONE

Hours later, Cutter gestured at a highlighted bright dot on the radar. "We've almost caught up. That's what a hard burn will do. I assume that's her since that's the only ship in the area. I've already started decelerating, so we don't overshoot her."

Erik started at the dots on the display, leaning over from his seat. "Is she giving any indication she's going to try to run?"

Cutter shook his head. "Nope. If she were going to try to run, it'd make sense to start her burn now while we're decelerating."

"Are we sure she can detect us?" Erik shrugged. "We're on the edge of effective sensor range." He looked at Jia.

"She can unless she has terrible sensors, and do we really think a woman who is wealthier than some colonies taking a fancy elite yacht is going to have crappy sensors?" Jia frowned. "She knows we're coming. She's choosing to run for a reason, but we'll have to get closer for decent communication. I don't think we want any delays, given the situation."

Erik leaned over, frowning at the radar display. "It's not like she has to worry about pirates near Earth. If she thought we were the conspiracy, she'd have every reason to run. It might just be that she thinks we're a random ship. No reason to change course."

Cutter laughed. "Could be, but that is an odd flight path. She's swung way out at a weird angle from Venus and away from the standard lines. That's actually kind of dangerous. If something bad happens, it'll take longer for people to get to her, and we're obviously on an intercept course. I'm not trying anything fancy here other than catching up, Blackwell."

"The farther she is from stations, satellites, or other ships, the less chance of assassins marking her location. It's not crazy that she took an out-of-the-way flight path if she left before she knew she was specifically being targeted." Erik sucked in a breath. "Damn. I don't want to spook her, but she knows about or is doing something that made the conspiracy go all-in on killing her. There's no way I'm letting her go hide out on the frontier. We just fought through a pile of monsters, and she's *probably* the reason. We deserve to know why."

"Then we close in and hail her." Jia smiled. "What's the worst that can happen? It's not like we're going to find out she's got a secret Leem jump drive."

"With our luck?" Erik raised an eyebrow. "We might find out that exact thing."

"Okay, okay." Jia waved her hands. "Let's just close the

gap and see what happens. If she's got a jump drive, it might be nice to have a spare."

"Attention, *Northern Phoenix*," Erik transmitted. "We need to talk to you about the incident on Venus. I repeat, we need to talk to you about the incident on Venus." He stared at the colorful data windows filling the control console, hesitant to add the next part but unsure what else he should say. "This is Erik Blackwell, formerly of the 108th Assault Infantry murdered on Molino by the conspiracy. We have things to talk about. I'd suggest you slow down, and we meet to talk about them. We can help each other. I understand if you're worried, but we just handed the Ascended Brotherhood a big ass-kicking. Parvati is safe, and the Brotherhood is down a lot of Tin Men."

Emma frowned at Erik. She'd shifted her holographic outfit to a pressure suit. "Are you sure giving up all that information is wise?"

"If she knows about the conspiracy, then she knows we're not friends of theirs." Erik shrugged. "And if we want her help, there's no reason to hold back now."

"What if *she's* a friend of conspiracy?" Emma folded her arms. "Announcing that one of her greatest foes is following them might not be wise."

"Screw that," Erik snarled. "I'm tired of playing defense. You don't win a sphere ball game that way, and you don't win a war that way. We're going to crack this shit open with effort and strength, and that starts by not dancing around, doing everything safely and by the ID book."

Emma turned toward Cutter. "Mr. Durn, I'd suggest preparing to adjust power for the grav shield and weapons. I'll take the liberty of informing Raphael and Lanara to prepare for battle."

Cutter nodded. "It's time to show you people what I'm getting paid for."

Erik cleared his throat. "*Northern Phoenix*, this is Black-well again. We know Sophia Vand was supposed to be in the hotel that was bombed. She doesn't have to worry. The *things* responsible were all taken out. The Brotherhood lost a lot of resources and men. We made them pay for every innocent person they killed."

"Erik Blackwell, the Last Soldier," responded a woman, her voice elegant but cold. "As you just reminded me, you're the only survivor of Molino, or at least, the only one who was out in the field that day."

Jia's mouth twitched. She didn't say anything but nodded to Erik to tell him to continue.

"That's me," Erik replied. "Is this Sophia Vand?"

"Yes. I suppose lying is pointless, considering you're chasing me through space like a dog chasing its favorite toy." She let out a long, melodramatic sigh. "More than that, you've managed to determine both my presence on Venus and my presence aboard this vessel. I'm assuming it's because of that toy AI you're borrowing from the Defense Directorate."

"Something like that." Erik's stomach tightened. He didn't like her tone. There was a possibility she was a victim of the conspiracy but otherwise a bitch, not unexpected from a scion of privilege who could buy and sell colonies.

"Is Miss Lin with you?" Sophia sighed. "Why am I even asking? She was on Venus with you, so there's no reason she wouldn't be. The indefatigable, vicious pair of attack dogs who have carved through so many enemies in their time together. It's almost *absurd* when you think about it."

"Sure," Erik replied. "But setting that aside, you and I have something in common, and I'm hoping we can help each other."

"What could that possibly be, Mr. Blackwell? No offense, but we're from two very different worlds." Sophia sounded faintly offended. "Other than us both being human and born on Earth, we're nothing alike."

"We've both been targeted for assassination by a dangerous conspiracy," Erik replied, now unsure of what he was thinking. "I think we could help each other."

Sophia laughed, the sound tinged with cruelty. "Do you honestly believe that?"

"That depends on you and what you have to say. You might be rich and powerful, but you also had to run away... well, like a dog with her tail between her legs from a ragtag group of cyborgs we carved through like Jia's roasted duck."

"Really?" Sophia sounded intrigued. "Is that what you think?"

"We should activate the grav shields," Jia whispered. "Just in case."

Erik shook his head and cut his comm. "Not until we're sure. The minute we look hostile, this is over, and we might not regain her trust."

"You know how you could help me, Mr. Blackwell?" Sophia asked.

"I'm willing to listen. I think I've proven myself against the conspiracy and their allies like the Ascended Brotherhood."

Sophia snorted. "Oh, that's convenient. It sounds from what you've said like you've finished off the Brotherhood. It saves me the trouble of having to do it myself."

"See? We can help." Erik tried to inject levity into his tone, despite the tension building in his neck. Sophia didn't sound like a woman scared and on the run. She sounded condescending and arrogant, like the assassination had been a mere inconvenience.

Jia's fingers danced across the controls. "Bringing up grav shield." She pointed to a data window displaying a rough outline of the *Northern Phoenix*, along with several fluctuating colored bars. "She just activated her grav shields."

"Shit." Erik killed his mic and scrubbed a hand over his face. "She's got grav shields in a small ship, too? Of course she does."

"Do you know what happens when you leave a problem to linger, Mr. Blackwell?" Sophia asked.

"Slowing more," Cutter reported. "Preparing for evasive action, including hard lateral burn." He took some deep breaths. "And here I thought this job would end by eating delicious snacks on the festival day."

"You concentrate on flying." Jia tapped on another set of controls. "Emma, please handle point defense. I'll handle primary weapons. We have to expect she's got a full crew onboard splitting tasks."

Erik gritted his teeth. He didn't want to destroy Sophia's ship, not until he had answers, but he also trusted

Jia's instincts. "What happens when you leave a problem to linger?"

"It metastasizes like a cancer," Sophia replied, her voice trembling with barely concealed rage. "I understand now what has happened and why you aren't dead, despite previous efforts. Those I trusted interfered with my plans, and that's unacceptable. One pathetic soldier and one little girl can't be allowed to derail all of my plans. All of *our* plans."

That was enough. Erik's heart rate kicked up.

"It's you," Erik growled. "You call the fucking shots? Or at least you're up there, and some of your lackeys got a little uppity?"

Sophia let out a venomous laugh. "You're nothing. You're worse than nothing. You're a ghost who refuses to accept that he died along with his soldiers. It's absurd what you've done. You've chased us across the galaxy to avenge minor sacrifices for the greater good? *THE GREATER GOOD!* Do you have any idea how many people die each day, Mr. Blackwell?"

"Those were good men and women, you bitch!" Erik's anger cut through the conversation. "They swore their lives to defend the UTC, and your little pet cyborgs hired and supplied mercs to murder them."

"For a soldier, you're curiously sentimental. Men and women die in war all the time. That's what a soldier's meant to do: *die*. If it brings you some small comfort before your imminent demise, note that they died in service of a greater cause. It wasn't pointless murder. It might sound quaint to a man who spent time as a detective, but you were all in the wrong place at the wrong time. It was nothing personal."

Erik scoffed. "Greater good? Does that include turning people into twisted ass-alien hybrids like the Agent? What about those Tin Spiders?"

Sophia sighed. "How simplistic, Blackwell. You're mistaking tools for goals. Both the Brotherhood and that man had their uses, and they were customized appropriately for them. Of course, I wouldn't want all of humanity to become like the Brotherhood or the Agent."

"She's deploying weapons," Jia announced, her brow knitted in concern. "And decelerating."

"The traitor led you right to me, didn't he?" Sophia asked, the pitch of her voice rising. "But it's too late. I received the delivery, and soon you'll be dead at my hands. I already know who is responsible. It's another cancer I let metastasize. She will die soon. Don't worry, once I confirm who is loyal and who isn't, they're out. Whatever *she* has told you is lies. You're no different than the Agent or the Brotherhood. You are tools to be expended. You think killing me is going to stop anything? You're so foolish and naïve, it pains me. The best thing you could have done for your species was die on Molino with the rest of your pointless scum."

"You think because you have some toys on your yacht, you can win?" Erik took a deep breath and forced a chuckle. "You're not the only one with surprises." He nodded to Jia. "This is your last chance to play nice before we start slapping you around."

"Spare me the threats. You will be a footnote soon, you ignorant little soldier."

"Deploying turrets and loading torpedoes," Jia reported.

"Yeah, I'm an ignorant little soldier," Erik continued. "But you know what being a soldier means, Sophia? It means I've fought. I've risked my life. I've killed men with my own hands when they were trying to kill me." He scowled in disdain. "It's easy to order someone else to do your dirty work, but I was on the front line for thirty years, fighting and risking my own life alongside my soldiers. What about you? Is this little bombing the first time you've been seriously threatened?"

"You are unimportant." Venom filled Sophia's voice. "One man and one woman can't stand in the way of progress. Now do humanity a favor, Mr. Blackwell, and die for it. Die for *me*."

"She's turning," Cutter announced. "And comm terminated."

Erik strapped his harness on. "Unfortunately for her, she doesn't realize I can't die here."

"I wish I had your confidence, Blackwell." Cutter tightened his harness. "This is a nice ship, but it isn't a battleship. You've got me, so your odds are decent, but just saying."

"You don't understand." Erik smiled, but it didn't reach his eyes. "I can't die in space like a Fleet punk. I'm Assault Infantry. When we die, it is with our boots on the ground."

"I want to die old in bed, surrounded by beautiful women." Cutter shrugged. "I don't care if it's in space or on a planet."

Jia nodded toward a data window. "From what I can tell, they aren't much more heavily armed than we are. We have a slight advantage because unless I'm mistaken, they've got two laser turrets and two plasma turrets. If we take potshots at range, we can win."

Erik didn't need to be an expert on piloting to interpret the sensor readings. The *Northern Phoenix* was turning to fight.

"I like the plan where we stay away from the bigger guns." Cutter nodded quickly.

Jia looked at Erik. "Keep in mind, if we take that ship out, we're losing a major lead."

He shook his head. "There's no way we're going to be able to board her, and I don't consider it losing a lead. You heard her. She's one of the people behind the conspiracy. Screw the Brotherhood. They were just errand boys. It's time we took down someone important. If they were desperate and making mistakes before, that'll really send them running, and then ID can give us more targets."

"You're sure?" Jia locked eyes with him. "I'm in, no matter *what*."

"I'm sure."

"Blackwell," barked Lanara over the comm. "Are you idiots strapped in?"

"Yeah, why?" Erik asked.

"I've been working on something with Emma. You see, I noticed the efficiency ratio for the external grav emitters was off by 0.2 percent, but the tolerances were as high as 0.5 percent. At first I thought, that's an idiotic waste of power, and I fix—"

"Get to the damned point, Lanara!"

Lanara grunted in frustration. "The point is I can give you thicker grav shields over certain parts of the ship temporarily without frying the emitters. Raphael can help me, and Emma's the only one fast enough to redirect the energy on the fly. It's going to weaken internal gravity, but we'll be deploying more impressive shields than we would otherwise be able to do."

Erik grinned. "Finally, some good news, and we have the dispersing nanofilm, right?"

"It doesn't make us invincible, Blackwell. And that nanofilm is far less effective against plasma attacks, but you guys do what you need to do, and we'll do what we can to support you. I can't die yet. I haven't finished even a tenth of my planned modifications."

Erik nodded to the control panel. "Give me control of the bottom turrets, Jia."

She raised an eyebrow. "I'm technically firing, but there are a lot of systemic aim assists built in."

Erik winked. "Think of it as another Emma situation. Computer thought plus human instinct, and if we're both concentrating on separate sides, it gives us a better chance."

Jia tapped her control panel. A virtual control pad and buttons materialized in front of Erik.

"She's coming in," Cutter shouted.

"Keep us out!" Erik ordered. "Stick to the plan. Let's show this bitch how we do things."

CHAPTER FIFTY-TWO

Sophia's ship came in at a steep angle, the laser turrets coming to life. The beams were invisible, but the sensors of the *Argo* marked them and the narrow misses.

The belly of the *Argo* was exposed, which meant Erik had the shot. He opened fire, doing his best to lead and letting the aim assist help him, but advanced systems calculations and instinct could only do so much against a target thousands of kilometers away.

It was absurd if he thought about it too hard.

It was like throwing a dart at a man blocks away.

Erik held his breath during Cutter's hard burn of the thrusters. He was feeling the loss of most of the gravity compensation, but the move helped the *Argo* approach the *Northern Phoenix* from the top of the enemy vehicle. Jia opened fire, small puffs on the sensor display marking hits. The *Argo* shook as Cutter peeled off and the enemy's laser turrets sought their revenge.

"Minor damage," Lanara reported, sounding annoyed. "They've got beefy lasers for their size, but the grav shield strengthening helped. I'm having to reroute power, but I hope you hit them harder than they hit us."

Jia gestured to a stream of debris clearly visible in the IR feed and nodded to Erik. "We got a nice hit. They're bleeding, too."

Sophia's ship spun, the lateral thrusters as impressive as the ones on the *Argo*. A collision warning sounded as a torpedo streamed away from the ship.

Sweat beaded Cutter's face as he accelerated, doing his best to loop around and beat the torpedo. He fired lateral and vertical thrusters to spin the ship and change their position relative to the torpedo while doing his best to not let Sophia come in below or on top of them. The enemy projectile broke into ten smaller projectiles, each speeding toward the *Argo*.

"She's got scatter torpedoes?" Erik grimaced. "Damn it. I didn't expect that nice a toy."

"She's rich." Jia retorted.

"So is your family," Erik replied.

"You aren't dating me for torpedo money."

"Well, true. But.." The ship shook slightly with the rapid firing of the point-defense lasers, all guided by Emma.

Two of the torpedoes vanished from the radar and close-range lidar. Six more disappeared in the next couple of seconds. The last two continued closing uncomfortably on the rear of the ship.

"Any time now, Emma." Erik tried to focus on his firing, blasting away at the *Northern Phoenix*. "I don't think a grav shield's going to help much against a direct torpedo hit."

The ninth smaller torpedo disappeared. Cutter's abrupt spins and lateral thrusts wreaked havoc on Erik's stomach.

He hadn't felt like this since being in a drop pod. The tenth torpedo disappeared from sensors, but not before the explosion sent a tremor through the *Argo*.

"Debris from plasma explosions hurts this ship, too," Lanara complained over the comm. "Primary thrusters have taken some damage. Rear grav emitters damaged. Do that enough times, and we'll lose enough thrust that you'll notice. Moments before we die."

"Run us right down her throat, Cutter," Jia ordered. "We're not going to win a war of attrition. I'll make her turn, and then you turn toward her."

Cutter nodded, a huge grin spreading. "Oh, I got you. Let's do some crazy shit. Fine by me. If I'm going to die here, I'd rather it be quick."

Jia narrowed her eyes on the sensor displays. "We will not be the ones dying out here."

The *Northern Phoenix* spun toward them, burning hard, the flight path a wide curve. Their laser turrets continued firing, a couple of shots clipping the *Argo*.

"Well, even if we do, it was a good run." Cutter changed course.

With the *Argo* now angled perfectly, both the top and bottom turrets could open fire. Jia slapped the torpedo control to fling torpedoes in rapid succession, launching four of the explosives toward the enemy ship. As predicted, the *Northern Phoenix* changed course, and their point-defense lasers opened fire.

"We're going to get close enough to scrape the paint," Cutter shouted as the *Argo* barreled toward the other ship. "Don't wet your pants."

The top plasma turrets of the *Northern Phoenix* flung

their blue-white death. Cutter tilted the ship back and forth, giving the lateral thrusters a good workout while Erik and Jia pulsed their lasers. Their superior attack angle let them bring all their weapons to bear, and the repeated laser strikes pushed through the enemy shield to rake the hull and penetrate one of the plasma turrets. It blew up with the kind of understated explosion a lack of oxygen produced, but its debris cloud shredded the back of the ship.

A plasma blast slammed into *Argo*'s side. A violent tremor shook the ship, and a shrill alarm sounded.

"Hull breach!" Cutter shouted. "Activating temporary seal. We're down some thrusters, too."

"Lanara, Raphael," Erik barked. "You okay?"

"Am I okay?" Lanara yelled. "You just let them blow a hole in my damned ship! The self-repair isn't going to cut it, Blackwell."

Erik nodded to Jia. "Yeah, she's okay."

Cutter's jaw tightened. "I can compensate for the loss of thrusters, but we've lost a lot of maneuverability."

Jia nodded at the sensor display and the trail of hot debris leaking from the *Northern Phoenix*. "They don't look like they're in much better shape."

She magnified the visual feed. There were multiple holes in the top of the ship, some starting to seal. The explosion of the plasma turret had taken the top laser turret with it.

"We've won." Erik grinned. "Just keep us on top of her, Cutter, and we'll finish this."

The pilot nodded, letting out a sigh of relief. "For a second there, I thought we were toast."

"Emma, broadcast this every way you can," Erik ordered. "I want her to hear it."

"Feel free to taunt her, Erik," Emma replied. "It's not petty when you've proven yourself superior. You might be both fleshbags, but you're the better fleshbag."

"Power down and prepare to be boarded, Sophia," Erik transmitted. "We've got all our weapons, and we're on top of you. You've lost."

"Fortune doesn't favor the bold, Last Soldier," Sophia replied, the transmission weak and full of static. "I realize that now. It favors the foolish. Know that you've won today, but your victory will be like ashes in your mouth. Whatever aid you've received is temporary. She'll turn on you too, and if the universe is designed as well as I believe, I'll laugh where I'm going next."

Erik scoffed. "If the universe is designed as well as *I* think, you won't be doing a lot of laughing from hell. Now, slow your ass down and drop your grav shield."

"Not today, Mr. Blackwell. Not today. There are worse things than death. You'll find that out soon enough."

"Power surge?" Jia's eyes widened. "Cutter, show them our ass and burn! Emma, guard it!"

With a powerful thrust and a lurching spin, the *Argo* accelerated away from the *Northern Phoenix*. The yacht's magnificent explosion added a small star to local space for a glorious span of seconds and a new cloud of debris to threaten navigation.

"I would have loved to have asked her some questions," Erik blew out a breath. "But I'll take not dying."

Cutter wiped the sweat off his face. "Yeah. We're not dead. Nice." He nodded a couple of times.

Jia nodded. "Not yet, anyway." She frowned at the spreading cloud of debris on the sensor displays. "She might be dead, but now we know one person associated with the conspiracy. We still have a lead."

"Yeah." Erik let his head rest on the back of his seat. "Today, true justice for the Knights Errant has begun.

CHAPTER FIFTY-THREE

March 22, 2230, Neo Southern California Metroplex, Private Hangar of the *Argo*

Jia didn't like the smirk on Alina's face as the other woman stepped into the cargo bay. The ID agent surveyed everything with an amused glint in her eye. It was like she was an aunt visiting her naughty niece and nephew.

Erik leaned against his MX 60, a bored look on his face. Alina had informed them on their way back to Earth that she'd debrief them fully once they'd returned.

They'd spent most of the trip back trying to avoid the angry Lanara and the less angry Raphael, who insisted they tell him exactly what they were feeling during each second of their fight.

He claimed it was important for posterity, and he was taking notes for a future book series.

Jia gave the man credit. He didn't seem to care that he'd come close to dying in a ship-to-ship battle in the middle of deep space.

Fanboy bravery could be an impressive thing.

"You had the transport for far longer without scratching it." Alina gestured around the cargo bay. "You barely get this thing and there are holes in it. That's the problem when you give people guns. They want to shoot them at something."

"Hey, not our fault Sophia didn't want to be reasonable." Jia shrugged. "I think we could use more firepower in the future if we're expected to deal with ships like hers."

"I'll see what I can do, but there are limits to what I can give you without it being too easy to detect." Alina clapped. "But enough teasing. I don't know if this passes into the level of a Herculean Labor, but both of you, at the least, were Perseus. You slew something far more frightening than a Gorgon." She sighed. "That said, you also left a big, obvious mess on Venus. That's going to take a lot of effort to clean up."

"A mess?" Erik pushed off his flitter. "We sussed out a plot to sink a city, stopped it, took out a horde of Tin Men, and killed some weird-ass half-alien freak. I don't think that happens quietly, no matter how prepared you are."

Alina nodded. "I suppose it doesn't. I would have preferred it if you'd used a different method of tracking down the enemy, rather than making it obvious that you were there. The ID is doing its best to downplay your involvement, but of course, people are making the obvious connection that some bizarre incident occurred, and it was conveniently stopped when the Obsidian Detective and Lady Justice were in town. If the conspiracy didn't know you were still fully in the game before, they do now."

Jia shrugged. "I can sleep with that."

"I know it's a long shot, but did you get anything from any of those Tin Men or the Agent?" Erik asked.

Alina furrowed her brow, a dark look in her eyes. "You didn't leave a lot of the Agent, but Priya and some of the other local agents are working indirectly with CID to collect evidence. No identified DNA from the Brotherhood cyborgs and all of them did their standard internal self-destruct. The ID now has custody of the remains of the Agent, but I will note that although you two turned him into confetti, we have some viable DNA samples from him. Our best analysis resources aren't on Venus, so his remains are being transported to Earth, but initial genetic examinations suggest he wasn't lying, or at least, he has DNA structures not consistent with him being one hundred percent human. No one was able to find a PNIU on the scene. I'm not sure if you two blew it to bits, or he disposed of it on the run."

Erik frowned. "There's always some way these bastards can sink lower. Maybe that's what was on Molino behind that locked door—a lab where they were cooking up new monsters."

"It could be." Alina shrugged. "But based on what both Sophia Vand and the Agent related, the main people behind this were born human."

Jia snorted. "I don't know if that makes it better. It'd almost be more comforting if this was a Leem plot rather than knowing there are human beings out there constantly pushing to see what kinds of new monsters they can generate for their plots."

Alina walked over to a mini-flitter and ran her hand over the seat, wiping off dust. "It just means we need to keep doing what we're doing. This was a noisy win, but it was a win. Based on our continued analysis of the intelligence from the New Year's raids and other recent collections, we're confident that what you fought on Venus was the last major force of the Ascended Brotherhood. We think we've even found their production facility."

"You do?" Erik rubbed his hands. "When do we hit it?"

Alina gestured at his chest. "You're not done healing up from Venus, and we don't need you two this time. The suspected facility was in Botswana, with an emphasis on 'was.' There was a massive explosion earlier today at what, according to public records, was a remote specialty hospital. All our intel pointed toward it being the production facility."

Jia sucked in a breath in irritation. "They're covering their tracks."

Alina nodded. "Probably, but if they're not going to use full-conversion cyborgs for a while, I'm not going to complain."

"What now?" Jia asked.

"If we can take what Sophia said at face value, we might have gotten in the middle of some sort of internal power struggle." Alina folded her arms. "That's useful intelligence right there. It means whoever this conspiracy is, despite their vast resources, they aren't operating in a unified way. Which means the more we can uncover, the more we can use that against them. That might be why they've closed up shop on the Ascended Brotherhood, and knowing Sophia Vand was part of this conspiracy gives us a useful lead to work. The ID might have to walk softly around her contacts, but now it's just a needle in a haystack rather than a needle at the bottom of the ocean like it was before."

"Do you have any jobs for us?" Erik asked. "I didn't get hurt that badly. We should move while we have the chance."

"It's not that simple, Erik. Sophia Vand wasn't your standard rich person doing shady deals on the side. The ID, the CID, and intel elements in the DD will be working together to dive into things, but I doubt we're going to be lucky enough to find data somewhere that's an official list of evil deeds. That woman had a lot of high-level contacts, including the Prime Minister. This is one situation we can't go all Blackwell and Lin all over everything without causing trouble we can't handle."

"'Go all Blackwell and Lin?'" Jia rolled her eyes. "We get results." She pointed at herself and Erik. "That's why you recruited us, remember?"

"Yes, you get results, and you make a lot of noise." Alina smiled. "I'm not complaining. You two did well. We might not have won the war yet, but we've won a major battle. Erik needs to heal, and the ship needs repairs. Enjoy your time off." She turned to leave but stopped. "Oh, and just so you know, there's no indication that anyone has reported Sophia Vand missing. The Fleet is investigating the explosion in that area, but we've pulled strings of our own, including falsifying the satellite records tracking the *Argo*'s departure from Venusian space. For now, someone other than us is interested in making it look like Sophia Vand is alive and still conducting business. We can use that to our advantage."

A door slid open, and a scowling Lanara stepped

through. She flipped Erik and Jia off before continuing mumbling numbers under her breath.

Alina raised an eyebrow. "What was that about?"

"She's still angry about us putting holes in the ship." Erik laughed.

CHAPTER FIFTY-FOUR

Julia waited patiently as the holographic images of the members of the Core appeared one by one around the table, all except Sophia. There were no surprises. Ivan and Farad looked weary and angry, but Shoji and others wore amused smiles.

"Thank you all for joining me." Julia faked a sad look. "It is a dark time. For the first time since Sophia's creation of the Core, one of us has fallen."

Ivan stared at her, calculation in his eyes. "Before we discuss the further implications, do we know if the artifacts she was picking from your people were lost?"

Julia sighed. "Some were lost, but I was only able to deliver a partial shipment. I'd worried about that at the time, but it seems like a fortunate turn of events now."

Farad leaned forward, trembling with barely concealed rage. "But Sophia was the one taking the lead on the analysis of the Hunter artifacts. Do we know where she has the rest of them stored?"

"I'm looking into that," Julia replied. "For obvious

reasons, she kept them well concealed, but I have my sources."

An olive-skinned woman in a dark dress looked at the members. Constance. Julia couldn't remember the last time the quiet woman had said more than yes or no at a meeting. Her personality belied her intelligence and dedication to the cause. That made her dangerous in her own way.

"I have other concerns." Constance sighed. "It's unclear to me why the last remnants of the Ascended Brotherhood were on Venus. I was under the impression they were to keep quiet while they replenished their strength. The Agent was also present on Venus."

Julia averted her gaze. "That's something I'm not sure about, but I've taken certain unilateral measures due to my concerns about what happened."

Farad sneered. "You were the one who destroyed the facility in Botswana, weren't you?"

Julia nodded. "I did what I needed to do to protect the Core. From what little I've been able to determine from my spies, they confirm what the media is reporting. There was a plot to sink Parvati, and the Brotherhood played a key role. The government is suppressing the existence of a major faction of cyborgs involved in the incident, and there are no public reports of the presence of the Agent, let alone his nature. However, there are many questions that remain unresolved, especially since the Last Soldier and the Warrior Princess were there." She frowned. "I'll admit to perhaps misjudging their level of threat in the past."

"You're saying you believe they killed Sophia?" Ivan asked.

"The timing is too coincidental overwise, but I fail to

understand the nature of the Brotherhood and the Agent's scheme on Venus as well." Julia frowned. "We've allowed them great latitude in the past, but there have been too many lapses of security. Given the severity of the losses and the attention that would have come with the destruction of the city, I decided to move quickly."

Farad glared at her. "That wasn't your decision to make."

"Do you object to the results or the process?" Julia offered him a smile. "We've lost Sophia, and I begin to wonder if her schemes caught up with her."

Ivan nodded. "My agents have independently confirmed much of what you've told us."

"As have mine." Shoji unfolded a fan and waved it in front of him, a coy smile on his face. "I've long questioned whether it was wise to entrust one member of the Core with so many artifacts. Sophia was responsible for the creation of the Ascended Brotherhood, and they were first and foremost her tools, as was the Agent. None of us can deny we've doubted the wisdom of some of their uses in recent years. I will give my eternal respect to Sophia for her creation of the Core, but it's obvious to me that she lost her way."

Ivan rubbed his temples, cold fury in his eyes. "We need to use all available resources to recover the remaining artifacts Sophia had under her control. Once that occurs, we can figure out the safest way to distribute them. If this incident has taught us anything, it's that we must be more careful about how and in whom we vest power. We've already suffered a major setback by losing any of the artifacts."

"The Fleet might recover some, but it'll be hard to extract them. I'd prefer it if the remaining artifacts she was meant to pick up were handled by others." Julia's mouth twitched. "I will make arrangements to have them split amongst you."

"Why do you give them up so willingly?" Farad laughed. "Are you afraid, Julia? Of the Last Soldier and the Warrior Princess? You thought they were a minor irritant, and now you think they will come for you as they did for Sophia?"

"I fear for the plan. Those two are annoying, but after what happened on Venus, the ID and others are undoubtedly looking into people and places they did not know about before." Julia closed her eyes and took a deep breath. "We're at a crossroads. A tragic one, but a crossroads nonetheless. I would suggest we adopt a different strategy, one that involves more cooperation and coordination among us, and less compartmentalization. We don't know if we lost what we needed when Sophia died."

"What you are suggesting risks the entire Core," Farad replied. "You were always a proponent of operating as we have."

"But hiding everything risks the plan." Julia gestured around the table. "We can't be sure if it was Blackwell and Lin who killed Sophia, but even if they were the executioners, it was others, such as factions in the Intelligence Directorate, who set them up for the death. We've become arrogant, and we've forgotten our vulnerabilities."

"Agreed," replied Constance.

Others nodded. Ivan and Farad looked like they didn't believe her, but they eventually nodded as well.

"Let us reorganize." Julia smiled. "Let us collect our

resources and take stock of what we have. We all know there isn't as much time as we'd like, so it's important that we unlock the secrets of the artifacts before it's too late."

"Very well." Ivan adjusted his tie, the fury abating from his face. "My people will be in contact soon about the surviving artifacts. I see no reason to continue this discussion until then." His hologram disappeared.

With a polite nod, others began disappearing until only Shoji remained. Julia tapped her PNIU to verify the single feed before nodding to him.

"None will challenge you openly, but all suspect you." Shoji closed his fan and tittered. "You realize that, don't you?"

"But you just supported me, and the efforts I've made have produced the necessary evidence." Julia smiled softly. "It might not be compelling, but it's enough to take advantage of their doubts. And it's not as if I'm lying. Sophia's arrogance and monopolization of the Hunter artifacts *was* a threat."

"Be careful, Julia. Beware of Farad and Ivan. What you've set in motion can't be undone."

"I know that, old friend, but we both knew this day would come." Julia smiled. "There is no success without risk."

"True, but death awaits us all, even those of the Core." Shoji disappeared.

Julia stood and smoothed her dress, then stepped away from the table and out of the room. Two rooms away, she smiled as she surveyed DNA-locked crates sitting atop her favorite oak table. She let out a satisfied sigh.

The universe had bent itself to her will. She'd spent

much time and effort arranging to cover up Sophia's assassination with the mysterious terrorist attack. If the plan had succeeded, the Brotherhood wouldn't have been directly implicated, and the Agent would have been able to cover his tracks. It would have appeared as if Sophia had died in an unrelated terrorist attack.

But the Last Soldier and the Warrior Princess had interfered. They hadn't reacted as she would have preferred, and they'd complicated things, and some of her greatest pawns were now gone. If anything, it'd worked out better because they had taken the bulk of the suspicion off her. It created enough uncertainty and chaos that she could take advantage of it.

Julia knelt in front of the crates. Sophia would have realized she was given fake artifacts the moment she returned to Earth, and now all Julia had to do was distribute a handful of them to the rest of the Core. It was a calculated gamble, but she would maintain the bulk of the artifacts, including the most promising ones. The Core needed to be polished. They'd become no better than the corruption they sought to replace. She would be the one to lead humanity into the new era after consolidating her power.

She reached toward a crate and stopped. Her hand was shaking. Absurd. It was almost as if she were afraid.

An automated, encrypted emergency transmission from Sophia's ship had confirmed her fate, although some of the data sent with the transmission suggested she might have destroyed the ship herself.

Sophia didn't die on Venus. Her ship had left Venus, but that wasn't what bothered Julia so much. She should have died on Venus, not fled the planet to be slain by two overzealous children.

Sophia had eluded Julia's trap, but how? The Agent could have betrayed her, but if that was the case, Sophia would have sent something to the others to implicate her. Somehow, at the last minute, Julia's plans had twisted in on themselves, and not knowing why meant she couldn't correct the problem for the future. She wanted to believe the universe loved her, but perhaps it was nothing more than blind luck.

Julia stared at the beautiful snowcapped mountains surrounding her home. She couldn't be afraid, not of the mild uncertainty the Last Soldier and the Warrior Princess represented. She'd held out some small hope that the Agent might be able to recruit them, but his violent end on Venus proved he'd failed.

It didn't matter. She wasn't a normal woman. Like a cursed maiden in a fairy tale, she had let the dark, almost magical power of alien technology grant her life far beyond what even the best human technology allowed. She was over a hundred and sixty years old and had witnessed the birth of humanity's journey through the stars. Even as they mouthed the platitudes, the rest of the Core no longer remembered why they needed to live so long, but she did.

Julia would do whatever she needed to do. When it was all over, if only she remained of the Core?

So be it.

Erik ran his hand through Jia's silky black hair as she rested her head on his chest. They lay in bed together, relaxing after some *fun* exercise.

Jia yawned. "We shouldn't have done that." She nuzzled his chest. "You still are healing."

"Yeah, well, I'll have to be a lot more damaged before I turn a naked you down." Erik grinned and kissed the top of her head. "It's finally happening. It's kind of weird to think about it. I never knew how it would happen, if it'd be all at once, or it'd be individuals I needed to track down."

"Some rich woman sitting at the top of the pyramid? Somehow that's not a big surprise." Jia rolled away and onto her stomach. "You know what's still bothering me about all this?"

"Don't tell me you're worried that we didn't arrest her." Erik frowned.

Jia scoffed. "She was trying to blow us up at the time. I'm not feeling bad about blowing her up first. No, it's that we have the means and opportunity, but we don't have a motive."

Erik nodded slowly and looked toward the wall. "Yeah, I know what you mean. It might be that they were breeding alien mutants at Molino, or it could be something else, but I don't get the end game. What does someone that rich and powerful get out of being more rich and powerful? Her family's been rich for centuries. It can't be that she needs anything she couldn't have already bought or otherwise acquired."

"Yes." Jia shifted onto her side. "But I didn't mean to depress you. If there's one thing I've accepted lately, it's that the Lady loves you and has decided to throw major advantages your way. Otherwise, we both would be dead."

Erik grinned. "Don't worry. I'm just friends with the Lady.

Jia smirked. "So you say."

"You believe we'll figure out the motive and all that in the end?"

Jia nodded. "As long as we keep doing what we're doing."

Erik offered her a wide grin. "I'm planning to seek and destroy. If the government wants to throw new toys at me to make it easier, all the better."

"And after that?" Jia looked hopeful.

Erik opened his mouth to say what she obviously wanted to hear, but the words wouldn't come out. It wasn't that he wasn't filled with hope. Taking Sophia and the Brotherhood down was a major success no matter how they looked at it, but a war wasn't over until the last battle.

"And after that, we'll see what life brings," Erik murmured and turned toward her. "Whatever it is, it'll be something good."

**Another planet closer to Earth than Erik's moon gives
up its secrets, providing Erik and Jia with clues that
could lead to the answer to one of the questions he has
been searching for.**

*What was hidden on that small moon that his people were
killed for?*

Along with the clues, an unexpected question pops up.

*Could an unfriendly but extinct species of alien not be
extinct, as presumed?*

**Both want the truth—but is the effort to reveal the
truth good for humanity?**

Two years ago, a small moon in a far-off system was set to be the location of the first intergalactic war between humans and an alien race.

It didn't happen. However, something was found that many are willing to kill to keep a secret.

Now they have killed the wrong people.

How many will need to die to keep the truth hidden?

As many as is needed.

He will have vengeance, no matter the cost. *She will dig for the truth, no matter how risky the truth is to reveal.*

Pre-order One Dark Future for Delivery on August 21, 2020

Thank you for reading not only this book, but through to these *Author Notes*!

Where do we go from here?

Ok, so we JUST finished the <secret clandestine project> that is the ship for Erik and Jia. It took many more weeks than planned, but like always, it looks amazingly cool. Big thanks to Cody, Gene, and Sasha for getting a premier product ready for the future covers.

The ship is shown on the new cover of book 09. Go check it out (and of course pre-order it at the same time. Just a little slip of the mouse and CLICK, pre-ordered!)

The amazing attention to detail is so cool to see. I can't wait to get the file where I (who has little to no skills with 3D software) can play with the ship on the screen. I won't admit to making little ship noises whatsoever.

But it might happen. Who will be around to prove I did or didn't?

We just got news: wear your masks! (Yes, I hate doing it, but do it anyway.)

So, here in Nevada, we have been "open" for twenty days or so. Our sister state California has had a mandatory rule to wear masks inside for a week now, and Nevada has followed in their footsteps. I can't say I'm surprised since we needed it (both the effort to stay healthy and the requirement to wear it.)

With so many people coming to Vegas throwing caution to the wind (and they do), without a state law, it wasn't going to happen.

Too many people cooped up for too long, and Vegas is for gamblers anyway. Gambling with not wearing a mask is just another type of gambling, I figure.

Do they say it?

Ok, this is book 07, and I can promise you secret special words will happen by book 08. I can't tell you the why because it's a surprise. Then again, I'm not admitting what the words are, either. So, you can assume I mean the obvious words, but then again…

I'm a fiction author – we lie for a living.

THANK YOU!

Thank you so much to all of you who are following this story and buying the pre-orders every single book. Your support (and reviews) help us continue pushing forward and bringing more fans into the family.

Go Erik! Go Jia! Go YOU!

Ad Aeternitatem,

Michael Anderle

CONNECT WITH MICHAEL ANDERLE

Michael Anderle Social

Website:
http://www.lmbpn.com

Email List:
http://lmbpn.com/email/

Facebook Here:
https://www.facebook.com/groups/lmbpn.opusx/